Enough Is Enough

Also by Mark Lawson

Idlewild
A Novel

The Battle for Room Service
Journeys to All the Safe Places

Bloody Margaret
Three Political Fantasies

Going Out Live
or, Are They the Same at Home?
A Novel

MARK LAWSON

Enough Is Enough

or, The Emergency Government

A NOVEL

PICADOR

First published 2005 by Picador
an imprint of Pan Macmillan Ltd
Pan Macmillan, 20 New Wharf Road, London N1 9RR
Basingstoke and Oxford
Associated companies throughout the world
www.panmacmillan.com

ISBN 0 330 43803 4

Printed and bound in Great Britain by
Mackays of Chatham plc, Chatham, Kent

For

my children

William, Anna and Benjamin

with love

DE	KH
MF	RA

7os

Permissions Acknowledgements

The publishers gratefully acknowledge the following for the use of copyright material: 'Here I am, floating in my tin-can' from 'Space Oddity' © Onward Music Ltd for the World. Used by Permission; 'Seasons In The Sun', Music Jacques Brel, English lyric by Rod McKuen, Reproduced by kind permission of Carlin Music Corp., London NW1 8BD on behalf of Edward B Marks Music Company; 'The Stranger Song' Words & Music Leonard Cohen © Bad Monk Music. Sony/ATV Music Publishing Ltd All Rights Reserved; 'Suzanne' and 'Everyone Knows' © Leonard Cohen, courtesy of Sony/ATV Music Publishing Ltd; 'Hold Me Close' by David Essex; *The Cure at Troy* by Seamus Heaney, published by Faber and Faber Ltd; *Dad's Army: The Complete Scripts of Series 1–4* by Jimmy Perry & David Croft, published by the Orion Publishing Group; 'The House at the Edge of the Wood' by Mary Wilson from *Selected Poems* published 1970 by Hutchinson. Every effort has been made to contact other copyright holders of material reproduced in this book. If any have been inadvertently overlooked, the publishers will be pleased to make restitution at the earliest opportunity.

Author's Note

Although every main character apart from one is an historical figure, this is a work of fiction and the people in it, even when they are recognisable names and faces, are behaving according to the conventions of a novel rather than a biography or newspaper.

In particular, because the story deals in part with the spreading of gossip, disinformation and half-truth, it is important that any claim about an individual should be judged across the whole novel rather than on isolated comments.

While all the main events are based on published or recorded sources, some of the accounts are contested and the structure of the book is intended to reflect these disagreements. An Afterword expands on sources, method and liberties taken.

M.L.

Contents

Contents

Part Three

1969

Lessons in Enemies

Part Four

1972/1974

Men of Destiny

Part Five

1974/1975

Slag/Bitch

Part Six

1976

Kick a Blind Man

Part Seven

2004

Everybody Knows

Part One

1911 / 1924

Boys of Destiny

'Delayed reaction' experiments have shown that memory, however it may be determined physiologically, is far better developed in the primate than in the lower mammal, and other experiments have also clearly indicated that monkeys and apes are superior to other animals in their adaptive behaviour.

Solly Zuckerman – *The Social Life of Monkeys and Apes*

1

Uncle Alfred's Boy

WHEN HE WAS TEN, he learned two lessons in cruelty. Decades later – finally in a position to inflict suffering rather than endure it – he would remember both, although he was tempted to repeat only one. These educations in pain involved a hairpin and a goldfish.

It was the first time she had hurt him in this way, but his mother's actions had the swagger of planning as she eased the makeshift scalpel past her brow and pulled the folded handkerchief from her pocket. She ran the hairpin along the crisp edge of linen like someone grinding a knife.

At first, he feared that she was coming for his eyes – how terrible to think that there had been enough evidence in their time together to suspect that she might – and so it was almost a relief when she merely dug her weapon into his left ear.

Nanny had once warned him never to put anything smaller than an elbow there – briskly recalling small boys almost deafened by marbles burrowing towards the brain, retrieved only by excruciating operations – and so he noted, again without surprise, maternal inconsistency in this matter.

She twisted the hairpin twice, widening its wings for greater purchase, as if it really were a surgical or dental instrument.

'It stings, Mama,' he complained.

'Oh, Snow, don't go on so!'

His mother's smiles were rare and oddly timed, often seeming not to fit the conversation, so that he wondered if she might be deaf. Now it was the health of his own hearing that concerned him as, grinning in malicious vindication, she withdrew the probe, examined its tip and wiped it on the handkerchief.

Expecting to see spots of red on the cloth, the boy felt almost grateful to see only a smear of brownish yellow. The closest his mother seemed to come to love for him was inflicting terrors slightly lesser than the one expected. After a minute of ridiculous optimism, in which he thought she might settle for torturing him on one side only, Mama began to investigate his other lughole.

This proved a richer seam – in two wide smears on the handkerchief, now looking like the flag of some obscure African dependency – but he gasped at the lunging thrusts. Now she wound a corner of linen into a slightly softer drillhead and made a second advance down each shaft. Then, after twisting a point at the other end of the handkerchief, she licked it and dabbed at the sites of her excavations.

Next she began to line up his nostrils. He tensed for the admission of the hairpin, but the operations here involved only fabric and were, by her standards, almost tender. While we forget the smell of our mother's milk, he thought, we will always remember their spit.

Waiting to find out if this was her final invasion, he wondered why she had pioneered the torture on this particular morning and could only conclude that, even in a family which was run on distrust and suspicion, she was particularly nervous of her brother.

Disappointingly, Uncle Alfred showed no interest at all in these newly cleaned ears and nose. If the old man had ducked down at once and begun a cataloguing of wax, he might at least have admired her foresight, which was not the perfect emotion for a son to feel but could have formed the basis for something like a business relationship. But all his uncle did was to pat him casually on the forehead.

'Still have that sovereign safe, eh, Snow?' he boomed. (Around the time of Snow's fifth birthday, he and his cousins had been given a gold coin – full of Latin words and the numbers 1905 – to mark their terrifying relative's entrance to the House of Lords.)

'Um, yes. Yes, sir,' was all he managed to say.

'Good. Gold's about all you can rely on, the world as it is.' Uncle Alfred gestured to several newspapers, spread out across a short, squat mahogany desk. 'Poor men watch their money, rich men watch their gold.'

His uncle's thumb jabbed down, smudging the wet ink, but the sentences could still be read. PEERS CONCEDE VETO ON COMMONS LEGISLATION.

'Torn the balls off the Lords, Snow. Though even the dullest of them is a better man than Asquith. Don't tell Mama I said balls. Though why the bloody hell not? You've got them, I hope.'

There was another sentence, which you called a headline, about RIOTS in somewhere called LIVERPOOL and what the HOME SECRETARY had said. But now Uncle Alfred moved between him and the news. He saw the fat head coming down and, from memories of his mother, flinched, but then he felt the gentle fingers in his fringe.

'Not white anymore. But I vote we still call you Snow. I know chaps who went to the grave with the name they were given in the perambulator.' The fleshy hand patted his head. 'And up like a wallflower. What sort of nosebag has that sister of mine got you on, eh?'

Like all very tall young boys, he had learned to slouch, aware that he was getting ahead of himself. In caveman days, this was probably a precaution against being sent to hunt or fight too soon. But, even leaning forward, he felt too high against his uncle, a tubby, pugnacious man who seemed to have had his desk designed to flatter his own dimensions.

Old men frightened him. They wore those sharp shirt collars, sticking upwards, which he always thought must cut their necks. He wasn't sure what he should be doing as his relative seemed to become distracted by something on the front of one of the newspapers. Uncle repeatedly hit it with a thick finger, as if to erase the phrase. Then, seeming suddenly to remember his guest, he spun round.

'But you're too young to have to worry about the Germans.' He had a different way of saying that name, so that it sounded more like 'Chairman', a word his mother sometimes used about the uncles. 'Let me show you this.'

Snow associated home with stone floors – and footsteps with Mama charging towards him – and so he enjoyed their soft, soundless progress across this room. Papa talked of the carpets sold in Persian bazaars and he thought this must be one of them. They sploshed across it to the far side of the room, where there was a large glass tank, in which two fish of different sizes swam. He was thrilled by this first childish turn in the day's entertainments.

'You know what this is, boy?'

'An aq . . . aquarium, sir.'

'Yes. Although fish tank would have been a satisfying *English* equivalent. And, in a way, you're only half-correct. Or, alternatively, twice right. It's a *divided* fish tank.'

Uncle Alfred leaned closer to the glass and his nephew – from interest, but also from fear that he now dwarfed the adult even more – copied this position.

From the new angle, it was apparent that each fish – one long, brown and bulbous, the other small and reddish – floated in its own square of water and weeds. He could now see that a fifth, inner pane of glass formed a see-through wall between them.

'A pike. A goldfish.' His uncle's tone was proud and loud, like a fishmonger of living species. 'At least until . . .'

The old man reached down – his fat thumb disturbing the water and causing the smaller fish to twitch with a useless premonition – and pulled the central panel from the tank. The gesture was reminiscent of a party magician and its effect was the same – disappearance – as the pike darted across its new, expanded territory, sharked its jaws and then swam a satisfied lap of honour around wider seas which it now ruled alone, until his uncle thumped the middle panel down again to show that there were limits to piscine power.

'A lesson from the deep,' said Uncle Alfred. 'Life is like that.'

For the second time that morning, a family member flapped a handkerchief towards him but, already schooled in dry-eyed terror by his mother's cruelties, he didn't need it.

'Capital. Your brothers blubbed at that. It may be that you're the tough one that we need.'

Returning the unneeded material neatly to one pocket, Uncle Alfred pulled from the other a gold coin, which he pressed into his nephew's hand before continuing the arc of his own fingers into a valedictory pat on the head.

'Remember the gold. Remember the goldfish. These lessons I have left thee with.'

As Snow came out through the vast dark-varnished doors – held back for him by a man whose only purpose seemed to be to swing them one way or the other – his mother advanced on him with the pointed breath-wet hankie held out like a sword, and he feared a reappearance of the hairpin. But she just briefly polished his forehead.

'Great black smudge there,' she complained. 'You look

like a blessed Hindu. He never remembers his fingers are always covered in ink.'

(Next spring, at Winchester, he noticed two boys carrying the same mark and wondered if their uncles were press barons too. But it was nothing as exotic. They were simply Roman Catholics on Ash Wednesday.)

The hairpin became part of his mother's repertoire of care, reliably applied on the night before a return to school or visit to family. Decades later, in a twist on the figure of speech, his ears really would burn when he thought or spoke of her.

He would always remember the goldfish as well. And, though few were yet familiar with genetics, he never forgot how first his mother and his uncle had terrified him and worried that there might be something lying in his blood, like typhoid in the water.

2

Uncle Harold's Boy

HOW HE HATED shaking in the dust and drafts above the gutter in that fancy hanging pram. Stopping and cornering were the worst. He thought of bike and sidecar separating, like in the comedies at the Saturday morning pictures. Da called this one the Precision but it never felt very precise to him.

Thrown sideways as they turned into a long, wide street, he shielded with one hand the jagged scar, still intermittently stinging, in the part of his body which his parents and the doctors always called his stomach but wasn't quite. The other hand clasped to his head the baggy flat cap which he wore for Sunday services and other best.

Both moves were complicated by his fear of kicking the family's precious Box Brownie, which – too big for the tool-box on the back of the Precision – lay at his feet.

Da, who loved numbers, spoke of the Precision in figures – 596cc, three-speed gears - though don't worry, young man, we'll not be needing all that unless a large man comes after us with a wood-axe. But, even at this speed, his eyes were too foggy – our Marjorie always said he'd need glasses, ha ha – to read the street sign, although it began with G. GOW something.

'The University,' his father shouted. This was one of the words always spoken at home in a special way, as if there was some kind of fancy capital letter at the front, like in the big high Bible the elders read at Chapel. That was another of those words. So were School and Scouts.

This way of travel frightened him – another sharp corner, and another, his hand twice jumping to the roughened skin above his plucked appendix – but he liked the way that being able to buy it lifted them above the other families.

And it was good to be so on his own. It felt like being lonely in a nice way. His da had two children, but the motorcycle only carried one. Sometimes he terrified himself with the fantasy of a Precision with a double carriage, the great fifteen-year-old lump of their Marjorie thumping into him at every corner.

He was glad that his sister hadn't made this trip. The best would have been just him and his mam but she didn't ride a motorcycle and London was seen as business for the boys.

His mam and da insisted that his sister was proud of him. The arrival of a brother coinciding with her seventh birthday, she had been told that the baby was a 'special present'. Marjorie sometimes said it herself to her friends. But children outgrew special presents, and last year, on holiday at Filey, she had thrown him fully-clothed into the sea.

The humiliation of standing in a sopping, salty flannel suit while new clothes were brought for him had been like wetting his pants to the power of ten. They hadn't even raised a row with Marjorie, swearing blind, in that way parents, teachers and football referees had, that they hadn't seen what happened.

After several more bumps – and worries for his wound – they stopped for their dinner at an ABC cafe.

'We're in Westminster,' his father announced, almost allowing that word the special capital letter as well. He asked if he could have the sausage and mash and was told that not only could he but he should. 'We need to work on covering those bones. I never thought we'd have a thin 'un in this family.'

Harold had never liked being fat – lads thought you were slow and would only let you go in goal for football – but now he felt floaty and weak, which was no better. Even buttoned up, his flannel jacket flapped in front. 'You're a ghost of yourself,' his mam had said when he came back from the hospital. The expression had frightened him, but he knew what she meant.

'Are they good?' his father asked as he ate the sausages, which came in gravy paler and thinner than his mam's.

'Yes, thank you, Da,' he answered, assuming that to be the right answer.

'Not as good as proper Yorkshire ones,' he was reminded. 'How are you finding the bike, son?'

'Very comfortable, Da.'

'I feel I haven't quite the hang of the corners yet. But the Beardmore Precision is a splendid machine. Quite a revelation, after the Banshee, though you never rode on that. Apart from the side-engine, how many cc?'

He didn't have to think; it was imprinted. 'Five hundred and ninety-six, Da.'

'Good. Apart from that, the main distinction is an integral fuel tank.'

Integral fuel tank. Sometimes he heard words and knew they ought to be remembered. He thought of his memory as a series of drawers, still mainly empty, and pictured this information dropping in and then the tray sliding back.

'Three hundred and five multiplied by two hundred and seven!' The command made the cafe a classroom. He put aside the sausages for the sum.

'Come on, son. Mastication and mathematics should be possible simultaneously.'

But he cleared his mouth of food and shut his eyes. The trick was to make your brain a blackboard. Chalk-scrape, columns, carry-overs and then: 'Sixty-three thousand, one hundred and thirty-five, Da.'

His answer was followed out by a rasping burp, probably brought on by swallowing the sausage too quickly and the worry. A passing waitress laughed as she heard.

'Satisfied customer,' she said and patted him on the head. He hated being laughed at. It was just like Marjorie.

'Excuse you,' his father laughed. 'But that were pretty nippy for a nipper too. Now ask me one. Don't mind about how hard.'

He chewed some sausage slowly, as if he was thinking of a zinger, although he was really just hungry. 'Three hundred and fifteen,' he asked, trying to sound like a teacher, 'divided by one hundred and eighty-nine.'

He had a school-friend whose da, once a fairground boxer, liked to invite all comers to hit him as hard as they dared. These divisions and multiplications, he already understood, were Herbert Wilson's equivalent.

Mr Mathematics, the Fabulous Human Computing Machine, made a neat cut and chew from his own food, plaice and chips.

'We've to be home by sunset,' he dared to prompt his da, a phrase often aimed at him when he was stuck on a sum.

Clearing his mouth of battered fish, then theatrically sipping water, Mr Mathematics announced, to his imaginary fairground crowd: 'One point six – to the nearest place. Of course, the flaw in the arrangement is that you have no way of knowing if I'm right or wrong. Except that we've brung you up to be honest as well as clever.'

Now his father began to chant a string of words which would have bewildered a German spy at a neighbouring table: 'Mutch, Wood, Bullock, Slade, Wilson (no relation, more's the pity),' the list began. Perhaps a stranger would have thought Da was a teacher, remembering the register. 'Watson, Richardson . . . carry on, lad . . .'

'Mann, Taylor, Swann, Islip,' the boy completed the challenge. He tried not to look cocky. Mam didn't like him being 'on show'.

'And which season is that?'

'1919–1920 Cup Final.'

'Result?'

'Aston Villa 1, the Town – swizz – nil.' His father seemed to expect this answer, so he added: 'After extra time.'

'Played at . . . ?'

'Stamford Bridge.'

Again, this seemed to be taken as what any reasonable person would know, so he quickly pulled out the trays in his brain until he saw something shiny and surprising. 'The crowd was fifty thousand and eighteen.'

His father nodded and then – a rare event – repeated the gesture, so that it looked as if someone had just knocked him on the bonce. Harold suddenly thought of the Sunday school lesson about how each of us is special to God.

'Good lad. Glad to see I'll not be the only elephant in our clan.'

Both his parents were famous for their memories in different ways. Da could give you all eleven players in every Town team ever fielded while Mam, who always said she'd forget her own head next, got through the day with notes of what she was doing next fixed to her pinny.

Over pudding – apple pie with custard which, like the gravy, seemed thinner and duller than his mother's – the interrogation switched from sums to history.

'Who's the Prime Minister?'

'Mr James Ramsay MacDonald.'

'Good. And in whose interest was he elected?'

'Labour.'

'How many Labour administrations have there been?'

'This is the first.'

In their house, Labour was not quite a word like Chapel or Scouts but it was still always said in a Sunday-best voice.

'All right,' said the question-master, standing. 'Let's go to Mr MacDonald's house.'

The stodge now sticking out his stomach made him feel less ghostly but also made him worry that the scar might rip with another journey in the low-slung bucket.

'Are you still thinking of buying a car, Da?' he asked hopefully, imagining smoother travel (although admittedly with Marjorie big and bossy on the shared back seat).

'I do have my eye on an Austin 7. But there's the question of pennies. The best years for Huddersfield were when the world wanted bombs.'

He never quite understood what his father meant by this phrase, which he said a lot. The end of the war should have been a good thing, but it had somehow been bad for Da.

As they puttered past a house five times the size of school, his father shouted: 'Buckingham Palace. I think we'll be forgiven for not standing in the circumstances.' When they swung into a cul-de-sac, he couldn't read the sign, but didn't have to because his driver-guide proudly announced: 'Downing Street.'

He had expected soldiers guarding the entrance, or at least a line of peelers, but they were able to park by the kerb and walk up to the door as if this was their own home. Already imagining an article about this outing for the *Children's Newspaper*, he shoved important details into the desk in his head: a raised front step, scrubbed to a cleanliness which would have impressed even his mam; bricks smaller and darker than the white, wide stones of their house; a vertical strip of three bells for visitors.

Above the door, in front of a seven-petalled window, hung a sloped rectangular lantern of the kind seen outside police stations. As well as the article for CN, he was now contemplating a model, snapped on Da's camera and sent to *Meccano Magazine*.

As he stood beneath the famous number, his father was folding out the Box Brownie. Worried about what might happen if the Prime Minister needed to leave or arrive, Harold stood in front of the well-kept step. His da told him to straighten his cap, and then his leg.

'You look as if you want to run away, lad.'

'Da, if I send an article to the paper, might I have the picture?'

'We'll see. I fancy your mam'll want to send it to your Uncle Harold.'

(This uncle – his mother's brother, 'who you're called after' – was a bit like Ramsay MacDonald but in Australia. When the boy impressed his parents with something he had done or said, they always spoke of telling Uncle Harold in a letter.)

Marjorie, when shown the photograph, joked about her little brother getting above himself, but it became known in the family as the Picture. Two years later – when the boy sailed to Australia with his mother, driven to the docks in Da's new Austin 7 – it was shown to Uncle Harold.

The old man, who had a desk much bigger than a teacher's, said: 'Let's hope it's a prophecy.' It was a word he had only heard in church.

Part Two

1968

The Emergency Government

My Bill has now been read a second time:
His ready vote no member now refuses
In verity, I wield a power sublime,
And one that I can turn to mighty uses.
What joy to carry, in the very teeth
Of Ministry, Cross-Bench and Opposition,
Some rather urgent measures – quite beneath
The ken of patriot and politician.

W. S. Gilbert – *Iolanthe* (first version)

3

The Turn of the Screw

HE WAS about to tap his pipe on the desk to empty it, but stopped when he saw the butterfly, which made him hope that summer had finally come. It hovered round the cross-hairs of the window in his study on the second floor of the only home in Britain better known by its number than its street.

The insect settled on the sniper's bullseye where the four bars of white-painted wood met. Since Dr King, he had often imagined his own head cross-hatched in a rifle's sights. Dallas and now Memphis. Did you know? Was there a moment of realization before your skull blew up?

Those poets his wife liked rhapsodized about butterflies, but this one was nothing special in colour, its greys outshone by the wood's glittering vanilla. Yet, to a tired man, it still felt like a blessing.

The Prime Minister watched the insect, admiring the perfect stillness or, perhaps, the simplicity of its responsibilities.

The visitor slowly flapped its wings. This movement reminded him of something. Trawling his exhausted mind for a metaphor – it felt a physical effort, like forcing jammed drawers – he was worried when he finally retrieved it: applause. The flapping of wings reminded him of hands clapping. Was this the effect of power on men? Imagining respect from insects?

The Prime Minister turned from the window and looked across the room. He raised an eyebrow at Marcia – a prompt to resume their conversation – but she seemed to be asleep, or at least had closed her eyes, her head tipped back against the top edge of the armchair, feet stretched out, high-heeled shoes skewed off sideways underneath them. Her hands shielded the belly which kept its secret well, even at six months. He scolded himself not to mention his own tiredness to her again. Staying up late with his boxes was nothing beside the way a baby seemed to drain a woman from within; he had seen it twice with his wife.

He thought that if a spy had been watching this scene, examining transcripts or fish-eye film – a possibility he had often considered – they might make much of the boss's kindly smile at his napping assistant. And stockinged feet in an office suggested relaxation, if not intimacy. Was it because it suggested closeness – or because we feared letting out our smell – that we exposed our feet to so few people? Well, let them gossip. If the press went too far, there would be an Arnold letter.

A scratch at the back of his throat became a cough, which he tried to bury under a breath in case she really was asleep, rather than not speaking to him. (Worried that the spasms in his larynx were something nasty digging in, he had asked for the doctor to be got. But Joe said it was just that Downing Street was full of dust. The downstairs rooms were like the excavations at Pompeii.)

Capitalizing (just a metaphor, brothers, I assure Conference) on a rare moment in which he was not being watched – at least officially – by anyone, he used his reflection in the window to smooth down hair which, at fifty-two, was eight-tenths silver but still plentiful enough to be ruffled by the double hand-rake which exasperation raised in him. It was a gesture he felt himself making several times a day now.

He experimentally tensed his jaw so that the dewlaps in

his window image vanished. When his time was over here, however that happened, they would need a photograph for the wall. History would know his fat face. He had only once looked thin and that was in the Picture.

While he admired his new tight chin, the butterfly, as if disgusted by this vanity, jumped away. Perhaps it had a premonition that the tranquillity was over because, as it took flight, a buzzer sounded. Marcia opened her eyes, jolted forward and was soon standing in her shoes with impressive speed for a woman in her condition.

There was a tricolour strip of bulbs above the door: red, green, white, like a personalized traffic light. When he pressed a button on the desk, the raspberry shimmer became mint and two men – Henry and someone else he wasn't expecting – came into the study.

WHEN Henry James pushed open the door, slowly, as if worried about what he might reveal, Bennett saw one of Britain's most famous faces sitting at his desk – fiddling with that no less familiar pipe – and one of the nation's most whispered names standing in attendance, a tall woman stooping forward, presumably to hide the signs of the child she thought nobody knew about.

This tableau made him think of a downmarket version of Renaissance paintings of the Angel Gabriel and the bashfully maternal Mary: Wilson was serene, masculine power, Marcia trembling feminine mystery.

'Prime Minister,' said Henry James. 'This is Mr Bennett from the Royal Mint.'

Shaking hands was more complicated for this politician than for most. He fussily transferred the pipe from right hand to left before greeting his visitor with a firm, dry grip.

'Have you met Marcia Williams?' asked Gabriel, indicating the Madonna.

She gave him one of those gawky smiles, too many teeth for the jaw, which made you think of stables and how the quality of English dentistry should not be given much emphasis in the next Labour manifesto.

'The Keeper of the Diary,' Marcia further identified herself.

Whatever its smoking role, the Prime Minister's pipe also seemed to serve as a conductor's baton, orchestrating his conversations. Now it waved them towards a sofa and armchairs set away from the desk.

Bennett, who had voted for Douglas-Home from tribal pull while knowing that Wilson was the more intriguing figure, reflected that he seemed exactly as you imagined – the pipe as constant a symbol as a comedian's prop – and yet somehow an impostor: shorter and thinner than television made him. To a voter who knew him only from the radio, though, there would have been no double-take. The soft Yorkshire speech – treading equally on each word, like a careful dale-walker – was as much a part of Harold Wilson's personality as the tamping of tobacco.

'So you have some money for me, Mr Bennett?' asked Wilson. 'Though not a pound and not in my pocket.'

Henry James and Marcia laughed at once. Bennett was slower because he had censored from his own planned remarks a similar reference to the devaluation of the previous year and the Prime Minister's televised gloss, which had been lashed to him as a catchphrase by Conservatives and cartoonists. For weeks afterwards, at the Mint, you would hear employees putting on a flat-cap accent and murmuring: 'It does not mean that the pound in the pocket is worth fourteen per cent less than it is now.' This turn was, like the Chancellor's lisped r's, an impersonation almost everyone could do.

He was surprised to find Wilson inviting such humour, but assumed it was pre-emptive jesting, like someone joking about the size of their nose.

Bennett took from his briefcase a small black display box and set it on the table. Flapping back the lid, he felt like a jeweller playing up to fiancés.

'A medal?' wondered the Prime Minister. 'I could do with one. I always feel short when I meet General de Gaulle. His chest rattles like he's stolen all your cutlery.'

This time, everyone giggled. The columnists Bennett read in the *Times* were often vicious about Wilson's jokiness – 'Rather more in the tradition of the Glasgow Empire than the British Empire' – but, as a recipient, it felt like kindliness: putting people at their ease.

The fingers into which the Mint man now placed the silver coin were surprisingly pudgy. Bennett had a flash of a fat boy at school.

'The third of the three pre-decimal coins, Prime Minister,' Bennett explained. 'The fifty pence.'

'Which is, what, the half-crown? Fifty pence. Though people will say pee, won't they, pretty quickly?'

Wilson touched each of the edges in turn; gently, as if he feared they might cut him. He turned to his press officer: 'Seven sides. I could use that, Henry, if we decide to join the Common Market. The Six plus us.'

'Yes,' said Henry James. Smirking internally at one of the shorter verbal forays under that name (imagining Downing Street press releases consisting of a single, one-page sentence, relentlessly qualified), Bennett looked at Wilson and thought:

if you decide to join the Common Market. You're running towards them like overripe Camembert but the General won't have you.

Wilson, suddenly a rugger referee, spun the coin in the air, then flicked it to his secretary: 'Here you are, Marcia. Don't spend it all at once.'

The Keeper of the Diary ran the edge along one wrist: 'Probably dangerous, isn't it, Harold? First currency you could use to kill yourself.'

The Prime Minister smiled but his eyes qualified his amusement. It had been a darker comment than he wanted. Marcia flicked the coin to Henry James, who caught it neatly, viewed both sides, then bounced it back towards his boss. It was a simple catch – in cricket, the batsman would be walking back already – but Wilson's hands, though cupped, were never under it. The fifty-pence piece rattled against the coffee table.

Wilson, Bennett noticed, looked slumped and humbled, taking the fumble as a much greater failure than it was. As the great literary namesake retrieved the coin and handed it back, the Prime Minister staged a distraction. Flicking it over, he glanced at the girlish profile of the woman whose government he led.

'Glad it's got the Queen on it. You know that Wedgie Benn thinks we should get her head off the stamps? Off his head, more like it.' The PM went on speaking, as if he wanted to put still more distance between himself and his slip. 'Henry tells me people are already calling the five-penny and ten-penny ones Wilson's Washers. I wonder what they'll call this.' His fleshy thumb tried the seven edges. 'Wilson's Screw?' he offered.

Mrs Williams's face had a naturally startled aspect but

now Bennett thought of women petrified mid-sentence by the lava from Vesuvius. Henry James, showing a sudden fascination in a pamphlet on the table, was silent but Bennett could imagine the censored paragraphs starting in his head.

Wilson, so keen on jokes, showed no sign of having spotted this one.

4

Pray that Fred West
Lives Forever

TO CELEBRATE the heart transplant, he lit another cigarette. He hardly had the puff for it, having run the final mile after the bus was blocked by a student demo heading for Trafalgar Square. The yells of 'Hey, hey, LBJ!' sounded disconcerting amid London stone and he contemplated a novel about an Englishman who is kidnapped, drugged and wakes up in America. Or was that too Kafka?

It was their third day of waiting for the patient to die and Storey, who had been getting the best spreads, had been elected unofficial dean of the cardiac hacks.

'Ah, Bernard,' said the fat fireman from the *Telegraph*, who had a Kingsley Amis sort of name: John Dixon? James Dickens? 'They gave you a good show this morning.'

Dixon–Dickens was holding a folded-over *Mirror* and enviously indicated the front page: HEART MAN GIVES A WINK AND A WAVE.

'I know. I'm lucky. Cudlipp's first rule of journalism is write about what the readers have or what they want to have. So you can't go far wrong with hearts. I'm just worried how we're going to top it today.'

'That's right,' said the joker from the *Manchester Guardian*. 'It would have to be a conjugal visit from Mrs West to get on the front again.'

The man from the *Telegraph* revealed the real reason for

his flattery by pointing between Storey's fingers: 'Would you have a spare one of those by any chance, Bernard?'

Storey instinctively tightened his grip on his cigarette. 'I've only a few left. And they've all got my name on them. It's been a long day. I've done two jobs this morning.'

Dixon–Dickens was middle fifties, almost twice Storey's age. Please, God (deceased), he prayed, let me not still be a news desk poodle in twenty years' time, left on the desk as colleagues claim columns and specialisms.

'Christ, they work King Cecil's men, don't they?' editorialized the *Guardian*.

'Oh, come on,' the *Telegraph* insisted. 'I'm sure there's something in union rules. Duty to a gasping comrade. I'd even buy them from you on a piece rate. Couldn't run to a pack this morning. My good lady's devalued the family budget. And it certainly does affect the pound in my pocket.'

'She's probably right.' This was Reuters, serious and shy, like many of the wire reporters. 'My brother-in-law works in the Square Mile. The rumour is that the Yanks are going to pull the plug on gold by the end of the summer.'

'Our abacus man says the same,' the *Guardian* agreed.

'And then Britain's back to barter by the winter,' predicted Reuters. 'Goodnight, Mr Wilson.'

'And *no* thank you,' added the *Telegraph*.

Storey was alarmed by this economic pessimism. It was not that he was a Labour man. He now despised Wilson as much as most of those who had voted for him. But his personal finances were so precarious that he needed Britain's to be buoyant. In the hope that a good deed might win him some kind of cosmic sympathy, he pushed one of the last Capstans into the mouth of his *Telegraph* colleague and lit it.

'Good man, Storey. If you ever need an alibi – adultery, expenses scam, whatever – I'm your man.'

As on previous days, a crowd had gathered outside the National Heart Hospital to cheer on Frederick West in his quest to break the rules of nature. A doctor had told Storey that the hospital had seen nothing like it since Peter Sellers had his coronary.

Now the waiting spectators made a noise like the final rushed discussion and sweet scrunching before lights go down in a concert hall or theatre, as two white-coated doctors and a sort of backing group of nurses walked out onto the steps. The snappers shouted and jostled as the TV crews blocked the view with their giant cameras and bloated microphones. The telly boys, once also-rans, now ran the show.

In the brief silence before the statement began, you could hear the whispered, rhythmic Latin of the monk and the nun who had kept a vigil on the steps since the operation. While the pious among the public observers were asking that Fred West should live forever, the professionally religious were present as objectors, asking God's forgiveness for a world in which the hearts of the dead beat in the chests of the living.

Over the marathon rosaries, the top doctor began: 'Gentlemen of the press, members of the public, I am delighted to tell you that Mr West has completed his most satisfactory night and his most active morning yet. He was able to eat a little more mashed food and sipped a glass of sherry. Yesterday, as you know, he was able to wave to Mrs West through the glass partition. Today, they were able to hold hands and speak.'

Perhaps, in cave days, when the first ever storyteller invented the genre of romance, a report of such a simple human gesture had produced a response as strong as this, but Storey could not otherwise imagine it. The people cheered and whistled.

'Mr West was able to walk ten feet without assistance

from his bed to the chair.' Another football roar, for a toddler's achievement by a man of forty-five. Beside his shorthand record of the medical facts, Storey scribbled: 8th Age? He wondered if the Shakespeare speech could be rewritten to add a third childhood after the second. But Cudlipp might consider that 'college stuff'.

'I'm very pleased that Mrs Frederick West will tell you the rest.'

Storey was sure he heard a boo. It was presumably a church objector to the violation of the body or possibly, these days, a women's libber objecting to a wife being designated by her husband's name. The crowd of nurses parted like girls at the Folies Bergère to reveal Josephine West, a small woman with a dark perm which gave her the appearance, like so many of her generation, of an unknown sister of the Queen.

'How long did you spend with Fred?' shouted the fireman from the *London Evening News*, who the others all called the Rioja Monster.

'Fif . . .' Her voice too high; a nervous cough. 'Fifteen minutes.'

'What did you wear?'

Mrs West, 45, from Leigh-on-Sea, Essex (as Storey had described her to five million readers three days running), looked perplexed and used her big handbag to point at her matching jacket and skirt. A doctor leaned over and spoke to her quietly.

'Oh. Oh, right.' If the television news were in colour, you would have seen her blush. 'I had to put on a gown and things. A mask and gloves.'

'What did he say?' Storey shouted.

She reddened again and revealed: 'As soon as I walked into the room, he said: "Hi, Kid." That's what he usually says to me.'

Storey knew the next question Cudlipp would want put and asked it, though he felt his voice instinctively changing in pitch, as if he were pretending to be someone else: 'Did you kiss him?'

'Heart transplants and flowers,' muttered the Rioja Monster behind him.

'No,' Mrs West admitted, her embarrassment increasing. 'I hadn't been told not to. But I thought it was taking things too far the first time. It was exciting enough without that, though.'

Knowing that he had his eight paras of colour easily, even a punt for the front on a quiet day, Storey relaxed and started another gasper. It could not have been often, outside of pornographic cinemas in Paris, that an individual human organ had received a round of applause. But in the pale May sunshine in front of the National Heart Hospital, the crowd enthusiastically clapped the news that man had gone behind God's back.

THEY MIGHT serve bog-water gin-and-bitters here, but it was not an uninteresting pub. Special clientele they must get, just around the corner from the National Ticker Clinic. The leggy blondes and chaps in leather-patched jackets must be *Carry On* nurses and Kildares. So the rest, overdressed and fumbling with their Woodbines, would be relatives, anaesthetizing their fear or stiffening themselves for life alone. Widows must come through at quite a clip.

Wright sipped his g-and-b, gambling it might have settled in the glass. Filthy drink. But then he wasn't here for the beer; he was here because of the wire-tap. Office joke.

When the saloon door opened, he knew it was his mark. There was a basic pride in spotting your quarry as soon as they breathed the same fug as you. On a black-bag job, it might decide if your next encounter with English soil was horizontal or vertical. On a watch like this, it was merely decent trade-craft.

The mark did not, in fact, much resemble his picture in the *Mirror*: the one in which he held a big white telephone to his ear. Why were hacks always photographed on the blower? He assumed it was supposed to make them look clued-up and ever ready for a story. Well, there were two problems with that. One: hacks didn't know an inch of what went on in Britain. Two: you needed to be careful on telephones because people might be listening.

Locking on to this mark was a Spanish driving test, anyway. Storey came in holding a notebook and a copy of the *Mirror* with his bleeding-heart story all over page one and went straight over to the Brideshead Boy.

IF SOMEONE says yes, ask why; if someone says no, ask why not. Another of Cudlipp's rules: it was a journo's business to be cynical. But that morning Storey's professional scepticism had been defeated. He believed he had seen the future: the renewable human.

By 1990, say – 2000, at the latest, though such dates seemed stupid, Stanley Kubrick – if you had used up your heart or liver, they would give you a new one. The National Health Service would be like a garage, trading yourself in when you felt a bit rusty under the bonnet.

In this mood of bodily optimism, Storey went to smoke and drink with his friend who only had one lung. Waugh was sitting in the corner, blowing out smoke at a rate which would have been heroic for someone with the full set of bellows. As usual, he was smoking no-handed, cigarette clenched between his lips, scribbling in a notebook while holding a newspaper cutting in the other hand.

'Column or novel?' asked Storey.

Waugh looking up, blinking piggily, one of many mannerisms which made you think of his father dead-batting Freeman on *Face to Face*. As now did the high, stuttery Edwardian voice, which would have better fitted someone four decades older than twenty-eight: 'Ah, Timmy. D-d-dear boy. It's just some notes for the Spec.' He pointed to a full pint glass on the table in front of the bar stool Storey had just taken. 'I got your drink in on the basis that you were bound to arrive eventually.'

'Yes. I'm sorry, Bron. I . . . the heart thing started late.'

'That's fine, Nigel.' It was Waugh's way to call you any name but your own. Too systematic and inventive to be forgetfulness, it presumably came from a fear of boredom and cliché which extended even to vocative conversation. 'Is Mr West still ticking over?'

'Apparently. He was able to sip some sherry today.'

'Really? It seems rather a palaver to strip an unfortunate Irish labourer of spare parts merely to allow another chap to drink Harvey's Bristol Cream. At least the wretched Dr Barnard in South Africa is using the hearts of Negroes to keep Afrikaners going, which maintains the Frankenstein traditions of science. He'll die soon, you know, your Mr West. The French and American recipients have gone already, a fact our papers are ignoring in their euphoria, although I'm glad they're giving you such a good show on it.'

Waugh brandished that day's *Mirror*, chuckling maliciously. Storey feared that his friend was going to point out some syntactical calamity or embarrassing typo in the transplant splash but he flicked to the centre pages and dangled the double-page spread like a sopping towel.

'The Super Seventy-Five,' Waugh read in the throaty tones of dog-track enthusiasm which he had used to personify

Cudlipp's *Mirror* when he and Bernard had worked there together. 'One of these seventy-five faces is the face of Mrs Britain, 1968. The face of the "young British wife and mother at her best" who will win the *Daily Mirror*'s 5,000-guinea award.'

Waugh indicated the two pages of passport-style photographs of housewives with bobs, beehives and perms. 'I have been wondering, Bruce, if I should impregnate a select number of the contenders in the interests of improving the pedigree of the working classes. Mrs Boniface of Patching, Sussex, aptly named, has an inviting grin and Mrs Titmus of Solihull a certain housemaidish simplicity. You might share the siring with me if you were not so entirely occupied with your sweet colleen.'

Storey was recently enough married for even this oblique reference to Moira to give him a button-popping hard-on. The memory of the taste of her suddenly pricked his tongue and he damped it with beer.

'It's very Cudlipp,' Storey admitted. In their time on the paper, he had always been more comfortable than Waugh with the *Mirror*'s populism and reader-involvement: an extension of the principle of local journalism that, if you printed the names of all two hundred people at the flower show, each horticulturist might buy a copy.

Waugh, though, was a satirist, by instinct and example. Storey thought that if his own father had been a famously brutal humorist and journalist he would not himself have written comic novels and mocking columns, but Bron felt a royal duty to carry on the line.

Storey asked: 'What are you sermonizing on this week?'

'The Sandhurst Administration, I think.' A questioning face from Storey won the explanation: 'The possibility of a

British coup d'état. At what point would the country get into such a mess that it might be run from one?'

'Are the army seriously talking about it?'

'People are talking seriously about the possibility that they might be talking about it. I hear that the Shetland Islands has been selected as a camp for political detainees.' Waugh stared at Storey's emptied pint glass. 'Do you think you'd better get some more drinks in before a chap in epaulettes comes round to implement a curfew?'

'I . . . I'm sorry, Bron. I'll get you one. I won't myself.'

'Really? You're not listening to all that humbug from American drunks?'

'The way the wine flows on the backbench, there are advantages in being less pissed than the subs. I've got to file twice this afternoon.'

Waugh grimaced at this industry: 'They work you hard in King Cecil's mines. Spare-part heart and what else?'

'The desk sent me to Hornsey first thing. Demo at the College of Art. The students declared a state of anarchy and occupied the principal's office.'

'Only occupation most of them will ever take part in!'

Most men, thought Storey, remembering the suburban schoolteacher he tried daily not to be, caught themselves imitating their father. The difference with Waugh, as with other dynasts, was that the model was generally recognizable, so that he gave the impression of someone trapped by accent and mannerisms. Bron was like a literary Prince Charles.

'Better than some of the stuff on the list,' Storey defended reporting which Waugh doubtless found boring. 'The desk threatened me with inflatable furniture. Your living room at the mercy of a pin. At Hornsey, they had all these banners.' Flapping through the pad until he found the shorthand record of the painted bed-sheet he half-remembered, he quoted:

'When the finger points at the moon, the idiot looks at the finger. Is that philosophy or bollocks?'

'I've seen lesser balls on a bull, Hector.'

Storey, who had secretly found the slogan poetic, avoided a disagreement by going to the bar. Waiting to be served, he changed his mind and decided he needed another beer himself, then, paying, wished he hadn't. He seemed to have much less money than he expected and was left hopefully patting his jacket like a fake major in a film. The pound in your pocket.

His friend had used the interlude to scribble another few lines. Bron had a facility in journalism, as well as an income, which Storey coveted. Obsessively sensitive to the possibility that rivals were becoming famous, he wondered if he had deliberately been drawn to a colleague who already was, whose success could be credited to nepotism.

If Evelyn Waugh had been Storey's father, he felt that he would have hated and resented him. Bron seemed not to. Even the episode of the rationed bananas was made into a tale of paternal boldness rather than savagery.

To ease the post-war diet of denial, the government had sent one piece of the forbidden Caribbean fruit to each child in Britain. Evelyn had sat his brood down at the table and consumed the entire ration with cream and sugar.

Rather than growing up, as many might have, to become an Oedipal greengrocer, Bron seemed to enjoy the shock and disapproval the anecdote generated in others. If he ever seemed hostile to the man who had loaded him with a large name and example, it was only in his scatological account of Evelyn's death, leaving a small pile of shit on the floor at Combe Florey after his coronary on the bog two Easter Sundays back.

Setting down their refill beers, Storey saw that his friend

had torn a piece from the *Times* about Biafra, an obsession of Bron's which represented an exception to his general taste-outraging provocations. He had talked about writing a book. Fearing that he might talk about it now, Storey challenged him: 'No decent gossip at all. Is it you or the world that's got nicer?'

'Neither's very likely, is it? You just catch me at the research stage. I'm working on a truly nuclear rumour.'

'Which you won't tell me?'

'Which I will for one of these.' Bron reached across and pulled a fag from the packet. 'Don't look like that. If the Yanks abandon gold this summer, the *Mirror* may be paying you in cigarettes and nylons by the winter.'

'OK. What have I bartered for, then?'

'The Prime Minister's secretary is pregnant. And he's the father.'

'Bollocks!'

'When the political correspondent of the *Spectator* fingers the biggest scandal since Profumo, the idiot looks at the finger.'

'Where did you get it?'

'It came into the *Eye* from one of the Commons offices.'

'So why has no one written about it?'

'She's convinced the Parly boys that it's a private matter. The baby, that is. As for the father, it's very 'ard to prove' – Bron switched to the Andy Capp parody he employed for northerners in general – 'that 'our 'Arold's 'ad 'er. Although I tend to the view that he did, in the absence of other obvious candidates willing to volunteer for that terrifying mission.'

As Storey began to reply, Waugh, who habitually affected a look of indifference, suddenly seemed to be drawn with mischievous interest to something happening across the room. Storey feared that he had become a 'bore', a category dreaded and catalogued by Bron in another continuation of his father's spirit.

But the other journalist leaned forward and whispered eagerly: 'Nigel, that white-haired man over there has been staring at us intermittently ever since you came in. Do you think he might be a homosexualist?'

HE HATED trailing the *Mirror* man because the bugger took the bus. What you wanted was a quarry who drove himself fast in a decent marque or caught cabs. Wright hadn't been on double-deckers since he came back from the war. He supposed Storey took them to save money for his flutters, although, as they seemed to be crossing the whole of sodding London by Omnibus, this journey might not feed many steeplechasers.

If Wright had been the betting man, he would have put money on Storey going into the *Mirror*, but at Holborn Circus he took another bus towards the river.

They were heading down the Embankment now, passing London Bridge. Wright wanted to stand up and ask the passengers to bow their heads in shame. London Bridge is falling down, falling down. But the song was wrong. They had pulled it down, broken it up to be sold to America.

From the lower deck – Storey would have a better view from on top – he could see the huge blocks lying on the quay, like some puzzle for a giant kid, numbered so that the Yanks (Jews, too, probably) who had bought it could put it back together. Bridges were supposed to cross water but not in the hold of a bloody boat.

He was working up a version of this bluster – ending with a shout about how we'd all be in the same boat soon – when his target appeared on the stairs. Wright, who had settled himself on one of the long seats downstairs for the club-footed and the pudding club, turned his face away – just in case the *Mirror* man had clocked him in the pub – under the pleasant enough cover of trying to tell if the secretary girl sitting opposite, in one of those fanny-bandage skirts they all wore now, belonged to that set you read about who liked to feel the air on their hair.

His investigation was still inconclusive when Storey flicked the wire for the next request stop. They were deep in the bumhole of nowhere. Wright wondered for a moment if his target had another secret in addition to the one they already knew. But a minute later he crossed a road and went into one of those sad brown shops with nothing except a name on its front.

5

King and the Queen

KING DREAMED OF needing less sleep. Biographies of great men confirmed they were frequently insomniacs, resenting the night, stretching the day: to become a man of your time, it was necessary for time to be defeated. This bothered King. The one obstacle to his certainty of his destiny was this contradictory fondness for his bed.

There was Churchill, who put on his pyjamas in the afternoons, but his naps were to sleep off alcohol and to allow him to play the owl later on.

The exceptionally long Rolls-Royce – one of a limited line, an English riposte to American stretch limousines – left the office in Holborn by 5.30 p.m. except in times of crisis quite beyond delegation. After a light dinner closer to a child's teatime, he was in bed – savouring the wide, high quiet of the Wren house and the river's soothing shush – by 8 p.m. and asleep within sixty minutes, no matter how exciting the biography he was reading, regardless of its insistence on how the great man under discussion worked until his last candle guttered. He had only rarely heard Ruth return from a concert.

Even as he endured these rhythms – enjoyed them, in fact, for they refreshed him – he was troubled by this mystery at the centre of his self-image. As the lives of exemplary leaders piled up in his two libraries – one in Hampton Court, another in the Holborn office – he had never found a historical model for somnolence, except in the most degenerate years of Henry

VIII and George III. And King, though his most recent birthday listings in the newspapers had reluctantly conceded sixty-seven, considered himself much fitter than the former – particularly since the weight lost for the portrait – and immeasurably healthier in the head than the latter.

As the swollen Rolls pulled away from the Pavilion and paralleled the placid Thames, King played his daily game of trying to read the newspapers as if he didn't already know what was in them. What might an uninitiated citizen – handing over his five pennies to the vendor – make of these pages?

In this guise of theoretical ignoramus, King considered: HI, KID! BRITISH HEART-SWAP MAN'S FIRST WORDS TO HIS WIFE AFTER A GLASS OF SHERRY. And: BOULTING TWIN AND HIS THIRD WIFE GET DECREES. There was a big picture of Hayley Mills on a yacht, cropped to favour her legs. The splash – ARMY BOYS IN WALK-OUT OVER 'BULL' – was perhaps unfortunate, given their visitor that day. Twenty-three cadets had gone AWOL from Aldershot, objecting to being marched too hard. So even the army was not inoculated against the national malaise.

Still, an efficient edition. No buyer would resent his 5d. Human interest, female beauty and hand-wringing: the classic Cudlipp formula. On page two, King found an attack on builders – which always pleased the punters – from the elevated perspective of Mountbatten of Burma, who, opening a new marina in Hampshire, had outlined 'terrifying examples of incompetence and indifference' during the construction, including the loss of all the fittings for the toilet block by British Road Services. King imagined his putative simpleton nodding in recognition and reflecting that Mountbatten was one of Britain's too-few heroes.

Apart from the heart-transplant man, each piece of news, it seemed to King, would encourage his notional know-nothing to hide his life savings in a suitcase and bolt the homestead doors. Cock a bloody gun as well, probably. If he were to look out of the Rolls's window now, he should see revolution in the streets, for the second time in his life.

But when he checked through the glass to his left, London was troublingly calm. Commuters buying their newspapers – just the kind of humble subjects whose minds he was trying to enter in this exercise – did so with an attitude which could not be claimed as resignation but rather gentleness. The City's pinstriped infantry looked a long way from turning their furled umbrellas into weapons.

The chauffeur's soft-shoe braking outside the tower snapped King from his pantomime of being average. But entering the *Mirror* building, he adopted another disguise: invisibility. He was pleasurably certain that no one saw him as he crossed the lobby and aimed the elevator towards the ninth-floor penthouse.

'The aquarium man's in the office,' advised his main diary girl. 'Mr Cudlipp rang. And the Bank needs to talk to you about a meeting.'

Both secretaries were grossly overdressed, as if expecting an emergency wedding. Like a layabout bachelor putting on a show for a girlfriend, Britain was happy to be drab until the Queen came around.

King himself had dressed in the chalk-lined three-piece he would have worn for everyday meetings; as he had warned the Archbishop of Canterbury at luncheon the previous week, he always started his studies at rock bottom. A title did not entitle anyone to reverence: they had to earn respect.

So, an hour later, it was not nerves at all (as he heard the kinder observers had suggested) which led him to dispense with the 'Ma'am' when he met the sovereign in the *Mirror* lobby.

'Cecil King,' he said.

KING AND THE QUEEN was the perfect headline, Cudlipp thought, as he watched his Chairman standing with Elizabeth II in a thunderstorm of flash-bulbs from the in-house smudgers.

Except that the sentence gave precedence to a newspaper owner over a head of state and might encourage the view, already growled in the places where hacks drank, that King had ideas above his payroll. THE QUEEN AND KING, he revise-subbed the phrase. But then Victorian sticklers would write in, complaining that the paper had over-promoted the monarch's consort.

In the fifteen years since the coronation, every royal profile Cudlipp had ever run had contained a line about the Queen seeming surprisingly petite to those who met her. But today, smiling up at King's six foot five, she comically resembled the twelve-inch porcelain figures of the monarch sold in *Woman's Own*.

The contrast was even greater because, while many towering men apologetically bent their knees in greeting, King veered towards tiptoe when posing for photographs, using his stature to attack. Yet, though as socially noticeable as a barrage balloon in a bathroom, King ludicrously liked to insist that he could enter premises invisibly. While his many other peculiarities were well thumbed in Freud, this was an entirely original eccentricity.

The picture claimed for history, King, with a notably casual flap of the hand, steered the monarch towards the waiting line of staff and, first, the keen observer.

'Hugh Cudlipp, who runs the *Mirror* newspapers,' King

boomed, already looking bored in this role of strolling footnote. Cudlipp briefly held the white-gloved hand. Nervous of
pressing too hard, he pretended it was an egg. He noted a
navy-blue coat and hat. Jodi had threatened him at breakfast
with a wardrobe question later.

After the line of grip-and-grin – in which their visitor
reminisced about something she had once read by Cassandra
and seemed to recognize Marje Proops – King led the Queen
and selected attendant staff to the basement.

There was always a risk in allowing visitors to see journalists at work. It was both a strength and a weakness of
the breed that hacks were not reliably servile. The subs were
particularly suspect. Despite pre-emptive memos, Cudlipp
still dreaded Elizabeth II overhearing the classic *Mirror*
backbench back-chat: 'What cunt subbed this?' / 'What cunt
wants to know?'

So Cudlipp had suggested that they visit the presses. The
printers were theoretically rougher types but would wear a
tie and never dare to swear in front of their monarch.

'One thinks first of the *Mirror*,' said their visitor. 'But the
International Publishing Corporation owns many titles?'

Cudlipp noticed that King's air became less dismissive
at this invitation to compare empires: 'That's right. Twelve
British papers, eleven overseas, seventy-five bookstall magazines, one hundred and thirty-two specialist journals and
twenty printing plants. Five million people read the *Mirror*
every day, while a dedicated subscription list buys, say,
Halsbury's Laws of England or *Cage and Aviary Birds*. But
they're all our customers.'

'Though you don't breed budgerigars yourself, Mr
King?'

Cudlipp chided himself for laughing too loudly. All jokes
depended on timing and royal ones even more so, the time

in question being the hundreds of years in which the royal family had accumulated deference.

King's face stayed straight: 'No. Though I do keep fish.'

The next comment would have seemed a non sequitur to many but Cudlipp considered the possibility that the Queen had been exceptionally well briefed: 'You're the nephew of Lord Northcliffe. Is that right?'

King's chin-dip of assent became a bow of the head, which the monarch might have taken as reverence to her but which any board member of IPC knew was his usual salute to his uncle's memory.

'Ink in the blood,' said Elizabeth II, whose crisp, dispassionate delivery made her sound like a doctor giving test results. 'Obviously one has a certain interest in family businesses. One imagines that Lord Northcliffe used to give you the kind of tour you are giving me now?'

'That was a treat of childhood, yes.'

Cudlipp wondered if she knew how Northcliffe ended up. They had reached one of the rotary presses which, this early in the day, was like an aeroplane on the runway: stilled tin which seemed to tremble with potential power.

'One imagines it must make quite a racket at full tilt?'

Wreck-ett. Cudlipp found himself thinking of Henry VIII and real tennis. At Hampton Court, in fact, where his proprietor lived. King nodded at Cudlipp, who took this as an invitation to share a simile he had used with previous delegations: 'Yes, Ma'am. When the presses start in the late afternoon, a rumble fills the building from below: like the organ in a great church. I've likened it to being in a cathedral of technology.'

Constitutionally discouraged from ever shaking her head, the Queen alternated between a nod and the withholding of one. On this occasion, the head of state moved but she added:

'Although one wonders precisely who they would worship in such a church.'

King abruptly started walking again and the Queen, after a momentary hesitation equivalent to a full-scale row from anyone else, meekly followed. Cudlipp, Cardiff-born, had often found England's traditions prissy – and, as a journalist, his creed was mischief – but he still felt some horror at watching the Queen treated with such lese-majesty.

(Perhaps the headline should be: QUEEN CHILLED BY SNOW. Cudlipp had heard King's relatives use the childhood nickname, which the old man's hair made fitting again.)

He realized that his Chairman's favourite egalitarian epigram – 'I always start my studies at rock bottom' – was this morning being applied at its highest level yet. But a motto which might be taken from an American as democratic was, in King, another arrogance: he believed that no one was better than him. Cudlipp just hoped that Her Majesty would not suffer his boss on the subject of her government.

They stopped beside the proofreaders' table where the visitor King was honouring with his presence was shown a smudgy pull of that day's *Mirror* with the loops, dashes and stets of pencilled corrections. Declining to comment on the mutiny by young soldiers who had taken an oath to her, the Queen asked: 'Though one assumes that, despite these efforts, misprints still get through?'

The Chairman now seemed momentarily engaged: 'Indeed, yes. There are whole programmes on the wireless devoted to them. My favourite, though, remains a reference to the funeral of George V where, readers were told, a large *crow* sang "God Save the King".'

Although this was the best joke of the visit, it received the softest response because the procession of employees was more aware – or, perhaps, cared more – that this jest concerned the obsequies of the grandfather of their guest. The Queen interrupted King's chuckle at the typo by asking: 'At this stage of the day, how much idea would you have of tomorrow's front page?'

King slid his eyes sideways towards Cudlipp, who repeated the expression in the direction of Lee Howard. The *Mirror* editor, a beer barrel of a man with silvery hair Brylcreemed back, had lost his usual air of confidence: 'Sparing your blushes, Ma'am, this visit is a likely candidate. We also have a reporter at the National Heart Hospital. We have a piece by an eminent doctor suggesting that lung and liver swaps will be next.'

The current head of a family which was routinely allowed to swap one body for another nodded. 'Our prayers are with both families. For the rest of us, it makes Britain seem a lucky place to live.'

King suddenly stepped between Lee Howard and the Queen. The first comparison which came to Cudlipp's reporter's brain was an assassination, although the weapon King brandished – which Cudlipp had hoped would stay sheathed – was only arrogant obsession: 'In some ways, lucky. Yes, in some ways, Ma'am.'

This long-delayed use of the grovelling honorific suggested to Cudlipp that even King understood this intervention to be a risk. 'Although, as you may know, our newspapers have disagreements with Mr Wilson's government . . .'

Pages of Cudlipp's memoirs – perhaps now to be written rather earlier than he'd planned – flashed before his eyes. But the Queen didn't call for her Beefeaters and simply withheld any movement of her head as she said: 'That is what you say, Mr King. One's Prime Ministers are like one's children. Whether one is pleased or displeased with them, the sentiment must be applied equally.'

DRAINED by witnessing the desperation of others to impress, King was glad of the second firestorm of camera-light which signalled the end of the visit. He remained unconvinced that he would have appointed this cautious young woman to the position of monarch on the basis of competitive job interviews.

Her car, which looked much less impressive than his, had drawn up outside the *Mirror* building. As she wafted her hand above his, she said: 'Oh, Mr King, I understand we have something in common?'

'Is that right?'

'We have both had our faces on coins.'

'Ah, yes. That was . . .' He was determined not to show that she had rattled him. 'An anniversary gesture, merely.'

'Although one forms the impression that no one would think they had you in their pocket. Thank you, Mr King. You have a great deal of power. I hope you employ it responsibly.'

It was what everyone said to him and so, quietly mocking their lack of originality, he kept a standard reply: 'Oh, I have no real power. It's not like Lord Northcliffe or even young Mr Murdoch. I'm just the Chairman of the International Publishing Corporation. An employee. They can fire me any time.'

The Queen's impassive stillness signalled her doubts. This was always the way. He spoke the humble truth and not a soul believed him.

6

And Jesus was a Sailor

FOG AT NOTTINGHAM was not a possibility he had considered. Though chance was the point of the business, he had not imagined he was betting on the Midlands weather, until the 7.45 Evening Chase – on which he was relying to make good the hobbled donkeys he'd backed at Windsor – was cancelled because of poor visibility. The runners had gone to the post but been recalled. A new way of losing, when he already knew so many.

Tuesday afternoon had almost ruined him. In the 2.45 at Chester, Storey, loyal to his employers, had followed Newsboy and Bouverie of the *Mirror* onto Colonel Blimp, a decent 7/2 to steady the bank manager's hands, even though all the betting levies these days made it a bookie's pension. But Double Quick had won, as favourites only did when they rode without his hopes weighing on them.

In the evening three-year-olds' sprint at Alexandra Park, he had put two pounds he didn't have – the sharp glance of the clerk – on Pussy Pelmet, excited that the owners had sneaked the rude name past the stewards. He had held out for a win, but the filthy beast had finished second at 10/1.

'I'll tell you, Cecil King'll not send flowers when he kills you from exhaustion,' Moira said. It was half-past eight, his latest ever, except during elections or assassinations, when there was an excuse. She was oven-blushed and had the scent of vegetables that should have been served an hour earlier.

'I know. We have to wait until edition time on the heart man, in case he pegs it.'

Moira apologized that the dinner was from three tins: chicken chunks, peas and then peach slices: 'I'm economizing. I know you say it's inflation, Bernard, but I wonder these days if Harold Wilson isn't dipping into my purse himself.'

As they ate, she asked why he was so quiet. Unable to admit he was thinking about money, Storey tried to suggest he was preoccupied with sex, a fairly plausible diversion, by reaching under the table and touching his wife between the legs.

'Can a girl not eat her tea without someone clawing at her nether regions?' Moira complained, but she seemed pleased by this latest triumph over the nuns and so he reached inside her knickers. She pushed his hand away.

'You're wet.'

But this expert biological evidence was rejected with a slap and his hand was stinging when he placed it back on the table like a robber showing that he had no gun.

Under the guise of wiping chicken from his lips, he surreptitiously licked the finger she had refused. When he resumed eating, the chicken chunks which had scarcely met a hen seemed even more of a disappointment after the prospect of her.

Moira, trying to interrupt his sulk, asked: 'So what did the Queen say?'

'She came up behind me when I was typing. She said she thought the transplant was a fascinating story. But she'd have said exactly the same if I'd written that Harold Wilson wears a Gannex mac. I was just fighting the temptation to type a line of f-u-c-ks and see if she noticed . . .'

'Not that you're a man with a one-track mind. And what

else happened, Bernard? You're supposed to be a colour writer and you're giving me picture captions.'

'Oh, I don't know. She's a pleasant enough woman in a hat.'

'Really, Bernard.'

'Anyway, you're Irish. You're supposed to want to blow her up.'

'And, in Ireland, they say all English men are queers.'

He understood that it upset her when he seemed secretive. He didn't mean to be but he lived work so intently that he needed to close off at home.

'Anyway,' he said, conciliating, 'as I've told you all week, if you've got a King in the building every day, the visit of a mere monarch's not going to get you flapping your flag. I can tell you that the Prime Minister's got his secretary pregnant . . .'

'Dear God, can that be true?'

'Apparently.'

'So why aren't you writing about that?'

'It's felt to be a private matter.'

He stood up abruptly.

'And where are you going now?'

Something – the money problems or the feeling that she had taken a husband she couldn't understand – had made her start to speak to him with suspicion.

'Music.'

Storey went to the Ladderex, a quick-assembly shelving system that looked like a social application of scaffolding or an adult Meccano. These interlocking shelves were one of only two modish luxuries they had afforded for the flat and held the other: the stereogram.

'Oh, not that American misery,' Moira complained, when she saw the LP sleeve.

'Canadian, in fact. Poet, as it happens.'

Storey's corrective voice was gentle: these were moves in a seduction he still hoped for. He had intended that the needle would smoothly find the groove but it stuttered on the vinyl and he tried not to take this as an omen for his next intended friction between shaft and sphere. But now the soft melancholy – a cigarette-drenched lament – of Leonard Cohen's voice rose above the rattle of trains on the Central Line outside.

Storey finished his chicken and peas in five teetering forkfuls. He needed a gap in the meal for what he planned.

'He's no Sinatra, is he?' Moira auditioned for *The Critics*. 'Did he have bad catarrh when he recorded this?'

'You listen to his words, not the voice. And this song reminds me of you.'

The main room of the flat was so small that Moira was able to lean from the half-sized dinner table to the Ladderex and reach the LP, with Cohen's name picked out in two-tone orange above the photo of him looking like the brother of that Jewish actor in *The Graduate*. Dustin Someone.

More problematically for Storey, the lyrics of 'Suzanne' were printed on the back, turning a lover's compliment into a government inquiry.

Nominating a song to a woman was a proven romantic tactic but the difficulty was that the words, especially when written by a poet, were endlessly open to interpretation. Storey foresaw pitfalls and Moira soon spotted one: 'Really. *And you know that she's half-crazy.* Thank you very much.'

'Yes, but . . . *which is why you want to be there*,' he rallied. 'Listen, I really like the way he sings *tea and ornje*, not oranges.'

However, Moira's professorial approach to pop music had found another obstacle to the possibility of this being her song: '*And just when you plan to tell her / That you have no love to give her*. What is this? Divorce by LP?'

Storey now wished that either he had never mentioned the connection with her or had chosen another song. The problem was that Cohen's major subject as a songwriter seemed to be how to tell someone that you wanted to fuck someone else.

'No, no,' he countered. '*Then she gets you on her wavelength / And she lets the river answer*. It's Yeats with a guitar line.'

'It's Perry Como with a diploma, Bernard. God, they should never have sent you to college. What does that mean, then? *She lets the river answer*. Have they gone for a dip in the Liffey now?'

'It's a reference to, er, wetness. She floods him with, um, love.'

'Does she, then? Well, to you, Bernard, everything's a reference to wetness. Peach slices, probably.'

Which he was now hastily eating, trying to regain the initiative.

Moira reached for the record sleeve again: 'And what about this bit? *And Jesus was a sailor*. Him and Edward Heath, then. Yachting seems to attract the most peculiar types.' She picked up his quickly emptied dish. 'Do you want anything else? I've got tea but I'm out of *ornje*.'

'What?'

'Oranges. I'm trying to take an interest in your interests. Like Marje Proops always says in her column.'

'No.' He had seen his chance, call it an opening. 'All I want is.'

His wife now standing beside the table with the plates, Bernard dropped to his knees, flipped up her skirt and put his tongue to the spongy triangle from which he had recently been deterred. She was wearing navy blue. Although Bernard was weaning her from some of the teachings of the Sisters of Mercy, he had so far failed to contradict their theology of lingerie.

'Bernard, will you stop it? I've to do the dishes.'

The nuns, had such a situation been within their imagining, would have advised Moira to make firmly for the kitchen hatch with the plates, but this she failed to do. Taking the movement of her lower lips as a contradiction of the upper ones, he slid the thick blue garment down and continued unhindered by cloth.

'OK, will we go to bed, then?'

The plates were on the table again.

'No, here,' he insisted, through the sliding muzzle of her vulva.

'I'll be stiff as a board in the morning.'

'I am already.'

Reclaimed by Rome, she cuffed his head: 'Bernard, I do . . . hah . . . so often wish . . . yah . . . you'd never . . . oh, sweet Jesus . . . read that American book . . .'

And when he took her hands and gently pulled, she knelt and then lay on her grandmother's rug in front of the Dimplex coal-effect fire which would be their only heat when their first married winter came.

SHE wanted him to do this but she knew she shouldn't but she also knew why she thought she knew she shouldn't and so she let him.

Moira blamed the sisters – and, before that, her ma and da – for the commentary which always ran through her head when Bernard slept with her and made her feel like Molly Bloom.

At first when he'd tried to kiss her there – that first night in the lodgings at Howth – she'd been convinced she'd married a sicko. But, just recently, he'd shown her a book. It was American and you couldn't get it in England yet but the *Mirror*'s man in New York had sent over copies. It was called *Couples* and even the writer's name was like a punchline in a joke the dirty girls might have told you: Up-dyke, although she thought it was spelled with an i.

Bernard had shown her a page where a man licked a woman there until she 'came', which was another word he'd taught her. He'd then flicked to a chapter where it was the woman slobbering down there on the man, which she knew was supposed to be another lesson, but she couldn't get her head around it. Jesus. As it were. Even this private double entendre made her blush. It was a big enough thing – oh, do stop it, Moira McNamee – even to let him put it where the Church allowed under certain circumstances. Although obviously she worried that other women had done it to him until they got lockjaw.

Bernard stopped for a moment and wiped his lips on her thigh. When he'd first tried, it had tickled but she'd come, as it were, to understand what the dyke man's book was on about. Their name for what he was doing was 'American'.

'Your cunt tastes lovely,' her husband said. Had they always talked like this in England or was it just now with miniskirts and women's lib?

'Oh, good,' she replied brightly, although her personal view was that it couldn't possibly. Nothing she'd been taught at home or school had prepared her for the etiquette of this conversation. She wished he wouldn't use that word – which made her pray her grandmothers were deaf as well as blind in heaven – and, once before, she'd asked him not to. But then he'd said 'vagina', which just sounded ridiculous and made her think of Sister Peter shouting Latin nouns.

She felt the trembling in her legs, like when a bus went over a bump, which meant she was beginning to 'come'. Bernard knelt back between her legs and waited and she knew that he wanted her to get his kecks off. But she couldn't. There was something about it jumping out which made her think of Pandora's Box or was it possibly Lot's Wife. She was so wet down there that she worried about a mark on the rug.

As Bernard fumbled with his belt and pants, like someone trying to dress an angry child, old gloomy-pants Larry Cohen on the gramophone was singing something else. *And then taking from his wallet an old schedule of trains / He'll say I told you when I came I was a stranger.*

Great, isn't that just what you want to hear when a fella was about to empty himself inside you? They had done this most days since they married which – excluding the time she'd been bleeding but counting the honeymoon nights when they hadn't seemed to sleep at all – probably meant about forty times. What still amazed her was the way that her body seemed to divide down the middle. Her thighs and legs jerked as he entered her, so that it felt like sitting on the shoulders of a wrestler, watching the bout down below.

He pulled out of her. 'Oh, no, don't stop.'

'In a flood like this, the smart man wears galoshes.'

Raising herself on her elbows, she watching him pull the silvery square from his pocket. He must have got it when he went to the bathroom before tea unless, God help us, he carried them around in his trousers just in case.

'Do you have to wear one?' she pleaded. 'It's the ninth day.'

After the Abortion Act (God save them) and the Pill, the rest of the country ws just getting on with sex, but poor Bernard had chosen a Catholic. He had told her that Charnley in Rome insisted the Pope would give the OK to protection before the year was out, although she would prefer to wait for the white smoke. She had her eyes shut – as they always were during this – but she heard the twang as he dressed himself: the sound, in more innocent days, of a magician doing balloon-dogs at a children's party.

When they got going again, the wrestling contest was one-sided. His thrusts felt like a knee grazing tarmac.

'You were coming,' he said. 'You were coming.'

'I'm sorry. I . . .'

He pulled out of her and there was the noise of the party-origami bursting and shrivelling. To a child, the end of excitement; to her, the beginning. She felt flesh against flesh, then wetness doubling itself and jolts over which she had no control.

'I'm going to write to Pope Paul,' he whispered, 'and tell him you can only come without condoms. They'll probably make you a saint.'

She wanted him to hold her now, but the phone was ringing.

HE WAS worried that the caller would be Moira's mother, in which case the guilt would probably put his wife off sex forever and certainly fucking on the floor. But, when he answered, a male voice – posh, old-ish, like something from an RAF film – asked: 'Bernard Storey?'

'Yes. Who's this?'

His first thought was that it must be the night desk – perhaps Fred West had snuffed it – but no one at the *Mirror* spoke like this except the boss class. And this caller sounded grander than even Cecil King himself.

'I've got a story for you, Bernard.'

Part of the pleasure of sex, even for men, was the thinking back straight afterwards and you really didn't want to be standing in your socks and shirt-tails with a limp, dripping dick being teased on the telephone by a toff you'd never met.

'How did you get the number? I'm ex-directory.'

Bernard had once read that investigative reporters stayed out of the book in case of reprisals.

'Don't worry. In the way I've got it, your security can't be compromised.'

The phrasing of this made Storey suspect a government source.

'What's the story?'

Moira had pulled her knickers on and was taking the plates into the kitchen. Storey was disappointed; he already wanted her again.

'It's about a man called Worthington,' the disembodied wing commander told him. For once, in the evening, there was no crossed line. Perhaps Tony Benn had really sorted out the Post Office.

'And what has Mr Worthington done?'

'Many, many things. Mr Worthington is a man with many secrets.'

Storey was no longer thinking government sources, but nutter: those people who wrote to or phoned reporters and revealed Jesus Christ was back on earth and working as a bus conductor in Stepney. 'The *Daily Mirror* tends to need a bit more detail than that,' he said, considering whether to try to take Moira from behind at the sink.

'And I'm sure Mr Cecil King would expect a little more curiosity from his reporters.'

This mention of the proprietor reversed Storey's returning erection. If this was some buffer King had met at a party then, for the sake of his career, he needed at least to seem to take him seriously.

'If you call me at the office tomorrow, I'll have my note-books and so on.'

'No, I distrust telephones. Are you out on assignment tomorrow?'

'In the morning, I'm at a pub in Chiswick.'

'So it's true what they say about you chaps and drinking?'

'No, no. I'm writing about some new TV comedy series. It's where they rehearse.'

'Good, so you'll be following a story about a comedy with one about a tragedy. Which pub is it?'

When the BBC gave him the address, Storey had committed it to memory with an image of a giant chicken drinking beer: 'The Feathers.'

'Good. I'll meet you there at quarter past one.'

'How will I know who you are?'

'I'll find you. Courtesy of the *Daily Mirror*'s egotistical little habit of printing pictures of its journalists. I hope you haven't put too much weight on since marriage. Many men do.'

How did the caller know he was a new husband? Even if the toff was a friend of King, was it possible the Chairman would have spoken of, or even known about, Storey and Moira? He realized that the five essential questions Cudlipp held them to – Who? What? Where? When? Why? – had so far yielded low returns. 'I should have asked your name.'

'Call me Alphonse.'

Still wondering how 'Alphonse' – and what a poncey, made-up name that was – could possibly have known he was recently married, Storey went into the tiny kitchen, hoping to take advantage of the fact.

7

Number 10 Operetta

THE PLUMP, bustling figure marched around the borders of the garden. He was marking out a rectangle, striding down a long length of lawn past the flower-beds, then turning sharply on well-polished black business shoes, on which the falling evening sun sometimes flashed, to complete a quicker width. He left no footprints: it had been a dry week.

'He looks like a gardener who's forgotten his lawnmower,' chuckled Harold. A sudden, big blow of cigar smoke against the window – like a trumpeter hitting a top note – gave his rival a brief cloud-cover for his exercise.

'He does this every night?' asked Colonel Wigg.

'Apparently,' Harold said. 'Though of course I'm not always watching. Country to run and so forth.'

The three of them watched as Jenkins continued his strange parade-drill.

'Looks as if he's chanting something, my dear sir,' Wigg noticed. 'What is it? *I want to be PM, I want to be PM.*'

Ever since school, Marcia had enjoyed knowing the right answer to questions and savoured the thrill of efficiency as she explained: 'The Garden Girls say that he mutters the number of each step. It's a mathematical thing. He does exactly the same rotation every day.'

'Good to see your Chancellor taking an interest in numbers, I suppose,' Harold interrupted. 'Although I fear Wiggy may be right. Roy may have got stuck on the number ten. At his home – his country home – he walks around the tennis

court, apparently. How many socialists do you know who
play tennis and on their own court?'

'He's not a socialist, my dear sir,' twittered the ridiculous Wigg. His Hampshire yokel's accent made the Victorian
villain's act – 'my dear sir' – sound even more ridiculous.

'That was Harold's point,' she skewered him.

Her back felt like a door that needed oiling. At first, she
had blamed the pain and stiffness on the baby but now she
reckoned it was the effort of pretending not to be pregnant,
rolling her shoulders forward and hoping that the spreading
of her belly would be blamed on too many state banquets.
Through a combination of her dowager's hump and tentish
clothes, she believed that only two or three people in Number
10 even knew she was expecting.

She needed to sit down now and was shepherding Harold
towards the settee with her eyes when Colonel Wigg put
down his brandy glass on the side table, straight onto the
wood without looking for a coaster. It irritated Marcia that
Wigg no longer took the care of a guest but had the reck-
lessness of a resident. Of course, in the flat above the shop,
they were all guests, but there were levels.

As the creep walked towards the bathroom door, he said:
'Back in a minute, Prime Minister. Got to empty the ballast
tanks.'

It was the first time they had been alone since lunch and
Harold had obviously been waiting for the moment because
he quickly said: 'Marcia, that coin this morning . . .'

The words meant nothing to her at first and she was forced
to show him a grimace of ignorance that always felt like
failure.

'The new fifty pee . . .' Wilson's Screw, she remembered.
'When Henry James threw it to me and I dropped it . . .'

'Yes.' She regarded herself as a guide to his mind but had

no map for this ramble. 'You didn't hurt it and, if you did, the Mint have plenty more.'

'No, no. But anyone could have dropped it? I mean, Henry didn't . . . it wasn't a clean throw . . . to the left of me . . .'

'Oh, I'd have dropped it and I played lacrosse.'

She realized now that he was having one of his wobbles about his body. If they weren't careful, he'd be going on about the 'heart spasms' he'd started to feel before Prime Minister's Questions. As if to convince himself of the fitness of his fingers, Harold crossed to the gramophone and neatly ensured that the overture to *Iolanthe* filled the room. Wigg, back from his ablutions, rubbing his hands together so hard that it looked as if he was trying to pull them off, heard the music and asked, in that bark he had when he was posing as the spokesman of common sense: 'Is this the one with all the fairies in it?'

'Well, yes,' conceded Harold. 'But you might as well say that *Julius Caesar* is the one with all the Romans in it.'

Marcia and Harold had carried their drinks to the settee under the Lowry, but the colonel went back to the window and looked down: 'Is the Chancellor still square-bashing? Oh, yes. Extraordinary. Wound and wound the garden . . .'

Marcia saw Harold flinch at the third-form impersonation of Jenkins's speech-defect. This essential gentleness was Harold's weakness as a politician, though a virtue as a person.

Wigg picked up his brandy and flopped into the armchair on the right. He pulled a notebook from his pocket, like a detective facing witnesses.

'So, Prime Minister. The List. I hear that Dick Crossman gave dinner to Brian Walden last Thursday night.'

'Do we know what they were plotting?'

'No, my dear sir. But Walden's from near my neck of the woods – the Midlands Machiavelli, we call him – and he's known to be thinking aloud about the Next Leader. Meaning himself, presumably. Apparently, he ordered the most expensive course from the menu, then didn't eat it. Just to show he could afford it, I suppose. Funny bugger.'

'I think he'd better go on my little list, Wiggy.'

'And what about your neighbour, the garden-navigator, Chancellor Jenkins?'

'What are you hearing? Is Roy moving?'

'He's circling,' Wigg whispered, nudging a shoulder towards the window to underline the metaphor. 'Or squaring. He knows he'll only get one chance and he's terrified of ending up holding the coat for Callaghan.'

'OK. Put Jenkins in brackets for the moment. Sunny Jim as well. Though lower down. Devaluation will be a shackle round his ankles for a while yet.'

Harold leaned back and attacked his second cigar of the night as if he hoped to kill the glow by blowing. Marcia thought he looked Mafia like that. Sounded like it too, when he was with that nutter Wigg. There were people who called her paranoid but Wigg would look at you sideways if you said good morning.

'And That Bugger Brown?' asked the Prime Minister. He always capitalized the letters, so that it sounded like a title from the state. 'Where are his tanks?'

'His tanks are full to the brim with firewater, as usual. He had to be carried back to his flat after a division last night . . .'

'Ah. Yes, I'd heard that.'

Wigg looked briefly displeased that his master had other sources of gossip. His reaction would have been savage had he known that it was Marcia who'd passed on this whips' titbit. She guessed that the tableau of That Bugger Brown being stretchered back had been his prize nugget for the night.

'I wonder if Brown even needs to be on our list now.' Harold rolled a taste of brandy round his mouth so that his already pouchy face looked to be incubating mumps. 'If you're to have an enemy in politics, let him be a boozer.'

Harold reached for more brandy but Marcia had anticipated his move and so their hands bumped together and the bottle almost fell. The liquid at the bottom had a long way to jump and she tried to remember when they had opened this one.

'So Jenkins and Callaghan, in brackets, only. Not bad. Abu and Donnelly on the backbenches as ever. Slippery little Walden to keep an eye on. I fear, Wiggy, the Fourth Estate may detain us longer.'

The colonel flicked his notepad to a blank page, an empty ear waiting to be filled with whispered filth.

'Bloody Nora. As normal,' Harold dictated.

'Yes, Prime Minister. I'd taken the liberty of writing in Miss Beloff before you even said it.'

'Wood and Trethowan as well. Repeat offenders. Marcia, I want Thompson brought here. They call it a paper of record. Paper of discord, more like. Tell Thomson he needs to have tea with me. Tea, mind, not drinks. Drinks are for friends.'

Marcia smiled to show she accepted the assignment, although she feared making the phone call. Harold might see himself as the nation's headmaster, but the proprietor of *The Times* certainly didn't accept the role of a schoolboy whose English prep wasn't up to scratch.

'Thomson has a tape in his safe of Tony Crosland plotting with That Bugger Brown against Harold,' Wigg boomed. A flick of Harold's cigar was mirrored by the pencil adding Lord Thomson of Fleet's name to the list.

Harold pulled from his pocket the Xerox of the *Mirror* first edition Marcia had given him earlier.

'This is what George Gale—'

'George G. Ale,' interrupted Wigg, guffawing at a joke he'd lifted anyway from *Private Eye*.

'We must contemplate at the next election,' Harold quoted, 'a defeat of the Labour Party so overwhelming that it will almost be destroyed.'

'I've put him down, Prime Minister. I've put him on the list as George G. Ale.'

When he'd finished laughing at a stolen joke he'd just told for the second time, Wigg suddenly blurted 'King?' sounding, appropriately, like an underling asking a question of a monarch.

'Isn't it right that such an egomaniac should own a paper called the *Mirror*?' asked Marcia. Wigg's bark of a laugh counterpointed Harold's chuckle.

But he had two moods a minute these days and now, swiftly agitated, Harold brandished the cigar like a dagger and raised his voice to drown out an especially loud bit of Gilbert and Sullivan: 'You know I offered King Cecil a job once?'

Marcia remembered it: the summer of 1965, the gigantic press baron's arrogant head almost scraping the door-frames of Number 10.

'I sounded him out about being . . .'

'A Min of State at Trade,' Marcia prompted him. She shouldn't do it. It looked overbearing, but she liked people to see what a team they were.

'Seat in the Lords, of course,' Harold was recalling. 'King asked for time to think it over, then wrote to say no in a five-line note. I do not feel that this is a sphere in which I could employ my talents to best advantage.'

For his quotation from King's letter, Harold employed his all-purpose 'saddle the horses, Albert' voice: the cruel fluting

he used for the reported speech of ambassadors, civil servants, army top brass and Martin Furnival-Jones of MI5:
representatives of the Britain he felt was against him.

'King wanted a job in politics like a starving man seeing
wheat,' Harold continued. 'But he was holding out for a
bigger post. Foreign Secretary from the Lords, I reckon. I
wouldn't give it to him, so now he chips away at me in his
papers. In the States, a man like that would simply run for
President. Luckily, the British parliamentary system protects
us from the self-regarding chancer. Someone like King isn't
going to nurse a constituency for fifteen years and put in his
hours as a PPS. So he needs a surrogate to run against me.' He
glanced towards the window from which they had watched
the Chancellor's forced march. 'I worry that it's Roy.'

'Jenkins sees King through the Bank of England link,'
Colonel Wigg growled. Harold jabbed his Havana towards
the notepad again.

'Take the brackets away from Roy's name, Wiggy, and
write King's in big letters at the top. There's a line in *Iolanthe*
about a susceptible Chancellor.' Although the LP had reached
completely the wrong bit, Harold attempted a gravelly
recitative of his own: '*But there'd be the deuce to pay in the
Lords / If I fell in love with one of my wards! / Which rather
tries my temper, for / I'm such a susceptible Chancellor!*'

Perhaps it was the atmosphere of suspicion in the room
that made them all jump when the phone rang. Marcia
answered, then passed on what the doorman told her:
'Barbara's on her way up.'

Like a teenager smoking in the bedroom when a parent's
feet creak on the stairs, Harold stabbed the cigar in the ash-
tray, then stood and dropped it in the waste-paper basket,
jumbling the contents to force the evidence to the bottom.

As usual, Mrs Castle came into the room at a pace which

suggested that the bobby on the door had chased her up the stairs with his hand on her bum. She was one of those women – that Mrs Thatcher in the Shadow Cabinet was another – who always looked like a speeded-up film. It was if they were rejecting the languidness which people connected with femininity. Mrs Castle was wearing a chessboard dress with a grey jabot.

'Is that new?' Marcia asked.

'It is, actually. Yesterday, we'd been all morning on prices. I told the civil servants I was going to the loo and got Mollie to whizz me to Dorothy Perkins. The departmental drivers make black cabs look like bubble cars. When I got back, my pinstripes were standing looking panicked outside the lavatory and wondering why I suddenly had two bags.'

Mrs Castle kissed Harold on the cheek.

'Hello, Little Minister,' Harold said. He had always called Mrs Castle that. She was one of those small women who made men protective. Tall women like Marcia made them angry.

The new arrival smiled around the room: 'Marcia. And Colonel Wigg. *Lord* Wigg, I must learn to say.'

'Oh, I don't stand on it, my dear lady,' lied Wigg.

'No Mary?' the other woman asked and Marcia wondered if that was a swipe at her.

'She's giving a poetry recital,' Harold explained.

Wigg speculatively tilted the brandy bottle and tumbler towards the new guest.

'I think I will. Medicinal, if nothing else. I've had an abscess for nearly a week but it seems that cabinet ministers have no time for dentists.'

'You must go, Barbara,' Harold said. 'Thick black diagonal lines across your diary. I want no one who works for me jeopardizing their health.'

'You say that, Harold.' Putting her head back on the settee, Mrs Castle pouched her cheek, presumably pooling the brandy around the infected tooth, then flinched and swallowed. 'But all departments have their disadvantages. When I was at Transport, Mollie never dared speed anywhere. At Employment and Productivity, they all seem obsessed with being employed and productive.'

Mad Wigg, always bored when anyone except himself or Harold talked, was staring at his creep's sheet. Noticing, Mrs Castle asked: 'Oh, dear. Another of your Enemies' Lists.'

'Not exactly,' Colonel Wigg perjured himself again.

'Well, if it is, you want Denis Healey on it. Have you noticed him in cabinet, Harold? Always muttering under his breath and stabbing his blotter. Like the Balkan baddie in a spy film.'

'I've noticed,' admitted Harold. Wigg scribbled briefly.

'Harold, I wish sometimes you'd stop totting up your enemies and count your friends. We're here for you, if you need us.'

'I know that, Barbara. A Yorkshire lass. Though admittedly with a Lancashire seat.'

Marcia didn't feel that seat was flirtation, although the party nasties said that Mrs Castle could get whatever she wanted from Harold by wiggling her bum. But, just in case and before the honourable member for Blackburn could expand on her campaign for New Best Friend, Marcia asked her: 'How are you finding Emp and Prod?'

'Well, as I say, shock one's the workload.' Another swill of alcohol to anaesthetize her abscess. 'It's grand to have a drink. Ever since I brought in the breathalyser, people reckon I've taken the Pledge. Hand me a glass of tap water with a disapproving frown. Shock two's the cloak-and-dagger stuff.'

Harold had a soft voice and a hard one, for different times. But it was the latter which asked: 'By which you mean?'

'I suddenly found on my desk one morning security reports on the union. It never occurred to me. Ten of the AEF National Committee are communists, nine of them sympathizers and so on. The minister should know that they take part in secret meetings. I mean, you think of our spies smoking in some Moscow hotel behind a two-way mirror, not following pot-bellied shop stewards into pubs.'

Marcia turned Barbara's laugh into a duet of humour but Harold and Mad Wigg were looking as if they had just been handed the day's trading figures from the Bank.

'And how do you act on this information, my dear lady?' Wigg raspingly asked.

'Oh, not very seriously. James Bond stuff, isn't it? Brother No, I think of it.'

Harold frowned and Marcia noticed how tired his eyes were, even allowing for the usual pouchiness. But it was Mrs Castle he was looking at: 'There's an important distinction here, I feel, Barbara. You're right to dismiss what the security services say, but you should never dismiss the security services themselves. To them, it's against the natural order to have the socialists in power and they're counting the days until we're out. And, ideally, they'd like to name that day themselves.'

'Oh, Harold,' said Mrs Castle, though it seemed to Marcia that visitors should call him Prime Minister, 'I think you worry about them too much. They spend their days writing tedious reports for me on how many reds there might be in the Amalgamated Union of Engineering and Foundry Workers.'

'No, no,' said Harold. 'They're dangerous because the British think that this isn't that kind of country. But it can happen anywhere if good men are weak. Every year, when I watch them out on Horse Guards Parade, practising the Trooping of the Colour, I imagine them one day turning and marching on Downing Street.'

'I hear that the CIA are working on ways of poisoning Castro's cigars,' Wigg suddenly hissed.

'Well, at least you don't smoke those, Harold,' Mrs Castle giggled, while Marcia wallowed in her superior knowledge. 'But you should maybe keep an eye on your pipe.'

The telephone startled them again and she realized how bad their nerves were. She must have another word with Dr Stone. But Harold, who answered, was smiling when he replaced the receiver and told them: 'Pooh-Bah's arrived.'

THE police officer in charge of admission instructed him: 'You're to go right up to the flat, sir.' The ground floor of Downing Street was always quiet at night and now more than ever the many unusable rooms – he could see white sheets over the furniture through the door of the Pillared Drawing Room – lent the place the atmosphere of an empty stage set. Indeed, had he not recently seen a play staged against sheeted tables and chairs? Some anti-capitalist rant at the Court?

On the stairs, he started to cough and, worried that the dust was bringing on his asthma, patted his inside pocket for the bulky inhaler that always made him feel like an agent on a mission, carrying a gun. But even as he wheezed upstairs, he enjoyed the metaphor of the state rooms being riddled with dry rot.

He rose now past the ghosts of Balfour, Asquith, Lloyd George, Baldwin, MacDonald, Chamberlain. Mrs Wilson could be a strain occasionally – there was always the terrible threat that she might recite something – but she had indubitably been right to return to the original arrangement of the predecessor portraits decorating the main staircase.

(After the Macmillan redecoration, the house had become a mess from the aspect of decor. Turning a corner, one would stumble unawares on a Degas: £80,000 worth of painting hanging on some shadowed wall like a print of a pony given as a Christmas gift.)

The pictures were all black-and-white: engraved prints until 1922, when Andrew Bonar Law became the first premier represented by a photograph. The boycott of colour even after it became technologically possible gave community and coherence to a group of men collected together merely by the prejudices of successive generations.

Who would take the picture of Wilson to hang here? In his different moods, he might opt for Karsh of Ottawa (who would perhaps rip the pipe from Wilson's mouth as he had pulled the cigar from Churchill's to win a look of surprise) or an unknown Yorkshire wedding snapper. And which of his faces would the Prime Minister display? The jolly or the paranoid, the idealist or the dealmaker?

Goodman resumed his ascent – past the photographic phantoms of Macmillan, Eden, Home – and pushed through the open door of the flat to find Wilson conducting the cheery banalities of Sir Arthur Sullivan's music with his pipe. It was one of the least bad – *Iolanthe* – which at least boasted that Overture, with its almost Beethovenesque moments and one lyric – *lying awake with a dreadful headache* – which captured something of the insomnia of the top man.

The Prime Minister was mouthing along now to: *And who has dared to brave our high displeasure? / And thus defy our definite command?* In the armchairs were that long-faced clot Wigg and Mrs Castle, to whom God, knowing that she was to become a doctrinaire socialist, had so fittingly given red hair. Mrs Williams was beside the Premier on the chesterfield, hands folded over the child she liked to believe was a secret.

'Arnold!' exclaimed Wilson in greeting, then turned to his companions in this characteristic soirée of brandy and suspicion and winked: 'You may think that Lord Goodman is late. But I have given Arnold a special dispensation to arrive at nine instead of eight. So he can have a proper dinner. We once opened a tin of salmon for him here but he prefers to pick the fish for his tea from a tank. Arnold, have you had a proper dinner?'

' I have, thank you, Prime Minister. Arts Council matters.'

'A grant for the D'Oyly Carte, I hope?'

Half-turning towards the stereogram, Wilson conducted another burst of Iolanthe: a tobacco Toscanini.

'*Professional licence if carried too far / Your chance of promotion will certainly mar / And I fancy the rule might apply to the Bar / Said I to myself – said I,*' the Prime Minister crooned tunelessly in unison with the fictional Lord Chancellor.

'In my view, they should all be called *Patience*,' Goodman told him, dropping onto the empty second sofa opposite the Prime Minister and the Keeper of the Diary, as she liked to style herself. The lunatic gossip Wigg – now, extraordinarily, a lord and therefore, theoretically, Goodman's peer – mimed the pouring of brandy into a glass.

'No, no. Just a soda, please, Colonel Wigg. I need to settle my stomach.'

'So a large soda,' joked Wilson who, like many chubby men, was happy to have the comparison of the absolutely fat, Julius Caesar's dictum mistranslated via vanity. Let him have men about him who were fatter. Goodman noted that the brandy he had declined was given to the Prime Minister instead, who now said: 'Arnold, Wiggy and I have been talking about suing Nora Beloff.'

When Wigg had been sacked as Paymaster General and

put out to grass as Chairman of the Racecourse Betting Levy Board, with the secondary consolation of ermine robes, Goodman had hoped that the colonel's role as Wilson's Iago might cease but, apparently – and unfortunately – it had not.

'Ah, well, in that, Prime Minister, I have a potential conflict of interest. As Chairman of the *Observer* Editorial Trust, I could not act for you against one of the paper's columnists. However, addressing the question more generally, I also ask you to consider whether litigation is the best response to punditry, however ugly. The quiet word with Mr Astor is an approach I have attempted for you before. But it is my observation of journalism that each time you call for Miss Beloff's head her esteem with her editor rises. The dislike of a Prime Minister – perhaps, at this difficult time for the administration, especially of this Prime Minister – becomes a badge of honour for a political columnist. I might gently suggest that one element in the Prime Minister's – doubtless temporary – dip in the admiration of the public is the perception that he keeps things hidden: that he was not entirely open on matters such as the devaluation of the pound and Rhodesia. You are also seen in some quarters to have stalled on House of Lords reform. A recurrent thrust of Miss Beloff's often less than Johnsonian prose, as I read it, is that she accuses you of over-sensitivity and, let us say, a tendency towards . . . *opacity* in management. The use of a lawsuit to counter these objections might, quite unintentionally, be seen to confirm them.'

During this address – a denunciation, however curlicued – the Prime Minister had been sucking at his pipe with a vigour which suggested a suckling babe or something baser.

'You may very well be right, Arnold,' Wilson conceded, although the wide-eyed Wigg looked miserable. Goodman regarded this administration as essentially comic: Number 10

72

operetta, sung most lustily by the conspiratorial colonel and the always alarmed-looking Marcia, with that locket round her neck which the Westminster hearsay claimed to contain anti-depressant medication prescribed by the Downing Street doctor.

'You know my view, Harold,' said Mrs Castle. 'Ted and I are just getting back on our feet after that seven thou we had to shell out.'

'Indeed. Had I been acting for you, Mrs Castle, I would have advised you not to sue Mr Chataway. I commend to so many of my clients President Johnson's remarks about leaving the kitchen if you dislike the heat. An apophthegm which, of course, President Johnson has applied to himself over Vietnam.'

The Prime Minister coughed to reclaim the evening before seceding it again: 'I've asked Lord Goodman to give us a *tour d'horizon* – that's French for overview, Wiggy – of the challenges facing the government. Arnold?'

Goodman took the opportunity to haul himself from the regrettably deep seat and lower the volume of the long-playing record. The part about lying awake with a dreadful headache. Returning slowly to the chesterfield, he noted that Mrs Castle was masking a yawn with her hand; the question of whether women could ever match the stamina of men for politics remained moot. He took out the sheet of paper on which he had written, under the Goodman Derrick crest, his headings.

'You will know, Prime Minister, that I traditionally counsel you against taking too much notice of polling. While by no means ideal, a deficit of twenty – or however many – points to Mr Heath is, at this mid-term juncture, still recover-able. However, my psephological friends—'

'What was that word, Arnold?' asked Mrs Castle. He had

always admired her brain and hoped that she was either tired or posing as a proletarian for Wilson and Wigg.

'Ah. The scientific study of voting trends. It's a rather elegant derivation, in fact. From *psephos* – pebble – the rock on which elections were built. My point is that the pebble-counters tell me that up to a quarter of Conservative voters now favour Enoch Powell as leader over Mr Heath. As a child of immigrants myself, I would urge that this is one electoral statistic to be given weight.'

Goodman looked deliberately at Wigg, who had for twenty-two years represented the constituency of Dudley, deep in the Powellite recruiting grounds. Whatever was written on manifestos, there was no way of knowing what Labour MPs in xenophobic territories said on the doorsteps in order to cling to their privileges.

(Certainly, Wigg seemed resentful. He had, though, never liked Goodman, furious at his refusal to sue half the reporters and pundits in Fleet Street on the colonel's word. Wigg was obsessed with destroying people: 'Give me three hours and I can ruin anyone,' he liked to growl.)

Wilson, though, was almost rocking in agreement. Goodman had begun with this subject deliberately. Ostensibly, he and Wilson were opposites: lawyer and don, synagogue and chapel, Tory and Labour, bachelor and husband – perhaps even adulterer. Yet they found common ground as outsiders to the public world they served: Jew and Yorkshireman. For all his achievements, each knew that he gazed in hopefully from the wrong side of the glass.

'You're so right, Arnold,' Wilson said. 'Martin Luther King was killed by racists. And it could happen here – to me. The files MI5 lay on our desks every day say that the threat of revolution is from the Left. But it's the Right that I fear.

This nation's first dictator won't have long greasy hair; it will be short back and sides under an army hat.'

'Perhaps, Prime Minister. Although we may not yet be at the point of choice between which barber shop our tyrant favours. Beyond that, I am saying little new in observing that the prospect of a second devaluation – viewed by many in the City as imminent – remains the greatest . . .'

THE EYEBROWS seemed even bushier than usual: thicker still than those of that bloody troublemaker Healey. These days it looked as if Arnold had stuck an Elastoplast on a badger and pulled hard.

Mutch, Wood, Wadsworth, Slade, Wilson (no relation), Watson, he fluently recited in his mind. Wilson, Watson . . . Richardson. His fingers on the stem of the pipe were suddenly slippery. Watson, Richardson, Mann. He touched his brow with the back of his hand and knew his forehead would be glistening.

If this happened at the despatch box, as it had over devaluation last year and possibly once on Rhodesia, the Opposition scented weakness and started yelling for resignation. Watson, Richardson, Mann.

In childhood, the idea of his memory as a series of drawers had seemed right and inspiring. But for years now, in shivering anticipation of this moment, he had pictured a particular compartment in this neural bureau sticking or jerking open to reveal an empty tray. Watson, Richardson, Mann . . .

GOODMAN noticed that Wilson was grimacing. 'Yes, the prospect of, shall we say, subsidence in the American underpinning of sterling is indeed painful to contemplate, Prime Minister. I am not suggesting that President Johnson is fickle in his support, but the call of Vietnam on the dollar may lower the priority of supporting gold in the UK.' When Wilson had flown to Washington to meet Johnson, the President had ordered the White House band to play 'Plenty of Nothing', a joke about no British troops going to Vietnam. 'In an extreme case, President Johnson – or his successor – might force you to swap the solvency of sterling for our troops in South-East Asia.' But Wilson now looked so sweaty and unsteady that Goodman felt obliged to soften his prophecy: 'I am not saying, Prime Minister, that this is likely: merely possible.'

WHAT WAS the word? Mnemonics. But he had never needed them. Those adverts on the front of the *Telegraph*. Amaze your friends with your memory. He had always just been able to hammer facts into his head. Until this slip. Slip. He felt the firing of the neuron almost as a physical sensation, like a hiccup. Islip. That was it. Wilson, Watson, Richardson, Mann, Islip, Stephenson, W. H. Smith, the last-named player scoring the only goal from a penalty in front of a crowd of 53,000 at Stamford Bridge. Huddersfield Town 1, Preston North End 0. The 1922 FA Cup Final.

THIS WAS by the far the most serious section of his speech and yet the Prime Minister was all at once grinning. Goodman was glad that fate had not made Wilson a judge; barristers would never know which way a case was going.

'It's perhaps all too easy, Prime Minister, to laugh off Mr Heath. Public suspicion of a middle-aged bachelor, popular intolerance of a yachtsman: these are indeed prejudices you may hope to find amplified in the electorate. But I ask you also to consider this possibility. If, as opinion polls suggest, the voters are to some extent punishing you for their familiarity with you, then is there not a chance that they will reward Mr Heath for the novelty he brings to the ballot paper?'

'In the next election,' wittered the silly Wigg, 'Harold and Mary should go everywhere together. Message: our man's married. If Harold and Mary seem like bread and butter, Harold and Heath will look like chalk and cheese.'

'How can Heath make speeches about the family?' Wilson asked. 'Those that don't play the game shouldn't make the rules.'

'Where is Mrs Wilson?' Goodman asked.

'Poetry reading,' revealed Wigg in a tone which suggested that the word verse had its roots in perversion.

A rap on the door prefaced the entry of the first editions of the newspapers – Goodman wondered how many stories he had kept out of them today – carried by Henry James.

(Goodman liked to fantasize about other literary doppelgängers on the Downing Street staff: Jane Austen juggling plugs on the switchboard, George Eliot plumping up the cushions in the study after everyone had left.)

James flicked at the front of the *Times*, then had to reach for a handkerchief to rub the wet ink from his fingers. 'It's too late for these because of the time difference. But Robert Kennedy has won another primary.'

'Kennedy versus Nixon for the second time,' Goodman predicted the 1968 American general election. 'Tragically, a different Kennedy and, let us hope, a different Nixon.'

'He'll struggle to match Jack,' Wilson said. And no smile of self-deprecation was apparent as he added: 'I think of myself sometimes as the English Jack Kennedy.'

'Yorkshire Walter Mitty, more like,' giggled Marcia. Mrs Castle and the colonel didn't know whether or not to laugh, while Goodman again felt gratitude at not having married.

8

The House at the Edge of
the Wood

THE MAN FROM Scotland Yard seemed to be asleep and she tried to compensate by raising her voice and looking straight at him as she said: '*I'll never let thee go.*' As she had learned to do, she filled her mind with her darkest moments of the heart and went on: '*Ends all our month-long love in this? / Can it be summed up so / Quit in a single kiss / I will not let thee go.*' This declaration had no effect on the man at whom she had aimed it.

The presence of a detective at a poetry reading was, she assumed, a new experience for both policeman and audience. One of the newspapers had claimed that a 'well-known writer' had joked that the copper might leap onto the stage and arrest Mrs Wilson for crimes against literature.

From the tone of the remark, Mary suspected that it had been that foul-mouthed librarian, Larkin. The comment had not affected her confidence. It was quite enough for her to have the blessing of John Betjeman and she knew that, to some people, her poetry was just another way of getting at Harold.

The Friends' Meeting Hall was almost full: a bigger crowd, she had been told, than the Quakers ever brought here except for their AGM. Harold, who had miraculously transformed himself from the shy don she'd met into a conference orator, had advised her at recitals to choose a single member of the audience and deliver the speech to him or her.

Ideally, she would have picked out her husband but he was unable to be here, speaking of 'meetings' and 'security issues'. He had, though, promised to attend 'An Evening With Mary Wilson' at Foyle's next month, although, Harold being Harold, he had said that he would 'rather you were playing W. H. Smith. He was a great outside-right for the Town.'

'*I will not let thee go*,' she continued. '*Had not the great sun seen, I might; / Or were he reckoned slow / to bring the false to light / then might I let thee go.*'

John B had once commented that perhaps she hit the rhymes too hard when reading. He said that rhyming was the raisin in the cake, not the icing. She had wryly explained that, for her, it was the cherry on top. Her readings deliberately drew attention to the matched line-endings, to remind people what real poetry was. Verse without rhyme was like a window box planted with stones.

Her heart was steady now after those staccato moments there always were on starting. She chose for her notional single listener a distinguished silver-haired gentleman, with half-moon glasses, sitting on the aisle in the very back row. He had a slightly military bearing, but also a hint of something more raffish: the hair longer and more unkempt than an army barber would tolerate.

Knowing this poem well enough to look up from her typescript, she shrank the room, as Harold had instructed, to just herself and the stranger. He didn't quite seem the type for a literary soiree. For a start, he was a lone man, when most of those who came to hear her were bookish spinsters or middle- to upper-middle-class couples: the kind who, demoralized by thirteen years of Tory rule, had voted for the novelty of Harold and were now beginning to repent of the experiment.

Addressing the scatty, bespectacled bachelor, she finished the poem: '*I will not let thee go / Have we not chid the changeful moon / Now rising late, and now / Because she set too soon / And shall I let thee go?*'

She aimed on the final line for what Harold called a hand-starter: a raised, emphatic tone which told them you had finished and launched the applause. Because she was used to the sound which crashed across the hall like surf after leader's speech at conference her own receptions always felt inadequate, but the women in particular were smiling supportively and this warmed her.

'Robert Bridges. "I Will Not Let Thee Go",' she confirmed for her listeners. 'I'm preparing an anthology for a publisher at the moment and I'm a little surprised to find quite how many of my favourite poems are love poems. This is one of the most beautiful: the Song of Solomon. Oh, I know that some Bible scholars tell us that these words describe the mutual love of Christ and his Church. But, even though I am a Believer, I've never really believed that! I think that any woman who has known real passion is aware of what these verses really mean!'

A couple of the spinsters – committed churchgoers, presumably – looked mystified or scandalized. Sipping some water – she had rejected Harold's advice to add a splash of brandy, as the Chancellor did on budget day – Mary began to read: '*The song of songs, which is Solomon's. Let him kiss me with the kisses of his mouth . . .*'

CHRIST! They send you to a poetry reading and suddenly it's like being on the Vice Squad or something. Wright, who was wired up under his blazer, thought it might be a nice piece of mischief to turn these tapes over in the morning. He liked the idea of the girls in Transcripts typing up this torrent of biblical filth. There had just been a bit about breasts being like two young roes that are twins.

Wright wondered how many poetry readings had been attended by both a detective (who, incidentally, seemed to be asleep) *and* a spy. He really hadn't expected all this sex from Mrs Wilski. He had her down as the kind who only got moist between the thighs if she put on woollen tights.

That first one – about never letting him go – was pretty obviously the number one poem of a lady whose husband had just got his diary secretary eating for two. But all this Solomon was another side to her, suggesting that there was still good hot casserole at home if Comrade Harold wasn't snacking at the office.

She was also a more handsome woman than suggested by newspaper pictures – meekly poised behind Wilski as she waved from Daimler windows and Number 10 steps – or surveillance shots which, in the end, you had to admit made everyone look shifty. In person, though, she had a long, strong face which her swept-up hair made leonine and the kind of bold blue eyes which told you that they knew things. Knew him, it had sometimes seemed this evening. Her azure gaze had been fixed on him throughout the opening poem, as if she were hurling the words at him.

He hadn't wanted to be here but the rule in K5 these days was that if one of the Wilskis so much as farted the contents had to be analysed and filed. He had jested with Tony Brooks that while Mrs Wilski's poems never exactly seemed to be in English, it was a big leap of the imagination to believe that they were in Russian code. Even so, he became more alert when she followed the scriptural porn by saying: 'So far this evening, I've read verse I admire from the past. Following them with my own rather feels like serving your scones to Fanny Cradock.'

Wright imagined himself teasing them at the office that Mrs Wilski had made a fanny joke. He hoped that something worth reporting might come from her own poetry. So far all he had from tonight was the unexpected spectacle of the Prime Minister's wife reading smut aloud in public under cover of religion, although that might make a sarcastic little diary paragraph: a nudge about the Wilski–Marcia–Mary triangle. He made a note to tell young Storey from the *Mirror* next day.

HER MUSE had never offered her a novel, but she liked, when watching strangers, to imagine them as characters, attaching stories to them. The man on the back aisle, listening alone in half-moon glasses, she envisaged as a widower who perhaps hoped to find a second wife at a recital. But had he chosen such a venue because his wife had liked poetry or because she hadn't? Within the mystery of love, either explanation was possible.

She glanced at the tragic verse-lover again as she coughed away the nervous surge in her throat (always brought on by the thought of reading her own work) and explained: 'It goes without saying that I'm happy and privileged to be in London for as long as my husband's work keeps him here. But there will also be a time when we live elsewhere again. And that's what this poem is about. It's called "The House at the Edge of the Wood".'

She held the silence between title and opening line, which John B had once described as sacramental, and began: '*Sometimes, as I struggle through crowded rooms / Thick with tobacco and whisky fumes . . .*' She didn't stress this rhyme because it wasn't quite one.

'*And vapid voices shrilling high / In one continuous parrot cry / Suddenly, I can see it there / I can see the bluebells, can smell the air / And the evening sunlight slants in lines / Across my house at the edge of the pines . . .'*

YOU WANT to see the bluebells? You want to smell the air? You want to live in that house? Well, we'll drive you there. Wright realized that he had rhymed.

9

A Susceptible Chancellor

IF THERE WAS a crisis in Holborn Circus while he was away and Cudlipp or someone else came to the penthouse and asked 'King?', the secretaries would answer: 'In his counting house.'

He knew it was a joke they had – one of those rituals, originally designed to lift the tedium of the business day, that eventually became a part of it – but King, as he sat in the panelled and portraited council chamber of the Bank of England, was aware that he had nothing of the languor of the monarch in the nursery rhyme. In the ten minutes that the Committee of the Treasury had been in session, his resolution to be gentler than in previous sessions had been removed by the vast edifice of deceit represented by the Governor's speech.

'Mr O'Brien,' he interrupted. 'You report that we will announce a rise in our currency reserves of twenty-one million pounds during April. What is the true figure?'

O'Brien pulled off his tortoiseshell spectacles, the better to reveal the slow blinking which King's insolence had provoked, and wiped them with his handkerchief in an elaborate delaying tactic. In the silence, the Chancellor of the Exchequer began to attend to his own glasses in the same way, as if some invisible dust storm had engulfed the room: though the financial establishment of Great Britain might have dirty hands and filthy consciences, their goggles would at least be gleaming clean.

'Well, Mr King,' said the Governor, peering disdainfully

through polished lenses, 'I'm not certain I understand you. The figure of twenty-one million pounds is the one that has been agreed to be released.'

'Yes, Governor, but it's not an actual plus, created by trading. The sterling reserves have been artificially increased by massive borrowing from overseas: loans on which we may very well default. The true position – isn't it? – is that our contingencies dipped by a hundred million pounds last month and that we're losing gold at the rate of one hundred tons a day.'

Chancellor Jenkins, the bald pate atop his chubby face reddening from shame or hypertension, gave the small snort of self-admiration which tended to presage his well-wrought metaphors: 'I would perhaps share with Mr King and other non-executive directors an understanding which has helped me as a non-professional in the business of money. It is that economics is not a science but an art. And it is in the nature of the arts that they demand a certain creativity.'

O'Brien's smile was probably as tactical as King's withholding of one as he responded: 'I say this to the Governor and the Chancellor. If we were merely lying to ourselves about the seriousness of our plight, it would be reprehensible. But we are lying to the public. Mr O'Brien, it is barely six weeks since a cobbled-together quorum of privy councillors – meeting in midnight emergency session at Buckingham Palace – imposed a bank holiday on the gold markets while we begged down the telephone to Washington. At the time, the Governor referred to this as a "spell in the sanatorium" for sterling. Well, the fever of international speculation is not retreating and matron has called the doctor and the parents to the patient's bed. Four thousand million dollars of American medicine is pouring from the bottle. Our nation is now mortgaged to the United States, Britons are the tenants of the

President and – if Uncle Sam's piggy bank is smashed by Vietnam – they will be homeless!'

Governor O'Brien polished his spectacles again and King accepted that it might be a necessity this time as it was possible he had splashed them with his enthusiastic spittle. Jenkins – fingering his heavy black rims but trusting to his ophthalmologist's prescription as it was – spoke: 'One is tempted to applaud the energy, if not the sentiment, of that address. Mr King favours medical analogies and perhaps I can extend them by summoning up the image of the government's recent cuts in expenditure as a tourniquet. The haemorrhaging he describes has been slowed and there is the prospect of normal circulation being restored. The fact that the, ah, medical supplies originate in Washington, which for Mr King is an occasion of dismay, is actually of reassurance to this particular relative in the waiting room.' Jenkins gave his snort of self-applause again. 'Though it may further burnish my reputation as an Atlanticist, my opinion – my second opinion – is that sterling could be in the hands of few better surgeons than Secretary of the Treasury Fowler.'

'But the surgeon is sick!' King insisted. 'The dollar is no stronger than the pound and the US Army has its hands on every greenback. You're like an architect who draws a marvellous castle and then builds it on a cliff.'

'We clearly hope,' added Governor O'Brien, his still-naked eyes refusing to meet King's, 'that President Johnson's tax surcharge will clear the Senate.'

The Governor replaced his glasses so that he again matched his portrait in oils on the wall to his right, although the effort to suppress his anger made him look even more impassive than the painting: 'I am as resistant to the parallels you derive from design as to those you derive from disease. The Americans are our friends, Mr King.'

'Friends! Is it not ridiculous, Governor O'Brien, to apply the language of playground acquaintance to international diplomacy? The Yanks do not send good money after bad because of admiration but because of a political calculation that it is cheaper to defend the pound than it would be to defend the dollar after sterling had collapsed. If any of these medical metaphors has any point, it's that America's interest in us is simply clinical.'

'To summon what should perhaps be this meeting's final image from the infirmary,' the Chancellor said, 'I would also mention susceptibility. The pound is akin to a hypochondriac. The *malade imaginaire* need only read of fever for his temperature to soar. In the same way, rumour of sterling's weakness becomes reality. Therefore our responsibility is to reduce speculation.'

Listening to this rapid – *wapid* – welter of w-sounds, King thought that, if he had Jenkins's speech defect, he would steer clear of words starting with 'r'. But the Chancellor seemed to take the opposite approach: recklessly reciting 'Red Rabbits Run Rarely' and facing down the stares.

In which connection, King became aware of Governor O'Brien glaring straight at him: 'This may be the occasion to remind Mr King that nothing discussed in Council or Committee of Treasury is to be reproduced to outsiders either verbally or in print.'

Attempting to mirror O'Brien's basilisk impression, King replied: 'If anything holds me back from mapping out current monetary policy in my newspapers, it's that readers might take it as satire, not reportage.'

Concluding the meeting, the Governor said to Jenkins: 'Chancellor, I'll see you again at the trial.'

'Ah, yes. The trial. I pray we win it.'

This exchange mystified King; although he could think of

many reasons for the Chancellor to be hauled before the courts, he knew of no such proceedings. He must ask the news desk.

As the gathering scattered, the Wilsonian placemen went into a huddle with the Governor, casting glances in King's direction as he strode towards the lavatory which, with its oak dadoes and crisp folded towels, indicated that this was a place where money could be spent as well as printed.

Perhaps the irritations of the meeting had inflamed King's prostate, for he endured a dry two minutes at the urinal. It was one of many intimations from the grave that a man of sixty-seven received.

Hearing the door bang behind him, he hatched a plan to piss on the Governor's shoes, but it was the Chancellor who came in. As Jenkins fished out a prick which, according to gossip, was more active than you might think, King said: 'Watch it go down the drains. Like this nation's gold and reputation.'

'Although I have to say, Mr King, that, at this moment, I am unable to emulate the rate of release you suggest for either.'

There now threatened a urological stand-off, neither man able to pee with another beside him. Trying to visualize Alpine streams, or the London Fire Brigade dousing a blazing house, King said, without turning his head: 'I fully understand that you must play the White Man in Council. But we should talk. Wilson's finished.'

'That prophecy is your perception, Mr King. Certainly the evidence for it is not within mine.'

The porcelain echo of their words was now muffled by the splash of the Chancellor's successful emission. To be second at this sport was a particular male shame with which only impotence competed.

'Can you come by Holborn Circus tomorrow at seven?' he asked the Chancellor. 'I have more of that Château Latour you enjoyed so much at the lunch.'

'That might be very agreeable. As long as sterling does not suddenly require intensive nursing.'

Having emptied his personal reserves, Jenkins nodded a farewell and crossed to sinks so clean they could have doubled up the duties of the wide spotless mirrors above. The sound of water pouring over the Chancellor's hands had the desired mimetic effect for King and he finally peed in a satisfying stream, released from him with a heat that felt like bile.

10

Soldiers! That's What They Look Like, Wilson!

IN A ROOM above a London pub on a Tuesday morning, the last line of defence for British democracy was mobilizing. They were numerous but there was a sense of well-meaning amateurs fighting against a terrifyingly professional enemy.

The one they called 'Wilson' – silvery hair and a rather slow-arriving smile which never reached the eyes – was a recognizable type from office or political life: the lieutenant who thought he ought to be in charge. Now his superior – the fastidious bespectacled bank manager – gathered his raggle-taggle partisans around him and rallied them.

'Stand at ease!' he instructed them. 'I think you'll agree this is a great moment. A great step forward in our progress towards fighting power. It's very well timed because we take over the defence of a vulnerable stretch of our beloved land.'

Although the men he was addressing were essentially joke soldiers, their patriotism did not seem comic and it was hard for an observer not to be moved by their makeshift indomitability.

'Tonight we are responsible for England,' the bespectacled leader went on, 'between the Jolly Roger Pier and Stone's Amusement Arcade. We have fifteen minutes before we move off to the guard post at the Novelty Rock Emporium.'

Storey wondered if he could get away with a trick intro to the piece, giving the impression that this really was a meeting of some secret army, perhaps even deliberately confusing this silver-haired Wilson with the other one.

He was aware of being looked at and realized he was the only one in the room who had laughed at the last speech. He assumed it was because the others knew the punchlines now.

The director – David Something, he had it in his notes – stood up at his trestle table and shouted: 'OK. At ease!' Storey scribbled that down – a usable bit of production colour – but again his was the only smile, so he added a note about how the making of a television comedy involved repeating jokes until they ceased to be funny.

The director – also the co-writer, along with someone called Perry who sat smoking a Prime Ministerial pipe in the corner of the function room – had prematurely white hair, brushed forward with ambitions for a fringe. He was wearing glasses with thick black rectangular frames which made Storey wonder if a single optician served the entire English comedy establishment: they were exactly the sort that Eric Morecambe and Harry Worth wore.

Flicking two pages back, Storey discovered that the director's name was Croft or, to his actors, 'Crofty'. He was a genial man whose face seemed to carry a perpetual half-smile, which Storey guessed must be useful for dealing with actors.

'It's cooking,' Croft told his cast, who now lolled on bum-dulled plastic chairs, with the exception of the one who played the captain. The actor still stood in the position in which he had finished the rehearsal, with a military stiffness belying his pudginess.

The dimensions of the set which would eventually be built in the television studio were marked out on the floor with white masking tape, like a builder's version of the chalk that detectives used for corpses. In this case, the lines represented the walls of a 1940s church hall, running parallel to the brickwork and radiators of this function room above the Feathers pub in Chiswick.

Sometimes, the production manager had told Storey, they rehearsed in an actual church hall. In a margin of the notebook, he put a reference to art imitating architecture but knew it would never get past Cudlipp. College stuff.

He recognized the one playing the bank manager – Mannering – from *Pardon the Expression* and *Turn Out the Lights*, television comedies which had often flickered in the corner of the room during his attempts to persuade Moira that Pope Paul VI was not the final word on heavy petting. Arthur Lowe. The director was talking to him now: 'Arthur, can I say as softly as possible that you might move around the rehearsal room with more freedom if you weren't encumbered by a script?'

Again distressed that he lacked the kind of observation a Bron had, Storey noticed Lowe was the only actor carrying a slab of pink foolscap the size of a London telephone directory.

'He hasnae learned his lines,' said the tall Scottish one with the wire-brush eyebrows. 'He stuffs the script behind the radiator every night before he goes home. Says he willnae have this rubbish in the house. Only proper plays.'

'Yes. Although that's not entirely an accurate quotation,' said Lowe, glowering through horn-rims.

'Just a few notes on that, chaps,' Croft tried to change the tone. 'Arthur, the line you have when you and Johnny inspect the troops. "Soldiers! That's what they look like, Wilson." I feel you're still playing the irony of the line. The point is that Captain M really thinks they look like crack troops. He's a Walter Mitty, Harold Wilson type . . .'

'Wilson! Ah, I've been thinking of him as Clement Attlee.'

'Well, whoever. Play it as pompous and proud as you can.'

The big Scot sniggered and the spivvy one with the pencil-line moustache added: 'That shouldn't be a problem for him.'

When working on location pieces, although his showbiz journalism was thankfully spasmodic, Storey was always struck by the substantial overlap between character and actor. The transformational skills claimed for the profession were heavily underwritten by the tricks that casting played with recognition.

'OK, chaps,' the director said, 'we'll take a coffee break. Can we reconvene at the top of the hour? And if you're worried that the young man sitting on the chair over there is a German spy, I should tell you he's Mr Bernard Storey from the *Daily Mirror*. He's here to write a little feature about the series. So he may come and ask you one or two things.'

'I'll tell you this for free, laddie,' boomed the gloomy Scot. 'It's a ridiculous idea and it willnae work. People either want to forget the war or glory in it. They dinnae want to laugh at it.'

The usual *Mirror* rule was not to represent dialect phonetically – it offended readers who spoke that way, while mystifying those who didn't – but conventional spelling could not convey the staginess of this actor's accent.

As the cast scattered from the room, Croft came across to Storey with a concerned expression: 'Don't take too much notice of John Laurie. He's something of a professional pessimist. We cast him to be the Caledonian voice of doom and he's perhaps a little too good at times. Although – I don't know if this is useful for your piece – he's the only one of them who was actually in the Home Guard during the war.'

'Do you mind if I . . . ?'

Storey pointed at the notepad with his pen.

'Go ahead. Although my better lines are saved for other people.'

'It's the absolute simplest one I wanted to ask you: why a series about the Home Guard?'

'Well, it was Jimmy's idea originally. Script called *The Fighting Tigers*. But, speaking for myself, I think it works because there's something so English about it: Boer veterans and bank clerks waiting for Hitler with sharpened bicycle chains and cheese-wires borrowed from the corner shop. How old were you when war broke out?'

This guess hurt Storey; he always hoped he looked much younger than he was. 'Three,' he said, across a memory of his father, two years later, turning purposefully away from the terrace step on which his small family stood. His mother had spent the few minutes before Dad left suddenly cutting onions in the kitchen. Bernard had been in his twenties before he understood that this was so she could offer her son a cover story for her tears. Out reporting now, he always lectured himself: notice the onions.

'Well,' Croft was saying, 'well, then, you won't remember how desperate it was. A lot of the time, no one seemed to think we could possibly win, except for Churchill. At the risk of pomposity, I'd say that there's a vital difference between American patriotism and the British kind. In the US, it's about thinking that you're the best there's ever been. In the UK, it's about muddling through. I'd like to think that's what this programme is about. The bulldog with fleas is still a bulldog. A tattered flag still stiffens in the wind.'

When the director excused himself to discuss the next set-up with studio management, Storey went downstairs in search of some quotes from the actors. He was successful sooner than he expected. Standing in the corner of the first-floor landing – which stank so heavily of piss that you suspected some desperate drinkers had not quite reached the doors to the left, marked with silhouettes of top-hatted and crinolined figures – was the tall, bronzed one who always seemed to be smirking at the world.

Storey recognized him from *Hancock's Half-Hour* and every British B-movie he'd ever seen: John Le Mesurier, a performer who might have been a household name if everyone could pronounce or spell it. The actor's cheeks were now slightly flushed above the tan as he slipped a silver hip flask, thin as a wallet, into a trouser pocket. Notice the onions.

'Ah,' said Storey. 'Have all the others run away from me?'

'Oh, dear boy,' chuckled Le Mesurier. 'It's nothing personal. Most of them go down to the snug for a smoke. Poor Arthur's in there.' He stuck a thumb towards the door which bore the cartoon of the dandy. 'A martyr to constipation. Sometimes he's late back from rehearsal and the crew are lined up outside the door, like fathers at the maternity ward, waiting for a sound. I think Arnold may be in there as well. He has the opposite problem with his bladder.'

'Arnold?'

'Ridley of that ilk. Plays Godfrey, the ancient. Wrote rather a successful play, you know. *The Ghost Train*. Although you'd never think it to look at him.'

'And what did you do in the war?' Storey asked.

'Oh, dear. Now you sound like Lord Haw-Haw or . . .' There followed an odd sound-effect in which the actor's snort of amusement – a theatrical hah-hah – almost matched the name of the traitor he had just mentioned. 'I was a captain, would you believe it? Breeding could get you somewhere in those days. Although clearly not in acting or I wouldn't be here.'

'You don't think it's going well?'

Behind the easy smile, the eyes seemed frightened: 'It's a

disaster, my dear boy. I really can't tell you, oh, it's absolutely *appalling*, it can't possibly work. No, no, my dear boy, it's an absolute disaster!'

THIS MARK was so easy to spot that there was no pride in trade-craft. Even without the picture in the *Mirror* and the recce in the pub beside the ticker clinic, he could have been in no doubt about who he was meeting. The shorthand pad in the hand shouted Storey of the *Mirror* at your service, sir. And most people in pubs were meeting someone they already knew, so bemusement was a clue to someone seeking a stranger.

Wright raised his rolled *Daily Mirror* in a discreet Christie's gimme and smiled directly at the journalist, who came over to the corner table, facing the door. Always know their way in and your way out.

'Bernard Storey of the *Mirror*,' he identified himself in a voice of such pride that he might have been confessing to a ten-inch donger. British hacks said they were 'of' or 'from' a newspaper, Americans 'with'. Why was that?

'Good . . .' Wright checked his watch. Always clever to make them think they might be late. 'Afternoon. You should call me Alphonse.'

'Though that isn't your real name?'

'Why could it not be? Some bloody odd things happen at the font. Speaking of which, what's your holy water?'

'What? Oh, er, a pint of Director's, please.'

The landlord had to change barrels so Wright had time for a surreptitious shufti from the bar. Storey was tall – six one in socks? – with thick – might one even say crinkly? – black hair, swept back from the temples, perhaps to cover for a little bit of Yul Brynnering on top. There was a glow to his skin which Wright categorized as tan or possibly olive.

With the arguable exception of August, when there was sometimes enough sun to justify colour, pale skin meant honesty in England. An Englishman with a tan was lazy; a non-Englishman with a tan was an enemy. Skin-deep, people said. But skin told you things. Wright suddenly worried that Storey might be a four-by-two, although that name sounded more Rugby League than Hebrew. Even so, perhaps he should arrange to stand next to his mark in the heads.

IF STOREY had been writing up 'Alphonse' in a feature – imagine the smudger drops his camera on the way back, Cudlipp always said, and the reader has to picture them in twenty words from you – he would have invoked a family solicitor or doctor, but, if the in-house solicitor would wear it, one who might fiddle your will or slip you some mickey pills. The face was as pale as bread and cadaverous, made harsher by half-moon glasses worn at half-mast in that way favoured by people who told you off.

'Sorry about that Bombay Trains delay,' boomed 'Alphonse', returning with the drinks. 'They had to switch casks. Very rare example of a journalist scraping the top of the barrel, I'd say.'

He slid a mat in front of Storey and placed the pint on it without a drip: a gesture which might either be courtesy or a mere reflex from a career of ruthless efficiency. 'Alphonse' was sipping what looked like gin and bitters: an old colonial drink, perhaps connected to the reference to Indian railways. The man's slang also supported this, veering between tuck shop and veranda.

'How was your comedy?' the pseudonymous stranger asked.

'I don't know. They've got some good actors. Do you know Arthur Lowe?'

'I haven't seen much television, Bernard. I've spent a lot of time out of the country.'

'Anyway, the cast all seem very down on it.'

'They'll be slurring their words, I'd imagine. Half of them have been up and down these stairs like a clap-doctor in a cat-house. What's the programme about?'

'Oh, the Home Guard. Butchers and bank managers, practising war in the evenings.'

'Alphonse' had raised the glass halfway to his mouth but now replaced it on the table and looked at Storey as if he had just been insulted.

'My God. Even for the Bolshevik Broadcasting Corporation, that takes the biscuit. A comedy about the greatest generation this nation has ever seen! Why don't they just bloody have done with it and make a situation comedy about the French Resistance?'

This flash of temper added to the sense of anger behind the respectable appearance. Looking carefully now at the man opposite – onions, onions – Storey spotted that the wispy white hair was worn longer at the back than any bank manager or family doctor could risk.

'When you rang me last night,' he prompted, 'you said you wanted to talk to me about a Mr Worthington? You have a story about him?'

'Oh, files full.'

'So, what's the yarn?'

'Mr Worthington is a Soviet agent. In full view of the British public, he is running a communist cell from his place of employment, assisted by other Sov Bloc sympathizers in the same line of business.'

'And where does Mr Worthington work?'

'Whitehall.'

Having assumed that 'Alphonse' was a time-waster who

would eye-poppingly confide that some tramp in St James's Park was the Messiah – and agreeing to meet him only because he had threateningly mentioned Cecil King's name – Storey was now genuinely interested. It was just possible that 'Alphonse' had the information which all reporters dreamed of getting.

'Is Worthington the Fourth Man?'

'What? Oh, you think the story I'm giving you is Philby, Burgess, Maclean and Blank? Yes, I did say *Blank*. No, Mr Henry Worthington is absolutely the first man to do what he's done.'

'Why not just tell me?'

'Because it's secret information. But sometimes things slip out under pressure, as the tart said to the cardinal.'

'What kind of job does Mr Worthington have?'

'First Lord of the Treasury.'

Storey's first editor – a disappointed but clever veteran on the *Kent Messenger* – had told him never to show surprise during an interview. Higgins always said it was like when a girl asked you to stay the night. If you replied 'Really?' it might make her think she was being cheap. In the same way, too much enthusiasm might warn a contact they were being candid. The trick was to look interested but as if you expected it. So Storey responded to the job title 'Alphonse' had given him by saying casually: 'Ah. So Henry Worthington isn't his real name?'

'Henry Worthington is the name on his file.'

Storey bought time with a long slurp of beer but the rendezvous made sense to him now: 'So you're a spy? MI5?'

The other man also faked thirst to win space before answering: 'You're possibly familiar with the philosophical problem of asking a man outright if he's a liar. Enquiring of a chap if he's a spy invites the same difficulty.'

'Yes. All the papers ran it when he won in '64. Wearing a fur hat in Red Square.'

'No, *not that photo*,' the other man growled, in a way that suggested he might not merely be a desk spy but the kind that could break your neck by taking your pulse.

'Even the security services, Bernard, don't consider it sedition to keep your ears warm. This is a photo Worthington didn't know he was posing for. Though the communist floozies doubtless knew where the camera was pointing. Classic honeytrap, though personally I doubt that the honey of Moscow bees is quite the same on the tongue.'

'And what does this picture show?'

'Oh, we're hazy on bust size or the odds on her being a natural blonde. We don't actually have the snap.'

'Ah.'

'But, in intelligence, possession is not the law. We were told of the photograph by Anatoli Golitsyn. You look blanker, Bernard. KGB agent, defected to the Americans in '63. We called him Gollywog.'

Storey now didn't doubt that 'PW' really was a spy, who was reliably presenting what the spooks thought they knew. But this stuff barely had ten per cent of the electricity to start the presses.

'So, at the moment,' he objected, 'all you've got is a rumour of a photo which you'd need a second Russian Revolution to see?'

'I keep telling you. This is a menu. We're eating slowly so you can digest. In 1951, Henry Worthington resigns from the Board of Trade. You'd have been – what? – fifteen then . . .' This accuracy, he guessed, was to hint that there was a file on Bernard Storey or, more likely, Ben Storr. 'But perhaps you've caught up on that scandal in the cuttings library?'

'It was over budgets, wasn't it? Point of principle?'

'Those were the words he used. Although a man speaking in his second language risks inaccuracy. He left the government because he opposed a rearmament programme designed to help Britain fight the cold war. The expenditure had been requested by the Americans. But Henry was not prepared to take orders from them. Whose tune he was dancing to I leave to you.'

'But if the Soviets had managed to get a mole in the British cabinet, why would they tell him to resign? It's like passing back to your centre-half when you've got an open goal.'

The irritated pause before 'PW' replied suggested that this aspect of the innuendo had already been tested in the secret world. 'Because he would have been voting in favour of arms aimed at the Motherland. It's like asking the Jew to chew pork. Even if he was pretending to be someone else, he couldn't. The stomach would vomit it back. No, the Kremlin withdrew Henry to prepare him for the next push.'

There were two reasons why a man with a full bladder chose not to leave the room: because he wanted to hear the end of an anecdote or he feared the assembly would talk about him. It was the former motivation which now made Storey seal his urethra through willpower.

'No sooner has Henry handed back the ministerial limo,' the spy continued, opting for the present tense which stressed tension, 'than he's going round town in another smart motor-with-chauffeur, courtesy of an outfit called Montague My-Yah . . .'

'*My-Yah*?' Storey checked, although the only notes he was taking were mental. This was not the kind of contact who was dictating for your shorthand.

'M-e-y-e-r,' 'PW' clarified. 'A company which specializes in trade with the East. In the twelve years before he seizes the party leadership, Worthington goes to Moscow a dozen times for Montague *My-Yah*. And we know that he had a good time there. An *exceptional* time. Because at no point in that rush to Russia did our Henry ever report to the Foreign Office – he's still a Member of Parliament all this time, remember – that he'd received an approach from the KGB.'

'Well, maybe there wasn't one.'

Storey was playing the notional fair-minded *Mirror* reader at whom Cudlipp encouraged them to pitch their pieces.

'Bernard, the bloody Second Coming in this pub right now is less unlikely!' The MI5 man seemed to consider banging his glass on the table before acknowledging that you needed to be a drinker of beer rather than spirits for such melodrama. 'Right through the time that Henry's drinking home-made borscht more than London tap water, every British business-man who goes to Moscow is lucky to get through the airport with their zip still done up and knows perfectly well that all those mirrors in the hotel room aren't for him to check his parting. When they get back, they tell us who put the eye on them and it's flowers for Mrs Businessman and a little some-thing for their current account. Worthington takes his annual leave there for more than a decade and never once complains they've tapped him up. Now, why is that? Who notices if a house stinks? The resident or the guest?'

'So it's the dog that didn't bark?'

'Along those lines. The bear that didn't shit. Now Moira will be wondering where you are . . .' The file on Storey again slid invisibly across the table. 'So, Bernard, the big question. In 1963, Henry Worthington becomes leader of the party. Here, not there, I mean. How?'

Storey laughed, immediately creating a contrary image on the face opposite, as if in a trick mirror.

'The comedy's upstairs, Mr Storey. This is a serious busi-ness. A national tragedy.'

'I'm laughing because I can see the way this is going. Wilson got the Labour leadership because Hugh Gaitskell died.'

'The sad but inevitable outcome of a prolonged and well-publicized illness?'

'No. But it still doesn't mean . . .'

'How did Gaitskell die?'

'A sudden infection. A pain in the shoulder. He went into hospital with a fever and then . . .'

'Lupus disseminata erythematosus.' The spy suddenly sounded like a priest saying Mass. 'Don't ask me to spell it. Look in any hypochondriac's anthology under lupus. An infection known only in a few tropical zones. In none of which was Brother Gaitskell prone to holiday.'

The use of the label 'Brother Gaitskell' gave Storey some indication of how Conservative his espionage contact might be. He had been a fireman on the *Mirror* news desk at the time of the Labour leader's death and it was his memory that Gaitskell, who led the party's right, was more socialite than socialist, a ballroom-dancer known to his Hampstead friends as 'Gaiters'. But he continued to humour the spook: 'So how did – how do you think – Gaitskell got it?'

'He was poisoned by the communists, who wanted Wilson in. It was a KGB wet-job. Just before he became ill, the leader needed a visa for Poland. He went to the Embassy. There was a delay. They pressed elevenses – coffee and biscuits – on him.'

'And which was tampered with? The coffee or the biscuits?'

The question left Storey lightly but came back heavy: 'Our lab rats are convinced it was the drink.'

Taking this as a hint that his pint might have been spiked, Storey left it two-thirds drunk.

'I see I don't convince you,' 'PW' conceded.

'Professional habit. I keep imagining going to an editor with this. A compromising picture which is out of sight in Moscow. And gossip about Gaitskell which was knocked down at the time. A GP wrote a piece in the *Mirror*. An overwhelming internal meltdown. The tissue consumes itself. It happens – not often, thank God – but it happens.'

THERE WERE two kinds of hack: the urinal and the test tube. The first sort just took everything you gave them; the others filtered and separated out. Storey of the *Mirror* was clearly glass not porcelain. But that could be good. Urinals could make you lazy about your, well, leaks. Test tubes encouraged you to be scientific about your allegations.

'Would you like another pint, Bernard?' Wright asked.

'No. No, I'm fine.'

'OK. What I'm saying is: ignore the missing picture of the Moscow Blonde, believe that Gaitskell got a really grotty dose of flu. But the case against Henry Worthington is a pattern of behaviour. You know a man by his friends. And who are Wilson's? Kissin, Schon, Weidenfeld, Sternberg, Goodman, Kagan . . .'

Most hacks, by the end of this list, were asking where they could get their Aston Martin and invisible ink, but Storey was proving to be a test tube of the Nobel Experiment kind: 'Well, you can sit there reciting the Israeli football team until late in the night. But what point are you making?'

Israeli football team. Perhaps Storey was a snipcock after all and the lunch hour had been wasted.

'The point,' Wright insisted, 'is that these are men with allegiances elsewhere. Kagan and Sternberg trade with the East. It makes Prime Minister Worthington a security risk.'

'But at least some of the people you list are refugees from

the Soviet system. They're more anti-communist than you are.'

This objection had often been raised by appeasers in seminars at Leconfield House and Wright had learned that to argue back was to exaggerate its significance. He had also come to understand that the way to persuade a man of a theory was to shape it towards his own secret shame.

'Men have secrets, Bernard.'

'Ye-es?'

The hesitation was a foothold on the cliff of the *Mirror* man's resistance.

'Bloody bad luck. Fog at Nottingham. Although I don't suppose you can tell Mrs Storey of the *Mirror* that a freak of racetrack weather is the reason that when she puts her hand in her pocket in the supermarket she's bringing up lint. Men have secrets, Bernard. Which means that other men can get them to do things they may not want to do.' The hack was placid now so he made his pitch. 'Henry Worthington is finally a risk because he's a womanizer.'

'As I keep saying, a fantasy snap in some KGB album . . .'

'No, not that. There are gymnasts who've had their leg over less often than Henry. It's classic agent-running. The Soviets' hold over him is the risk of exposure. In April 1949, on a trade mission in Canada, he slept with Barbara Castle, then Betts.'

'Wilson's had Barbara Castle?'

Seeing that he had Storey's attention, if not yet belief, Wright added: 'And now Marcia's pregnant.'

He had expected shock but the journalist was nodding.

'You knew that?'

'I'd heard it.'

'From?'

'Sources. Is it true?'

'The question, Bernard, is: should a man who visited Moscow ten times in a decade and whose closest colleague is now mysteriously expecting – should that man be Prime Minister? I think that Mr Cecil King would want the *Mirror* to consider these issues.'

'Then why don't you just tell him?'

Storey was definitely clever: even insolently so, in that fuck-you way of the four-by-two. There was no other way; he would have to see his dick.

'Because stories come from reporters, Bernard, not proprietors. And hacks don't trust stories that come from the top floor. We prefer to get our news out in the usual way.'

A locked door throughout the conversation, Storey now seemed about to click and swing. For Wright, only one doubt remained.

'I'm desperate for the Gents',' his mark said. Wright followed him in.

STOREY emptied his bladder with the almost orgasmic satisfaction which came from delaying for half an hour after the first tremor in the nerve endings. But, standing back to maximize the splash, he became aware that 'Alphonse'/ 'Patrick/'PW' was leaning in and looking down.

When a smile of something like triumph crossed the other man's face, he began to fear that the meeting had been a ridiculously complicated queer pick-up or that – he had no idea why – MI5 was framing him. They would claim – perhaps the solitary old geezer at the next table had been a plant – that Bernard had made seditious comments about Wilson and then enticed the operative to the bog. But why would they need something on him when it was clear they already knew about the horses?

There was no hint of an arrest for soliciting as the two

men crossed to the sinks and washed their hands – side by side in time like piano duettists – and were soon distracted by a sound like ripping curtains from behind the door of one of the distemper-painted stalls. Many men might have been embarrassed by the noise they had made but, when the door swung back, Arthur Lowe was grinning like a politician who had just won an election.

'Ah, you're the journalist chappie,' he blinked at Storey through John Lennon spectacles. 'I wanted to warn you that my character's name is M-A-I-N-W-A-R-I-N-G. Chap last week put Mannering. Maddening.'

The journalist saw that the spy was glaring at Lowe as if the actor's own surname were particularly apt: 'I hope you realize that, if it weren't for the people you're laughing at, your bloody little comedy would be in German.'

Storey smiled sympathetically at Lowe as the secret agent left but the performer would have been more appalled to know that the journalist chappie next went straight to a telephone kiosk – nervous of being overheard on the pub pay phone – and rang the features desk.

He had trouble getting through, still unused to the new design, with a dial instead of the A and B buttons and the trick of pressing the coin in when you heard the answer at the other end.

Storey told them this *Dad's Army* thing would never make a piece – all the actors seemed to think it was a car-crash – then asked to be transferred to Cudlipp's secretary. He requested an appointment as soon as possible.

11

The African Library

IT WAS A striking photograph and looked handsome run across the fold but Cudlipp was concerned readers would think it was a story about family planning rather than politics. Pictured at a family picnic, Senator Robert Kennedy and his wife were surrounded by eight of their children.

Either domestic schedules or the current limits of Kodak focusing seemed to have prevented a snap of all ten kids coming on the market. But, as Lee Howard had joked down on the editorial floor, they were gambling that the readers couldn't count and running the head: 10 REASONS WHY THIS MAY BE AMERICA'S NEXT PRESIDENT.

'Is it time the papers came out for Kennedy?' King asked, aiming, as ever, for Caesar but, just as characteristically, invoking Little Caesar.

'Would it be smarter to wait, Cecil?' It was Cudlipp's tactic, a version of Evelyn Waugh's trick with Lord Copper, to stall King by offering him an option of greater intelligence. 'There's still the risk of a late run from McCarthy. As you know' – another device was to pretend that an idea quite new to the Chairman lay deep but briefly forgotten in his stock of wisdom – 'politics isn't like horse racing. You can only lay so much store by form and reports from the stable boy. Though, looking at that picture, there's no question that this runner is on his oats.'

The joke was a mistake. King was puritanical, despite a

second marriage or perhaps because of it: he perceived his libido as a weakness and disguised it.

'I think it's time the *Mirror* said: we back this man. I've a feeling he's his brother without the womanizing.'

From forty years in the ink business, Cudlipp had construed the rule that newspapers always exaggerated the size of their parish. On the *Dinas Powys Gazette*, they imagined that Penarth was listening. On the *Penarth News*, editors agonized over the likely reaction in Cardiff. Now, in London, he worked for Cecil King, whose delusion of influence ran to the belief that the world was waiting for a word from him. He considered how to tell the Chairman that the Bobby Kennedy '68 camp was not staring at the Holborn Circus chimneys, waiting for the signal. 'Shall we see how he does in Indiana tonight, Cecil? Our man in the States heard the gap was narrowing.'

'OK. But no jokes about all those children. We have a lot of Catholic readers.'

'Indeed. But Lee has commissioned a little women's piece about what it might be like to have a brood like that. Getting their breakfast, packing them off to school. With foreign stories, I always tell the editors: make the details lean over the garden fence. At this stage, the reader's much more interested in how you feed all those mouths than what he'd do in Vietnam.'

But King, whose interests were precisely the reverse of those of the theoretical reader, interrupted with: 'What have we got on Wilson tomorrow?'

The Schleswig-Holstein Question and the Irish Question were coffee-break crosswords beside the Wilson Question from King. Cudlipp stared at the aquarium as if his salary were lying beneath the rocks and weeds, staring at the large carp as it resentfully inspected the partition in the middle.

'Ah. It's been rather a slow day in domestic politics. Gold is holding.'

'By which you mean that the astonishing daily drain on the reserves is slightly stabilized . . . ?'

'You see, there, Chairman, I'm not sure how we'd take the story on. What I say to the troops downstairs is: no reader should ever for a moment think they've picked up last week's paper. Also, no real developments in Rhodesia. We do have a little piece on the Money page questioning Chancellor Jenkins's decision to ask the mortgage companies to extend the length of loans rather than putting up interest rates. But that's just good popular journalism. Would Jenkins put you under house arrest?'

King stood up abruptly behind the octagonal desk and paced the rug-covered promenade beside the tank. When trailing in debate, he liked to impose his height.

'Hugh, I don't think Jenkins' – King's slushy tongue, a result of affectation or dentures, made it Jenkinsh – 'is the story at the moment. I really feel the headline of the day, the week, the year is: WILSON MUST GO.'

Short of actually announcing that he had become a fish, Cudlipp could not plausibly gaze at the filtered water for much longer. The quickest answer he could think of was: 'The International Publishing Corporation does not schedule elections.'

But he had used variations of this delay so frequently in recent weeks that an area which had begun as King's backhand was now a fluent ground-stroke: 'Not general elections, Hugh. Or not yet. But it's quite proper for a Labour-supporting paper with five million readers to intervene in the party leadership.'

'Shall we see how the borough elections go tomorrow night, Cecil? As I say, it's a matter of taking the story on.'

'Hugh, how are you fixed on Friday afternoon?'

'I don't know. I'd have to shift things.'

'Clear it from three thirty. There's someone I want you to meet.'

Cudlipp, who had learned as a reporter not to show too much enthusiasm for what the other person was saying, had adapted that strategy in management to avoid demonstrating too little. But he would be wasting Friday – the heaviest day of the *Mirror* week, with three titles heading for the stone – talking to some bore the Chairman had picked up at one of his anti-government lunches.

It was way past the corkscrew hour now but King had taken leave of the grape at around the time his senses had also left him. As Cudlipp shuffled the page-pulls and looked apologetically and hintingly at his watch – a reporter on the *Mirror* had asked to see him urgently – King rumbled down at him: 'And, Hugh, another thing. At Court at the Bank of England yesterday . . .' Cudlipp realized he had failed to maintain the blank-sheet face for which he aimed. 'No, don't worry. I'm not going to tell you Treasury secrets. No. Just, at the end, that liar O'Brien told Chancellor Jenkins that he would see him next at the "trial". You don't happen to know of any of our financial establishment up at the Bailey or anything, do you?'

'No, Cecil, I don't. Although I'm sure, if they were, you'd be prosecuting.'

'That's a joke I've made in my own mind.'

'No. I don't know what that would be. I can ask around the City desk.'

'Would you, Hugh?'

He was going to suggest that King should simply have asked the Governor and Chancellor what they meant but understood why that could not happen: Cecil King could never admit in public that he didn't know.

ALTHOUGH it was the second Wednesday of May, the evening was a rehearsal for the coming summer and Jenkins felt hot as he hurried towards the rendezvous which was neither precisely a secret nor entirely an official engagement.

Because he resented surrendering any of the morning to his wardrobe, he wore the same sort of woollen suit across the twelve months. This was an efficient system through three seasons but foundered in the middle of the year: now only the uncomfortable constriction of the collar prevented sweat from dripping down his neck. Jenkins accepted that he had never been svelte but recent newspaper photographs had seemed to show a monstrous impostor. He would have to consider extending his circuits of the Number 11 lawns.

He had asked the Treasury car to drop him at Hatton Garden, hinting at a present to be bought, and walked to Holborn Circus, counting his strides so that the stroll might be classified as exercise.

At the front desk, there was a considerable fuss which, when he finally reached the ninth-floor suite, Cecil King explained by saying: 'Were they slow to let you in? Nothing personal, Chancellor, I assure you. The porters are slightly standing on formality. It's because a murderer was arrested here last week.'

'How alarming,' said Jenkins. 'Not one of the staff, I trust?'

A politician became so accustomed to others laughing at his jokes that it was a shock to find King looking as solemn as during discussions of fiscal policy at Threadneedle Street: 'No. It wasn't an employee at all. Rather someone who came to the building to turn himself into the police. A tribute to our journalism, in its way.'

Jenkins looked around the room and through the window to the distant, miniaturized London beyond.

'This tower's certainly imposing, Mr King. A passer-by would want to know who owns it. The *Mirror* used to be in Fetter Lane, am I right?'

'That's right.'

'Geraldine House. Named after your grandmother?'

This pleasantry was strategic, telling King that Jenkins understood his inheritance, with all that might imply. In the head now nodding gravely, with its wide forehead and spread nose, there was much of Lord Northcliffe. Even the silvery fringe which fell towards one eyebrow mirrored the position of the bronze locks on the statue of the press baron in Fleet Street.

(That curse of journalists had been a boon to biographers. Northcliffe, like his nephew King, had favoured living at the top of buildings, ending his days in a shed on the roof of the Carlton Gardens mansion, throwing five-pound notes over the edge. He died huddled in his hut with a gun in one hand and a Bible in the other, protection against the German invasion he considered imminent. Jenkins, who had feared repeating his ancestors' lives only in the matter of rank, wondered what it must be like to worry about duplicating their personality.)

The walls were so full of books that they resembled some vast but rather dull national flag, consisting of vertical strips of velour and leather.

'Did the books come with the office or from you?'

'It's my Africa library. First – and often only – editions. When paper-rationing slowed up the press in Britain after the war, we bought titles in Nigeria. I ran them.'

King gestured towards the oak-panelled sideboard – certainly antique, perhaps even Stuart – where a wine bottle stood on a silver coaster.

'Would a Château Latour be acceptable, Chancellor? It's the '58.'

'Yes, very agreeable.'

Jenkins would have been happier if the wine had been decanted but King poured directly from the bottle, placing the glasses on the table in front of two rather impressive armchairs where he indicated they should sit.

'Am I right to think these are Chippendale?'

'I believe so. The wing-chair is a Hepplewhite.'

As they sipped the wine and murmured tasting notes, Jenkins continued to look around the office, which resembled the residence of a Mogul in sixteenth-century Delhi rather than the modern business sense. The carpet, which felt to his shoes like snow, was a tableau of birds, trees and leaves picked out in gold and green. This – and two lavish mats – seemed to plead for the feet of an emperor.

'Architecture is scarcely even a tertiary discipline for me, Mr King, but I'm prepared to hazard Adam for the fireplace?'

'You're too modest, Chancellor.'

'An unfamiliar tribute.'

'Adam it is. You may know that this is a smokeless zone, so I required a dispensation for my chimney. It has a special filter. I believe the Beatles have the other fireplace licence at their Apple building.'

'I envy you those desks. Too much of my writing has been done at hotel dressing tables.'

'They're a matching pair. Mahogany. William Kent.'

The writing tables had been angled against each other to make an octagonal work-space, perhaps eight feet wide, at the centre of the room. Jenkins wondered if there was a

Freudian connection to King's sense of himself as a many-sided man.

'I envied the *Observer*, Chancellor, your article on the Luther King funeral. You should not rule out the *Mirror* as a market.'

'That's generous. Though one wonders if one's prose has the right, ah, wheel span for that gauge of track.'

'Oh, a piece by you wouldn't be for the readers. It would be for me. Cudlipp is proud of what we do. But I see it purely as a financial proposition. The success of the *Mirror* was due to the fact that it appealed to people who wanted something simpler than the *Daily Express*. But there comes a time when each paper has reached a lower level than the previous one, until you get down to bedrock. You can't publish a paper which appeals to people less educated and less intellectual than the *Daily Mirror*.'

Jenkins was surprised by this attitude: 'In politics, it's habitual to maintain the fiction that all of one's constituents are miracles of uncomplaining good judgement. I imagined the relationship between newspaper and reader to be similar.'

'Your face is on posters. Those who buy the paper may never know my name. I have the luxury of invisibility.'

'Is it a luxury or a deprivation, Mr King?'

'What makes you say that, Chancellor?'

'Your ancestor, Northcliffe, sought to make the news as well as print it.'

King turned towards the sizeable fish tank which was the one piece of contemporary furniture in the room. Facing his guest again, he said: 'Northcliffe also went mad. And I certainly don't intend to do that.'

There followed a silence which Jenkins regretted, realizing that he had steered the conversation with that slice of his mind which was a biographer's rather than a politician's.

'Do you ever tire of politics, Chancellor?' King asked eventually.

It was an interrogational technique he associated more with women. Do you ever think how nice it would be live in the country all the time? Is this all becoming a bit too complicated? These were questions which already had armies massed to march behind them. 'Well, I rather think that one must endure a great quantity of anything before lassitude becomes a risk. And my ministerial experience has just reached four years. Your question would frankly be better addressed to a Gladstone.'

'Even so, I would think that four years would be an eternity if passed in the service of a man unsuited for his office and with whom one disagreed on every major point. Wouldn't they, Chancellor?'

The constant use of the political title, Jenkins felt, was not to flatter the guest but to glamorize the host: stressing the level of men who accepted King's hospitality.

'Well, Mr King, you are assuming both an attitude towards a superior and the consequence which might follow from that position.'

He understood that he was being invited to sell his soul for Château Latour – of which King had not yet drunk a drop himself – but he needed to be careful. JENKINS JETTISONS WILSON in the *Mirror* at this juncture would be entirely destructive. Even so, it would be politic to hint at some distance from Wilson. 'You know, I think collective cabinet responsibility is a tremendously healthy intellectual discipline. It's not good to be agreed with all the time. A point my wife often makes. I don't know about yours.'

This was his second joke to prompt a reaction from the press baron that was more funereal than humorous. King's massive forehead creased with the effort of emphasis: 'I worry for this country under Wilson. Labour has a discredited Prime Minister and a cabinet – excluding your presence – far less impressive man for man than the board of IPC. Across the chamber, one third of the Conservative Party wants Enoch Powell as leader. I had Iain Macleod to lunch recently and he believes that Parliament is in peril and Britain heading for a right-wing dictatorship!'

'Really? I know the Shadow Chancellor's urbanity on fiscal matters. I'd be surprised if he were quite so apocalyptic on the wider politics.'

'Oh, would you be surprised?'

King stood and strode to the paired writing tables, where he jabbed down – his great height giving the impression of a man falling – on a bell of the sort which called service in shops. The penthouse doors opened and a secretary, significantly less forbidding than the Treasury species, carried in a large bound book which she handed to the Chairman.

King flicked to a page, then gave the open volume to Jenkins. A cabinet position – especially, at this time, the Treasury – was good preparation for being nervous of the contents of a document but Jenkins still felt a jump of wine and bile in his gullet as he saw:

Monday April 2nd, 1968.
Iain Macloed to lunch. He wanted to know how I saw things as I had been right all along! I told him substantially what the Bank had told me. Evidently, a crash was coming and equally evidently . . .

King's diary was typed on foolscap sheets. Jenkins guessed they were dictated and that his own confidences would be thundered at the bell-girl after he left.

He looked down the page and found what defamation lawyers called the words complained of – 'Macleod . . .

threatened . . . dictatorship . . .' – although he was amused but not surprised to note who had introduced the possibility of a democratic collapse: 'Macleod agrees with me that our Parliamentary institutions . . .' He was also appalled to read that his Tory shadow 'thinks Denis Healey the ablest of the Labour ministers; Roy Jenkins is too keen on popularity.'

The closest corollary Jenkins had to this ridiculous situation was the moment at home of confrontation over the note of soft handwriting and ambiguous content found in a pocket or drawer.

'I'm not trying to prove a point, Chancellor,' King insisted, towering beside him like the functionary waiting to take away the inked agreement at a treaty signing. 'It's merely that, at times like these, we need to be sure who thinks what.'

'I am grateful for the elucidation,' Jenkins told him. As if in reward, the Chairman poured another glass of Latour, leaving him caught between his palate's desire for the tang of slightly bitter raspberries and his mind's call for absolute clarity in this moment of some danger to his reputation.

Serving in a cabinet which had a historically unprecedented quota of diarists – Crossman, Castle, Benn – Jenkins was trained in speaking for potential publication and that must be his tactic now. He returned the journal to King, who placed it not on top of one of the writing tables but in a drawer, which he then locked with a small key.

As the press baron sat down again, he lifted his own glass of – as yet untouched – wine, though still seemed reluctant to drink from it. (The Foreign Office, in its pamphlet on overseas hospitality, warned about two-speed sommeliers as a method of embarrassment.)

'The job of Prime Minister should be yours.'

King, who always spoke deliberately, was now so slow that he resembled a wrongly played LP. He was savouring the baptismal solemnity, lifting his drink in a toast which never reached his lips.

A moment for the memoirs, Jenkins thought. But would the biographical irony for the future reader be that King's presumptuous recruitment was an early dress rehearsal or the last night of the run?

'There is no vacancy,' he said.

'Great men don't wait for a job advertisement.'

'Only fools or blind men sit in an occupied chair.'

This trading of aphorisms changed the feeling of the meeting, which was clearly over, although the handsome bracket clock – eighteenth century? – marked out another quarter-hour before the shaking of hands. King became at once more courteous but also less attentive.

'Chancellor, Hugh Cudlipp told me that one should always ask a journalist the details he left out of a piece; the things he felt he couldn't print. He says that the East has censorship, the West has self-censorship. The Luther King funeral – was there anything you held back . . . ?'

'Ah. It's a shrewd observation. I believe journalists call it over-matter, don't they? There was, in fact, one story where tact stayed my hand. The walk from the Baptist church to the burial took four hours. It became a sort of slow-motion protest march. At one stage, I was walking alongside Robert Kennedy. He said: "You know why LBJ isn't here, don't you? Just frightened of being shot." At first, it seemed such an offensive thing to say about the President, but then I realized it was such a brave thing to say about himself. We look away when we see the Dallas pictures on television. So for him? At that point, we made a left-wheel, leaving me between Bobby Kennedy and a building which looked uncommonly like a book depository. It may, in retrospect, have been one of the most perilous episodes of my career.'

'But leaders need courage,' King said, letting the comment settle in the room. 'I told Mr Cudlipp only this evening that the *Mirror* will put its weight behind Robert Kennedy.'

CUDLIPP'S office might seem to an outsider to be surprisingly modest but an insider understood that it was drawing attention to itself by being so. The secretaries said that King's digs down the corridor were fit for Suleiman the Magnificent. Cudlipp seemed to have settled for paper, telephones and hospital carpet as the theme of his suite.

The only flourish was famous *Mirror* page ones framed on the wall. One was not yet two months old, as if to reassure Cudlipp that he was still moving forward: a photo of a white seal looking up hopelessly at the trapper's steel baton and the headline: THE PRICE OF A SEALSKIN COAT.

Other trophy frames shouted from the past. The front-and-back wrap for Gagarin, with the headline MAN IN SPACE used at top and bottom of each page. There was the rebuke to Khrushchev – DON'T BE SO BLOODY RUDE – and IS THIS THE PROMISED LAND?: that election-day headline – over a picture of a mother pegging up washing in the cramped backyard of a tenement slum – had encouraged the voters to turn out the Conservatives four years ago and replace them with Wilson.

Storey was impressed that the editorial director had so speedily agreed to see him and said this as soon as he sat down at a conference table so covered in paper that it looked like a teller's desk on election night.

'Yes, well, you should really be seeing Lee. But I'm assuming this is about him. In which case, I remind you that journalism isn't politics. Disloyalty is rarely rewarded. Your complaint had better be massive and valid.'

'Oh, no. It's not about Mr Howard. Just the contact who gave me this said to go to Mr Cudlipp or Mr King.'

'Ah. And you plumped for John the Baptist? You think you've got a big story, do you?'

'I think it's something you should know.'

Imagine the smudger smashes his camera: twenty words from you is all we have. How would Storey have summed up Cudlipp? Well, he had lively eyes and the core of his personality was warmth, although he had a notorious dislike of men with beards or cripples of any kind. Men would enjoy his company in a pub and women would be flattered to dance with him and this easy communication must be the key to his popular journalism. The one contradiction to his image as a plain man of the people was a vanity about his hair, swept back and up as if in a tonsorial version of the eyeshades which American editors wore in films.

'The difficulty is, Mr Storey – name like that you had to be a journalist, I guess – the difficulty is that our stories are not always as big as we think. Sometimes they are. When I was a kid, my brother Percy told me the local clergyman was a bigamist. Percy's first ever exclusive and he was right. I asked him how he knew and he said he just did. Well, sometimes, sometimes not, I've found. I just give you this warning. As a young man – boy, really – on the *Penarth News*, I was sent to Cardiff to report on the Messiah, they said. Three thousand words. Well, three thousand words, Messiah. It just had to be the Second Coming. Cardiff was an unlikely venue admittedly but then perhaps Bethlehem was not exactly Mecca. And, you know what, Bernard, it turned out to be a lot of people singing about God. Scarcely front-page news, especially in Wales. After copying out most of Grove's *Musical Dictionary*, I was still fifteen hundred words short. So I printed the name and address of every member of the chorus.

No other edition of the *Penarth News* has ever sold so many. But, you know, it wasn't the scoop I thought it was.'

It was a rare pleasure to be laughing naturally at something a superior said, despite the gentle menace of the story's moral. Because accents had always been regarded as a handicap in the British establishment – although Harold Wilson, for example, now exaggerated his – Storey had never previously realized how Welsh Cudlipp was. He Londoned up in public, although his roots were there, if you listened carefully, in the elongation of certain words: chorus, occurrence.

Conscious of Cudlipp's frequent injunction that a piece could always be shorter (except, presumably, his anecdotes), Storey presented as headlines what the three-named stranger in the Feathers had told him: Wilson's treachery and womanizing overseas, his secretary's pregnancy, Gaitskell's poisoned coffee, the possibility that the British Premier was a Kremlin agent.

Cudlipp nodded several times: a movement which had no effect on the auburn visor of his coiffure.

'And you think he was MI5?'

'He knew things about me. My wife's name and so on. My, uh, hobbies. And I'm not in *Who's Who* or . . .'

'You will be if all this turns out to be true. So the man you met was obviously a paranoid clairvoyant or a spook. Bernard, I want you to think carefully about this. What do you think the story is here? The facts the man in the pub was telling you? Or the fact that this man was telling you these things?'

Storey felt like a contestant on an American game show, the car or the holiday depending on his answer. If he got it wrong, he would become one of those hacks who drank their days away waiting for a particular executive to die in the hope that their career might resume.

Finally, he filed his reply: 'What I – what we – need to find out is why they're putting these things about now.'

'Good. Because I don't know about the rest of it but I can tell you now that Harold Wilson is not the father of Marcia's child. As it happens, I know the chap who is.'

Storey decided that he was too junior to ask the father's name, which was almost certainly the sensible decision, but meant that he then began to torment himself with the thought that it was Cudlipp himself. 'I also have to say, Bernard, that Harold Wilson is a most unlikely Soviet agent. I always think that the key to his success in politics is that he isn't actually very political. He believes what he needs to believe at any given time and has – or had – the gift of getting people to think that he genuinely thinks it. Whereas Philby, Burgess, Maclean and whoever – you may not be able to give them credit for much but they were genuinely communists. It would be murder running Wilson as an agent. You'd never know which side he was on. Thank you, Bernard. You were quite right to come to me. There's no question of wasting police time here.'

'Should we – should you – tell Mr King?'

For the first time in their conversation, Cudlipp's eyes withdrew their keen amusement. Storey at first feared that the anger was aimed at him but a firm handshake – the free hand coming round to rub the knuckles – contradicted that impression.

'I don't think Mr King would need to be told any of this.'

HE HAD chosen a telephone kiosk in Notting Hill. A gang of nigger kids – with that big, tall swagger that made your car keys tremble – was coming out of a youth club. There were parts of London now where you could be in a foreign country. He couldn't, though, risk ringing from Leconsfield

House. With everyone mole-hunting, the listeners were pretty much taping your farts in the bath these days.

Although he had the number on a scrap torn from the *Mirror* Letters page – in the tobacconist's, he had bought *The Times* as well, in case they got the wrong impression of him – Wright fumbled the first connection, unable to press in the pennies when he heard Storey's voice. His sense was that these new telephones were less efficient. He missed the simplicity of the lettered buttons. When his second attempt connected, he thought of the photo of his asset holding the big white telephone.

'Storey. News desk.'

'Ah, Bernard. It's Patrick White.'

'Oh. Hello, "Alphonse".'

'Bernard, Cecil King has two desks joined together in his office. The top left-hand drawer of the one on the right as you look from the door is always locked. Now why do you think that is? Is it possible that it contains news far more interesting than anything printed in the *Mirror*? Have you got that, Bernard? The top left-hand drawer of the one on the right.'

'Yes. But I . . .'

WHEN the telephone in the main house rang after 10 p.m., it was either business or bad news or sometimes – as on the night when the negro American preacher was shot – a combination of the two. On the way to the table in the hall, she turned down Mahler One on the stereogram.

'Pavilion House.'

'Is that Dame Ruth?'

'Yes. Who is this?'

It was a well-spoken individual. At any other time of day, she would have assumed he represented one of her charities.

'Dame Ruth King?'

'Yes. Railton, also, depending on context.'

She hoped for the click of Cecil picking up his bedroom extension, though he often disconnected it now. He seemed to need more and more sleep.

'Your husband is a man of destiny. Look after him.'

'I'm sorry. I . . .'

'Tell Cecil King he is a man of destiny.'

The line went dead but, it seemed, respectfully so, not aggressively, like one of those men who called to ask what undergarments you had on. She turned up the Mahler as loud as it would go but Cecil always said he could kip through a civil war. She would tell him in the morning.

12

As the Sob of the Breeze
Weeps Over the Trees

FOR TONIGHT, he had chosen *Ruddigore*. The duo's first flop, it suited his mood of ruined promise. His first term had been *The Mikado*, the second *Ruddigore*. As Wilson waited for the doctor, he tried to mock-conduct the music with his pipe. Unusually, this relaxation failed him. He found himself keeping time not with the orchestra but his own thumping pulse, which he felt as a trembling in the neck.

'I told you not to have MI5 as your last of the day,' Marcia reminded him. 'They always upset you.'

But, whatever his secretary liked to believe, not all political problems were soluble by drawing a line with an arrow on it in a diary. He could meet Furnival-Jones over a leisurely lunch on a birthday during which he also won the football pools, and the Head of MI5 would still cause palpitations.

'I don't think it's about appointments, Marcia.'

'Well, let's see how you get on without the Keeper of the Diary, then.'

Marcia was like the weather fishermen most feared: calm to cyclone in a moment. One cartoon-frame after she had been smiling at him from her chair, she was already in tears and at the door. She was carrying her handbag, which meant it was a force two storm-out rather than a force one, in which she was unable to leave Number 10 without coming back to the study for her stuff.

'Marcia, you're tired. You're tense about the vote tonight. We all are. I don't suppose your ... condition helps either ...'

'Oh, it's Dr Mitty now, is it? Why do you always call for Joe Stone if you're such a medical expert yourself?'

The strap of the handbag was over Marcia's arm, which she raised so that she looked like a domestic version of the Chancellor on Budget Day. She tapped the glossy black leather.

'It's all in here, Harold. One phone call to the *Daily Mail* and you're finished.'

With this increasingly familiar threat, she left. She would be back. The single advantage of a climate which turned from sun to rain without a hint of thunder was that the showers gave way to warmth with equal speed. The pity of it was that she had been right. Meetings with the spooks always left him uneasy and unwell.

Wilson had been suspicious before even meeting the spy chiefs in '64 because he was still not entirely convinced that the security services hadn't murdered Gaitskell, hoping to bring in that ardent anti-communist, Brown. He felt that MI5 had not expected Wilson to win either the leadership or the general elections and now couldn't forgive these results.

At their first encounter in Number 10, MI5 had admitted the telephones of some of the cabinet were tapped. The top men undertook that it would stop but what did a promise mean from a secret organization that officially did not exist?

He had initially found the spooks useful during the seamen's strike two years before – the evidence of communist cells in the unions had shocked him – but the revelation that he had welcomed this surveillance had lost him credibility with the Left of the Party.

Next, an attempt to keep secret an aspect of national hygiene – that all cables from overseas were opened and read before being sent on to the public – had become a full-scale stand-off between Downing Street and Fleet Street, forcing him to sacrifice Wiggy from the cabinet.

Tonight, Furnival-Jones had been at his most insidious, spinning some shaggy-dog story about Jeremy Thorpe and a young chap who posed for magazines. Scott, was it? Wilson had wryly pointed out that the Liberal leader had been married twice, which seemed excessive to cover an interest in men. He had challenged F-J (as he wanted you to call him) on where the information came from and was told: BOSS.

But wasn't it obvious, he had argued, that the South African spies – with their ridiculous James Bond-ish acronym – were targeting Thorpe because the Liberals opposed apartheid? He could not let the spies bring Thorpe down. Even now, he believed he could keep the party together, but if he failed he might need a Liberal coalition.

The record had reached the brilliant patter-song – in which three performers raced each other, Grand Prix singing – and he closed his eyes to listen: '*My eyes are fully open to my awful situation / I will go at once to Roderick and make him an oration / I shall tell him I've recovered my forgotten moral senses . . .*'

Wilson tried to transport himself to the comic Cornwall of Gilbert and Sullivan's plot. But the spies had even ruined that for him. Now, when he thought of Cornish cliffs and the Scillies beyond, they were disfigured by the brace of hundred-foot satellite dishes installed for the Americans at Bude and the hut on the bluffs at Nancekuke, where nerve gas had been researched after the war. The spies seemed to delight in siting their ugliest activities in places of the greatest beauty.

There was a knock on the door and he hoped for a contrite Marcia but his encouraging shout admitted Dr Stone.

'Good evening, Prime Minister. Are you in the wars again?'

'Oh, hullo, Joe. I'm probably just being silly again. But earlier I thought I felt a . . .'

'A "heart tremor"?'

'I thought so. Yes.'

'Let's have a listen, shall we? Shirt off.'

As Wilson disrobed, he noticed that Joe was overdressed: white dinner jacket, black tie, scarlet cummerbund.

'Oh, I'm sorry, Joe. I told them not if you were busy. Did I get you out of dinner?'

'Theatre. And we'd just got home. Don't worry. I always say there's no more fitting place than this for a Gladstone bag.'

Joe was lifting from the grip his holy trinity of instruments: the stethoscope, spirometer and sphygmomanometer.

'What was the play?'

'*The Royal Hunt of the Sun*. You'd probably quite enjoy it. Time when people believed their leaders were gods and so on.'

'And sacrificed them on slabs, didn't they? Politics is never simple.'

There was something humbling about sitting in the Premier's chair in his vest. He thought of the man who walked alongside the new Pope, muttering that he would become dust.

'Did you enjoy it, Joe?'

'The setting was spectacular. But it's a strange thing about theatre. People say: isn't it amazing that they did a sunset? But there's never actually a moment when you think it really is the sun going down. Your quiet night in with G&S is probably more the ticket. Although do you mind if I turn it down?'

After hushing Dame Hannah's ballad, the doctor, as usual, blew on his hands before applying the blood-pressure cuff. This gesture was not necessarily hygienic but indicated the kindness that was the reason Wilson had chosen his GP and then promoted him to this role.

'Is Mary not around?'

'Another poetry reading. Public can't seem to get enough of her. I keep telling her she should stand in the next election.'

'We mean to go to one. "The Isles of Scilly" is our favourite.'

Putting on his Home Service voice, Wilson quoted from the poem: '*Nature is not more gentle here / Than in the city's crowded core; / For suddenly dark clouds appear / Great waves beat up along the shore.* Personally, I think nature probably *is* more gentle there.'

'What an extraordinary memory you have, Prime Minister.'

Why had Joe suddenly mentioned memory? He wondered if the doctor had spotted something and began secretly to recite: Mercer, Goodall, Barkas, Redfarn, Wilson, Steele, A. Jackson, Kelly, Brown, Stephenson, W. H. Smith. Jackson had scored but had been unable to prevent Blackburn winning 3–1 in front of a crowd of 92,041 at Wembley. That was 1927–28. The season he started at Royds Hall Grammar on the scholarship.

Satisfied that his mind was intact, Wilson now worried about his body as Joe squeezed down the sleeve and said: 'We'll try it again in a while.'

'Is it bad?'

'As I've told you, one reading can be misleading. Blood pressure and triple jumps: best of three.'

Next it was the stethoscope, so cold against his chest that he always feared it might reverse its purpose and stop his heart.

'Steady enough now. Show me on the table with your pipe what the rhythm was when you had the "spasm".'

He banged the briar faster than the patter-song – so hard that baccy spattered the red boxes – then slowed down to loping, irregular beats like a child playing hopscotch.

'How alarming that you were alone when this happened.'

'Oh, Marcia's around. She's working somewhere.'

Joe handed Wilson the spirometer and he blew into the tube three times. Medical tests were the only examinations in his life which he always dreaded and had frequently failed.

'OK, put your shirt on. I'm going to take my tie *off*. And prescribe a little medicinal brandy as a first resort.'

As the doctor poured two glasses – parsimonious, presumably medical, measures – *Ruddigore* came to a muffled end and he lifted the stuttering needle before delivering the drinks.

'Any chest pain?'

'No.'

'I'm not Robin Day or Ian Trethowan. You have to tell me the truth. Any chest pain?'

'No. Although I should have stabbing pains in the back, the way my colleagues are behaving.'

'Good. That there's no pain, I mean. Normally, I'd ask a patient if they were under particular stress. But there's not much point with you.'

'Why? Because I'm unusually gloomy?'

'Because you're Prime Minister.'

'Well, you probably saw in the papers this morning the Scottish local-election results. I expect I've similar to come from the English shires tomorrow. Tonight's turned into an all-night sitting of the Finance Bill because my friend at Number 11 – maybe accidentally, perhaps deliberately – didn't put a timetable on it. If we fail to pass it, the government will fall. Tell me straight, Joe. If I have to resign, do I have health grounds?'

'You won't be going that way. Your lungs are a little more congested than I'd expect from a pipe-smoker. If I didn't know better, I'd think it was cigarettes. But the heart sounds are fine. It's hard not to notice, though, a certain rumbling lower down. Tell me, are you still breakfasting courtesy of the member for Aberdeen North?'

(Ever since Wilson's election, this backbencher had sent him an annual gift of smoked fish from his constituency.)

'Yes. We still have some left.'

'What you think of as "heart spasms" is almost certainly your breakfast kippers coming back at you. The guts and the heart often feel the same from the inside. The racing pulse is what, I believe, American medicine calls a "panic attack". Do you have a brown-paper bag?'

'What? To wear over my head so my enemies won't know who I am?'

'Next time the rat-a-tat happens, breathe slowly into the bag. I could give you more pills but the bag works better. Now, do you think I should go and see Marcia?'

THE Prime Minister was attending quietly to his boxes in the study when the duty press officer brought him the first editions of the next day's papers. Mr Wilson had advised his Private and Political Secretary, Mrs Marcia Williams, to go home early because she was feeling unwell.

In contrast, there was no doubt about the Premier's own health. Earlier in the evening, he had a routine consultation with his private doctor, Joseph Stone. The doctor was impressed with his overall fitness but gave advice on dealing with the mild indigestion that had been troubling the Prime Minister. The physician commented afterwards that he wished all his patients were as sturdy and stoical as Mr Wilson.

As the Premier smoked his familiar pipe and sipped a hot milk drink, he was listening on the sound system recently installed in his study to the new BBC pop music station, Radio 1, which he enjoys as it keeps him in touch with young Britain.

The press officer drew the PM's attention to some stories in the newspapers. The *Daily Mirror* gossip column 'The Inside Page' reported that an urgent telegram from the Chairman of Newcastle Transport Committee to Mrs Barbara Castle, Minister for Employment and Productivity, had failed to reach her because the Post Office had no record of the address of the recently created ministry.

A laughing Mr Wilson told the aide to check with Mrs Castle if this were true. If it were not, he might need to have a word with his old friend, Cecil King, Chairman of the *Mirror* owners, IPC.

The press officer went on to advise the Premier of the latest news from Indiana, where former Attorney General Robert Kennedy had won another victory, although less decisive than some had predicted, in the presidential primary in that state. Mr Wilson, who was a friend and admirer of the assassinated President John F. Kennedy, said that he was thrilled by the possibility of a second Kennedy in the White House. He joked, however, this did not mean he would be encouraging his sister, Marjorie, to enter politics.

The Prime Minister invited his press officer to stay for a mug of cocoa. Though politely declining, he did stay to listen briefly to the radio. The Premier commented that the Beatles were one of the best things about the new Britain.

When the press officer left to go home, Mr Wilson was heading in the direction of the connecting door which links Numbers 10 and 11 Downing Street. Such was his dedication to his office that he doubtless had an appetite for late-night economic debate with Chancellor Roy Jenkins.

NEVER a friendly house, Downing Street was even lonelier as midnight approached, with all but the duty copper and overnight telephonist gone home.

He found himself humming the ghost song from *Ruddigore*. *As the sob of the breeze weeps over the trees, and the mists lie low on the fen / From grey tombstones are gathered the bones that once were women and men.*

He tried the door that linked the downstairs rooms to the Chancellor's apartment. It was open. Taking his Huddersfield FC key-fob from his pocket, Wilson locked it.

13

Better Than Churchill

ONE MEASURE of historical development was mankind's changing knowledge of his own face. Our most distant ancestors had first glimpsed their image in a river's reflection. The subsequent steps of recognition had been paintings, mirrors, photographs and X-rays.

King was among that small group of men who had seen themselves regularly on television – a portrait which was disconcerting because it corrected a mirror's reversal while falsifying size – but there was a greater and ancient satisfaction in being painted. Television glistened but then vanished. It was not a medium that would ever mount retrospectives. Yet even if a canvas were taken down from the wall, there was the dream of it being found in an attic centuries hence.

'I hope, in the end, I turn out better than Churchill,' King said.

Even in repose, Sutherland's features were creased – was it a qualification for an artist that he should have a paintable face? – but the lines multiplied at this mention of his most famous but unseeable creation.

'Not meaning to be rude, but it's something I prefer not to discuss. I suspect it's rather as if, Mr King, a dinner guest asked you to list the court cases brought against your papers for defamation. Not that I regard the Churchill portrait as any kind of libel. It was not a failure of artistic depiction but of psychological honesty by the family. What they called "cruel" was truth. Your newspapers are thrown away each evening. It happened to me with one painting.'

'At the risk of flattering you, Mr Sutherland, the man you painted was the man I knew. But truth would be a useless defence; it was not a commodity that bothered Churchill. In '41, he threatened to close the *Mirror* and the *Pictorial* down. "Cassandra" had attacked the war effort. He sent me a letter, accusing me of malice and lowering morale. I asked to see him and he agreed that day. He shouted that we were rocking the boat. I argued that we were describing the state of the sea, not creating it. After an hour, he ordered me to leave or my papers would attack him for wasting the nation's time. An air raid had begun and so he insisted that I took his government car to my office, where I gave Cassandra no instructions to hold back. Other wounded letters came. I think Churchill perceived that I saw him as the wrong leader for the times.'

'Well, you were wrong about that.'

'Was I? For how can we know how different the outcome might have been with someone different at the helm?'

Fearing a portrait showing him with an open mouth, King stopped and concentrated on his own mental sketch of the painter. There was nothing of Van Gogh or Picasso about this artist. He was not wild or mad in dress or manner. The voice was slightly high and light for a man, with the occasional word slowed and almost sucked like a sweet: cru-ell, lie-bell. Was that Welshness, though, or affectation? A dapper man in shirt and slacks that would pass at a summer party – no sense at all of his favouring clothes that could risk paint dribbles – he seemed, in the way of creative types, just a little bit queer.

But whereas Ruth's music people usually were, King suspected Sutherland wasn't but had merely adopted the habits of the artistic locality, like taking off your shoes outside an Indian temple. What seemed specific to his own profession was the gaze. Through half-moon rims, he gave the impression of looking under your skin, like a natural radiologist.

It would be so easy to lean round and see the oil sketch progressing on the easel but he understood he must not. His Northcliffe uncle, when he gave the boys a parting gift, made them close their eyes as he placed a coin in their palm.

'Why did you choose to paint me, Mr Sutherland?'

The artist gave that little wiggle of his shoulders: part of the arse-bandit act.

'Well, I was commissioned by the International Publishing Corporation. Mr Cudlipp, is it? We met him through Hans and Elspeth Juda. Do you know them?'

'I rarely go out in the evenings.'

'Mr Cudlipp wants to hang you in his boardroom.'

'I understand Hugh's interest. I was speculating about yours. I doubt that Graham Sutherland accepts every invitation to put a chap on canvas.'

'That is true. You know, I'm really only a weekend portraitist. I only ever painted the Somerset Maugham because he was my French neighbour and he asked me to. I simply couldn't find a way into it until, one day, I looked at him and thought: *face is landscape*. Of course, Willie's visage was more geological than most.'

'Mmm. A "wedding cake left in the rain".'

'Well, that was said of Auden, actually.' King flushed at being corrected by this mock-ponce. 'Although it more than applied to Willie as well. Meringue in a storm, even. And, looking back, I have, I suppose, gone for men with something of earth and rock about them. Max Egon, Adenauer . . .'

'And what loam or limestone am I?'

'Oh, one seeks to avoid the cliché of the man-mountain.

But I doubt that I've ever painted anyone taller and broader, so that becomes a calculation. You may know that I tend to use an exceptionally narrow canvas? My decision is whether to expand the space or let you brush the edges. And people will doubtless have mentioned your eyes? Their piercing quality.'

King feared a giant with a one-mile stare was taking shape in oils across the living room.

'I happen to know this, Mr Sutherland, because I had to approve the expenditure: there was never any possibility of this being a surprise. I noticed in the correspondence that you charge £5,000 from the waist up but £10,000 for a full-length portrait. Why, pray, are legs so expensive?'

'Oh, I'm far too old to be painting pants all day. Especially pinstripes. I was pleased Mr Cudlipp concluded that posterity doesn't need to see your knees.'

King saw the opportunity to bring up the one subject he wanted to discuss: 'You mustn't paint me too slowly or you'll find that even five grand will scarcely keep you in turpentine. Get Cudlipp to pay you before Wilson devalues again.'

Once more, the artist gave that little shake of the torso like 'Teasy Weasy' Raymond and those other Chelsea queens.

'Oh, I'm not much good to you on politics. We live in France. You'd probably get more sense out of me on de Gaulle.'

What was it that made us long to share our secrets? Against all sense, King had an urge to tell the artist capturing him for history that he was mobilizing against Wilson that afternoon and the Prime Minister would be gone by Saturday. But then he remembered what Wright had once said about social discipline and turned the conversation to Dame Ruth instead.

THE SUBJECTS always asked him why he had chosen them, except for Churchill, who had come to see immortalization as his due. If he had revealed his true criteria, then all of his portraits would have recorded a grimace of vanity and anger as the sitter reacted, for his subject was man in his final state, awaiting the grave or grace.

Sutherland chose to paint faces which had been tested, the expressions of men who had known responsibilities and temptations. It was possible this came from his Catholicism, a creed which took most interest in a man at the moment when he ceased to be a work in progress, but he had always been drawn to the old. In his forties, when he had painted Maugham, the connection was speculative. Now – at sixty-four, only three years younger than his subject – the portraits had become a dialogue about dying.

Sutherland turned away from King, then looked back quickly as if his name had just been called. It was a way of tricking himself into a fresh impression. Because he chose to paint faces of character, the risk was always caricature. King's height, wide nose and eyes like sunlit sea lured one towards a cartoon. Exaggeration, however, must always be resisted. Many viewers had questioned whether Willie Maugham really held his neck like an ostrich with tetanus but he had painted what he saw. Picture the figure precisely and you captured the spirit.

The press baron was beginning to flex his fingers, as if he hoped to be allowed to shift his hands. Sutherland allowed sitters to choose their position – if you picked a pose for them, you might as well scribble on a false moustache – but, once selected, it must be kept. Prince von Fürstenberg had sat with one leg over the other and, though gangrene became a real fear, that was how he stayed until the sketches were complete.

King had leaned back in the chair with his hands clasped

across his crotch. And, while most big men held in their tummy, this sitter thrust his forward as though it were a trophy given for good living. Sutherland had worried about the long-term comfort of such a pose, but this was the attitude the subject wished to show the future: a man who knew his weight and threw it around. The artist also noted that, unusually for a man, King had not undone his jacket to sit down. Was this an Edwardian fashion – like old men who belted their trousers almost at their chests – or a barrier: a buttoned-up man?

People also always wanted to know if you liked your subjects. Artistic affection, though, was a complex matter. A painter's interest might legitimately run skin deep. He had shared the national gratitude to Churchill but found him an irritating sitter, absurdly sensitive about his hands. He had expected King to resemble Beaverbrook – for his prejudice was that newspaper tycoons were a narrower genus than doctors or painters – and they certainly shared a habit of bombast.

Two minutes into their conversation, King had begun an anecdote about a man – well spoken, obviously not a nutter – ringing the house the night before and telling Dame Ruth that her husband was a man of destiny.

Much of their chat had been about the subject's wife – commendably uxorious on King's part but, in practice, potentially boring – who seemed to be a woman of unusual powers.

'Dame Ruth,' King announced, in a voice that was more of a lullaby than the boom his huge frame seemed to threaten, 'once felt unwell on a flight to Manchester. The stewardess served her a cup of tea and asked if she felt better. Absolutely out of nowhere, she heard herself say, "I should be quite all right now if we hadn't burst a tyre." Shock and consternation in the cabin and the cockpit, before a safe but bumpy landing achieved on the remaining wheel. The pilot took my wife aside and asked: "How did you know I'd burst a tyre on take-off?" She replied she didn't know but that it had come to her at the moment she felt unwell. Dame Ruth, you see, is what they call a "sensitive". She has extrasensory perception. Another time, in a hotel in County Donegal, she woke in the small hours with a nightmare about fire. The place burned to the ground three weeks later!'

Sutherland hoped he managed to avoid aeroplanes and accommodation containing Dame Ruth, although her husband now disclosed an aspect of her supernatural talent which might be socially useful: 'She has been aware of this gift since childhood. If she was late for a train, she was able simply to will it to stay in the platform.'

Before there could be any more about the sitter's life with Madame Nostradamus, Sutherland used his customary settler question: 'Tell me about yourself in two hundred words or so. Imagine you're at a job interview, a balloon debate. A biography no bigger than a postcard.'

'It can be a useful exercise,' King conceded. 'I did something similar once for a book about Fleet Street. Well, let's see.'

He shifted his feet and placed his hands level in front of him, as if on the ledge of an imaginary lectern.

'The pose, please, Mr King.'

'Ah, yes.' As often with Sutherland's sitters, there was a visible shock at taking orders, but then obedience to the cause of art. 'Is that it? All right. Cecil King: a user's guide. I think people have certain expectations of a "press baron", driven by money or publicity. But I am essentially a shy introvert. Northcliffe gave his name to a company, but there is no King group. I function best as an employee of a large organization. I am not particularly interested in money but am principally concerned with politics and using my publications to exert influence in directions which seem to me important.'

There was so marked a change in the eyes now that artistic honesty called for Sutherland to stop and begin another picture, but you could not control everything a sitter did.

'Because my photograph is in the *Financial Times*,' King continued, 'people see me as a conformist. But I am not. I run into trouble because I tend to see things with a fresh eye regardless of the accepted point of view. Also, I am *Irish*. This is overlooked because I have no accent and am not Catholic. But I am still more at home in Dublin than anywhere else.'

Sutherland empathized with this resentment. He was a Welsh painter – Pembrokeshire lay like a primer under all his pictures – but England had a way of claiming everyone in these islands as the English, especially if you had any measure of success.

'Finally,' King concluded his survey of his personality, 'I have a considerable store of general information which, at the risk of immodesty, I have not found matched in any other man. The consequence is that my judgement is always based on knowledge. I'd say that was under two hundred words.'

Sutherland had taken part in mock elections at Epsom College and King's contribution was reminiscent of such events, except for the difficulty of guessing which party the candidate represented. The speech had most resembled a manifesto for leadership of the world.

The sketch was finished. The next decision was the background colour for the canvas. Though not a 'sensitive' – no hotel could hope to use him as a fire alarm – Sutherland believed to some extent in synaesthesia. He filled in a painting with the shade that best represented his impression of the subject. For Maugham, it had been yellow, a royal colour in the Orient which meant so much to that author.

King tried to project power, which suggested a backdrop of purple or red. Or the black – marking something dark and dangerous – which he had used for Beaverbrook. At the Judas' supper, where the commission had originated, Cudlipp told Sutherland that, to mark the fiftieth anniversary of the *Mirror* in 1963, King had minted a bronze medallion with his own face in the monarch's place. So there was an Emperor complex here.

But he had detected something else below the swagger: a current of rejection and dejection. If he gave his portraits titles other than the nominal ones, he would have written under this picture: An Uncertain Egomaniac.

Grey, this face was saying to him. Grey.

14

The Excellent Raincoat
Company

IN THE 2.50 at Chester, the Oulton handicap, Bouverie in
the *Mirror* was going with Hard Man, although the horse
was out at eights, way down the betting. Maybe the tipster
had reached the stage where he needed to win big to reach
anywhere near even.

This was certainly Storey's reason for chasing the same
hope. Although he had begun to dash across London by bus,
looking for bookies where his face was less well known, he
was now establishing a pattern even in these out-of-the-way
places. Today the clerk had smiled at the sight of him and
popped his eyes at the size of the flutter when Storey staked
two pounds: now his standard gamble only weeks after such
a wager would have called for extraordinary form or a solid
whisper from the stable.

When he left the shop, there was sweat on his face, which
soon met rain and then more perspiration as he was forced
to rush to have any hope of punctuality for 'Alphonse'.

A day that had earlier promised to be a warm-up act
for high summer had given way to showers and Storey was
glad of his raincoat, although he had felt some resentment
when Moira had nagged him to take it that morning. The
moment had seemed too much to come from the other side
of marriage: what would be left between them when the sex
had gone.

'I hope that's not Gannex,' said 'Patrick White', who'd come into the City Golf Club and, ignoring raised hands of recognition from at least two other guests, crossed straight to Storey. The dripping rain from 'White's' umbrella made the raincoat even wetter as it hung on the back of Storey's chair.

'What I earn at the *Mirror* runs to Burton's,' Storey told him. 'But it's going a bit far, isn't it? Even having it in for Wilson's raincoats?'

'Gannex is more than a mac to Worthington,' insisted 'White', sitting down, although noncommittally on the edge of the bench, like a man soon planning to go for a piss or a pint. 'Gannex is the link to Joseph Kagan.' The spy pronounced the name *Yo-Seff*, in that Establishment way of flagging a foreigner. 'Kagan is in this up to his lapel buttons. He may even be Worthington's control. Anyway, like our friend in Number 10, he's certainly waiting for a rainy day.'

'Pretty unlikely cover for the Soviets, isn't it,' Storey persisted, 'a factory in Huddersfield making macs? I mean, I know they say the KGB uses poisoned umbrellas as weapons – what's the deal with Gannex macs? Are there bugs sewn into the seams or . . . ?'

'Does it not occur to you, Bernard, that a cover operation would, by definition, be unlikely?' This was another of the flashes of anger of the kind he had seen at the Chiswick meeting. It struck Storey that 'White' probably shouted too often to be a really efficient spy. Heads at neighbouring tables had already turned, prompting 'White' to continue in a whisper: 'I mean, the Kremlin isn't going to set up a little boutique on Kensington High Street called I-Spy. Do you happen to know, Bernard, what was one of the major front companies for Soviet intelligence in Continental Europe before the War?'

'No. But I sense the way this is going. Burberry? Pac-a-Mac?'

'No. The Excellent Raincoat Company. So how ridiculous, is it, actually to think that Gannex might be cut from the same cloth? And think about that cloth. What is it that makes Yo-seff's waterproofs so special that Henry Worthington puts one on every time he sees a camera?' This time, the spy didn't risk facetious answers. 'A special insulating fabric: wool on one side, nylon on the other. A process quite unknown in any British laboratory. Why? *Moscow know-how*.'

Storey still found it hard to understand why the Russians were so keen to keep the British dry before taking over their nation. It would surely have been cleverer to take advantage of their inferior rain-gear and invade in winter, maximizing the Soviet experience of Siberia. But 'White' was a man for whom conversation consisted of documents offered for stamping, so Storey restricted himself to: 'Can I get you a drink?'

'No. I have to buy them. Club rules. I'm the member.'

'Ah, right. Odd sort of place, this. How long's the bar, for a start?'

Storey pointed to a serving surface which, although the tables in the room would barely have seated one hundred people, looked long enough to allow an entire sell-out audience at the London Palladium to order interval drinks at once.

'I believe it's fifty feet,' 'White' explained. 'It was originally parallel to a driving range, with a cinescreen of bunkers and greens and so on.'

'Oh, I see. I assumed the City Golf Club was a joke about the kind of people who come here. A nineteenth hole in town for bosses who can't get to Buckinghamshire in time.'

'No. No, not at all. It was literally a golf club in London. Wheeze of an Etonian called Arbuthnot. But it soon became clear that the clientele were more interested in lifting their arms than swinging them. The driving range rusted and went but we were left with a beer-hatch the length of a fairway. I'm surprised you've never been here. We have a lot of the ink-trade in.'

'Not from my end of the payroll. I know that Cudlipp is a member. And that's John Junor over there, isn't it?'

'Jonah, yes. One of our keenest golfers. And you know who that is?'

'White' indicated a small man, who was responding with a fillings-flashing giggle to something Junor had just said to him. The laughing stranger wore the kind of glasses which looked as thick as a shop window and made you think the next step would have to be white sticks. Storey didn't recognize him from a photo byline.

'No. Who is he?'

'Raymond Jackson. You're still looking blank. If I say JAK?'

'Oh, right. He docs fantastically right-wing cartoons of Harold Wilson in the *Evening Standard*.'

'A Gillray for our day, I'd say, Bernard. He's one of ours.'

'Yours?' Storey did not initially trust his understanding but had come to realize that 'White' was no Lenny Bruce. 'Seriously? The *Standard*'s cartoonist's a secret agent? I mean, Christ, how does it work? Is there an extra picture in invisible ink you only see if you iron it? What's his mission? Caricature Wilson into resignation?'

'We don't say agent. We say asset. We have someone at every newspaper, let us know what might be coming out.'

'Who is it at the *Mirror*, then?'

'What are you drinking? I should get them in before the lunch-time rush.'

'Oh, er, do you know if they have Seeger's Egg Flip?'

'God, what's that? Some kind of advocaat?'

This was, in two senses, a flip request. Storey guessed his new source was someone who saw personality in surface – judging a man by what he wore, smoked and drank – and, keen to seem uncooperative in a scheme he found bemusing, he had chosen the most ridiculous tipple he could think of.

'I don't know. I saw it advertised in a magazine. If not, then a glass of whatever red wine they've got going.'

WRIGHT asked the barman to show him the bottle. Seeger's Egg Flip – according to the label – was 'a mixture of full-strength Australian wine and eggs'. He almost retched at the prospect. It was the sort of thing a secretary drank at the Christmas bash if she was planning to grant the boss admission to her knickers. Storey from the *Mirror* might not be a snipcock but perhaps he was a poof.

Wright carried the frothing, purplish concoction and his own gin and bitters back to the table where the journalist was flicking through the *Mirror*.

Wright tapped the front page headline:

PRISONER SNATCHED FROM HOSPITAL BED
P.C. Coshed As He Guards Patient In Ward 23

'Did you read that, Bernard? Six men burst into the ward, bundle out a bloke in his pyjamas. This is the country we live in. Grandpa goes in for a hernia, bloody lucky not to have a seizure.'

'I wish I'd written it, actually. Good yarn.'

'We long ago gave up hope of this government keeping us safe in our homes. But there's still a certain expectation in our hospital beds.'

'Gangland thing, isn't it? Blag goes wrong, someone needs stitching. Get him out before he's asked too many questions.'

'I'm glad you're so sanguine about the state of the nation,

Bernard. I just hope they never make you Home Secretary. You make Callaghan look quite tough.'

'I'm saying it's contained between the bad guys. There are obviously turf wars going on – they finally got the Krays yesterday . . .'

'Yes. I read your little bit this morning on it. Served on a plate in their mam's council flat. I hope there's a Jack Ruby out there somewhere for those buggers. Save the taxpayer.'

Wright raised his glass in a toast to a contract on Ronald, Reg and Charlie. Storey of the *Mirror* took a sip of his eggy claret and grimaced, either at the political sentiments to which he was being asked to drink or the peculiar brew itself.

'You know what they say about mixing grape and grain?' Wright teased him. 'You've got bloody vine and hen there, which must be worse.'

Wright had decided that Storey was too headstrong to be of long-term use but choosing assets wasn't central casting; they happened to have an emergency where Storey worked. But there was still no sense that he was theirs. He needed cementing.

'Did you talk to Cudlipp yesterday?'

'Yes. He saw me.'

'And what did he make of our story?'

'He said that Harold's not a daddy. Except with Mary.'

'So does he say who Marcia's been hiding in her tunnel?'

'He wouldn't tell me.'

'Then he's bluffing. There's only ever been one interior decorator competing for that contract. Did you get the impression he'd tell King Cecil?'

'I had the sense he wouldn't.'

Storey's lips were purpled from the Oz eggnog, giving him a drag-act aspect.

'What exactly did he say, Bernard? Think carefully. This is the final round in a "Win £20 a week for life" quiz.'

The journalist half-closed his eyes in a dumb-show of focus. These bastards panicked without their shorthand notepads. Wright was trained for a world where the only archives you dared carry with you were in your mind.

'I think,' Storey said, 'I think it was, "I don't think Mr King needs to be told any of this." '

'Really? That was the form of words? That exactly?'

'I believe so.'

'Good. Now, Bernard, do you remember what I told you? The top left-hand drawer of the desk on the right as you look from the door of King's office. Listen. It has a rhythm to it. The top left-hand drawer of the desk on the right. You need to have that in your head like a nursery rhyme.'

Storey, who had always been so cool and smirky like one of those pointy-heads on *Late Night Line-Up*, was suddenly almost banging the table, like a union boss told he'd have to give up the big car and office and go back to work.

'It's more like a bloody fairy tale,' he hissed. 'Just tell me, Mr "Patrick White", who didn't write *The Tree of Man* but penned instead "The Ballad of Henry Worthington", a rather lesser work of fiction. Just tell me, "Mr White", why I would be stupid enough to break into my proprietor's office on the say-so of a stranger who insists that the cartoons in the *Evening Standard* are some kind of secret code?'

This moment was always so sweet: when an asset thought they were definitely saying no but you knew you had the key to turn them.

'Why? Colonel Blimp and Pussy Pelmet, for a start. Yesterday, it was Angel Child and Happy Guy, wasn't it? I'm starting to think that if the handicappers really want to wreck a horse's chances, they should just get Bernard Storey to back it. None of that fussing about weights and so on. I've known a lot of wives, Bernard, one of them my own. I'm sure Mrs Storey is desperate for a Servis twin-tub or whatever. She must wonder where the money's going and I don't suppose she'd be thrilled to know. Although, it might actually be getting beyond that. It might be Mr Barclay who asks the hardest questions. Or even Mr Bailiff.'

From the way Storey looked at it, the Seeger's Egg Flip could have been hemlock.

'The top left-hand drawer of the desk on the right,' Wright repeated.

THE TANNOY in the shop was so rattly – worse even than British Rail announcements – that the commentary always teased the punter with the possibility that his horse was heading the field before the winner turned out to be a mount which sounded similar when shouted in excitement.

In the 2.50 at Chester, for example, Hard Man was easily confused in the race-caller's roar with Bartang and even Drake's Drum and so it was only when the result was confirmed in chalk on the blackboard that Storey finally accepted he had a winner at 7/1.

A BROTHEL didn't want to look like a brothel, so it tried to seem nicer than that. There were whorehouses with better curtains than restaurants, anything to put the neighbours off the scent. But betting shops, which didn't want to look like betting shops, seemed to be trying to look like a knocking shop where you were guaranteed to get the pox.

The front windows were painted out brown but, even so, it managed to look duller inside. Wright had checked the interior decor earlier that week (muttering about the Official Secrets Act and palming fivers across the counter as he told them that he was positively vetting a Mr Bernard Storey for a government position) and found stools which looked built to give you piles and sheets of newspaper used as wallpaper, like in an army khazi.

A colleague in D branch, who knew the colours of every jockey in the country, had told Wright that the shops were actually required by law to put you off. The government, who wanted the money from the betting levy but had to buy off the Church and the pledgers, had written into the Bill in '63 that the shops should look like shit.

They had certainly succeeded. Storey, though, was coming out of William Hill as if he'd just had the time of his life in there, which could not be good, could not be bloody good at all.

15

Men Don't Make Passes at Girls Who Are Skinny

THE CHAIRMAN telephoned from his 00 extension – a managerial vanity which combined a hint of Bond with a nod to Omega – just after twelve and used his usual preface: 'Cecil King. Let's have a chat, shall we?'

But when he arrived in the office brandishing two newspapers rolled into a baton, and with the tread of a Frenchman making wine, Cudlipp wondered at the sin about to be denounced. It turned out to be another rant on sanitary towels.

'Hugh, in the car on the way here, I read the *Mirror* and *The Times*. Editorially, I really think a boxing judge would struggle to give the decision. But advertising! Into Lord Thomson's coffers goes their full card-rate for a whole page from Debenham & Freebody. Advertising mink coats. And what do we have? Colour pictures of Farrow's Processed Peas, Lazenby's Best Red Salmon. And – I had to look twice, Hugh, to be sure – Dr White's.'

Betraying the prejudices of his generation – admitting to only one item which might go into a lady below the waist – King instinctively dropped his voice on the scandalous brand name.

'Tampax, actually, Cecil. And you should be glad. Since women got the vote, it's been the long dream of Fleet Street to print a paper they might read. That ad tells us Wardour Street believes it's happening here.'

King's way in an argument was rarely to interrupt an answer but never be swayed by what he had heard. He continued now, as if Cudlipp had just apologized: 'And if it's not sanitary towels, Hugh, it's fat-cures. Look at this!'

The Chairman flipped to a page of the *Mirror* which had paid for many wages: perhaps even a portion of King's. 'Read that!' he instructed, in the tone of an optician keen to close up for the day. Too irritated by being made to play his superior's stooge to rootle for his specs on the desk, Cudlipp bent and squinted and then read out, as casually as if he were reporting on Jack and Jill's journey: 'Men Don't Make Passes At Girls Who Are Skinny'.

As if they were sharing sheet-music in a choir, King leaned over and read his lines in a censorious tenor: ' "Super Wate-On. Fruit supplement to build you up. Emulsion – strawberry flavour. Tablets – banana." Is this the best way we can fund our company? Through the bleeding and feeding of secretaries?'

'But isn't it more positive, Cecil, to think that we have made a paper which is read by stenographers who wish to be more hefty? I'm sure Lord Thomson of Fleet would give his butler's right arm to have a readership of underweight typists. *The Times* advertises furs because that is what their readers buy for their wives. We carry ads for processed peas because that is what our readers eat. Tinned vegetables get you five million buyers a day; skinned animals three hundred thousand. I think I'd settle for a can of Farrow's.'

'You're as clever as ever, Hugh. You bring the discussion round to supermarket food and make it seem quite reasonable. But my objection was to feminine unmentionables in a daily newspaper.'

'Objectionable to who? We'd none of us be here without menstruation.'

Cudlipp realized as he employed it that this contention was questionable; it was the interruption of the monthly cycle which gave us life. If he had been typing a piece, the sentence would now be a wire-fence of XXXXs. But King was unlikely to start trading gynaecological detail with him and, in fact, this latest reference to the female body seemed to have terminated the conversation.

'I understand – obviously I do – the arguments of commercial expedience. It's just that I sometimes wish I ran a paper I could leave open on the table in the drawing room.'

(Like much about King, this prurience about newspapers could be traced back to his mother: Geraldine Harmsworth, mad Northcliffe's sister. At the end of dinners, King handed out anecdotes about her cruelties like cigars. The story which always made Cudlipp shiver was a torture with hairpins carried out under the guise of cleaning out the ears.

The son was in general a disappointment to his mother and she held his publications in contempt. Cudlipp had once been summoned to see the proprietor's mother when he ran the *Sunday Pictorial*, a title Lady King especially despised. He had asked Margot – King's first wife – how the publication might be made more palatable to her mother-in-law. Advised that the matriarch's ideal in journalism was *Horse and Hound*, he had, against all other editorial instincts, packed the *Pic* that Sabbath with stallions.

Lady King seemed appeased that her wayward child had equestrian instincts as well as clean ears and the fact that the paper's circulation remained unchanged the next weekend convinced him that readers were either loyal or apathetic.

But, though the *Mirror* was bought by a tenth of the nation, King still dreamed of appealing to a reader who had been dead for a decade.)

'You're thinking of leading on the local elections tomorrow, Hugh, I suppose?'

Cudlipp tensed. He knew that King prided himself on the rarity of his editorial interventions but infrequency was no guarantee of merit; no one ever praised a volcano for spacing out its eruptions.

'Well, yes. If the Scottish results yesterday are any guide, Labour might be losing a dozen boroughs or more. We've a special report from the Paris peace talks but – short of North and South dancing a can-can together at the Moulin Rouge – that's not going to throw anything up for the front.'

'Yes. I think it's time we got properly involved in the Vietnam War.'

Fearing that his Chairman was about to urge support for America's colonial folly, Cudlipp asked, as sharply as he dared: 'You mean Britain should send troops? Wilson couldn't get it past his party even if he wanted to, which I doubt.'

'Oh, no, no, no. The *Mirror* should. Both sides need to hear our voice.'

It was King's habit to keep his suit jackets fastened: the vanity of a man fatter than he wanted to be. And so the gesture he now made – removing a scroll of paper from his inside pocket – was more elaborate and protracted than it would otherwise have been. Later, Cudlipp wondered if the delay had been a deliberate attempt at theatre: the slow fiddling with buttons equating to the dial of a safe.

King unfolded the sheets of foolscap (a strange and beautiful word, Cudlipp always felt, referring to a watermark of a jester's hat on an ancient make of paper) as though he was leading a delegation at the Paris talks and this was Ho Chi Minh's ceasefire agreement.

'Hugh,' he said, 'I'd like you to read this. I think it might make a striking page one for tomorrow.'

Cudlipp tried to hope that some grandee or minister summoned to the emperor's den on the ninth floor for posh red wine and the thoughts of Chairman Cecil had arrived with an article in draft.

But he had feared for months that this moment was coming so the byline – clearly peck-typed by a big man's two fingers rather than a secretary's hands – did not surprise him:

By Cecil H. King, Chairman of the
International Publishing Corporation

As Cudlipp read, it became clear that Vietnam was not the only country in which his boss wished to intervene.

King left him with the text and said that he had two urgent letters to dictate.

16

Mr Jenkins Changes Trains

LENIN, leaving Switzerland in a sealed train, had presumably been spared the sight of the faces on the platform of the proletariat he claimed to serve. Chancellor Jenkins, however, denied the protocols imposed by the German government of 1917 on their inflammatory passenger, was forced to endure the furious glares of commuters denied access to the first-class compartment.

Jenkins had first been alerted to this particular beneficence of ministerial office by Dick Crossman. The security services were nervous about state papers being read in public and such worries had multiplied since the D-notice fiascos. Thereafter, a cabinet member who so much as opened his red box on a train necessitated the evacuation of the carriage. Thus a national neurosis about security facilitated an individual's desire for privacy, permitting ministers to travel between London and their constituencies in splendid isolation.

Although it was actually his intention to read Gladstone's *A Chapter of Autobiography* – this rereading combining his interests political, literary and numerical, for it was exactly a hundred years since first publication – Jenkins had indicated to the train guard that intense ratiocination on Britain's gold reserves might be taking place. Though this gentleman evidently felt some resentment at the prospect of Chancellor Garbo, he duly blocked the corridor and growled about 'security' to those who waved their first-class tickets in his face.

An elected official should perhaps feel concern at the possible loss of votes from those denied their seats beside him but Jenkins doubted that those who paid the highest fare would vote Labour in any eventuality. When the train was well clear of New Street, he pulled down the blinds, becoming, in this small respect at least, a fellow traveller of Lenin's, then lifted half a bottle of Château Latour and a corkscrew from beneath sheaves of Bank of England briefs containing the information that all investments including fine wines were probably doomed. This vintage demanded to be drunk from something grander than a plastic picnic cup but the crude vessel did not dilute the liquid's therapeutic effects.

The day's official business had begun with a fractious cabinet, erratically refereed by a Wilson at his most determined to smell rats in every corner. Delivering the now familiar tirade about the importance of avoiding leaks, the Prime Minister had stared at Jenkins directly. Afterwards, Barbara had praised his coolness under such innuendo but he feared that what she took to be forbearance was, in fact, exhaustion. The Finance Bill Committee had continued until breakfast.

(Long after the debate had become a game between two players who knew each other's shots too well, Macleod and the Tories had launched an ill-tempered filibuster designed to deny the Chancellor his restaurant table and bed. They had succeeded to the extent that he had feared falling asleep in cabinet which, with Wedgie, Barbara and Dick all rumoured to be keeping diaries, left the risk of being known to post-erity as a political Rip Van Winkle.)

As they were walking to their cars, he had told Barbara he hoped the cabinet leaker, whoever it was, would not tell Fleet Street that he had been rather narcoleptic in the meeting. It was an unsubtle tactic – like someone with intestinal difficulties asking if the dog had made the smell in the room – but being the object of suspicion among his colleagues had begun to unsettle him.

Catching the 2.15 from Euston to Birmingham brought him no respite from the apparent status of pariah. He had thought it proper to visit his constituency on the day of the municipal elections but was barely out of the taxi at Stetchford when he was informed of the prediction that every ward would be lost. Intending to present himself as the figurehead of the ship, he now felt himself exposed as the Jonah who brings storms and drownings and needs to be thrown overboard.

The experienced politician knew defeat was inevitable when voters refused to look him in the eye, and on his brief watch outside the polling station there were enough squints and focusing difficulties to keep the eye-doctors of the Midlands in business until the millennium.

'Thank God it's not a general election,' George Canning, his agent, had said, driving him back to the station for the London train.

'I rather share your relief on that point. Although the results of municipal elections tend to be a caricature of the national mood rather than a reliable likeness.'

'You say that, Roy. But it's Harold Wilson they're giving out about on the doorsteps, not any of our local councillors. Since devaluation, they wouldn't trust him to look after their cat without killing it or selling it. And, frankly, would you?'

It increasingly seemed to Jenkins that an ambitious politician was like a spy. He had a cover story – the loyal colleague – and must make that lie his life, aware that anything he said might be reported or recorded. People spoke to him in code and he must reply to them, depending on who they were, using the same cipher or another.

'I fear, George, I am unqualified to comment on the Prime

Minister's viability as a guardian for a pet I do not, in any case, possess.'

'There's a lot of support for you here, Roy.'

'That's kind. And it's why I wanted to show my face here today. Take my part of the blame.'

'It's not you they blame.'

But as he returned from Birmingham, Canning's exoneration was small consolation for a day of failures which seemed to presage others. The claret, even from its cheap beaker, and though the air-blown heat of a railway carriage was no sommelier's idea of room temperature, achieved at least a portion of the warmth it brought in happier surroundings and chosen company. He turned to the words another politician had written a century earlier, aged fifty-nine, twelve years older than Jenkins, but with his greatest years of public office yet to come.

Gladstone had lost power four times, and retrieved it on three of those occasions, filling in the intervening periods with theology and tree-felling and schemes for the redemption of young women that these days would receive an earthier interpretation in the *Daily Mirror*.

Yet this optimistic memoir was a false model for a politician in 1968. In the nineteenth century, electoral defeat had been a semi-colon rather than the end of a sentence but it was now impossible to imagine Wilson and Heath serving turn and turn about as Gladstone and Disraeli had, while the wilderness years of Churchill and de Gaulle served as contrast rather than example to the modern power-seeker. That will o' the wisp which was the highest office offered itself only once and, in seeking to grasp it too early, Jenkins might tighten Wilson's hold.

At a knock on the blinded door, the Chancellor drained his drink and built a ziggurat of files and papers over cup and bottle, placing a piece of foolscap stamped SECRET upper-most, in case a passenger had come to argue over the exclusion of the general populace. The intruder, however, was the train guard. After admitting him, Jenkins turned the confidential paper over in a gesture intended to harden his claim on the compartment.

'Sorry, sir. We've been told to stop the train at Didcot Parkway.'

'Ah. That's rather inconvenient.'

'It's for you, sir. You're to take a phone call on a secure line.'

He had been informed – again by Dick Crossman – of this slightly sinister privilege of ministers: an unscheduled halt for the train and the walk to the stationmaster's office for the call from Whitehall and the offer of tea in a big blue-and-white striped mug. A civil servant had once told him that in the days before train drivers had radio links, the locomotives would slow down through the station and a split potato would be thrown to the guard, with a note pushed into the cut.

The train began to brake.

The question of whether his first fear in these circum-stances had been for his children or for sterling was one which long occupied him afterwards.

HAROLD wanted Marcia to telephone Didcot at precisely the time agreed but she argued that, whatever the other achievements of the Wilson administration, they hadn't quite yet made the trains run on time and so it was better to wait a few minutes. When she felt Harold was actually counting the seconds, she rang and the voice that answered was bluff and solid, the kind you would cast if they ever did *Thomas the Tank Engine* on television.

'Didcot Parkway Station. Stationmaster's office.'

'Good evening. I'm calling from the Prime Minister's office at 10 Downing Street. Is the Chancellor with you?'

'Yes, Ma'am.'

She smiled at the formality, although it was not displeasing. Jenkins could be heard saying, in what television crews called 'off-mike', 'That's most awfully kind but I was well refreshed on the train.' She thought: you won't have got claret on the London–Brum run. Anticipating the moment when Jenkins would be handed the receiver, she transferred the call to Harold, enjoying the perfect choreography of such moments.

As the Prime Minister said, 'Good evening, Chancellor,' Marcia moved to the chair against the study wall and picked up the extension. Civil servants listened on the second phone because they didn't trust the politicians but the Prime Minister invited her to eavesdrop because of her integrity.

'I'm sorry to get you off the gravy train, Roy.'

'I recommend the hospitality of Didcot.'

'Probably more your kind of people there than Birmingham.'

'It is not a distinction I made. Obviously, Prime Minister, one's mind turns at once to the possibility of crisis.'

'Roy, I'm calling you to ask you what you know.'

'Ah.' In the pause, she could hear behind him the echoing nonsense of a station announcement. Then Jenkins again: 'I feel rather at a disadvantage, Prime Minister. I had assumed I was to be the recipient of information on this occasion, not the giver.'

'It's not an essay, Roy. It's a telephone call. You don't have to talk like Macaulay. Are you saying that nothing's going on?'

'Well, I would find it easier to guarantee the absence of

activity if we could narrow down the field of which we are speaking.'

'Wiggy says there's a plot. Fleet Street's full of rumours that my enemies are moving against me. What do you know?'

'As you discovered in tracing me, I have spent most of the day on trains. The London tom-toms make a rather muffled sound in Birmingham and even Didcot.'

'Why did you go to Birmingham?'

'One doesn't want to become known in the constituency as Macavity. Your voters in Huyton have the compensation of your greater visibility elsewhere. I decided to visit the scene of the crime.'

'And what offence would that be, Roy?'

Harold was so sharp with his answering. Marcia thought he should get his own television show – sort of PM Simon Dee – when he decided to leave office.

'The decision of the populace to rob us of their votes municipally.' She had to admit that Jenkins had the gift of the gab as well but he didn't speak to the people. It was what Harold always said about Enoch Powell: the jokes sounded translated from the Latin. 'Prime Minister, even the commendable equanimity of the English might eventually be tested by this unscheduled stop. Did you have a specific request?'

'I need a show of confidence. Wedgie's going on television to debate with Quintin Hogg. As for you, I don't care how you do it – interview, speech, letter to the good people of Stetchford – but I want you to come out strongly for me.'

'Prime Minister, my problem is not with the sentiment but the public expression of it. I feel rather that the sudden application of a buttress implies a house that is in danger of falling down.'

'It's the owner of a house, Roy, who decides the renovations. And who lives there.'

Afterwards, Harold sucked triumphantly at a cigar. Marcia imagined the Chancellor's face at the other end of the line, the colour of red wine.

17

Worried of Hampton Court

THE PENCILLED SKETCH of page 1 of edition 20,022 of the *Daily Mirror* – Friday May 10, 1968 – was dominated by three words, in 56 point, underlined, across four and a half columns: ENOUGH IS ENOUGH.

This headline had been dictated – like the text which would fill the space below – by an employee of the International Publishing Corporation making his front-page debut at the unusually late age of sixty-seven.

The chief sub was grumpy: it was an ugly looking splash by the standards of those that had won them bronze plaques at black-tie dinners. 'We can do better, Hugh,' he had said but Cudlipp had spun some garbled US-guru speak about how the message was the medium.

He wanted the next day's front to be unusual: looking to the attentive reader as if the paper had been taken over by a madman – which, very probably, it had – and the staff were getting out the edition under emergency conditions.

The MD of IPC had found out somehow what was happening – the drawback of managing a newspaper was that the place was full of journalists and no rumour remained exclusive for two minutes – and telephoned in a frenzy to urge the stopping of the presses. But Cudlipp, making his voice more level than he felt, said: 'Frank, Cecil craves his day in the sun. We need to let him have it. You can't prevent weather.'

Now Cudlipp nudged aside the page-pull to uncover a pair of envelopes with legendary addresses. The destinations were professionally typed, although 'Urgent and Personal' had been added in the sender's hand. Inside, Cudlipp knew, was the Chairman's heavy deckled stationery: rough-edged paper for a man who prided himself that his tongue had that texture.

Cudlipp's many roles for Cecil King had not included messenger, so he was unsure what to do. A sense of occasion seemed to preclude sending a *Mirror* despatch rider in a snowball crash helmet, throttling into Downing and Thread-needle Streets on a mud-crusted motorbike. You didn't tuck history into a saddlebag next to the cyclist's sandwiches.

He considered playing postboy himself but alighted on the flattering excuse that he might be recognized in both these places of high state. He rang the deputy editor, who answer-barked: 'Bryan Parker.'

'Bryan, I've a problem. There are these two important letters.'

'Can they wait until tomorrow, Hugh? We've just put the Old Codgers to bed.'

'No, no. Not for the Letters page. I wouldn't usually ask an executive to be a postie but I need two crucial envelopes delivering.'

'To where?'

'SW1 and EC1. A Chancellor Jenkins and a Governor O'Brien . . .'

'Phew. From you?'

'No. I communicate with these people, if at all, through the leader columns. Our Chairman is attempting a more direct dialogue. You'll guess that he's not sending Valentines. Bryan, I'm offering you a little walk-on – make that drive-in – part in history. Are you on?'

'Sure. The first few pages of tomorrow's newspaper seem to be out of our hands.'

'I know. I'm sorry. It's the way it has to be. Bryan, don't use an office car for this. Hire something from outside.'

'Christ, Hugh. Bit Le Carré, isn't it?'

'Perhaps it is.'

In fact, Cudlipp had just read *The Looking Glass War*. And, as he replaced the receiver, his headline-writer's mind told him that the spy-book phrase would make a perfect title for the vanity-driven drama just beginning. But the Chairman had already chosen his own gloss: Enough Is Enough.

SENT TO Kent to write a piece about a new form of transport, Storey was let down by an old one. Although he had tried to display the cynicism that was a journalist's first duty, the Hovercraft had thrilled him: the sudden sensation of floating as air rushed into the cushion and the cabin trampolined into the sky, the eyes surprised by their sudden height as the vehicle headed out across the waves, like a boulder skimmed by a child on the beach.

Storey scribbled in his notebook – with a hand jolting from excitement as well as motion – that it was as if the experiences of boat, train and plane had somehow been combined.

'Britain is literally going somewhere,' the PR man shouted over the wind and the slightly frightening rattle of what the experts seemed to call the skirt. 'With the Hovercraft being launched this year, Concorde being tested and the Victoria Line under way, this country's transport system will be the model for the world by the twenty-first century!'

Having recorded in shorthand this evangelism for travel, Storey was several times tempted to scratch out the passage from his notes during a train journey from Folkestone in which the carriages mainly seemed to be moving backwards. This was apparently to avoid the path of a failed engine blocking the tracks. He fantasized about the 4.15 rising on a giant football and rolling over the obstruction.

(Even before the delay, he was irritated. As he'd left what was apparently called the Hoverport, an employee handed him a scrap of paper with an unattributed phone number. The prefix wasn't Holborn – Mayfair, he suspected – so couldn't be the news desk with a prize assignment. Storey felt gloomy confirmation rather than surprise when the voice that answered was 'Alphonse' or 'Patrick White' or whichever fancy-dress costume he was playing in today.

'Bernard! Did you enjoy your bounce across the Channel? It seems to me the giant flying lilo's not a bad idea, except for the risk of sabotage. Terrorism with a big hatpin. I mean it as a joke. But does the Sov Bloc?'

'How did you know where I was?'

'Would you ask Sinatra how he holds a note?'

'I suppose it was your mole at the *Mirror*, whoever that is.'

'Did I say we had one?'

'Yes. Now, are you ringing with old lies or new ones? I'm running out of coins.'

'Tonight, Bernard. It needs to be tonight. The ball's taking more pace on the green than we thought. The top left-hand drawer of the desk on the right.'

When the pips interrupted, Storey pretended that he had run out of money. The spook with two names yelled some final words of his own which Storey almost convinced himself were not Secret Ray and Princess Galina.

On the day of their meeting in the Chiswick pub at the rehearsal for that terrible television comedy, Storey had been unable to understand why MI5 had chosen him. Now that two bets he'd made in an unknown betting shop in Folkestone had been shouted down the telephone from London, he understood that his recruitment was a transaction in a perfect currency of untruths: in the world of White/Alphonse, secret men blackmailed men with secrets into finding out the secrets of other men. The only mystery was why the spy – the 'asset' – supposedly already on the payroll of the *Mirror* could not accomplish the burglary at King Cecil's office himself.

Storey was reluctantly coming to the conclusion that the espionage plant was Cudlipp, someone too close to the target and with too much to lose if discovered. The consequences of this explanation were both depressing: the greatest popular journalist of his day was a print-world Philby and Storey had been chosen for the mission because it wouldn't matter if he was sacked. Expendability was as important as his betting in making him an asset.)

His gloom made it even harder to join a party which was well advanced by the time he reached the pub at 10 Fetter Lane that the *Mirror* staff called 'Winnie's' after the landlady.

When Storey had joined the paper six years before, the editorial floor had resembled a speakeasy. The most coherent words were written – and the most sensible spoken – before lunch. The paper surfed towards the streets on a wave of white wine from the executive fridges of Cudlipp and others until Chairman King – who the gossips had down as a repentant piss-head – declared the office dry. The veteran revellers cheated for a while with hip flasks and mugs of coffee smelling more of Dublin than Brazil but gradually the drinking had become an inebriation race squeezed between the early and late editions.

Storey entered this frenzy of false male friendship sober and late. Drink brought some men briefly together but pushed them further away from those who hadn't drunk enough. Newspaper anecdotes Storey knew so well he could have set them to music were being repeated to trainees and casuals who might not know the punchline: 'When we were at Geraldine House, there was a reporter called Romilly, nephew of Churchill's. He was so ashamed of working for a tabloid that he used to tell people he worked for the "newspaper of the times", which is what the adverts called the *Mirror*. He hoped people would think he'd said the fucking *Times*.'

Pint glasses and pewter mugs banged down on the bar, sliding in the slops of previous performances of this ritual. Those hacks here who had least irritated the printers might receive a version of this ceremony: 'banged out' with tools on the metal trays of type on the day they retired. Storey promised himself he would have left to write his novels years before he qualified for that privilege.

Snigger from the backbench, nicknamed for his cartoon laugh, spotted Storey as he pushed through the edge of the scrum to buy a pint.

'Multi, how was the big blow-up boat?'

'It's a good yarn. Nice pix. The smudger was wetting himself.'

Pubic from sport, fingering his stringy goatee, shouted: 'You did the Hover thing, Multi? Must be like fucking a rubber doll all the way to Calais.'

The sexy redhead from features – the new wank-fantasy for all the men in the office – twisted her mouth dismissively and told Pubic: 'Calais? I doubt if you'd last to the end of Folkestone Pier.'

Glasses banged the bar again. 'The first time I had sex, it was over in thirty seconds,' a revise sub from news was hollering. 'But I've got better now.' A laborious pause, copied from *Rowan and Martin's Laugh-In*. 'I'm much quicker.' More beer was lost in admiration of this gag.

'You don't want to boast, sweetie.' The voice – a throaty

baritone – came from the middle of the ruck. 'More and more of the letters I get are about PE.'

'Physical education?' queried Dogbreath the copy-taker.

'I tell you, it's no laughing matter,' the phlegmy tones continued. 'It used to be men who wrote to me about premature ejaculation. Now it's women. I tell you. You men need to get better in bed or your women will get men who are.'

This prophecy of cuckoldry silenced the men sufficiently to allow the speaker, though one of only two women present, to take the floor.

'Now, I've a bone to pick with you chaps.'

'You can pick my bone any time you want, Marje.'

'Slim pickings, I'd expect.'

Storey pushed closer to listen. While evenings at Winnie's were dominated by people who were legends only in their own heads, Marje Proops was a true Fleet Street diva.

She passed her white cigarette-holder – as familiar a prop as Wilson's pipe – to Pubic, who reverentially held it for her. Mrs Proops had freed her hands to fumble in her bag for something which now turned out to be a letter. Straightening the paper with one hand – an action rattling the bangles on her wrist – she retrieved the cigarette-holder and warmed up her vocal cords with a draw. Her smoking apparatus was only partly for show – it was also supposed to have some filtering effect – but its limited benefit was obvious as she began to speak in a voice which would have placed her at the darker end of a male voice choir. 'This letter arrived this week and was marked up for setting by my trusting deputy until my old nose smelled mischief.'

Despite her massive lenses – so large and square that they seemed designed for protection from heavy welding rather than the clarification of print – Mrs Proops still moved the sheet of paper closer to her face before she read.

' "Dear Marje, I have so many problems that I don't know where to start. My mother hated me and my uncle went nuts. He ended up shooting imaginary Hun from the roof of his house." ' Some of the older men were laughing, recognizing the reference. ' "My mum's problem was that she never forgave me for living. Our home was in Ireland and we were sent back to school in England on boats. Because it was 1918, she always booked on separate ferries. As I had a picky housemaster, who hated boys coming back late, I swapped tickets with my younger brother, Bobby. His boat was torpedoed by the Germans. I have never quite recovered from the feeling that it might have been me; my mother never got over the feeling that it should have been. More recently, I have begun to worry that I may be going mad like my uncle . . ." '

Mrs Proops managed to fold and place the letter in a pocket while also finishing her cigarette.

'Luckily, even before I got to the sign-off "Worried of Hampton Court", I knew enough of our distinguished Chairman's biography to clock what was going on and avoid leaving myself dependent on Proopsie's pension. Now, which of you buggers was it?'

Hal E. Tosis from features raised his hand, to backslaps and beer-banging.

'A more subtle joke, I grant you,' the agony aunt admitted, 'than last week's "HC" from Dinas Powys who was worried he's caught a social disease from a sheep.'

This prompted Storey – who only endured these boozy evenings in the hope of putting down some marker for a promotion with a sozzled boss – to ask: 'Isn't Cudlipp coming over tonight?'

'Hardly,' Mrs Proops growled. 'They're laying down sandbags on the ninth floor in case Wilson sends round the army.'

'What's happened?' Storey asked.

'Christ, Bernie,' laughed Dogbreath. 'Good job you're not a reporter.'

A carbon of an article was passed down the bar. Surprised by the byline – Cecil H. King – Storey read it in the way that journalists learned, speeding over the sense, slowing when he detected a key sentence. Reporters were taught to arrange their information in literally descending order of importance because, on the stone, over-matter was trimmed from the bottom up.

King – spared both journalistic training and any fear that his story might be shortened – had ignored these rules. Starting drably – 'The results of the local elections are fully confirming the verdicts of the opinion polls and of the Dudley by-election' – the author kept his energy for the end:

> We are now threatened with the greatest financial crisis in our history. It is not to be removed by lies about our reserves, but only by a fresh start under a fresh leader.
>
> It is up to the Parliamentary Labour Party to give us that leader – and soon.

Storey thought of what 'White' had said on the telephone to Folkestone: the ball's taking more pace on the green than we thought.

'This is – what? – a signed leader-page piece?'

'No, front. Turned to three. Big mug-shot of King Cecil where Lee usually has a girl in a bikini.'

Their Chairman's attempted overthrow of the PM already seemed old news to most of the group. The boys from sport had returned to their favoured subject of which of the female staff they'd like on the end of their cocks.

'Christ, have you been down to the fashion department? The smell of cunt in that room. It's like a fifth-former's finger after a dance. I blame the miniskirt.'

'You think dicks smell of roses?' asked the redhead.
Though Storey had read about feminism, he had not appre-
ciated that it might involve women matching men drink for
drink, filth for filth.

'Another one, Multi?' Storey was asked.

'No, no, I promised to be home.'

'So did I,' added the agony aunt, buttoning up her coat.
'Proopsie's not entirely safe with a hot-plate.'

As they left together, Mrs Proops touched his arm:
'Bernard, isn't it? Are you sure you're OK? You suddenly
went very pale and worried in there.'

Storey laughed. 'I suppose it's the perfect opportunity to
confess my deepest worries. Like Henry Ford offering to look
under your bonnet. But, no, I'm just bushed, keen to get
home.'

'I know the feeling. I used to be amazed that my post-bag
contained such astonishing numbers of unhappy women. But
an evening in there and I see why.'

At the top of Fetter Lane, Storey was about to turn
towards the *Mirror* building when he remembered that he
had told Britain's most famous scourge of domestic deceit
that he was pining for his wife.

'I think Cecil King can stand me a cab tonight,' said
Mrs Proops, peering towards Smithfield in search of a For
Hire light. Storey thought that taxis must loom up like
buses through those specs. He was suddenly worried that
she might offer to drop him somewhere so he quickly said:
'It's later than I thought. I'd better ring Moira before I get
the tube.'

Mrs Proops's unexpectedly broad smile was presumably
in recognition of a level of husbandly devotion which rarely
cropped up in her correspondence. Feeling guilty about being
the recipient of this false tribute, he then became concerned

for the famous columnist's eyesight when, dialling home from the phone kiosk on the corner of Holborn Circus, he was sure that he saw her ignore two cabs with lighted signs. He was checking whether she took the next when he was distracted by Moira's answering whoop of good news when the coin went in.

'Bernie, you'll never guess what's happened?'

Pregnant, he feared, remembering the fuck on the rug without a johnnie.

'What? That was going to be the first thing I said to you.'

'Oh? What's yours?'

'You first.'

'The bank rang!'

'Christ!'

'No, real smiley this time. All "Mrs Storey", like they were my cleaner, not the other way round. The manager thanks you for the "ample provision of new funds" to your account. So King Cecil's finally shelled out on those expenses, has he?'

'Yes,' Storey lied, then – really earning his first spy's wages – doubled the falsehood: 'What I was going to say is, I've got to stay late. Big political story.' He knew that the subject bored her so she would not ask what. 'They're remaking the whole front page. Cudlipp wants the entire desk on hand.'

'Poor love. You can wake me up when you get in.'

That code between them was the dirtiest the convent-girl got. But, for the first time in his adult life, Storey had no interest in the prospect of sex. He had walked into the telephone kiosk as a *Daily Mirror* reporter but left as James Bond.

Walking towards IPC House, he was shocked to see Mrs Proops still leaning hopefully into the street and so stopped and ran down the steps to the Underground like the Husband of the Year.

PEOPLE thought of agents as a funny little club but all of us were spies and liars in our way. Standing in the shadows of Shoe Lane, Wright would never have expected such high entertainment as the game of charades between Storey of the *Mirror* and Dear Marje.

They should get a Christmas special this year instead of Morecambe and Wise. The funniest bit was when his asset came out of the telephone booth and found Queen Tampon still hanging around, gazing into the dusk but not daring to put her bloody arm in the air, just in case Hymie Driver spotted her and stopped.

As soon as Storey ducked down into the Underground tunnel, Dear Marje turned and, in heels a woman of that era really shouldn't have been wearing, teetered across the street into the *Mirror* building. Proopsie would have a long wait for his tea tonight.

Storey left a gap of two minutes – not quite spy-school rules but it would do – before reappearing at street level and visibly congratulating himself that the sage of the snatch had got her cab.

Watching Storey fumbling for his staff pass as he returned to work, Wright heard an imaginary whistle blowing for the beginning of the game. In his mind, he saw a rugger ball punted high into the air and two teams running towards a catch. Come on, England.

THERE WAS still one more side of *Iolanthe* to play and he thought it would have to wait until Saturday. But, as he was putting on his raincoat and looking for the pipe, Henry James came in to say that the car door was jammed again.

Wilson had always insisted on British vehicles in the ministerial fleet – from the fine motive of patriotism and the impure hope of votes in Midlands constituencies – but he now sometimes feared that the policy was becoming impractical.

Bill was always purring about the advantages of the Daimler Limousine for government business, which was all perfectly true once you successfully got into it. At the moment, this process was complicated by a rear left-side door which seemed to have been fitted on a Friday afternoon by a workforce who had been told there was money under the bar in the pub.

Wilson had hung his Gannex back on the peg and was holding the needle above Act II – '*When in that House, MPs divide / If they've a brain and cerebellum, too / They've got to leave that brain outside*' – when Marcia came in, holding three typed sheets. His first assumption was that it must be his speech for Bristol, but if so, then the look on her face suggested that he would be announcing the end of the world.

'Gerald got this from one of our remaining friends at the *Mirror*. It's tomorrow's page one.'

There were three distinct shocks – like the escalating stages of his heart spasms – as he read first the headline, then the byline and finally the sentence:

Mr Wilson and his Government have lost all credibility: all authority.

'Enough damn well is enough,' Wilson said. 'Get me Jenkins on the telephone.'

Marcia, after dialling the Chancellor and asking for him in the sharp voice he always enjoyed when she applied it to others, reported: 'Apparently he's at dinner.'

'Using a long spoon, presumably.'

The structure of the plot came to him abruptly in the way that an algebraic equation sometimes solved itself. 'That's it.

He'll be having a meal with that bugger King. Tell the Garden Girls to trace King, wherever he is.'

When Marcia had instructed the switchboard, he asked her: 'Should I cancel Bristol?'

'No. Business as usual. Otherwise, they'd say Northcliffe's nephew kept you in London.'

'I don't know, Marcia. Should I be turning my back on them?'

'Staying looks weak, going looks strong. This is no time to fucking wobble, Harold.'

Feeling Marcia's hands on his shoulders, he feared that she might actually shake him. He knew that he should rebuke her for speaking in this way but there was a part of him that needed it.

The extension rang, and though Marcia reached for it he lifted the receiver himself, saying firmly, 'Prime Minister,' as if the words might be a curse against his enemies.

'Mr King's not at the paper, sir. The lady who answered at home says he's already in bed.'

Wilson looked at his watch. Dogs and toddlers were still up.

'It's me they must think is asleep if they expect me to believe that.'

As they tried to leave Downing Street – Bill had finally dominated the unruly door-lock – their way towards White-hall was blocked by another black Daimler turning in. He was at first pleased by this chance to challenge the Chancellor so early but then saw that it was not a ministerial vehicle but the Daimler Double-Six, most often seen in the fleets of funeral directors.

'Why's someone sent a hearse to Number 11?' asked Marcia.

'It must have arrived early. A sudden burst of efficiency in the British service industries just when you don't want it.'

His joke, though, hid a pulse-quickening unease about not understanding what he was seeing. They watched as the undertaker's car parked and a middle-aged man, dressed not in pall-bearer's black but a camel-hair coat, got out of the driver's seat and walked unchallenged past the Number 11 bobby to knock on the Chancellor's door. A suit and face of civil service grey appeared briefly and, after nodding at a comment from the off-duty mortician, took possession of a letter. The messenger then reversed his journey from doorstep to car to street, finally allowing Bill to head for Bristol.

'It seems queer to me that people can just drive in here,' Marcia complained. 'Especially since the assassinations in the States.'

'In Britain, we like the romance of it. Approachability.' He was thinking of an eight-year-old child riding up to the Prime Minister's door in a sidecar and believing ever after that it was his duty to return. 'And the fact of the matter is, Marcia, that most leaders aren't shot by people they don't know. They're stabbed by people they do.'

HIS MOTHER was trying to kill him, her hands round his neck. When he woke, he found his own fingers pressing at his jowls, a defensive reflex in those last moments of sleep when a dream feels real.

Other people would tell King of the exam dream or the naked dream which recurrently interrupted their nights but his unconscious wasn't troubled by difficult studies or mis-placed pants, saving its nocturnal churning for the possibility of being strangled by a mama long departed.

Although he had been in bed before nine – welcoming but also fearing the increasing ease with which he slept – he found it harder than usual that night to put himself under again after the nightmare of Lady Geraldine as a living killer. The speeding of his mind was caused by thoughts of other motion: the rolling of the presses in the Holborn basement, the racing of the trains carrying the papers north.

Newsprint faded and was pissed on by cats but the ink of history books was thicker. Imagining these dates in 1968 being chanted one day by children in a well-run Britain, King turned onto the side where he had less feeling of his heartbeat, closed his eyes and tried to find a place in his dreams where his mother could not reach him.

ON A murder story he had covered in his provincial days, a detective had said that there were two kinds of alibi that raised suspicion. False ones, obviously, but also plausible stories which the suspect shouted about too loudly. Why, for example, might someone tell their neighbours in enormous detail what they had watched on TV and eaten for tea the previous evening?

Finding this advice impossible to follow on his first night as a criminal, Storey made a great show of putting on his coat and informing Gorbals as he passed the backbench that he was going home.

'You're working late tonight, Bernie,' the night editor said.

'Yeah. I wanted to type up my notes from the Hovercraft thing. I'm fireman tomorrow and there's something about bad news and Fridays.'

'I don't think I'd take my kids on the Hover, Bernie. As far as I can see, it's the same technology as the French letter. And that's why I've got kids in the first place.'

'They've always worked for me. Anyway, I'm off home. See you tomorrow.'

Storey imagined the spike-monkey later telling the police: 'He seemed ever so keen to tell me where he was going.'

Briefly delayed at the lifts by a sub heading for the bog – 'All right, Multi? Next time you write us something, don't swallow the dictionary first' – he checked over his shoulder like someone in *Virgin of the Secret Service* before pressing the up arrow rather than the down.

It was quarter past ten. There was no risk of meeting King – famous for going home long before the first edition – and the cleaners started on the office, working from top to bottom, at eleven. After an incident in which a couple of Mrs Mops had disturbed Lardy and Clap fucking on a fashion-department desk, Cudlipp had sent a memo: staff who absolutely couldn't keep their hands off each other were advised to be in and out by 23:00 hours.

Stopping at the ninth floor, Storey worried about the loud-ness of the lift bell. The building felt empty except for the subterranean presence suggested by the rumble of the presses in the basement. (When they had first moved to this HQ, Storey had assumed that the tremor was the Central Line tube until he learned that it was the roar of stories being born.)

Passing the legal department, he heard the loud, happy voice of a woman who he'd have told a court was Mrs Proops if he hadn't known that she took a taxi home long ago.

Storey stopped and put a thumb to his wrist. He would have needed an official Mexico Olympics stopwatch to record his heart-rate. Even dictating copy close to deadline with no notes, he had never felt as panicked as this.

He turned a corner and was in King's court, the door to the penthouse ajar behind the desks for the two secretaries. Storey realized that he had never considered the possibility of the room being locked but that was the risk MI5 took in trying to turn newshounds into gumshoes.

Even years of gossip in Winnie's about the splendour of King Cecil's palace didn't stop him feeling shock. It was more like an embassy than an office, with bowls and other antiques displayed on a towering dresser.

The carpet was so lavish that it felt like walking on art: respect as well as the fear of being overheard – the only noise was the bubbling of water in the large aquarium – made him tread softly as he approached the fabled octagonal desk: two angled antique tables touching at one corner to create an eight-sided space, with a v-shape between them for King to sit. This object had also been much discussed in the pub but again hearsay had been no preparation for the vast mahogany altar.

The top left-hand drawer of the desk on the right. Above his target, he found a stack of papers. With the natural self-absorption of the human species, a condition even worse in journalists, he imagined reading 'Storey must be promoted' or 'Storey must be fired'. But the Chairman would never know of this sparrow's fall, unless the toppling happened to take place in King's own office. As a precaution against this outcome, Storey left the documents untouched, distracted by a leather-bound appointments diary beside the blotter. He flicked it open to the week that might include the date of his final payment from the *Mirror* before he went to jail.

The Chancellor had been for evening drinks earlier in the week and there had been board meetings, one of them delayed by a morning appointment in Harley Street. But what most interested Storey was a less familiar London address in the entry for the following day: 2 Kinnerton Street, 4.30 p.m. Beside it, in black ink, was a capital letter M and then, in blue, presumably a later addition, the word *Zuckerman*.

As Storey copied these details into his notebook, he felt like the hero in a thriller: a parallel regrettably emphasized when he heard shoe-clop and conversation in the corridor. Perhaps the whole 'Alphonse' business had been a set up, a joke like the 'Dear Marje' letter supposedly from King. They'd now tipped off security and his hopes of being political editor were over. Except that surely no clown from features could know the name of every horse that ate his pay cheque.

Desperately, his only coaching for such a moment coming from the movies, he flattened himself against the wall in a place invisible from the door: the far side of a massive oak dresser. He was glad that some espionage sixth sense had made him leave the room in shadow, relying on the light from the flickery filaments in the corridor.

The voices of a man and a woman drifted in, talking in the way of people who have been drinking; enthusiastic yet also hesitant, like actors who had just learned a script.

'Kiss this.'

'I might if you lick this.'

'Ugh, that's disgusting.'

He recognized the voices: Gorbals and the redhead from features.

'Sauce for the goose and so on. This is feminism, sweetie.'

'You're on the Pill?'

'I told you. This is feminism. Christ, you're about to come on his Persian rug. Give me that.'

Watching other people fucking was a common fantasy and Storey had not been spared it. But, as he listened to the couple's competitive breathlessness and watched their shadows on the wall become one larger, shaking shape, the only tingle in his prick was a need to pee from fear.

A loud grunt of release was followed by a clearly female sigh.

'Were you all right there, lassie?'

'I was just thinking that you remind me of a nuclear missile.'

'Really? Why? Because I'm so big?'

'No. Because you're a Minuteman.'

'Fuck you, lassie.'

'Oh, if only you had.'

Storey heard slidings and slippings: presumably the replacement of knickers, trousers and shoes. One heavy pair of retreating feet was followed by a softer step. He waited until the trembling in his legs lessened enough to leave the hiding place.

The papers had been scattered across the blotter and there was a patch of darkened wood in front; the glistening archipelago of recent sex. Storey wiped it with his handkerchief; not from respect for his employer but because, if a flathead came in now, he would be taken for a disgruntled hack who had broken in to wank on the Chairman's antiques.

If this was a spy movie, then it sadly lacked the scene in which the hero is given the ballpoint penknife or wristwatch jemmy. He had given no thought to opening the desk. The proprietor's letter opener lay alongside the blotter with restaurant neatness and Storey seized it with relief before also grasping that the necessary dent in the expensive timber would lead to his immediate identification from fingerprints. He had approached the task less like a burglar than a pig rolling in mud.

He protected his fingers with a handkerchief far too late. The jismed linen felt manky but, while the cops could separate us by the ends of our fingers, they couldn't trace you from your spunk. Storey pulled at the drawer to test the level of security he must seek to beat. The shock of its being open was so great that he prat-fell backwards like a cartoon character hit by a door, squeezing a testicle against the arm of King Cecil's padded chair.

In the drawer was one manila folder, which he opened to reveal a sheet of paper, amateurishly typed with XX-ed corrections:

THE EMERGENCY GOVERNMENT
First administration – 1968
Prime Minister / First Treasury Lord – M?
Chancellor of the Exchequer – Alfred Weinstock?
Deputy PM / Lord President – Cecil. H. King
Dept of Economic Affairs – Alf Robens?

Lower portfolios had been allocated to half-recognizable names that Storey connected with ATV, EMI, ICI and other establishment acronyms.

Years before, Cudlipp had crossed the word 'surreal' out of Storey's copy as 'college stuff' but there was no other description for this document except those inevitable lines of dialogue in a thriller – 'You're mad, completely mad' – directed, in this instance, silently to the absent occupant of the baddie's lavish HQ.

On the wall, there were two portraits of Northcliffe: a solemn oil picture and a newspaper cartoon. Looking from one to the other, Storey reflected that this had been the press baron's journey: from grandeur to caricature. Now the nephew was following those footsteps.

And who was M, who would become PM? Storey's first thought was Marje Proops, who would at least run a benevolent tyranny with cigarettes sold at historically low prices. But there was no way King would serve under a woman.

Then the obvious candidate – one of British history's leading representatives of the letter M – came into Storey's head. Oh, Jesus, this was serious.

SINCE HIS love of wine and dining had become what the Left of the party liked to term an 'issue', he had endured a forced acclimatization to the lesser Italian restaurants of Westminster. No political editors would stoop to eat in places such as these. The veal had been agreeable enough but the avocado-pear hors d'oeuvre had been of a consistency suggesting the recent cultivation of a new variation called avocado apple.

A book usually removed the sadness of eating alone. But, finding his eye returning for the fourth time to the same Gladstone sentence, he was forced to accept that he was distracted by more proximate political battles. After the loss of the previous night to the Finance committee, a return journey to Birmingham with its stressful interruptus at Didcot and now a bottle of a 'house' wine which was more soporific than a superior vintage, the red boxes awaiting him at the residence seemed even less than usually inviting.

He decided to leave them until morning but, back at Number 11, a residual ministerial diligence caused him at least to check there was no Washington telegram announcing that the pound was worthless and the President owned Britain.

Such a crisis had not transpired but an unopened envelope lay on top of the boxes: a paper-clipped civil-service memorandum revealed it to be from Cecil Harmsworth King. Jenkins began to read it three times but, finding the sense as clotted as the Gladstone autobiography had been, he opted to sleep off his tiredness and trust to fresh morning attention.

THE holy sisters always said that sex, if they mentioned it at all, was a gift from God, although what they really meant was that it was a sort of book-token you used to give a present back to Him: a child.

But the world had taught her that sex was a gift you gave to a man. They even liked to unwrap you. In the war, it had been a going-away present. There had been stupid girls at school who handed it out just as a thank-you for being looked at. Letting Bernie do it had been her reward to him for wanting to marry her and, these days, for silly things like mucking out that guttering or – tonight – for sorting things out at the bank.

As soon as he got into bed, Moira pressed herself against him so that he could feel her readiness. He was always going on about how wet everything was. Sometimes she thought he should have been a blessed weatherman. But tonight was different. It wasn't exactly that he pushed away but he'd never felt like that against her ever, soft as a mouse. She remembered her mother saying once that Auntie Kathleen should have known her husband had a fancy woman because he'd stopped being demanding.

Soon, though, she wasn't worrying about that because he was talking in a way she'd never heard before, not even when he came home with a couple of pints on his breath, saying that they'd given him the 'splash' next day.

'The really ridiculous thing is that I actually didn't write a story about the Home Guard this week – well, in fact, a comedy about it – because I couldn't take it seriously. But now I realize I am the fucking Home Guard: a part-time soldier with a pitchfork trying to save the country from invasion.'

'What are you on about?'

'Cecil King is planning a coup d'état against Wilson. There's going to be a fucking blackshirt government. Someone called Zuckerman is helping them.'

'Bernie,' Moira asked. 'Have you been drinking?'

18

Machine-Guns on Street Corners

WHATEVER happened in the next few days his broadcast appearances would increase, and so he doubled his rotations of the Downing Street flower-beds: television somehow contrived to reduce the size of the speaker's mind while expanding the waistline. At least Jenkins was happily spared the fulminating face at the study window next door. Wilson was apparently in Bristol, once again being photographed in a hard hat to establish himself as a technocrat.

On the second circuit, Jenkins was able to place his feet in the imprints left by his shoes on the first turn. The dew had been especially heavy and so the best explanation was that his inner tension had encouraged a stamping tread.

Earlier, returning to the bedroom after shaving, Jenkins had found the newspapers laid out on the bed, as was normal, although he knew once he saw it that the *Daily Mirror* front page was anything but regular.

The photograph, the headline and the reference to 'lies about our reserves' rapidly revealed the folly of neglecting Cecil King's letter the previous evening. Reading it now with a steadier eye, although with a hand that suddenly rejected equilibrium, he understood the import that exhaustion had kept from him the night before:

> Dear Chancellor,
>   As I am becoming more involved in political controversy, I think it will be more convenient for the Bank of England if I resign from the Court.

This is, therefore, to tender my resignation, effective forthwith.

Yours sincerely,

Cecil. H. King

After setbacks, it was Jenkins's habit to imagine himself being taken through his actions by a prosecuting QC. 'The phrase "political controversy" did not alert you in any way, Mr Jenkins?' / 'I didn't fully comprehend it until I saw the next day's newspapers. I imagined a more, ah, languid timescale.' / 'And yet, Chancellor, he used the word "forthwith". Did that not suggest a certain urgency?' / 'It seemed to me a Victorian formality in correspondence. Like "sincerely" or "faithfully". People who end letters with those phrases are not necessarily genuine or steadfast. All I can say is that I *was* somewhat somnolent.' / 'Had you been drinking, Chancellor?' / 'I had not gone beyond my usual tolerance in these matters . . .'

In assuming that his future would depend on the moment he chose to seek power, the mistake had been to think that the timing was entirely his. Now someone else had shaped the occasion and he was doubly disadvantaged. Not only would Wilson assume his Chancellor's collusion in a move Jenkins in fact considered ridiculous, but the Prime Minister's position in the party was likely to be strengthened through attempted assassination by a press baron.

This internal cross-examination was interrupted by a yell from a secretary in the house: 'Chancellor, I think you'll want to take this call.'

He assumed it would be Wilson panicking in Bristol – or O'Brien at the Bank, fretting over the effect of King's article on the markets when they opened – but it was Barbara Castle, although he didn't initially recognize the speaker.

'It's this bloody tooth, Roy. I'm sure it's an abscess but we can't see a gap in the diary until next Monday. I'm getting by on whisky. The way things are, I'm not letting some other bugger go to the House for me.'

Barbara was not a political enemy, but nor did Jenkins delude himself that she was calling as a friend. Wilson alternated two styles of paranoia. When mildly suspicious, he telephoned you himself; in the severe form, he contacted an ally and ordered them to call you.

'Roy, have you seen the *Mirror*?'

'Yes, this morning.'

'You had no wind of it before?'

'I've always thought it customary to read newspapers on the day of publication.'

'Just Harold says you were slippery on the telephone yesterday.'

'I can assure you – and him – that whatever, ah, lubriciousness he perceived was not based on a knowledge of the future contents of the *Daily Mirror*.'

'Roy, he wants an immediate statement from you: supporting him and distancing yourself from King.'

'My dear Barbara, I rather feel that such pronouncements have a habit of appearing to answer a question that hasn't been asked and therefore giving the query some credibility.'

'Harold said you might come back at me with something about flying buttresses. He said his analogy would be that I can hope my tooth abscess will go away but we all know it will eventually have to be drained.'

For weeks, the torment of his morning walks had been whether and when to move against Wilson; now the Prime Minister had marched against him. 'You can tell him I shall start drafting a public letter to my constituency party. The municipal results a stumble, Cecil King an arrogant chisel aimed at a quite immovable rock and so on. Like St Paul to the Philippians.'

Except, Jenkins thought, that there had never been any risk of the Philippians writing back to disagree.

IT TOOK both hands to carry *Who's Who* from the shelf, the 3,415 pages making it more like a concertina than a book. Twenty minutes passed before a librarian arrived for work; Storey realized he was spending too much time in this building out of hours.

Laying on a reader's desk the vast dance-card of those who moved to the Establishment's tune, he flicked – or, more correctly, paddled – to KING. He wasn't sure what he was looking for: perhaps a home phone number (for a hoax call to cancel the 4.30 p.m. meeting with the mysterious 'Zuckerman') or simply a clue to the personal facts that the would-be revolutionary considered characteristic.

Alphabetical precedence had left the press baron wedged inappropriately between two diplomats: a namesake Cecil King, Ambassador to the Lebanon, and Charles King, who had served in Hong Kong, Vienna, Berne and Zurich.

Was there anything to be found in the boastful codes of KING, Cecil Harmsworth's entry: 'b 20 Feb, 1901'? So he was already past the age at which his paper's readers would be forced to tend their gardens. (Storey remembered indignation one night in Winnie's that King had restructured the entire company pension scheme to avoid retiring himself.)

A first marriage to Agnes Margaret Cooke, a canon's daughter, had spawned 'three s, one d', before her replacement by Dame Ruth Railton, a 'qv' beside her name marking them among the rare couples who both featured independently in these columns.

Another line specified '2nd class honours in history at Christ Church, Oxford'. From neighbouring entries, it seemed unusual to shout about anything except a first, so

King could be taken as either humbly honest or a tactical braggart, emphasizing how much more he had achieved than the contemporaries who had graduated higher.

An address was given – The Pavilion, Hampton Court – but with no T and number beside it. So all he knew about England's Fleet Street Cromwell was that he was an old man fearing superannuation who had prided himself on overcoming earlier failures. This was the basis of a newspaper profile rather than a Resistance movement.

When Storey turned to the Z section, the colossal volume became so unbalanced that the tiny slice of pages in his right hand resembled an overhang from the cliff of the other entries. This 26th division of those who ran the country was small and, filed between the 18th Baron Zouche of Norfolk and Adolph Zukor, Chairman of Paramount, contained a single ZUCKERMAN.

Sir Solly, b Cape Town, 1904. Chief Scientific adviser to HMG. Chairman of Central Advisory Committee on Scientific Policy. Publications: *The Social Life of Monkeys and Apes*; *Functional Affinities of Men, Monkeys, Apes* (editor); *The Ovary* (volumes 1 and 2). Address: The Medical School, Hospital Centre, Birmingham 15.

Storey regularly used *Who's Who* as the first call for an obituary or feature, and even through the telegrammatic house style it was usually possible to see the clear route of a life: type of person, kind of work. But this summary of King's presumed co-collaborator was confusing. He seemed to be a zoologist who also specialized in gynaecology. Storey wondered if children would one day burn a 'Solly' on May bonfires in celebration of democracy's defence.

As the librarians began to arrive, chuckling and grouching about the *Enough Is Enough* edition now needing to be cut and cross-reffed for their archives, Storey picked up the library telephone and, staying at the far end of the alphabet, called Waugh in Somerset.

'Bron, does Oswald Mosley have a house in London?'

'My dear Pierre, I didn't realize you were what we must now apparently learn to call ESN. After failing to make the East End his own little Berlin, they exiled themselves to France: the near-miss Hitler and the Mitford sister, as Noel Coward might have put it.'

'I know: it's the Mitford connection I'm thinking of. You don't happen to know if they have a London place at 2 Kinnerton Street?'

There was the wing-flap of Bron searching through his celebrated contacts book. 'I've no idea. I'm sorry, Hector, it's like looking for a pubic hair in the stuffing of a sofa. Anyway, what's the yarn? Is this King and Mosley again?'

It was so fucking unfair. Storey was the one who'd become a spy and yet everyone else knew more than him about everything.

'King and Mosley. There's a connection?'

'Cudlipp used to mutter that King was always trying to get him to run the old fascist's books. A flawed figure but perhaps with vital things to contribute: bore, bore, bore. I assumed your call was because the *Mirror* had bought serial in *Black Was The Shirt My Father Wore* and they had you writing the standfirst.'

'No. Just a tip-off. Probably just gossip . . .'

'There's nothing wrong with gossip, Dickie. It's often truer than the news.'

Feeling hopeless – his comparison with the Home Guard becoming ever less of a joke to him – Storey went to Cudlipp's office. The secretary outside was reddened with excitement.

He guessed it had been a morning of famous voices in her ear, celebrated names in the appointments book.

'Look, I know I'm small fry . . .'

'I'm afraid you probably are.'

'But something's come up. What he saw me about the other . . .'

'We'd be lucky to squeeze in the Queen. He's got meetings all day, mainly boards.'

'Just five minutes. Maybe around four thirty . . .'

'Well, it *definitely* won't be then. He's going with Mr King to an appointment outside the building.'

Cudlipp's assistant would have attributed Storey's drained, staring face to rejection from the diary but, as he walked away, he was contemplating the size of the conspiracy. If Cudlipp – who, he feared, was MI5's man inside the *Mirror* – was in on King's plot, then it was impossible to see why Alphonse/White needed Storey at all.

Unless he was the Lee Harvey Oswald, the patsy.

THE DAIMLER'S door had jammed again as they arrived at the foundry in Bristol. There had been a terrible minute when Wilson feared that the Saturday front pages would show him caged in his car, unable to fulfil the speaking engagement. He had already lit the pipe for the cameras and the car was fugging up like a Turkish bath.

Marcia, however, had somehow managed the catch and they had told the welcoming committee the delay in opening the door was a security precaution. With the riot police on the streets of Paris that very day against the students, you couldn't be too careful. Even so, it was all he could do not to include in his speech about the triumphs of British industry a sarcastic bracket excluding the Jaguar car company.

For the dedication of the zinc smelter, they insisted that he wore a hard helmet. They never sat right with a suit – making you look less like a worker rather than more like one – and he feared the headlines in the *Mirror* and the rest about Wilson only coming out with his tin hat on. This particular design had a sort of hairnet as well, which was worse.

Both before and after his prepared remarks at the smelter, Wilson asked Marcia if the Chancellor had issued his statement of support, but the answer was negative each time.

'Number 11 say he can't do anything until after the "trial", whatever that is.'

'God, is that today, Marcia? The Trial of the Pyx. There've been better days for it.'

(He was glad he was not Caesar, for no soothsayer could have seen good in this event coinciding with his crisis. In 1279 – he was relieved at this evidence of long-remembered facts still intact – the King had decreed that every moneyer in England must place in a locked box one silver penny from every 240 made. This was then tested by the royal authorities to check that the currency had not been debased.

Even now, the Trial of the Pyx ('pyxis' was Latin for box) still took place annually. A random handful of change was examined by a jury of liverymen from the City of London, who must pronounce whether the currency was sound. The event was now supposedly ceremonial, although there must be a risk this year that they would decide sterling should be hung.)

'Get me Jenkins now, Marcia,' he said. They raised a secure line from the office of the foundry boss. Jenkins was about to leave the Treasury and began in that way of his that seemed to relish simultaneously his cleverness and your stupidity: 'Ah, Prime Minister, you find me for the first time in the Chancellor's robes of office. The Trial of the—'

'Possibly wearing them for the last time as well, Roy. Have you issued your statement of support?'

'I've started on a draft to my constituency chairman . . .'

'That's loyalty by the long route, Roy. I want it as the crow flies.'

Marcia smiled at this directness and he felt his insecurities reduce; the way that a diet suddenly showed its success in loosened clothes.

'A statement now, Roy, could catch the lunchtime bulletins. The pound's going through the ground . . .'

'And an unscheduled encomium from the Chancellor to the First Lord of the Treasury might merely deepen the tunnel. You attach too much importance to a letter from me because you exaggerate the significance of the article by King. I suggest you view him as a Savonarola denouncing the sins of the improvident Florentines. In both cases, the public will turn on the preacher rather than the subject of his disgust . . .'

'I don't think we speak the same language, Roy.'

'Well, with respect, Prime Minister, let me try to bring our vocabularies closer. You follow Association Football . . . ?'

Hesford, Craig, Mountford, Willingham, Young, Boot . . . 'I think you know I do.'

'A Welsh father raised me in the other code. But I've gleaned enough from my son to know that a chairman's statement of support for the management is frequently a prelude to the, ah, heave-ho . . .'

Boot, Hulme, Isaac, MacFadyen, Barclay, Beasley. 'Except, Roy, that when it comes to the Treasury XI, I'm the chairman and you're the manager. King sent you a letter last night?'

'Yes. And clearly now I regret not passing on its contents.'

'Why didn't you?'

'Inattention, though not necessarily an excuse, is the reason. The night before I had scarcely slept . . .'

'I'm like a spider, Roy. I don't let myself sleep.' FA Cup Final, 1937/38, the actual result neither here nor there. The crowd: 93,357.

Leaving the robed Jenkins to hear the jury's verdict on sterling, Wilson turned to Marcia and said: 'Plots are like potholes. They're only dangerous when you haven't seen them. And I've seen this one.'

THERE were a hundred places on earth Wright wanted to be more than the London Golf Club. Even among licensed premises, it ranked low. He'd like to have been at a Silver Jubilee bash for an SOE mission. His expectations of this meet were as low as a cobra's bollocks.

Storey had dialled the number the assets were given for emergencies but he was only half a Joe, if that, so far and it would doubtless turn out to be like someone calling an ambulance for a scratch.

His asset was sitting at the table under the signed picture of Tony Jacklin, flapping through a newspaper you knew he wasn't taking in, the way that lovers and agents waited. He was reading the *Mirror* with its amazing front page. The phrase was something people said all the time; in England, especially. But personally, if you asked him, Enough was never bloody Enough. In anything that mattered, it was always more you wanted.

Wright barked at Storey without preamble, liking the startled reaction: 'Another mug of that purple stuff, then? I hear Henry Worthington's drinking hemlock.'

'Oh, "White"! Er, no. A half of whatever the beer here is.'

'Why the pansy portions, Bernard? Tastes better from a long glass.'

'I'm working this afternoon. For *two* employers, as it happens.'

'I'd let you buy them, if the club committee weren't quite so Comintern about it. I understand you're flush. Account-holder of the month and so on.'

While clearing more space on the table for his glass, Wright shuffled the *Mirror* to the racing page and left it upwards. DARDA WILL BE OUT TO RECOVER LOSSES.

With the drinks were on the table, Wright, sipping his own gin, tried to put his asset at ease: 'Wonder you need to come to me with your problems when you're on personal terms with Marje Proops!'

The aimless trails that weren't worth the bloody shoe leather and the Washington tip-offs that turned out to be all piss and maple syrup were worth it for these moments of showing someone what you knew. Storey stared back with satisfactory bafflement: 'What do you mean?'

'I saw you and Dame Douche on a pleasant stroll through the London dusk, both pretending to go home.'

'Both?'

Smart boy. Hacks were sharp. They listened and they noticed. That was both their up and their down as an asset.

'Both, Bernard. Soon as you headed down the Holborn hole, Lady Leg-Shave was dashing back to work like Solly on payday.'

Storey of the *Mirror* was looking like he'd need a diction-ary to scribble a note to the milkman. They said knowledge was power but the part you paid your green fees for was watching ignorance as weakness.

'What do you mean?'

'You didn't know, Bernard, that the Woman Who Knows has been fucking the legal manager for years now? It seems that old Proopsie doesn't float her boat. Perhaps he ought to write to "Dear Marje".'

'You were following me?'

Wright just busied himself with the intake of gin because that allegation wasn't worth the breath. But his asset pleased him with a bigger leap. 'When that desk drawer opened – the one King always keeps locked – I thought it was luck. But you'd been in there first, hadn't you?' Quaff, say nothing. The only good thing to come out of that whole darn game of poker was the face. 'Setting the cheese in the trap?'

'You're no mouse, Bernard. You do yourself down. Find anything interesting out?'

The Cabinet of all the Arseholes, 2 Kinnerton Street, the leader of the British Fascist Party claiming Downing Street: Wright listened as if it was news to him, which the last part slightly was. But then Storey said: 'He's meeting *Zuckerman* there. Some sort of expert on women and monkeys, as far as I can tell. Is he part of the plot?'

Sip and blank him, hug your cards. Don't let him know that he's thrown you. How the fuck is Zuckerman involved? South African Jew, saluted two flags before the one Britain flew. Casually as he could, Wright said: 'Maybe they wanted someone who was careful with money. I expect emergency governments set you back a bit.'

Storey was leaning across the table aggressively now, as if Wright were some piddling minister up against Robin Day: 'One of the many things I don't understand about this – up to and including why you need me at all when you've got Cudlipp . . .'

'Bernard, when did I ever say we had Cudlipp?'

'When did you ever say anything? So it's hardly the criterion. What I don't understand is that King wants to bring down Harold Wilson and you want to see the end of "Henry Worthington". So why don't you just let him get on with it? But it's as if you want me to stop him. MI5 should be papering its office with today's *Mirror*. It doesn't make sense.'

Top of the class, boy. Here was an asset who could count to ten and wipe his own arse. He would need watching.

'You're making a lot of assumptions, Bernard,' Wright told him. 'Now, do you need cab-fare to SW1? Or can you get it in expenses from our dictator-in-waiting?'

THERE WAS a joke about Brezhnev spending a day with his mother. He proudly showed her his huge office in the Kremlin, with the selections from the Hermitage on the wall and the fleet of Zils at his command, which now drove them in a mile-long motorcade to his dacha in the country with its private lake. 'It's lovely, Leonid,' she said. 'But what will you do if the communists get in?'

As they purred past *Evening News* and *Evening Standard* billboards howling a run on the pound, Cudlipp wondered if the self-declared nemesis of the Wilson administration should perhaps be travelling today in a vehicle more austere than this bloated Rolls. King, seemingly seeing no conflict between luxury wheels and revolt, turned to him and said: 'I don't think you'll regret being present for this, Hugh.'

People only used that phrase when they were contemplating the resentment someone else might feel, so Cudlipp asked: 'This meeting, Cecil? We're just getting his view of the temperature of things generally? State of the nation. Possible article on the leader pages: more the Sunday than the daily, Lee would consider him elitist. I mean, we're not offering him a seat on the board or anything?'

King gave him what Cudlipp's mother would have called a chapel look and murmured: 'I think this gentleman might be able to do the state rather more service than seven hundred words on the gold reserves or even a seat around the table of the International Publishing Corporation.'

Cudlipp let this go. An atheist ever since his brother had

divined that their rector was a bigamist, he was of the firm opinion that believers kept their faith by not really thinking about what they were hearing. Increasingly an agnostic to the doctrines of King, he had begun to adopt this approach at work.

He was singing hymns in loud counterpoint in his head as the Chairman began another of his lectures on the working of the personality: 'A man is like a safe, Hugh. To open him up, you need to know his combination. In the case of our host this afternoon, the vital numbers are one-nine-one-seven.' King repeated these figures, just in case Cudlipp had become a cretin in transit. 'One-nine-one-seven.'

THERE WAS no flag or plaque outside 2 Kinnerton Street to hint at its occupant. The tall Victorian townhouse was expensively nondescript. Uncertain whether he was a spy coat-tailing or a journalist door-stepping, Storey tried to project yet another identity: a loafing tourist or house-buyer waiting for an agent. An *estate* agent.

His eye primed for limousines or even outriders, he was surprised when the first car to stop outside the house was a black cab. The man who ducked out of it seemed to combine pugilism with intelligence: a stocky body and bullish neck tapered towards a high, furrowed brow framed by lively eyes and grey, corrugated hair. But Storey was embarrassed to admit to himself that he knew it was Zuckerman by the Jewish nose.

'Sir Solly?'

Storey – deciding that journalist was his most sensible disguise – was holding a notebook and pen, prompting Zuckerman to respond with his own questions: 'Yes? Press?'

'Ben Stringer from the *Daily Express*.' He had made up his alias on the model of Henry Worthington. 'We're asking a number of prominent public figures what they thought of Mr Cecil King's attack this morning?'

'And how did you know I'd be here, Mr Stringer?'

'Newspaper grapevine, sir. I think my proprietor's secretary may have gossiped.'

'Really? And why would Max Aitken know about this meeting?'

Bewildered until he realized that he was working for the *Express* – changing your name meant reinventing your memories as well – Storey blustered: '*Did* you have a view of Enough is Enough, Sir Solly?'

'I felt it was a resonant and timely phrase. But its moral should perhaps be taken by Mr King rather than Mr Wilson.'

Storey suddenly understood why the spooks recruited assets from the press: both professions specialized in telling when people were lying.

'Sir Solly, I have evidence that you are part of a conspiracy.'

Short of Storey announcing that he possessed ovaries or gills – and therefore all the great scientist's books must be rewritten – Sir Solly could not have looked more convincingly shocked. His general expression of amusement graduated to bemusement and then fury: 'Conspiracy? I don't think I've ever heard such balls, Mr Stringer.' Then there seemed to be an abrupt understanding. 'Ah! Unless you mean the Great Jewish Conspiracy? Does your proprietor fear a cabal? The underground Zionist government meeting over tea in Mayfair? Well, I don't think even the *Daily Express* would suspect the man I am here to meet of being Jewish.'

Zuckerman thrust his body forward, rushed up the steps, rang a bell and was rapidly admitted. The Home Guard was contemplating the pitiful state of its defences on Kinnerton

Street when a black official car of the kind Storey had always envisaged turned into the street.

As the passenger climbed a little stiffly past the door held open by a uniformed lackey – would that be a valet? – the flash of naval braid and hat badge and the rectangle of ribbons on the chest confused Storey. Had Mosley been so prized an officer?

But, as the bulk of *Who's Who* had made clear, M meant many men. The intended Prime Minister in King's dictatorship was Lord Mountbatten of Burma, Supreme Commander in South East Asia during World War II, last Viceroy and first Governor-General of India.

ALTHOUGH he was at home, his next engagement was, in effect, a business meeting. So he chose one of the light-grey worsted double-breasteds (leaving it, however, to hang unbuttoned because in recent photographs he had looked worryingly stout).

He once would not have been able to imagine a time of being glad to abandon his uniform but the epaulettes had felt heavy on his shoulders that morning as he shook the hands of disturbingly young cadets whose grip seemed at least three times stronger than his.

What he most needed was to soak in a hot bath but it was almost 16:30 and, though a chap could not expect to live his life without insults, he hoped never to be called untimely. President Johnson in Washington, though terrifically engaging in other ways, had hopelessly overrun his diary and made the British naval party three-quarters of an hour late for lunch.

His fingers were giving him gyp and the cufflinks flummoxed him so badly he thought of calling for the valet. But once one needed help dressing, it was full speed for the scrap-yard. Only when the sleeves were neat – symmetrical lines of white peeping out from the cuffs – did Mountbatten shout for his man. He stood against the wall of his dressing room between the Turner seascape and the wardrobe.

'When you're ready!' he commanded. His man held him by the armpits and half-threw him against the plaster. 'Again!' he instructed, and the procedure was repeated. 'Excellent!' he said. 'Are they in the drawing room?' He stood for a moment, waiting for the shakedown of his bones and then, to his satisfaction, walked in exactly as the half-hour was sounding.

The big chap, who would be King, stood up at once and exclaimed: 'Lord Mountbatten!'

'Dickie, please,' he beamed at them and quickly toured the table on a meet-and-greet, winking at Solly and stroking his arm. He shook Cudlipp's hand, saying, 'Hugh, I know, of course,' then found himself greeted by King with a double-grip. The massiveness of the man surprised him. He was like one of those warriors with their nose-bones who danced for Lilibet on her trips.

'I'm sorry it had to be so late in the day. I was taking a passing-out parade.'

'You keep yourself impressively busy.' This was King. He sounded posh but not quite pukka, as if he was putting it on somehow. 'Hugh was telling me of your involvement with – how many organizations is it now?'

'One hundred and seventy-nine at the last count, I believe. Well, since I left the Admiralty, what is one to do? I'm too old for polo. I still dream of bagging a thousand birds in one day but what with this blasted arthritis . . . So I go where people want me to go.'

'We were pleased to report your speech at the Lymington

Marina this week,' said King. 'I think we've all had experiences of shoddy British workmanship.'

'I hope you don't mean my speech! No, you're very kind, Mr King.' He left space for a 'Cecil, please', but it never came. 'It is the speeches I enjoy. When a room rises in applause, one understands just a little of what happened to Mr Hitler. It's among the most wonderful sensations in the world and I can quite understand people going mad on it.'

'The feeling that your voice should be more widely heard in national affairs is what led to this meeting. I understand Hugh came to see you at Broadlands and talked about leaders who might reinvigorate the British people, a need for a strong voice . . .'

'Yes, indeed, Mr King. I think I suggested the *Mirror* should get behind Mrs Castle. She's really rather a formidable lady. You know, people say the public wouldn't let a woman run the country. And yet they have such respect for Lilibet . . .'

'But, with respect, Lord Mountbatten . . .'

'I insist on Dickie . . .'

'Barbara Castle is hardly Queen Elizabeth II.'

'I'm merely saying that, as any old salt would tell you, it doesn't make sense to fire from the obvious positions. As Hugh, I think, understood, I was arguing that we may be looking for our leaders in the wrong places.'

'Ah, well, I think now we may be marching in step.'

They were interrupted by his man serving refreshments: tea for the men from the press, strong coffee for himself and Solly. Neither Zuckerman nor Cudlipp had yet spoken but then each was present as a sort of aide-de-camp.

Visibly relieved when the social pleasantries were over, King resumed his pitch: 'I read somewhere a detail of your family history which has always stayed with me. What to us was the "Russian Revolution, 1917" was to you, the Batten-bergs, the murder of "Uncle Nicky" and "Aunt Alix".'

Mountbatten bowed his head for the family dead but also because this was a topic on which he could still not absolutely guarantee the absence of tears.

'Indeed.'

King went on: 'I myself, though never having such a direct link to the history books, also lived through revolution. Though the dialect was educated from me, I am Irish. I was living four miles outside Dublin in 1916. I didn't learn about the Easter Rebellion from newspapers or history books but through the craic of people who had heard or even fired the shots. So, in our different ways, I suspect that neither Lord Mountbatten nor I have the traditional British complacency of saying: it couldn't happen here, bloody Revolution could not touch us . . .'

Solly, the rational scientist, and Cudlipp, the sceptical journalist, looked embarrassed by this passion. But Mount-batten's values were not those of the test tube or the news desk. He was a fighting man, raised to give and take command. What was it, he wondered, about deep-felt words delivered at white heat that made one want to follow a man?

DURING the thirty-one years that King had employed him, Cudlipp had observed numerous moods – good and bad – but awe had never featured until today. The man who boasted that he began his studies at rock bottom seemed genuinely impressed by the former First Sea Lord and final hero of the leased-back Empire.

(Although, as the afternoon continued, Cudlipp came to the conclusion that even this apparent deference from the Chairman was a form of selfishness. His personal ambitions required him to believe in Mountbatten, so he did.)

At first, however, he was more concerned with the impression his boss was making on the sea-dog. Cudlipp had been acquainted with 'Dickie' for decades, their connection not a friendship but a loose business understanding. Mountbatten was one of the few names instantly familiar in a headline, and as the only member of the Royal Family licensed to give interviews he was happy to supply such stories when he needed to raise money or his profile.

Almost the same age as King, the old sailor looked in much better shape. He sat with his back square to the chair, the chin at the end of the long, equine face shaved to barber's standards. Only a couple of liver spots encroached on a complexion polished by sun on sea.

Zuckerman, who had unsheathed a fountain pen to make notes, showed his impatience and disdain by failing to take any but Mountbatten seemed to be listening with complete attention as the Chairman of the International Publishing Corporation continued his oratorical journey from the riotous Ireland of his childhood to the potentially no less volatile Britain of the present.

'Our whole system of government faces disintegration,' King declared. 'The Bank of England pretends to the country and the world that our democracy is guaranteed by gold which it long ago sold. The same tired political faces play musical chairs in the cabinet room. Four Ministers of Education in four years; three Ministers of Fuel and Power in three years. Harold Wilson, a fresh and inspirational leader of the Opposition, has proved to be what we in the business world recognize as a classic example of a man promoted to a level at which his weaknesses are revealed . . .'

Zuckerman, still refusing to give these words the merit of a record, grasped his pen so hard that he seemed to be at risk of breaking it, as King continued: 'Wilson and his list of endlessly rotating cronies are ever more futile in the face of intransigent trade unions in the grip of the Militant Left. Soon the dockyards and the factories will rise in violent protest. I fear the police will be unable to quell the bloodshed. And so the army will step in. In London, Liverpool and Birmingham, there will be machine-guns on street corners. Enoch Powell – a talented man who, I fear, went a little mad – believed that immigration would be the trigger for the collapse of Britain. But it is my belief that the rivers of blood, which *will* flow, will have their source in Downing Street and the fact that Great Britain Ltd has no satisfactory managing director. Mr Wilson seems to believe that his job as Prime Minister is to keep the balance between the Left and Right wings of the Labour Party. What we need is a government which unites all those in this country who believe in monarchy and democracy and fear the rise of communism. The moment is coming for an Emergency Government, bringing together the best businessmen in the land under a renowned leader of men. I am here today, Lord Mountbatten, to ask if you would serve as head of such an administration?'

IN THE mess at Sandhurst, the officers had been discussing devaluation, the student sit-ins, the Bolshies in the TUC, the lack of leadership. One of the chaps had said that Britain needed a 'figure in the wings', ready to lead a National Government, as Churchill had. Yes, Mountbatten had agreed, but Churchill was a Member of Parliament. In fact, a member of the cabinet. He wasn't 'in the wings' but almost 'centre stage'. That was the objection. That was the objection.

A TALENTED man who went a little mad. The epitaph that King had wished to hang around the neck of Enoch Powell now waited to embrace his own.

For ninety per cent of the peroration, Cudlipp had been mentally rejigging editorial budgets. The rant was familiar from his Chairman's fireside chats: Merseyside's post office no less vulnerable to history than Dublin's, Muscovite shop stewards on the factory floor and so on.

It was only when King offered Lord Dickie not the expected op-ed article on why Wilson must go but the keys to fucking Number 10 itself that Cudlipp's ears opened, in swift syncopation with his eyes. You and whose army, Cecil? You and whose fucking army?

EMERGENCY was a word he liked, a term with a decent history. He had chaired the Emergency Committee in India. There, as later in Malaya, the word implied a route to a solution, not a permanent state of affairs. The Emergency Government of Great Britain: 1968 to . . . To when? The crucial point would be how long he held this job. In his career, he had been something of an expert in transition.

PRACTISED as he was in convincing listeners that Cecil King had not intended the meaning he might have conveyed, Cudlipp had only previously soothed troubled waters involving offended hostesses and hurt journalists. He did not possess the balm for application when the Queen's uncle had just been asked to take over the country. (And was a bromide lotion, in any case, required? Dickie had not yet rejected the offer.)

Mountbatten turned to Zuckerman: 'Solly, you haven't said a word so far. What do you think of all this?'

Even now, the scientist denied himself words, preferring the action of pushing back his chair and walking to the door. Holding it open, he spoke at length for the first and only time that afternoon: 'This is rank treachery. All this talk of machine-guns at street corners is appalling. I am a public servant and will have nothing to do with it. Nor should you, Dickie.'

Zuckerman seemed to wait for an answer from Mountbatten which now came: 'I agree with Solly.' Cudlipp glanced at King, who was glaring at the departing scientist as if it were the latter who had embarrassed the gathering.

THERE WAS a call box on the corner of Kinnerton Street and Storey kept finding himself near it, as if his subconscious considered it the solution. But who would he ring? His wife thought he was crazy and he had come to the conclusion that both of his employers knew more about what was going on inside the house than he did.

The dull brown frontage of a betting shop – not quite off-putting enough – was visible from the telephone kiosk, so he concentrated on avoiding that temptation, ensuring one victory in what felt like an afternoon of failure.

Twice, a policeman walked past and he wondered about stopping him. But what was the system for reporting a possible coup d'état? Did you tell a bobby or call emergency services? Storey imagined constables escorting the four conspirators – King, Cudlipp, Mountbatten and Zuckerman – to police cars. Kinnerton would join Cato as a street of sedition.

He spent thirty minutes walking in a wide, repeating loop – glancing up at the house, away from the bookmaker's, helplessly towards the phone booth – like a horse in the parade ring, no *not* like that – until, on one pass of Number 2, he saw Zuckerman coming down the steps, then scanning the street both ways for a cab.

Storey stooped to tie a shoelace as an excuse for not acknowledging the scientist but the ruse proved unnecessary. Realizing that he had twice ignored a shout of 'Stringer!',

Storey found Zuckerman standing over him and trying to catch his attention for a third time.

'Oh, er, Sir Solly. I'm sorry about my behaviour earlier. I may have . . .'

'No, I owe you the apology, Mr Stringer. Your talk of a conspiracy was not balls, though I was never a conspirator. In fact, should you wish to report this story in the *Express*, you should be aware that it was a treason involving only one. Think yourself lucky you don't work for Cecil King. Do you think Aitken will print this?'

'I think there might be difficulties with that.'

'Dog does not eat dog, eh?'

'Will you say anything?'

'Not publicly. Privately, I will speak to the Prime Minister. I think Mr King may discover that Enough *is* Enough. I'll remember your name, Mr Stringer.'

A taxi stopped for Zuckerman, who directed the driver simply: 'Whitehall!' Trying not to reflect on the career Ben Stringer might have had with the patronage of a leading member of the Establishment, Bernard Storey took the next cab to Holborn, to avoid a meeting with two people emerging from the house who did know which newspaper he worked for.

'*HOW like a man to choose a crowded train,*' she said, looking straight at him, '*to say that we must never meet again! / Or was it masculine low cunning / So that I could not make a scene / It might have been.*'

The air-force type with messy silver hair was in again. He must really love poetry, unless he had taken a shine to her. No, don't be daft, Mary. She suddenly worried that he might be a journalist. Harold had told her she must assume for the moment that anyone who spoke to her, even if seemingly friendly – especially if seemingly friendly – might be a writer from a newspaper, an enemy or both.

Harold had telephoned her in a panic from Bristol that morning, telling her to pack things up in the flat; they might be going. Mary had told him, as she always did, that the party wouldn't dare ditch someone who had given Labour their first victory for thirteen years.

But tonight, when she read from 'The House at the Edge of the Wood', she was even more careful than usual to stress in her preamble that this vision of solitude lay far in the future and entirely subject to her husband's timing.

'*Somehow, someday, I shall be free / To go to the place where it waits for me,*' she said to the single member of the audience she had chosen. She was pleased to see the long-haired wing commander nodding vigorously in appreciation.

HE HAD spent the last office hour of the day persuading an apparently famous pop singer – whose name now escaped him from blessed ignorance as much as client confidentiality – not to sue a newspaper over the imputation of homosexuality; ever since Mr Lee Liberace had somehow taken money from the *Mirror*, unmarried entertainers had viewed Fleet Street as a piggy bank.

When Goodman had hinted as delicately as he could that the crooner might indeed have Greek interests, the star had countered that Liberace was an absolute screamer. 'My dear boy,' Goodman had replied, 'I do not entirely like the idea that I am fat. I might well be hurt by a columnist who called me "Bunteresque". But, if I sued, I should be gambling on the jury's judgement of my silhouette.'

Goodman had suggested the singer and his 'business manager' consult Peter Carter-Ruck. There was a man who would represent Humpty-Dumpty over the allegation that he had suffered fractures.

So, as Goodman arrived at the Downing Street flat, he was in a mood which might perhaps be soothed by the Andante from the Mozart C Minor Concerto – which he now hummed to himself – but not by the lamentable G&S which now drifted down the stairs.

The Prime Minister's voice had been a dirge when he summoned Goodman by telephone earlier, so he was surprised to walk into a party which, if it were a wake of any kind, was of the Irish variety. The Prime Minister, that ridiculous bookie's runner Wigg and the Keeper of the Diary seemed tipsy and giggly.

Wilson was conducting – with a sizeable cigar rather than the famous pipe – a stretch Goodman recognized as *Trial By Jury*, which at least had the virtue of being by far the shortest of the Annoy Operas.

'Ah, the Lord High Everything Else,' the Prime Minister cried. 'A perfectly timed arrival. Perhaps you should join me in this one.' Wilson briefly sang along, in a phlegmy tenor voice, to the Judge's song: '*All thieves who could my fees afford / Relied on my orations / And many a burglar I've restored / To his friends and his relations.*'

It was by no means the first time that this quatrain had been dedicated to Goodman, no matter how often he had pointed out that he was a solicitor rather than a barrister and would, anyway, be much happier listening to a dripping tap. However, the Prime Minister's jokes tended to be strenuous and repetitive. He gave the impression of a man who was not naturally funny but had one day decided that a sense of humour would be a political advantage.

'Handled any good briefs today, Arnold?' wheedled Wigg, who looked flushed and triumphant, full of brandy. How often he now regretted keeping the story of the colonel's illegitimate son out of the press. Glancing dismissively at him, Goodman noticed that the secret father was at a disadvantage.

'I think Colonel – forgive me, *Lord* – Wigg needs to pay heed to Isaiah, chapter 6, verse 5.'

Wigg looked blanker: 'I'm not with you, Arnold . . .'

' "*Woe is me, for I am undone*"!' quoted Goodman. After a further delay in the working of his brain, the pride of the Totaliser finally looked down and attended to his gaping flies: 'Thank you, my dear sir!'

Wilson handed Goodman an inch of brandy, which he flooded from a little jug that was, unlike the bottle of spirits, almost full.

'You seem much happier than when we spoke on the phone, Prime Minister?'

'Yes, well, Arnold. That's because I've crushed the buggers who were after me. They tell me from the House that backbenchers are clambering over each other's shoulders to sign a motion calling for King to resign. And, by extension, for the Prime Minister to continue. My neighbour, Brother Jenkins, who likes to regard himself as one of England's finest writers, has spent all day apparently unable to get beyond the phrase "Dear Constituency Chairman". But now it's *he* who needs the letter of support from *me*—'

'Ah, a rhyme, Prime Minister,' cut in Wigg. 'Mary has a rival.'

Wilson ignored his jester's intervention. Goodman sensed that the colonel's influence was slipping. 'You know, Arnold, they said I was paranoid about plots. But the fact of the matter is, I wasn't paranoid enough. I thought King was plotting to replace me with Roy Jenkins. Even after watching my back for so long that my neck hurts, it never occurred to me that he was planning to replace me with Mountbatten of bloody Burma. You disappoint me, Pooh-Bah. You don't look shocked. Don't tell me you were in on it . . .'

It was not entirely clear if the last remark was a jest about Wilson's sensitivity or the re-establishment of the paranoia itself. Goodman explained: 'Sir Solly telephoned me this evening, vouchsafed a little . . .'

'Mountbatten had a map on the wall of his office, showing how it could all happen,' Marcia announced.

'I understand the maps showed where the machine-guns were to be mounted against the populace,' Wigg added.

'Ah, well, my impression from Sir Solly was that it was all at a rather more theoretical level.'

Wilson was expertly slicing and lighting another cigar. Goodman suddenly wondered if the pipe was merely theatrical business, then reproached himself for such distrust.

'I never thought Mountbatten added up,' the Prime Minister confided. 'My niece the Queen, chest that clanked if you hit him on the back. All that. But the man's a raving unilateralist, you know. More CND than half the Party Left. I'm surprised that King chose him. The army would have got a bloody shock with him in charge . . .'

'Poof as well, apparently.'

'Ah, well,' Goodman growled. 'There's no evidence of that, Colonel Wigg . . .'

'I'll tell you another thing about Mountbatten, Pooh-Bah. When they christened him, they gave him five names. Louis Francis Albert Victor Nicholas . . .'

'Your memory never ceases to amaze me,' said Marcia.

'Yes, well I . . . where was I? . . . where was I? . . .'

They all looked at Wilson in alarm until he gave a full-throated laugh to show that the lapse had been a joke. 'Five names, they give him. And he doesn't use a single one of them.

You have to call him Dickie. I will never understand the upper classes in this country.'

Wigg, playing brandy waiter, boomed: 'The word is that before Mountbatten goes out on show he gets his valet to bang him hard against a wall. I don't mean sexually. In fact, the opposite. He can't bear not to look straight on parade.'

'The vanity of the man. He must live in a hall of mirrors.'

And you, Prime Minister, thought Goodman, reside in a hall of distorting glass, mistaking the faces of both friends and enemies.

Henry James entered, holding sheets of teleprinter paper.

'Prime Minister,' he said. 'This is from Paris.'

Wilson, setting down his glass and cigar, read the wire copy with the swift, intelligent attention that was his best quality and the drinking and long repetitions of office had not yet wholly extinguished.

'What is it?' Marcia asked.

'The students have taken the Latin Quarter. They tried to storm ORTF, the broadcaster. They're holed up behind barricades, facing deep lines of riot police. The Embassy says it feels like the Second French Revolution. De Gaulle and Pompidou are considering whether to send in the army.'

'Do you know what they do?' Wigg lectured them. 'The students? They take a tricolour and rip off the white and blue, fly the *red* flag over their barricades. Showing their true colours.'

'It could happen so easily here,' predicted Wilson, with a shiver which may not have been merely for effect. 'The LSE marching on the BBC—'

'Bedfellows!' the rustic bookmaker interrupted. 'Bedfellows! More likely they'd march together on Downing Street. Left, left, left, left, left . . .'

'Even if the English temperament were not traditionally

loath to revolt,' Goodman interjected, 'we have the advantage that the Union Flag is so much harder to slice in the fashion Colonel Wigg describes. The students would be left at the risk of masquerading as the Red Cross . . .'

The communiqué on the anarchy in Paris rapidly reduced the Prime Minister's mood of half-cut triumphalism. His more characteristic suspicion restored, he asked: 'Arnold, should I sack Brother Jenkins?'

'Might not such a termination create a crisis similar to the one only recently resolved? Better surely a colleague in private debt to your tolerance than in public grievance over your revenge on him? Why strike against Mr Jenkins when his capacity to strike against you, if it ever existed, has been severely damaged by today's events?'

Wilson seemed to accept this wisdom reluctantly. But then, with a pop-eyed intensity that alarmed Goodman because he had seen it only at the Prime Minister's darkest moments, Wilson hissed: 'Arnold, do you want to know what's going on?'

'What's going on, Prime Minister?'

Wilson laughed. '*I'm* going on.'

19

Enough Is Enough

THE LIFT was full of vicars and a bishop got in on the second floor. Cudlipp assumed it was Rag Week at one of the London colleges, although no one seemed to be rattling a tin.

When another set of prelates was hanging round the stairwell on the ninth, he wondered if the Church had taken over the country in an ecclesiastical response to the recent failed attempt to impose a naval hero as national saviour. But there was no time to ask why IPC was full of sky-pilots because the board was waiting for him.

'Anyone know why it's like a vicars but no tarts party out there?' Cudlipp asked, as he walked towards the head of the table past the space on the wall where the Sutherland portrait of Cecil Triumphant was intended to hang.

'I assumed they were praying for our newspapers' relationship with Harold Wilson,' said Frank Rogers. Cudlipp thought: no, that one will be settled by human sacrifice.

'Where *is* Cecil?' someone wondered. 'Not like him to be late.'

Cudlipp began to answer that question with the act of usurpation of sitting in King's place. 'Good morning. This board meeting has been called in the absence of the Chairman. Because – under paragraph 100 (g) of the Articles of Association – it concerns the behaviour of the Chairman.'

*

THE problem with businessmen was that they craved the portrait but hated the sittings. That very word, with its implication of inactivity, was hostile to the drive that made them famous enough to be painted.

It had been true of King's fellow press baron Beaverbrook and also of Longman (books) and Paley (television). Because men with money liked to have what their rivals possessed – whether cars, women, companies or a particular oil painter – Sutherland now found himself at risk of becoming the Joshua Reynolds of the Stock Exchange.

From his reluctant interlude immortalizing tycoons, Sutherland had drawn the lesson: never try to paint the portrait of anyone who has conducted a time-and-efficiency study. He had begun to consider using highlights – little shimmers of the brush on the background – in an attempt to suggest the caged energy of his business sitters.

King was already ten minutes late, delayed by a telephone call, according to Dame Ruth, who had thankfully made no mystical pronouncements on the safety of travel or accommodation, confining herself to comments on the previous night's Gala Concert for the State of Israel. When he had asked after King, she had simply replied 'fine', the lie that sustained so much English conversation.

However, as he laid down drip-sheets in the subject's study, Sutherland was perturbed that he might have to abandon this canvas and start again. He could not think of a previous sitter who had undergone such a physical (and, he suspected, emotional) shift between sessions.

From the English press in Pembrokeshire, he knew that the arrogant capitalist of their first encounters was now a political bogey and journalistic joke and the man who appeared at the door cut a figure suggesting this fall into ridicule. King's chin and one cheek were clouded with shaving foam and this semi-Santa was wearing a pyjama top rather than the stiff grey jacket, all three buttons done up, that was half-recreated on the easel. He held a foam-flecked towel in one hand and an opened white envelope in the other. The image had distinct possibilities as a painting, though more Magritte than Sutherland.

'I'm afraid you'll have to paint me from memory,' King said. 'I have been summoned to London for a meeting.'

Turning to leave without any formal apology or farewell, he stopped and added: 'Dame Ruth tells me that you specialize in Crucifixions. Which may now be useful in my case.'

EVEN deep in Catholic Ireland, he had never seen so many priests. The lobby at Holborn Circus was a throng of dog collars: black-suited men with lassoed throats could be glimpsed every time the lift doors opened. King swore he saw a bishop by the ninth-floor fire escape.

Arriving at the penthouse, he asked the secretary: 'What is this, then? Judgement Day?'

'I'm sorry, Mr King. In what . . . ?'

'Herd of clergy in the building. Is *All Gas And Gaiters* on location?'

'Oh, that. You've probably forgotten, sir. You agreed last year. It's a post-ordination course for the Diocese of Southwark. They're learning about communications. Fifty new parish priests are with us for the day.'

Let his tragedy play out against a farce, then.

'Get me Cudlipp and Rogers up here at once.'

While King waited for the traitors to ascend, he sat at the William Kent tables and stared at the fish tank, trying not to think that he now viewed the fable of the carp and the goldfish from a different angle.

Pulling out the fob from his pocket, he selected a small key and tried to unlock the top left-hand desk drawer. Surprised to find it already open (he felt the falling of a shadow from the geriatric ward), he removed the cabinet list and made confetti of it. Fumbling with the buttons on his jacket – these are old man's fingers, dammit – he pulled out a different sheet of paper.

May 29 1968

Dear Cecil,

I have been instructed to inform you by letter of some decisions which have been reached by all your IPC colleagues. They were reached with great reluctance and solely in what we believe to be the long-term interests of the Corporation.

It has been decided that the retirement age for the Chairman of IPC should be sixty-five, in keeping with the rule laid down by you for all other directors; that you should therefore retire immediately as Chairman.

It has also been decided that I should succeed you as Chairman.

Then the writer of the letter – who attested to his sincerity in the signature of this execution notice – pushed open the door and was followed in by Rogers.

ONLY one chair had been set in front of the octagonal desk, as if to make clear that, for all the talk of the unanimity of the directors, this was between King and Cudlipp, who took the seat isolated for him, leaving Rogers to hover like a wine waiter during Prohibition. 'Good morning, Cecil,' he said. 'Pleasantries' was never a satisfactory word and even less so on this occasion.

'If such it can be, Hugh, when a man is sacked while shaving.'

'You've read the letter, Cecil. Are you now prepared to resign?'

King simply glared at him. Cudlipp thought of those prisoners of war who refused to talk. Rogers, perhaps feeling useless, tried to remedy his ineffectiveness by saying: 'I would like to say, Cecil, that all your colleagues hold you in high esteem and affection. We have done our duty as directors. But the affection . . .'

No longer pretending that he didn't speak the language, the captive said: 'An odd way of showing it.' But it was Cudlipp he had nominated as main traitor and interrogator and towards whom King now swung back his lighthouse beam of disillusionment: 'Resign? Resign today? Certainly not. It would look as if I had been found with my hand in the till. Certainly not.'

THERE was something different about Moira's hello kiss when he got home. She actually pushed her pussy against him, as if to say: your tea and then me. He knew why: the pound might be plummeting but their own sterling reserves were on the rise.

'Now we're a bit flush – seems they've not only given you a pay rise but an advance as well – I got a drop of something . . .'

She gestured to the table, where a ray of fading daylight picked out a strip of purple on the bottle. 'It's made of eggs and Australian wine, which sounds strange but it's quite affordable . . .'

'Yes, I had some this week. Tastes more omelette than grape, to be honest.'

'Do they sell it in pubs, then?'

'No, it wasn't a pub. Sort of a club.'

'What *sort* of club, Bernard Storey?'

'Oh, just somewhere a contact wanted to meet.'

She handed him a glass of the thick violet liquid.

'It was on the news,' she said. 'King Cecil's gone.'

'Yes. Do you know, it was amazing. On BBC1, they actually interrupted the racing to flash it.'

'And why were you watching the gee-gees in the middle of the afternoon?'

'Oh, the news desk like to have it on in the corner. Some of the subs are big punters.'

This new fluency in untruths still shocked him and he tried to suppress his pleasure at Moira's easy acceptance of the invention. She asked through purpled lips: 'Will it affect you? King going?'

'It could be good, actually. I mean, I've never even been in King's office . . .' So this was how lying took hold of a life. Fibbing was addictive. Once you got away with one, you found yourself looking for another opportunity. 'And I've often been in Cudlipp's. We know some of the same people.'

WHAT the hell would old Reggie Bosanquet do if they brought in colour? Even in b&w, you could tell he was a bloody strange shade: looked like a nigger minstrel. Wright would have called Leconsfield House Requisitions for another telly, except that he had passed Bosie once on the Strand and he was practically tangerine. Sun-lamp or what they called pancake.

(Bit of an odd 'un all round. A boozer, reputedly, which you could sometimes tell from the way he giggled through the silly bit at the end about ducks singing the Hallelujah Chorus or whatever. And, if that wasn't a toupee on his head, then a carpet-fitter had mistaken his bonce for a floor. His old man invented the googly, aka bosie. Laker and Benaud mentioned him just the other day on the cricket: Worcs v. the Touring Australians.)

But if Bosic looked darker than any Englishman should, King looked paler, as if he'd been painted all over, like the woman in *Goldfinger*, only white.

'Why do you think they dismissed you?' the minstrel announcer asked.

'Oh, I think it was a counter-attack by the Labour Party members of the board on what I said on the front page of the *Daily Mirror* a fortnight ago.'

'Now this really is an important question. Why did you sign it?'

'Because I thought it was important and I shouldn't hide behind the masthead of the paper.'

If you got on *News at Ten* for a bit of a boardroom reshuffle and some comments long ago gone to fish shops, then Wright couldn't imagine what they'd do if they got hold of 2 Kinnerton Street. We interrupt this programme . . .

Bosie asked King now: 'One always had the impression that you and Mr Cudlipp were friends. Are you still friends?'

The mouth was the only part of the ghost-white face that moved: 'I should have thought there was a certain chill about our relationship today, wouldn't you?'

'Yes, I would. That's why I asked you.'

'Yes, I think you are right. You know what Fleet Street is. It's a bit of a jungle. I mean, you know, it's not played like an old-fashioned minuet, is it?'

THE CARP was pushing hungrily against the partition, able to see the goldfish but denied by the glass. The smaller fish swam to the far side of its portion of the water, as if fearing that the division could not hold.

King raised his hand towards the glass sheet protecting the

weakling from its destiny. His fingers skittered on the surface of the water. Almost six decades had passed since a child of ten had been given a lesson in the nature of business and the business of nature.

He pulled his hand away from the tank and dried his fingers on the CHK handkerchief. He was not a man of words – no Cudlipp – but felt he had in some way broken the grasp of the past.

The goldfish returned to swimming circles, too ignorant or too innocent to know of its reprieve.

With dry fingers, King raised the monogrammed hand-kerchief – one of the symbols of the office he'd lost – which he now required for a second time.

20

Savoy Opera

SPEECH OF his life, speech of his fucking life. Until tonight, he'd never believed something Jack used to say: that there were times when it wasn't you saying the words, it was the words saying you. But that had been true in the ballroom back there. *We are a great country, an unselfish country and a compassionate country.* Lots of girls holding out their hands, singing a song with his name in it. America loves you.

Salinger and Rosie Greer had pushed him through. They'd promised he'd brief the press in a dining room. The *Times* of both coasts, guy from the BBC. They were going round the back way. Short cut through a serving pantry, apparently.

Everything was so loud. The songs from the ballroom and now the television somewhere, some kind of shout show from the count. Two long steam tables, a coloured chef reaching out to say: ya done it. They were in the kitchens.

Well, he was *sweet*, sweeter than anything the pastry chef at the Ambassador could make. Come too close to me, lady, and you'll put on thirty pounds. A guy was staring at him. Well, let him. Better get used to. Sound like someone banging a pan on the wall to say you're the man. Girl screaming. *Oh, no, not again . . .*

HE HAD never eaten breakfast anywhere as grand as this before. Thick pillars supported a stuccoed ceiling. The tables were set grandly enough for dinner, white tablecloths and napkins folded with army-sharp corners. The general sense was of a palace, although the atmosphere was broken by two jokey, Art Deco touches: a fish-pattern carpet and silver ashtrays shaped like an ornate toaster: a flattened oyster shell with a slot in the top for the ash.

His wife had made him buy a new tie – the ones he had were apparently either 'spivvy or hippy' – with 'the money from the latest pay rise'. Offered a drink while waiting, Storey chose tap water, frightened of the likely prices here. Fifteen minutes after the time he had been given, Storey began to suspect the whole thing had been a stunt by a sub pretending to be Cudlipp's secretary.

Then he felt a hand on his shoulder – distracting him from his attempt to be distracted from the *Mirror* racing page – and heard the enthusiastic, gentrified Welsh voice.

'Bernard! I know how irritating lateness is from the other side . . .'

'Oh, not at all, Mr Cudlipp.'

'Hugh, surely, by now, I would think.'

'I was beginning to worry there'd been a big news story.'

'No, no. Unfortunately. Quiet as a holiday Saturday back there. Bobby's just won the California primary but they'll not be chatting about that in Dinas Powys. Do you know the Savoy Grill? If you answer yes, I shall have to have your expenses investigated . . .'

'No. No, never.'

'Drink it in, then. Mm. Not many virgins in today. Most of 'em have sat here until they were sore.'

Cudlipp's head twitched both ways, like a bird seeking worms, stopping to nod at a red-complexioned diner three tables away who most resembled Leonid Brezhnev moonlighting as a circus clown: the Soviet leader's wild-animal eyebrows and slab of a face but the latter, in this case,

frequently animated by a grin so big and sloppy that it threatened to spill over his doubling chin.

'You know who that is, Bernard?'

'Denis Healey?'

'Yep. Politician's brain, boxer's balls. As opposed to
Crossman, who he's eating with: academic's brains, testicles
AWOL. If Healey's not Prime Minister one day, then *chapeau
de Cudlipp* will be a brief addition to the Grill menu.'

Cudlipp waved this document at a waiter to quicken the
order: he chose kippers and suggested that his junior should
as well but Storey was nervous of coping with eyes and bones
in company and so chose bacon, sausage and eggs; a child of
rationing, he still associated treats with meat. When Cudlipp
asked for his 'usual pick-me-up' and was brought a glass of
champagne, Storey felt both an envy and a fear of a world in
which men started boozing at breakfast.

A tall man, tightly bow-tied and trimly moustached,
stooped as he passed their table and said, in a soft voice with
a hint of a lisp: 'Hugh, I do hope you're not corrupting
another young journalist.'

'You know Frank Muir?' Cudlipp glossed the conversation. 'Very funny man. Scriptwriter on the wireless, mainly.
Do you know the story about the Little Green Book?'

'Er, no.'

Storey sipped at the coffee: poured from a silver pot without his asking. He coughed at a taste so strong he felt entire
beans had lodged in his throat.

'Auntie Beeb,' Cudlipp went on, 'distributed among her
many scriptwriters a list of verboten subjects. No jokes – no
cracks under any circumstances – about swearing, Royalty,
race, disability or homosexuality. Well, Frank is livid about
these heavy-handed restrictions. Next script he hands in, the

top line is: " 'Fuck me,' said the Queen, 'I think that one-eyed nigger is a poof.' " '

Cudlipp laughed so loudly that neighbouring eaters turned with enquiring smiles. They were probably further confused, like Storey, by the editor's sudden look of depression: 'The rumour's that Frank's going to one of the new ITV companies. Weak London Television or whatever it is. The "marketing" men tell me that TV is the future. That and "computers", damn machines. Do you know, they say there are fifty thousand of them in the States now? Now, I'm not averse to an odd turn on *The Editors* but I devoutly hope I'm under Welsh sods long before the goggle-box becomes the *Mirror* of tomorrow. Indeed, I do believe the Antichrist himself is among us.'

Storey followed the swing of Cudlipp's gaze to a corner table, where a thin, intense man was stroking a Havana as lovingly as if it were his own dick. When he removed the cigar to make a remark, followed by a laugh, Storey was struck by how much thinner the face looked than on television, although the rodentish quiver of the lips was the same.

'That's David Frost, isn't it?' Storey asked.

'Sshh! It's very important that one of us doesn't recognize him. You know he's twenty-nine? The only cure for his pointless fame is a starvation diet . . .'

Cudlipp continued to defame the TV star but Storey didn't hear because 'Patrick White' had just arrived. Unusually for entries to this celebrity restaurant, Storey was the only diner to turn his head this time. He tilted his eyes in recognition but his spymaster passed without a glance. Initially relieved that Cudlipp had shown indifference to 'White's' arrival, Storey then worried that both his employers might have been bluffing.

But, if so, Cudlipp was an Olivier quite lost on journalism

because he suddenly said, with no sense of a sequitur: 'Bernard, I thought we should talk after all this business with my, ah, predecessor. When you came to see me on that day, with the stuff the funny people were feeding you about Wilson . . . have they tried to give you anything else? Anything about King?'

Storey used the buttering of a bread roll to cover his hesitation. Was this a trick, in which Cudlipp was testing Storey's discretion on behalf of 'White'? But the latter, at the London Golf Club, had seemed untroubled that his asset had confided in his newspaper employer. Even so, Storey could scarcely admit to the new Chairman of IPC that he had once ransacked the office which went with the job.

'Has the address "Kinnerton Street" ever been mentioned?' Cudlipp pressed. 'Ah, I can tell from your reaction it has. Right back to sheep-stealers in Penarth, the hardest thing is to learn to lie with your eyes as well. And you know about Mountbatten too?' Storey again tried to stare noncommittally. 'Ah. That as well. Bernard, let me tell you something. If you do know, it's better that I know you know. Then, I might owe you, see. How many people have you told?'

The hero-worship that young journalists felt for Cudlipp often held an element of fear. When he strode across the newsroom, stooped slightly forward so that the shout could arrive before he did, a fag or Havana clamped in his mouth, his charisma was always slightly menacing.

Storey chewed bread as slowly as his mouth allowed, thinking melodramatic thoughts about the final meals of condemned men. He finally admitted: 'Just my wife.'

'Well, that's fine. Long as you stay on the right side of her. Bang up to date with the housekeeping and so on. I'd like to keep this hidden behind the *Mirror*, as it were. Newspaper boss goes crazy, seizes front page, gets his cards – a business can ride that out. Top man tries to put Queen's uncle in Number 10, the shareholders might ask a few more questions. Between us, Bernard, I'm surprised it hasn't leaked. Apparently, the *Express* had a reporter on the story. Mysterious type called Stringer.' This time, Storey managed a gaze that said he had stolen no sheep. 'But he's never written it up. Unless, which is one advantage of the Wilson administration, they slapped a D-notice on it.'

Cudlipp was about to speak again when his mouth hung open in the appalled yawn which, in horror films, meant that the protagonist had just seen a corpse walking across the room. And life was more or less imitating cinema because Storey, as he turned, was forced to adjust his look upwards to take in the looming bulk of Cecil King, pinstripe jacket triply closed over buttoned waistcoat.

In greeting, the two former colleagues spoke each other's names as if they were items ordered in a greengrocer.

'You look well, Cecil.'

'Then a month of feeding the rooks and killing weeds must be recuperative. I should join my host, Hugh. I think we shall next meet at the Annual General Meeting.'

'A lot of interest this year, Cecil. We've taken the Café Royal.'

'So I understand. The Napoleon Room.'

'Mm. With the Marie Antoinette Annexe for overflow.'

As King crossed the room, Cudlipp chuckled: 'Not much works in England. But the manners still do. In Chicago, we'd have shot each other. Why are you looking like that, Bernard?'

'I just hadn't expected to see him.'

But the real reason for Storey's own Hammer double take was that, at a table in a far corner, Cecil King was sitting down with 'Patrick White'. He missed whatever Cudlipp was saying about the AGM and a final showdown with King.

'Bernard,' Cudlipp resumed their conversation, 'you've shown a lot of gumption, some of the stuff you've found out in the last couple of weeks. Do you happen to know who the Secretary of State for Agriculture, Fisheries and Food is . . . ?'

Where the fuck was this going? What had farmers to do with spies or journalism? 'Oh, God. Fred . . . Fred some-one . . .'

'Fred Peart, you're thinking of?'

'Yes. Exactly.'

'Who certainly did hold the post until last month's reshuf-fle, when it went to Cledwyn Hughes. Well, you got the wrong answer half-right and I've certainly appointed politi-cal correspondents in the past who would have struggled to do that. Bernard, I'm planning to talk to Sydney Jacobson about getting you on the Parly staff. Is that a thought which appals?'

But the pressure of first tension and then release – and the suddenly unpleasant smell of the eggs cooling and congealing on his plate – proved too much for his bowels.

'Excuse me, is the Gents' . . . ?'

JUDGING from the splashes coming from behind the door, Storey of the *Mirror* was dropping rocks into a pond. Wright was beginning to fret about how long he could reasonably stand drying his hands on that big white piece of linen.

The bolt finally slid back and Storey came out of the stall. He looked ashamed in the way that people had when you met them after crapping, worried about the smell they'd left and the prima facie evidence they had an arse.

'Bernard!' Wright exclaimed, old friends meeting by chance during ablutions.

The hand-wallah rushed forward and gave Storey a flat white towel, then retreated far enough along the vast bathroom for Wright safely to whisper: 'Out there, it was good that you blanked me. In here, it's suspicious if you *don't* know me.'

'But what if Cudlipp . . . ?'

'Cudlipp doesn't know me from Adam Faith. Introduce me as your turf accountant or whoever.'

'So Cudlipp isn't your man at the *Mirror*?'

'Good Lord, no. We couldn't tap up him. Far too much his own man.'

Nudging Storey's elbow, Wright steered him past the linen coolie – tipping the boy for them both because these assets often had money worries (office joke) – and into the empty bar area, unused at breakfast, between the khazis and the restaurant.

'So are you blackmailing King now?' the reporter hissed. 'Though I don't really see how. He must have more money than MI5.'

'Some of the assets take money. Others like posh lunch and the sense that they're serving their country.'

Ignorance is weakness and Storey was a day-old kitten whose mama wouldn't give it the tit.

'King is *yours*?'

'Well, as a hack, Bernard, you'll know the palaver about not confirming or denying.'

'Cecil King is an *agent*?'

'Well, when people talk about agents, it always sounds so formal. A holster bulging under the armpit and a certain pedantry about how their cocktails are agitated. We prefer to think in terms of friends. Cecil King is a friend. You're a friend.'

Running an asset was like giving them a jigsaw. It had a

picture on the front they were creaming to complete but then they discovered that a couple of big pieces had dropped out of the box. He watched Storey trying to make the shapes fit together.

'But I got the impression you wanted me to stop King's plot?'

'Bernard, I'm going to tell you a story. About horses. A man owns two mounts. And they're up for the same prize. But one nag is – frankly – better than the other. And that isn't the only factor to interest a betting man. The second-best horse has a bit of wildness in him. He might suddenly rear up and scare the other runner: the one that ought to win. So, all in all, it might be no bad thing if the lesser gelding were to fall before the big race.'

That smarmy young bugger from the only show on television that got close to the truth about Henry Worthington – Frost, was it? – passed, on his way to the bathroom, presumably in the vain hope of wiping the smile off his face, although even the Savoy was unlikely to have the towels for that operation. The TV personality grinned at Storey and Wright, either because he thought he knew them or assumed they would know him.

Turning back, Wright saw that Storey had taken advantage of the cover of Frost to get away.

WHEN he got back to the table, his untouched food had gone. Storey assumed that Cudlipp must either have eaten it or taken offence at the delay but his host now clicked his fingers and the plate was returned under a silver dome, which was lifted to reveal the still unappetizing breakfast.

'I asked them to keep it warm for you. You were in there so long I thought you'd gone Liberace with that friend of Cecil's. I can tell you it's infuriating not knowing who he is.

I'm used to recognizing the whole clientele of the Grill. You didn't happen to chat to him in there?'

'No.'

Storey was finding that lying was like a sport or a hobby; a sense of progress gave you pleasure.

'When his friend was away, I caught a sight of Cecil off guard for a moment, not putting on a face for anyone. And he looked *broken*. I could blame myself for that, I suppose. Except that I think that whatever snapped in Cecil broke a long time ago. He used to fret about why he slept so much, nightcap on by nine and so on. And I wanted to say: look, you know, narcolepsy, and don't try to print that word in the *Mirror*, is the number one fucking symptom of serious depression.'

The Chairman scraped the last flakes of kipper from his plate and then seemed to hold them in his mouth until they melted. Cudlipp had stopped the conversation in order to eat but also perhaps for other reasons. In the talk of King's hidden unhappiness, Storey had a sense of a man scratching a scab. Cudlipp projected a relish for what he did and how he lived – happy in his skin, as the French expression had it – but he had been widowed twice, the second time by sleeping pills which might have been miscalculation or intent.

It had once been said that if you were ever frightened of Hugh Cudlipp in his office, you should think of him frightened in a coroner's office. He must carry the memories like lead in his bones. Or did all men secretly dream of their wives dying in middle age and leaving them free to remarry?

'When you go down to the House for us,' Cudlipp returned to their earlier conversation, 'one of the things I'd like you to do is to build bridges with Wilson and his gang. Being from the *Mirror* down there's going to be a bit like flogging the *Orangeman* in the Vatican for a while. There's a young chap at Downing Street called Kaufman, used to work for the *Mirror*. Maybe you could cultivate him. Of course, Marcia's the dream source for a Parly hack but she's pretty tricky.'

Storey took advantage of his recent elevation to ask the question: 'When I came to see you in your office, you said that Wilson definitely isn't the father of Marcia's kid. I don't suppose you're going to tell me who it is.'

Cudlipp suppressed a kipper burp, then smirked: 'No. I don't suppose I am. You know something I know, which is fine. But I'm your boss: it's good that I know something you don't know.'

The head waiter arrived unsummoned at their table and muttered: 'There's an urgent phone call for you, Mr Cudlipp, at reception.'

Left alone to dip toast in almost cold egg yolk, Storey was finally allowed a Poirot moment of reflecting on 'White's' revelations. The story of the two horses in the same race – a metaphor calculated to rattle a gambler – could only mean that King's plot against Wilson threatened to jeopardize a more official treachery.

King had gone beyond his orders. He was meant to ensure that the *Mirror* printed editorials dicking the Prime Minister but instead he'd booked the Royal Lancers for a bloodbath in the Mall. The spooks had used Storey to investigate and expose the rogue asset and blow his credibility. MI5 had wanted the plot to continue and implode.

And yet, by telling Cudlipp, Storey had surely threatened this strategy; the younger and wilier of the two newspaper tycoons might have told his superior not to be so stupid, preventing the humiliation of King the spies desired. Except.

Storey realized how clever the scheme had been. The main aim had been to find out if Cudlipp suspected his boss was

MI5, which – 'I don't think Mr King would need to be told any of this' – he clearly did. 'White' had gambled that Cudlipp, even if made suspicious, would not intervene. If he had realized that King was backing Mountbatten to run the country, Cudlipp would still have done nothing. He could only gain from his superior destroying himself.

The game 'White' played relied on seeing others' weaknesses. Storey's gambling, Cudlipp's ambition. They had turned these forces against their expendable asset: King.

And yet, unlike for Poirot, this was not the end of the story but the beginning of another. The weaker horse had fallen to clear the track for the thoroughbred: the plot against Wilson on which the security services were betting.

As Cudlipp came back to the table, flushed by something other than 9 a.m. champagne, he was already waving to the waiter for the bill.

'We'd better get back to Holborn Circus smartish, Bernard. News desk will need all the hands they've got. Bobby Kennedy's been shot.'

AFTER this month of assassinations and attempted regicide, Storey was woken at midnight by a call from the desk.

'Multi, can you get back here? One of your special subjects has died and we need a piece.'

'Wilson?'

'No, of course not fucking Wilson. The transplant guy. Fred whatever. Fred . . . *West*.'

So the dream of the renewable human was over. We would have to get by with the hearts we had.

Part Three

1969

Lessons in Enemies

The flowers are so gay, and the grass is so green,
The gardens have hedges, the pavements are clean,
The policemen are tall, and the people are neat
And sometimes they smile as they walk in the street.

Mary Wilson – 'On Returning Home'

21

Spilt Ink

MAKING HIS handwriting tiny – suspecting that all the diarists in the cabinet tried to read his notes upside down – he scribbled on the blotter: J. Harold Wilson.

That was how his name would be printed in the papers if he were American. President J. Harold Wilson said on Tuesday – no, said Tuesday, that was another of theirs, the lost preposition. These Yanks claimed to be classless but then went all Eton and Harrow about initials.

Every memorandum about the visit had referred to President Richard M. Nixon. Just as it had been Dwight D. Eisenhower (back in hospital this weekend after another coronary, surely the last). The M was for Milhous, Nixon's mother. That was another thing over there. He would have been Seddon, shrunken to President J. Harold S. Wilson said Tuesday. If they could, they made you just initials, like a code: JFK, RFK.

Britain's plain Harold Wilson turned his attention to the words of Richard M. Nixon, President for just a month after easily beating RFK's dull substitute, Hubert Humphrey.

'Let me turn now, Mr Prime Minister, to the question of student unrest in Europe.' Stoo-dent. Yurr-up. Nixon brushed his hand over that strange little separate square of hair which grew on his forehead and darted his tongue over lips which looked chapped. Wilson recognized in the President another leader who had been forced to teach himself public speaking, not a film-star politician like the Kennedys.

'It is easy to speak of youthful exuberance, of how political unrest is something with which our young people inevitably experiment: along with narcotics and fornication. Let me say that I see no reason for levity about any of these three although, for the moment, let me concentrate on protest. I would go as far as to say that anarchy on the campuses of Western Europe is weakening my hand in any negotiations over arms with Soviet Russia. The worst excesses of the French colleges have not yet reached America, but let me tell you that if they do my administration will not tolerate it.'

Brothers Jenkins, Healey and Wedgie Benn glowered at that. Nixon, though, grinned. He was an awkward man and one sign of this was a smile that seemed to happen at random, out of syncopation with the conversation, as if a bulb were timed to switch on at precise intervals, regardless of the light outside.

Nixon scratched his chin, with an audible rasp: despite all the cosseting a President got, he had a burglar's beard. Wilson had read the theory that Nixon's bristliness had helped Kennedy to look so good against him on television back in 1960. Campaigning was a catwalk now and not just in America. In the '66 election they'd made him change his shirt three times a day to look fresh for television. When he'd started, only your wife would stop you wearing the same one for a week.

'Mr Prime Minister, members of the cabinet, the remark is attributed to Marx that religion is the opium of the people. As a Baptist, I find the comment offensive; as a politician, I believe that the greater crisis in society today is that Marxism has become the LSD of the classroom.'

'Not just Marx, Mr President, Marcuse. *J'accuse* Marcuse,' Wilson intervened. Nixon smirked at him like he was

Jack Benny, though Mrs Castle and Mrs Hart looked grim. Judith said she had student sons and was reading Marcuse to understand them.

'The challenge to us all,' Nixon went on, 'is to construct a new religion – a new ideology – behind which our currently misguided young will march . . .'

Wedgie Benn raised his hand and was almost certainly on the verge of delivering a sermon about the Levellers when a bobby and a Secret Service agent burst in. They looked like creatures from different planets: the English policeman bald and fat in his uniform, the American gaunt and crew-cut in his dark grey suit.

'Mr President,' the latter said. 'We have to clear this room.'

THE WORD that the summit had been mysteriously inter-rupted – mysteriously been interrupted, Storey's internal revise sub told him – came from Waugh who, while going for a pee, had seen the cabinet trotting out into the lobby after they had been in with Nixon for only a few minutes. Though Bron affected amateurism, Storey was once more in awe of his colleague's ability to pick up stories: even a quick trip for a piss became copy for a column. Storey, in eight months as a political correspondent, had only ever been the beneficiary of more conventional leaks.

Green-baize tables had been set up in the Garden Room, now officially free of dry rot after years of redecoration. A stack of notepads, two telephones and three typewriters attempted to turn an entertainment room into a press centre.

These facilities were shared between the pol eds or pol corrs of the main newspapers, the Westminster columnists of the *Spec* and the *Staggers*, and the guys from the *New York Times*, the *Washington Post* and something called Knight-

Ridder, which sounded like a superhero from a comic book but was apparently a wire service.

The Yanks, who carried little portable Remingtons in monogrammed cases, were indifferent to the typewriters provided. The phone lines, however, obsessed them. The shootings of two Kennedys and Luther King had left them 'antsy' about how to file if Nixon was killed in England.

Now their concern was that the talks had been killed off.

'Auberon.' The Americans spoke the name with great solemnity, presumably taking him for some sort of lord or even a character in Shakespeare. 'Auberon, did the G-men seem panicked to you?'

Bron blinked: 'What would G-men be?'

'The Secret Service agents.'

'Ah. I asked Kafka's Castle . . .'

'Auberon, who is that?'

'Barbara Castle, she's a finance minister,' Storey explained.

'Auberon, does she have a middle initial?'

'I'm sure she would if she thought it would help. According to Mrs Kafka, the short-haired man said there was a "security situation".'

The three American reporters edged closer to the two telephones. The door opened and Storey predicted, 'This'll be Joe,' but, instead of the new Number 10 press man, they saw a tall, thin stranger who seemed to consist of different shades of grey: from the dark cloth of his suit to the neatly parted steel-coloured hair but, most of all, the entirely leaden complexion, from which all blood seemed to have drained.

'Excuse,' he began, then stopped, coughed and resumed: 'Excuse me, is Bernard' – pronounced Buh-*nard* – 'Storey here?'

When Storey identified himself, the visitor beckoned him closer with an imperious flick of the finger. The American leaned in close and spoke almost in a whisper: 'I'm Angleton. There's a story I'd like to share with you. Can you ring me at Claridge's tonight?'

'Are you a reporter?'

'Uh, sure. With the *Idaho Courier*.' Angleton handed over a card with the hotel phone number, urged, 'Call me,' and left.

'Who was the vampire?' Waugh asked.

'He says he's got a story for me. Which means it will be mad or libellous or both.'

'But you never know. Bakers would never despise dough. And hacks should not look down on gossip. It's where we start.'

Knowing that he was now doomed to ring Claridge's, Storey expressed surprise to the guy from the *New York Times* that the *Idaho Courier* would cover Nixon's visit but had received only half the reply – 'Well, you know, Buh-nard, I'm not sure if . . .' – when the deputy press secretary came into the room.

Joe Haines, with his short hair Brylcreemed back and wire-rimmed spectacles hardening an already strict expression, had the look of a fourth Kray brother, although the very opposite morals, operating as journalistic judge and jury over the reporters whose ranks he had so recently abandoned: Storey had known Haines as the *Sun*'s man on stories he was covering for the *Mirror*. It was said that Marcia had selected him for Number 10. She and Wilson believed they were being denigrated by the papers and wanted a press man who might bully the hacks.

'What is it?' Waugh asked. 'Did Harold drop his pipe and start a fire?'

'As you all know, sparks only fly from his ideas. And I expect the BBC will say that the Chancellor was lighting his farts or something similar. But, no, President Nixon's address to the cabinet has been interrupted because there's an intruder on the roof.'

HE GUESSED it was demonstrators again, like the students who'd thrown pennies at the windows of Claridge's all night. He'd briefed Ziegler to tell the press that the P had slept through it all but the fact was that he had been kept awake, even though he was tired from the flights and had left DC already weary after the long nights with Kissinger on the secret response.

'Will it be students, Mr Prime Minister?' he asked. He felt that he should use formal titles in front of the cabinet members, although they had been 'Dick' and 'Harold' the night before at the country house, the Brits' Camp David, which he at first thought was called Checkers, like the dog, until he'd seen it printed on the Visit of the President sheets: Chequers.

'It's possible, Dick, though we're well protected here.'

Wilson was indicating a pair of policemen in those blue domed helmets, standing behind the black door that seemed to lead right into the street. Why were English cops so goddam fat? The one he'd met at the Parliament building – the guy Ziegler had the idea of giving the White House pen to – was even called 'Tubby'. You would never think from the level of security that this country had endured a revolution in its history.

'Mind you,' the Prime Minister was saying, 'I expect the BBC is already broadcasting that the room had to be evacuated because I broke wind. I can assure you, by the way, Dick, that we've put in an official complaint over the coverage of the arrival yesterday.'

Ziegler had briefed him on this. An anchor at the BBC had criticized the visit, accusing Wilson of 'hogging the limelight' and of using expensive press secretaries to hide the truth. Wilson's flacks had complained to the broadcasters and now it was all over page one of the paper they called the *Mirror*.

'The word is that Dimbleby's going to apologize,' Wilson told him.

'Dimbleby? Is he the guy that did Churchill's funeral?'

'No, no, no. Richard's dead. Brain tumour.' Nixon had noticed that his host frequently mentioned illnesses and wondered if he was a bit of a sick-noter. 'This is his son. The Boy David.'

'Really? In British broadcasting, does the job pass down the family line at death?'

Wilson laughed: 'Well, not officially. But that's very good, Dick. I might steal it for the next time we're baiting the Chairman.'

Since Dallas, the Secret Service, at times like these, always formed a circle round the P, facing outwards, so, while the cabinet members conversed in throngs around the room, Nixon found himself alone with Wilson beside a fireplace. There was chessboard tiling on the floor and watercolours of Victorian London or oils of wigged aristocrats hung on the red-painted walls.

'Do you have to watch the CIA and FBI, Dick?' Wilson suddenly asked him, dropping his voice as if there might be a microphone in the carriage clock on the mantelpiece between them.

'What do you mean by watch?'

'Spies – and so on – making trouble for you? What we call dirty tricks.'

'The trick is for the President to know more about them than they do about the President. Do you feel threatened, Mr Prime Minister?'

Wilson was now leaning as close as if they were trying to

have a conversation at a ball game but, even so, Nixon could hardly hear him above the buzz from the gossiping politicians.

'Dick, I think they're trying to destabilize me. I shouldn't be at all surprised if this intruder on the roof has some connection with them. Embarrass the Premier in front of the President.'

The CIA, who had told him that Wilson was a Commie spy, would say that the British leader's claim of persecution by his security services was double bluff. But Dick Nixon had seen through Alger Hiss and it was hard to believe that Wilson was a Russian front. In their bilateral, the Prime Minister had practically begged him to keep US troops in Europe, whatever the demands of Vietnam.

Nixon lowered his own voice and advised: 'I think there are two rules of survival for a politician. Point one: know who your enemies are. Keep a list of them – paper or brain, doesn't matter – but keep it permanently updated. Point two is that you should always remember exactly what the other guy said. Keep a record if necessary.'

'You mean a diary or what?'

'Well, in Nixon's experience, a good politician always has a good memory . . .' He felt that fear flickered across the Prime Minister's eyes for some reason. 'But it may be sensible to keep another record.'

'Ha!' Wilson had restored his voice to its public level. 'The only records I keep are Gilbert and Sullivan LPs.'

Nixon, who considered the term 'small talk' one of mankind's most accurate descriptions, was delighted by this revelation of a connection between them and his enthusiastic smile must have given this away.

'You're a G&S fan, Dick?'

'Sure. In my college days, I was stage manager for a couple of productions.'

'Which?'

'*Pinafore* and *Pirates*.'

'Ah, I happen to be word-perfect on both of those, Dick.'

'I'd be surprised if I'd forgotten them myself, Mr Prime Minister.'

DURING the tiresome hiatus in the President's *tour d'horizon*, Jenkins was careful to position himself at the purlieus of the conversational pond – perhaps, alas, a rather shallow one – that had Barbara Castle at its centre. Wilson, isolated by the fireplace with Nixon, would almost certainly view these informal colloquies as cabals of potential plotters and so it was sensible to be spotted with an unquestioned loyalist.

Barbara was distracted: twice that evening, she had been called to the telephone over the latest strike at Ford's. Each time a messenger had come for her, Jenkins had wondered whether the summons was for him. Sterling remained mercurial, periodically lowered by another jeremiad in *The Times* from Cecil King, in retirement in Ireland.

But now Jenkins and Mrs Castle were turned away even from their diversionary topics for, as she told their little group: 'Flaming Nora, they're singing a duet!'

They turned, their movement matched throughout the room, towards the fireplace, where the Prime Minister was crooning: '*When I was a lad I served a turn / As office boy in an attorney's firm . . .*'

Jenkins clenched his face to avoid showing contempt for a social gaucherie which was entirely characteristic of Wilson. For all the inevitable vicissitudes in the Special Relationship, it was unthinkable that Churchill had ever sung indifferent operetta at Roosevelt. But, to his astonishment, Nixon,

flashing what had every appearance of being his least reflex-
ive grin of the evening, accepted the lyrical baton: '*I cleaned
the windows and I swept the floor / And I polished up the
handle of the big front door.*'

With improvisation that would have earned high marks
at RADA, the American President gestured at the appropriate moment to the gleaming black portal of Number 10,
then twisted the pointing hand towards Wilson, inviting him
to pick up, which he did: '*I polished up the handle so care-
fullee / That now I am the ruler of the Queen's Navee.*'

The chemistry between the two leaders more resembled
the centre court at Wimbledon than the stage at Covent
Garden: the duet was competitive, challenging the other man
to miss the return, which, to a small extent, Nixon now
did, in his next couplet. '*As office boy, I made such a mark /
That they gave me the post of junior clerk,*' he sang but,
by rhyming the final word with work in the American style,
broke the rhyme.

It was, anyway, the end of the performance because a
senior Special Branch policeman entered and crossed the
lobby, leading Wilson to remark: 'Oh dear, I think we may be
arrested for causing a public nuisance. The show is over,
ladies and gentlemen.'

Dick Crossman started a round of applause, which Jenk-
ins felt it politic to swell. The officer waited before saying:
'You can take your guest back to the Cabinet Room, Prime
Minister. The scare is over.'

'What was it?' Jenkins asked the sergeant. 'A student
prank?'

'Not a student, sir. A schoolboy.'

'Ah!'

There were two possibilities: a schoolboy unknown to him

had infiltrated Number 11 or – by the far the worse option –
the intruder had been resident.

'Age of fourteen, apparently. Clambered over the roof
from Number 11 to Number 10 to get a better view. You
might want to have a word with him.'

'Ah. I see.'

The amusement of a father clashed with a politician's
calculation of the embarrassment at being responsible for
this lacuna in the impromptu State of the Union address.

When they re-entered the Cabinet Room, Wilson, after
the narrowing of the eyes that generally signalled his jokes,
began: 'Though I have in the past sometimes feared an incur-
sion into Number 10 from the family next door, it was never
young Edward Jenkins I had in mind.'

He decided it would be unwise and churlish not to join in
the laughter prompted by Wilson's remark. The Prime Minister now asked the President to return to his meditation on
America's strategic interests.

The Downing Street catering staff had taken advantage of
the evacuation caused by the intruder to place silver coffee
pots on the table. As Nixon talked – 'Let me say that the position of this administration is to favour the United Kingdom's
application to join the European Common Market. In my
one-on-one with President de Gaulle tomorrow . . .' – Wilson,
with an instinct lying between the diplomatic and the maternal, poured his visitor some coffee, leaving the President the
preference of milk and sugar, which he nudged towards him
on a tray.

Nixon glanced down, nodded gratitude, then looked up to
resume his world-view – 'This administration and yours also
differ with President de Gaulle on the matter of US troops in
Europe . . .' – while diluting his drink with milk.

However, overestimating his dexterity while continuing to

meet the eyes of his audience, the President had mistakenly raised a crystal inkwell. Seeing this vessel unexpectedly tilted towards the beverage, Wilson, having presumably rejected the possibility of an eccentricity in the Californian diet, interjected: 'Er, no.' The President, possibly disoriented by what he took as the first hint of differences over NATO troop movements, became confused and succeeded in tipping the ink over his hands, his lecture notes and the cabinet table.

The President stared in horror at his stained hands. Sir Burke Trend, Cabinet Secretary, jumping up to summon governmental pumice stones and blotting paper, upended a jug of cream over his own trousers, either from clumsiness or in obedience to a Civil Service convention that embarrassment to a guest could be diminished by its replication.

As the Secret Service arrived with towels, the sleek agents now resembling waiters, Jenkins felt that he should try to break the silence.

'Ah, Mr President, in your predicament you somewhat resemble Pontius Pilate or Lady Macbeth.'

Arnold Goodman liked to claim that Wilson had only ever read one book for pleasure – a saga of Yorkshire life with little reputation outside that county – but he clearly understood Jenkins's literary references and, seeming to find them potentially offensive, glowered.

'Not that either is a precise historical comparison,' Jenkins stressed.

22

John Christ Angel Comes
to London

JOURNALISTS were killed by either their livers or their
lungs, so Storey had known some smokers. But Angleton of
the *Idaho Courier* seemed to have ambitions to become a sort
of human kipper.

Lighting his next cigarette from the still-glowing tip of its
predecessor, he kept in front of his face a constant fog which,
at its initial thickest, worsened a cough already occurring
every few words. The most phlegmy of these eruptions were
drenched in bourbon from a glass that he frequently lifted for
the barman to refill.

'You're lucky to get to stay at Claridge's with Nixon,'
Storey said, sipping a burgundy the American had ordered by
name, grimacing when his English guest had asked for a glass
of whatever red was going.

'Lucky in what way?' Angleton wheezed, suddenly sounding suspicious.

'When we travel with Wilson, Number 10 usually puts the
hacks in a hotel down the road.'

'Oh, right. Sure. Yeah, I generally get pretty close to the
President.'

'This story you said you had for me,' Storey prompted
him. 'Although I don't really understand why you can't print
it yourself . . .'

'Oh, well, that's because . . . excuse me . . .' Angleton's

voice had struck an unwanted falsetto note, which he lengthily tried to lower with coughs and alcohol. 'I'm sorry. Picked up some kind of virus on the airplane. The reason I came to you with this is that it's a story about England, really wouldn't play so big back home. Bernard, how long has the Third World War lasted?'

Unless the man opposite was a nutter, this was obviously a trick question, so Storey left it as rhetorical and let his host answer himself: 'The Third World War has been running for twenty-four years. It began on May 8th, 1945. It's a fight between democracy and communism.'

In his mind, Storey had given the *Idaho Courier* the weight of something like the *Sheffield Evening News* but it was hard to imagine a Yorkshire reporter lecturing a hack from the nationals in these apocalyptic terms. Perhaps, though, it was a reflection of their different systems. If a President had greater grandeur than a Prime Minister, then perhaps the status of a regional correspondent was also raised.

'Our opponents in this conflict – the Soviets – have staged their battle in three phrases,' the American journalist continued his editorial. 'They first penetrated Eastern Europe by invasion. Next, they achieved influence in Western Europe through the election of parties we are asked to call Euro-Communist, a euphemism that has always seemed to me rather like Safe Strychnine or Nice Diarrhoea. What we mean is Crypto-Communism. But, my friend, the most devious and dangerous phase was the election in at least two Western European nations of leaders who were, in fact, Soviet agents of influence. Your own Prime Minister, Harold Wilson, was put in position by the Kremlin. I have to say that I'm surprised you receive this information with a smile.'

Angleton began a bronchitic riff so loud and prolonged that it seemed likely to result in his lunch or even his lungs

staining the carpet of Claridge's bar. Reflecting on the madness, but also the familiarity, of the rant that caused these
spasms, Storey's first reaction was surprise that 'Patrick
White' should have attempted to spread his suspicions as
far as the *Idaho Courier*. Then he realized, with a slowness
lamentable in a hack but catastrophic in even a part-time spy,
that Jim Angleton, if that was his name, was not a reporter
for the Midwest American press.

This angry understanding was confirmed by the arrival
at their table of the white-haired spymaster, who drawled:
'Ah, good evening. Glad you chaps have met up. Should
I see if I can find you a cunning linctus for that chest,
Jim – you're a fan of cunning linctus, aren't you, Bernard?
Or are you treating it with whisky?'

JAMES Jesus Angleton. Christ, what a name. You couldn't
imagine folks calling their kid Jesus in England. The spicks
did it, although they said it Hey-zeus, which was different. If
the cousins used the same rules of 'light cover', then presumably his alias was John Christ Angel.

Jesus was apt enough for Angleton, though, because he
had the look of someone who had died at thirty-three and, in
this case, missed an Easter Sunday. Cigarettes were the nails
in his cross. Could barely say hello without sounding like the
orgasm of a porn-film whore. Instead of buying him a drink,
you wanted to stand him a cylinder of oxygen.

'Oh, hi, Pee . . .' wheezed Angleton but Wright cut in with:
'Patrick White.' Jesus H. Angleton registered slight surprise
at this name and Storey of the *Mirror* seemed to have picked
up the syllable of the given name, which Wright really wished
he hadn't. Running an asset was like having a dog. It was
good if he could do tricks but mainly you just wanted him to
walk, sit and shit.

Storey was staring at Wright like his dick was hanging out of his zip.

'So, who is this, then, "Patrick", if he isn't from the *Delaware Bugle* or wherever?'

'Bernard, I'd like you to meet James Jesus Angleton, chief of CIA Counterintelligence Staff.'

'Pee . . . Patrick's told me a lot about you,' John Christ Angel spluttered through his consumption.

Storey of the *Mirror* was looking ready to shoot a Kennedy so Wright smiled and said: 'Congratulations on the lad, Bernard. Rough old world to be born into but we're all the time trying to make it safer for him. What've you christened him?'

'Er, Dermot.'

'Your late father-in-law's name. That's touching. Wondered if you'd call him Cecil. Pretty much nine months, isn't it? Must have put it in the oven during all that?'

The happy daddy, though, seemed to want to change the subject.

'You said two? At least two,' his asset asked the cousin.

'Excuse . . .' A volley of coughs, like firing squad with sputum shooters. 'Excuse me?'

'You said "at least two Western European leaders" were Brezhnev's men. You've claimed Wilson. Who else?'

'Ah, ah, ah . . .' Another blue-movie climax. 'Willy Brandt of Germany.'

Wright nodded strongly to signal to Storey that he was getting the hooch from the top of the bottle but the hack snapped: 'And how do you know this? Because he wears red socks on holiday?'

'No, no. Intelligence. The, the, the . . . excuse me . . . the . . . the . . .' Oh, big boy, big boy, you're making me come. 'The Verona material . . .'

While the God-boy from across the pond fumbled for a bicycle pump to fill his lungs, Wright murmured a footnote: 'Soviet ciphers from WWII. London and Washington have been decrypting them for years.'

John Christ Angel could now spare the air to add: 'Brandt, though, is just part of the background pattern. It's Wilson I want you to focus on.'

'But "Patrick" here's already told me all this. And I didn't believe him.'

'Which, Bernard, is why I wanted you to meet Jim. I know how partial you and Mrs Storey are to things American.'

Storey was a cocky bugger but, at that, he looked like a politburo boss told he would get the same bread rations as his people. Wright imagined him visualizing spies watching as he went apple-bobbing in the Irish forest.

'Buh-nard,' the Yankee son of God rasped. 'Pee . . . Patrick and I shared the handling of Anatoliy Golitsyn . . .'

'Gollywog,' Wright added.

'. . . when he came over from the Soviets in '63. We had him first in Langley but he wished to come to Britain . . .'

'Mrs Golitsyn had nightmares under her skirts. Her curse was like a haemophiliac's nosebleed,' Wright remembered. 'Someone had told her the best snatch-doctors were in London. While Harley Street's finest hunted around in her Russian muff, I put the world to rights with "John Stone". That was the cover name Jim's boys had given him . . .'

'You know, that's classified. Are you really sure you should . . . ?'

'I trust Bernard like I trust my right hand, though both do a certain amount of wanking around. As a result of what "John Stone" told us, London opened the "Worthington" file. Our American cousins started . . .'

'Operation Oatsheaf,' God-boy managed to say and was

even able to continue: 'You say you doubted what . . . our MI5 source here told you. Let me tell you, my friend, that American intelligence is firm on this. In fact, new information from a Polish defector-in-place is that Mossad was isolating lupus as a virus in the years before Gaitskell was murdered . . .'

'Now you're saying the Israelis killed the Labour leader?'

This was new to Wright but made perfect sense. The Wilson administration, after all, was government by snipcock. But John Christ Angel was already breaking that tablet of stone.

'No, no, Buh-nard. No one's saying Mossad killed Gaitskell. But if Tel Aviv was cultivating lupus, then it's logical to assume the KGB could have been as well.'

'Wilson's a wrong 'un,' Wright reiterated. 'It's as simple as that. No one who had made twelve trips to Moscow should have become Prime Minister!'

'His election expenses were paid by Kremlin gold,' came confirmation from the CIA.

'You know Marcia's pregnant again, Bernard? Their second's due in June. That's why she wasn't at the Nixon thing tonight. Under the doctor.'

'This is mad stuff!' Storey of the *Mirror* was on his feet as quickly as a shop steward during productivity discussions. 'As it happens, a friend of mine who works for *Private Eye* . . .'

'The Brideshead Boy, you mean . . .'

'Says the father of her kids is the political editor of the *Daily Mail* . . .'

'And you think that's a *more* likely story, Bernard?'

'I'm going.'

Jesus looked peeved, snapping, in a tone that was anything but Christian: 'Well, I'm telling you that this is the song the Camptown Ladies sing . . .'

A PENNY hit his head, with a sting so sharp he thought it had cut him. But though his fingers found wetness on his brow it was only the sweat that had collected there during his meeting with paranoiacs from both sides of the Atlantic.

The line of police was losing ground as it tried to shove the ruck of anti-Nixon protestors beyond coin-chucking distance from the hotel front. Storey knew that he should talk to cops and students and file a piece but the instincts of an enthusiastic reporter had been engulfed by the worries of a reluctant spy. So he wandered, absorbed in self-pity, along Brook Street towards Grosvenor Square, from where he could hear the yelling of another demonstration outside the American Embassy.

The allure of the espionage world was that it suggested the possession of secrets but, in the encounter with 'Angleton' and 'Patrick'–Peter, Storey had come to understand that it meant the loss of all your private knowledge. Angleton's quotation from 'The Camptown Races' revealed that he knew the weakness that had made Storey an agent. 'Patrick' (probably Peter) had known about Dermot's birth and why he had that name. Most disturbing, though, was the reference to his 'American' interests.

The most tolerable possibility was that they had merely read his many cuttings about the US, the secondary terror that spooks had broken into his home and seen the shelves of American fiction there. The worst interpretation was that the flat was wired and the secret state had actually been bugging their cunnilingus.

And apart from stripping him of his privacy, the double briefing at Claridge's had removed Storey's indifference to the Wilson allegations: not because he believed that the British Prime Minister or the German Chancellor really were on the Soviet payroll but because the monstrous gossip now seemed to have deluded two – perhaps at least two – intelligence services.

Naked in the invisible world, Storey headed for the bus that would take him home to the son whose name and birth date had been filed away by spies. But, then drawn in by a peripheral flash of brown hoardings, he walked towards the first secret he had kept from his wife. His luck today could not get any worse.

THE London air was suffocating. It was a wonder Limeys didn't carry tanks on their backs like divers. Peter Wright was always saying it was better – they'd just passed this Clean Air Act – but it was still like being in Dickens, the sky all smoke or clouds or both. People kept telling him it was the cigarettes that wrecked his lungs but it was England.

'Thank Christ I can stop calling you Patrick,' he said to Wright. 'Confusing, isn't it? At the Agency, we mainly use our real names. Nobody knows who the fuck we are, anyways.'

Wright waved to the waiter for another of those pink gins he drank. Angleton tilted his bourbon glass to show the guy it was dry. Sipping the refill, he asked his British counterpart: 'The reporter? You're sure he's tenable as an asset? He seems a little, well, dismissive. Is he discreet?'

'No, he's not, old boy. Which is the point. There are targets you choose because they keep their mouths shut and others because they open them as wide as a Korean street-walker. Storey talks. And we want the ballad of Henry Worthington sung from the battlements. Even if he's telling people it's ridiculous, maybe he'll tell someone who thinks it's not. Where's Nixon on this?'

'Tricky Dick says Wilson's more anti-communist than he is. We haven't yet convinced him that's a classic tactic of distraction. Like the Prague Spring.'

'Well, exactly,' Peter Wright agreed with him. 'Where are you on Kissinger?'

'Nixon's not sold on that either. We've shown him every page of the dossier. I mean, a German Jew for alarm bells one and two. A German Jew who speaks of making peace with Russia and China and – this is the olive in the martini, Peter – insists on meeting their officials alone. I think that's the clincher, isn't it? If he went and fucking married Mata Hari, he couldn't send a bigger signal.'

Angleton stopped and looked around the bar but there was no one he recognized from the Presidential party or the embassy; just a few old Brits hoping to buy a fuck from a younger woman with a couple of drinks. He leaned towards Wright and whispered: 'Kissinger's going to bomb Cambodia.'

'Remind me, Jim, are you at war with Cambodia?'

'The North Vietnamese have training camps there. If we can't get the enemy, we go for the enemy's friend and hope the American people won't see the difference.'

'Bravo! Little yellow buggers won't see that coming! Funny, though, that wasn't on the brief we got of Nixon's Chequers chat with Worthington.'

'It wouldn't be. It's eyes only Dick and Henry. Aren't our leaders sweet, the way they think they have their secrets? Kissinger and the Pentagon mapped it out on Monday. Met in Air Force One on the ground in Brussels, while Nixon was at NATO. They decided the plane was "secure". But secure from who?'

The shouts of the long-haired college Maoists outside reached the pitch of a scream but the whinnying of police horses could be heard above them. Why the fuck did the British cops think that jockeys could stop a riot? Let's see how long the 'ideals' of these mop-heads would survive the sight of a gun.

What Angleton had to say needed to be whispered but he was forced by the noise outside to speak louder than he wanted: 'Peter, I've got new information. I can't tell you precisely from where. But let's say down Mexico way. The final proof that Wilson is a Soviet agent-in-place.'

'Well, that's cracking, old chap. Let me have it.'

'Peter, if we pass this on, I need your solemn promise. That London will tell no one.'

'No one? Well, I'd think the Queen and the *Daily Telegraph* might have a right to know, for starters.'

'I'm serious, Peter. If I tell you this, then it never leaves the files of MI5.'

'But that's bonkers, old boy, isn't it? It's like having a fifteen-inch dick and becoming a monk. Why can't we tell anyone?'

'That's the deal, Peter. Take it or leave it.'

'Leave it, then, Jim. Call this kettle and pot, old chap, if you want. But is it possible that you're taking this paranoia and secrecy too far? If you can't trust me, who can you trust?'

But Angleton had trusted Philby. Philby, his best friend in London before Wright, had also called him 'old chap' and drank with him in hotels – all varnished wood and heated towel rails – and lied to him that they were on the same side. Fool me once, shame on you; fool me twice, shame on me. That was why he couldn't breathe in London. You felt Kim's work everywhere. Wright and he both believed that there was another mole, a second Philby, in British intelligence now. Wright had tried for years to find him. Angleton suddenly saw, bright as a flare in a prairie sky, the possibility that Wright had failed to find the traitor because hunter and hunted were one and the same. Kim's work.

'I'm sorry, Peter. My rules or no game.'

'Well, I wouldn't worry, old chap. The way things are

going – the pound and the brothers in the car plants and so on – 1970 will be the last date on Henry Worthington's grave. Operation Oatsheaf closed.'

Angleton had the very rare and worrying experience of being told something he didn't already know. There had been nothing of this in the cables from London Station.

'Next year? You're that close to exposing him?'

'He's exposed himself. As it were. Oh, missus, don't.' Wright often did this, sometimes seeming to be addressing phrases to an unseen third presence in the conversation. Angleton wondered if he was wired and speaking in some kind of code to Control. 'No, Jim, this is no secret. Harold Wilson's going to lose the next election.'

Part Four

1972 / 1974

Men of Destiny

The shining eyes and claws
Of all the hunted creatures
Are sharpening for a kill:
Crows and wolves and vultures
And every animal
That was my victim ever.
I'm at their mercy now.
This is my last stand
And I haven't an arrow even.
All I've left is a wound.

Seamus Heaney (after Sophocles)
— *The Cure at Troy*

23

The Temple of Glory

HAVING DINNER with Hitler – a Führer who had survived to live out his old age in exile – was, he supposed, the nearest historical equivalent to these meals.

'C'est la maison ici, Monsieur King?' the driver asked.

'Oui. C'est là,' he agreed, pointing down the lane towards the house. King deliberately made no attempt at a native accent. He had disguised his facility for the language as a precaution against the driver making conversation all the way from Nice. He preferred to read his day-old *Times*, with its horror stories of Heath's futile obduracy against the unions.

'Le Temple de la Gloire!' exclaimed the driver when they were close enough to read the name-stone.

'Oui. Il étais fabriqué par un général de l'Empereur Napoleon.' King lacked the interest and probably the French to explain that the successful general had commissioned the building to celebrate victory at Hohenlinden in 1800. King assumed that the general in question had been either humble in victory or short of funds because the home he had raised as a trophy was modest and economical: living accommodation in a small central block, with stunted rooms on either side containing bedrooms and necessities.

Drawn by the sound of the car, his host stood on the steps of the portico. Although the early spring air still held a nip of winter, he was wearing an unbuttoned shirt, as usual, presumably because the polo-necked sweater had caused him such problems in the past.

In old age, the face was still recognizable from the news-reels and campaign posters: the square, flat brow and bloated nose which – if you hadn't known him and his views – you might have thought was Jewish. The moustache, which most men would have shaved off as an act of distance if not disguise, defiantly remained, though grey and roughly trained. The height was always a surprise. While it was true that most men seemed little to King, he thought of Tom as a particularly small man, perhaps because of some historical connection with Hitler and Mussolini, pint-pot demagogues.

The French peasant housekeeper served pink champagne in the first-floor drawing room, sent into a flurry of shrugs when King insisted on water. (Tom always forgot his guest's temperance, perhaps because his survival mechanism was to deny himself memories.)

'Cheers, Tom.'

'Your health, Snow.'

There was drink King missed and drink he was glad to miss; he had always considered pink champagne somehow juvenile, the strawberry taste recalling fruit cordials.

Diana was away in Paris seeing lawyers (King recalled a reference in *The Times* to a television film about the Mitfords and wondered if that was what concerned her) and Dame Ruth was occupied with concerts in London, so the two men would eat alone. But King was in some ways happier with this arrangement. In the absence of the women, both more sociable and anecdotal than their husbands, the lunch would have the feel of a political summit: Chequers, Camp David, the Temple of Glory.

Tom, however, was initially disappointing, laying out oft-heard exonerations as if King was a hippy interviewer from the BBC. He insisted once again that he had never been anti-Jewish or pro-German, nor approved of the violence to which some of his supporters had resorted. 'I know this,' King tried to silence him, although it was his opinion that Tom protested too much. It was only over lunch – a rabbity cassoulet dished up with a claret that the crone again tried to force on him – that the conversation reached affairs of state. 'The sense we have from here, Cecil, is that the centre cannot hold in Britain.'

'Yes. It remains my view that a world financial crisis is inevitable, even with Wilson gone. I made the point in Paris to Pompidou, who remains irritatingly sanguine on the matter. In Britain, there is also the distraction of prospective anarchy. The student body is docile but Heath has been bombed into direct rule of Ireland. My own view is that Dr Paisley is the kind of strong leader Ireland needs but this opinion is not widely shared. As you know, Tom, it has long been my opinion that Britain must ultimately depend on military discipline. If our troops are bogged down in the six counties, the communists may see their opportunity. Increasingly, I see it as the oddest – and perhaps luckiest – aspect of our present century that the Russians and the Chinese fell out with each other. If they had fallen in together, think what power they might have wielded.'

'What do you make of Edward Heath, Snow?'

'Dame Ruth is fonder of him than I am. She says he's knowledgeable about music. My point is that the Soviets will not be deterred by our Prime Minister's record collection. He's certainly a more cultured man than Wilson. I lunched at Heath's Albany flat and he had the most exquisite collection of porcelain figures of horses from the Spanish Riding School in Vienna. He cannot, though, ride those into battle. I see him as no exception to the general crisis of leadership.'

King's host nodded vigorously at this and there appeared for the first time during this encounter that curious look in

his eyes that came and went. It was a certain cloudy occlu-
sion, like an instant cataract, that, strangely, Enoch Powell
also had. Was it this tic that gave such men the name of
visionaries? Certainly, it was in the moment of the wild light
in the eyes that Tom, an old man living in France, became,
again, Oswald Mosley.

'I think you're right, Cecil, in your certainty of an emergency. The present times remind me of the 1930s. There has
been no economic setback as apparent as 1929. But perhaps
the devil will arrive in disguise this time. I think you are right
that a moment of vacuum is approaching. We must be ready.'

This inclusivity wrong-footed King. Was it really possible
that Mosley saw his way back? King had once considered
him for a position (Minister for Europe, perhaps) in the
Emergency Government but his favoured cabinet ministers
had all considered this beyond the pale. And that was when
the disparity in their status permitted King to be charitable.
Now he must be careful of their being seen as ridiculous
twins, a Dad's Army of lost leaders.

'Do you still see yourself as a player, Tom? It's been a long
time.'

That fogging of the gaze again: 'I'm seventy-five, Snow.'
Only four years older and yet King associated him with
ancient days. 'Adenauer came to power at seventy-four and
was still influential at ninety-one.'

'There's hope for us all, then, Tom.'

'What do you miss most, Snow, since they, ah, deposed
you?'

It was the loss of influence King most abhorred. The feeling that millions were listening to him, that he could give
orders to thousands.

'This risks sounding sentimental, Tom, but the sense of
making a difference is what I regret. I thought when I retired

that some charity would ask me to be chairman. I was ready to be useful but no one asked me to be.'

While King picked at some near-putrid cheese, Mosley smoked. His hands were trembling, from nerves or simple age or maybe Parkinson's. The son – a fashionable novelist, apparently, who King had seen on television – had a terrible stutter and the seed of it was there in the father's speech: a little shiver at the beginning of some words.

'I often w-wonder, Snow, w-why is it that you come to see me? Not, I assume, just because we are both Wykehamists.'

'Hah! Hardly. I have made a point of avoiding – or thwarting – those who prospered at that frozen place of doorless lavatories.'

'That is, I agree, a particular humiliation. So, if not Winchester, w-why?'

Because King had made a secret study of Mosley and Powell, hoping to emulate their patriotism and charisma but not their mistakes. Because there was so little leadership of any kind these days that even abandoned mavericks were to be learned from. Because, in truth, he knew what an eye-catching entry the old blackshirt might make in the index of a published diary. 'Because, Tom, I suppose, I hate the way that men are written off in England. Even before it happened to me.'

King looked carefully at a watch that – he omitted to tell his host – had once belonged to the uncle who in 1934 had backed the British Union of Fascists on the front page of the *Daily Mirror*, therefore earning his nephew's contempt but perhaps transmitting a dangerous lesson in editorial impact.

'I'd told the driver to come back about now, Tom.'

'But it's barely afternoon. There are many things I still hoped to discuss.'

'I should have liked that. It's just that it's a long trek back and . . .' Reluctant to show weakness in front of another man he decided, knowing that their acquaintance could not survive the betrayal he was planning, to give a final gift of intimacy. 'It's just that I find I turn in earlier and earlier these days. It's not unusual for me to be asleep by dusk.'

'Oh, dear. Are you ill? Have you asked them to look at your prostate? That starts with tiredness.'

'No. It's not that. I'd always wondered why I . . . why I needed so much night. I'd always hoped to be one of those men who played poker until midnight, then rose to gallop their horse at four. It was something Cudlipp said on the day it all ended. That needing sleep was a primary symptom of depression. I now fear that he was correct. All my life, I failed to enjoy things while I had them. It means that there is no consolation of memory when they're gone.'

Though Ruth had insisted that such admissions were therapeutic, he had not found his one particularly helpful but, in the see-saw way of human nature, Tom seemed to have gained strength from his friend's declaration of weakness.

'We must be ready, Snow,' Tom said, the last words of their long friendship. King looked into the trancelike stare without reply.

Mosley waved from the portico as the car flattened the tracks it had earlier raised in the gravel. Was it just fancy that he seemed careful not to raise his right arm too high?

'C'est un ami, Monsieur?'

King feigned deafness behind *The Times*. He imagined the anger – the ostracizing hatred – of Tom and the others when the Diaries were published and they realized they had let a spy into their life.

24

Extra Time

HESFORD, Craig, *Mountford*. Mountford. Craig, *Mountford*. Mountford. Wembley, anyway. Definitely Wembley. 1–0 to Preston and after extra time, which was unusual. Hadn't happened since. Had happened before to the Town, when he was a babbie.

Hesford, Craig, Mountford. It began with a W, didn't it? Shadow of his own name. Wil. Will. Willingham. Hesford, Craig, Mountford, Willingham. Young? If only. Hesford, Craig, Mountford, Willingham, Young. Young. Young.

'I expect most of the people in here are asking for extra time, Doctor.'

'"Mr", in fact, Prime Minister. I'm sorry, when you say "extra time" . . . ?'

'What we were saying about football. I thought I . . . You know that thing where you think you've said something and . . .'

Oh, don't give me that look like a tick on a list. This isn't a symptom. Ever since I was a little lad, sitting at table with Mam and Da and Marjorie, I'd have a thought so strong I'd think I'd spoken it. Mary had it too, said poets went into a sort of trance. A lot of them smoked things, though.

Willingham, Young. Boot. Always an easy one. Born to be a footballer, Da used to say. One thousand three hundred and two multiplied by seven hundred and seven, Harold. Quick before she brings the custard. I have noted my honourable friend's question and, with his permission, will place an answer in the House of Commons library in due course. Young, Boot. Boot. Name of the first man you beat, though different. The 13th Earl. Hulme. Hesford, Mountford, Willingham, Young, Boot, Hulme. Missed one. Hulme was seven.

'Prime Minister, I'm going to ask you a series of questions.'

'Sure. That's what I do. PMQs. They say I never answer them but I'll do my best for you, Doctor . . .'

'When did you first become aware of the deterioration you mentioned to Sir Joseph?'

'I'm sorry. What was the question?'

(Eric had said that timing was about knowing when not to speak as well as when to come in. There were the woofers, the word-play, they got straight away. My aunt's got a Whistler. Now there's a novelty. And then there were the slow-burn jokes that were about letting it grow. That ticking look again.)

'That was a joke, Doctor. Mister. When I did *Morecambe and Wise* the last time, Eric said I had a future in it. Perhaps I'll need it, depending on today. What were we saying? Figure of speech. What it was was – what I said to Joe, Sir Joseph Stone – was . . . Ma always used to call me and Da the Memory Men. Marjorie called us – by which I mean me, I seem to be getting more Yorkshire these days – the fat little abacus. What it was was I've always had football teams off pat. Huddersfield Town's FA Cup Final teams . . .'

'Really? With respect, Prime Minister, I wouldn't think they'd take up much brain-space . . .'

'What? Oh, no, when I was growing up, it wasn't like now. It was a surprise if the Town weren't in the Final. Five times between . . . in the '20s and '30s. I think the Pope – it is the Pope, isn't it? – has a chap who walks behind the throne, whispering that all this will go. Me, I think of Huddersfield Town.'

Mutch, Wood, Bullock, Slade, Wilson. Wilson. Wilson. Stamford Bridge, anyway, that year.

'I see. Tell me, were they in the Final in, say, 1925?'

'Um, let me see, er, no. They *were* in . . .' Easy one, Wall Street Crash. '. . . in 1929/30.'

'And what was their team that day? Can you tell me now?'

'Ah. Righto. They lost to Arsenal. Turner would have been in goal. Turner, Goodall, Spence, Naylor, Wilson . . . Wilson . . . Wilson. I keep wondering if it's significant, Doctor, that it's my own name I get stuck on. Like trying to hang two coats on the same peg . . .'

'Overload. Yes, it's an interesting image. Is that what it feels like when it happens?'

'What it most feels like, to be honest, no jokes about the pound in your pocket, please, is when you've lost your wallet. You put your hand in your coat, knowing it's going to be there because it always is, and . . .'

That was the best he could do. It was exactly like that: the same heart and stomach spasms when you felt the absence.

'And when did you first feel that you were losing recall?'

'Oh, when we were back in Opposition in 1970. I knew there were some teams I couldn't do anymore so I stuck to the others. When Heath got into trouble, I even wondered if I should stand.'

'Obviously, I know more about you than I do most patients, but did I read somewhere – I sound like Mr Michael Parkinson, don't I? – am I right that your mother died young . . . ?'

'Younger than my da. But he made eighty-nine. She was seventies. It was cancer, in the end, but . . .'

'But. Had her doctors ever mentioned dementia?'

'Her doctors? *Doctor*, you mean. I'm the first in my family to have more than one. I'd say Mam was forgetful.

It started as a joke. Later, you found you'd stopped making the jokes . . .'

'Do you find you're drinking more than you used to?'

'Well, how do you know how much I used to?'

'I wouldn't need to. I'm simply asking you if you feel the present quantity is greater?'

'No, you're right. As a mathematician, I should have known that. What I say to people is . . .'

'So people have raised it with you . . . ?'

'An eyebrow here, an eyebrow there. Is that a line from G&S or have I made it up? What I say to people is that this time as Prime Minister I'm more relaxed, know where the bodies are buried. So I might be more inclined to sip a glass of brandy with my boxes of an evening.'

'Sip. Glass. Are these firm terms?'

'Oh, I'm sure I'm better than Churchill. In that respect. A Prime Minister couldn't function properly if he were drunk, I'm sure.'

'Do you sleep well?'

'No. But no doctor could help me there. Our four years in Opposition, Joe Haines once said he'd discovered what it was like to sleep for eight hours without being woken with bad news.'

'In Sir Joseph's notes to me . . . you have frequently complained of anxiety?'

'Again, I may not be an ordinary patient. I don't mean in terms of being important. But . . . there's an old joke which is no joke to me. I'm not paranoid: people really are out to get me.'

'Prime Minister, I think we should do some tests.'

Boot. Hulme. Hulme, Isaac, Macfadyen, Barclay, Beasley. 1–0 to the Villa. After extra time.

Part Five

1974/1975

Slag/Bitch

And in that town a dog was found,
As many dogs there be,
Both mongrel, puppy, whelp and hound
And curs of low degree.

Oliver Goldsmith – 'Elegy on
the Death of a Mad Dog'

25

Lady Slagheap

WHEN STOREY came out of *Mirror* HQ in a white flannel suit and matching jockey cap, Wright assumed his asset had turned queer or mad or both. The hack got into a vintage convertible – a Bugatti, Wright would have wagered, had he been the betting man – where he was joined by a young woman in a floaty hat and the kind of dress that they called flapper but should have been slapper.

Following them through traffic in a cab, Wright thought it looked like a wedding. The girl, however, was certainly not the solid colleen who had rights on Storey's Y-fronts and, though surveillance had slackened off from the days when they practically had his backside tapped, a divorce or even a supernumerary screw would still have made a page in his file.

The Bugatti stopped in Oxford Street. When Wright, from a doorway far too close to be good trade-craft, heard Storey shout, 'Hello, old sport!' apparently at random passers-by, he felt a shiver of ignorance, although it inevitably took him some time to recognize the sensation.

THOUGH the seriousness of the situation was not in doubt, some cheer came from the blessed absence of satirical light music from the stereogram.

'Prime Minister, it is always my duty to say to a client that the law in Britain means that litigation for defamation most resembles an experimental medicine. Beneath what seems to

be a rapid improvement in the situation may be hidden symp-
toms of a deeper damage.'

'Sue them, Arnold.'

THE SECOND phone call came, like the one that had
started the whole saga, at breakfast time. Patrick White
seemed to be an early riser. Or perhaps, thought Storey, who
had become an expert in suspicion if not spying, it was easier
to record calls at a hotel and his home than at the *Mirror*
office, which was regularly swept for bugs since the circulation struggle with the *Sun* had begun.

'Bernard,' 'White' began, as soon as Storey answered. He
never bothered with 'Is that?' or 'Can I?' 'Sorry for it being
thrush-fart and all but the yarn is getting better by the minute.
I have accounts of Slag Ltd for the last two fiscal years. Yours
for not even a thank-you.'

'I've told you. Even if the stuff you give me stands up, the
desk won't want it. Every time we move on this story, Lord
Goodman lumbers into view like Frank Cannon chasing a
drug baron.'

The light in the hall flickered and Storey heard Dermot
cheer from the kitchen. His generation were the new Vic
torians, Heath's three-day week and power cuts making
electricity a miracle again.

'You couldn't speak up, could you, Bernard? I'm on a
station.'

'No, I can't speak up. You're a secret here, it might amuse
you to know. '

'Look, why's the *Mirror* pussyfooting? The Millhench
letter is a direct link between Wilson and Mrs Slagheap's
brother.'

'Yes. But the fact that a name is on something doesn't

mean it's real. You sign letters to me "Patrick White" but that's not who you are.'

'So you're suddenly Isaiah Berlin? Bernard, Mrs Slagheap's brother is married to Lord Kagan's secretary. Tell me you think that's just a love-match. Bernard, did I tell you, I know someone who met Lester Piggott at a Newmarket do? He was full of a mount called . . .'

'You're flogging a riderless horse there, "Patrick". I've left the William Hill stable.'

'Really? Oh, everyone likes a flutter.'

'Not as much as you liked a flutterer. I don't run in your colours anymore.'

'Bernard, you can have this for free. No obligations, just, in the rest-home at the end, you don't want to be thinking that you missed the British Watergate . . .'

Storey put down the telephone. Though they were becoming used to the strange, chirruping ring – no longer confusing it with birdsong and rushing downstairs to find the instrument silent – the receiver still felt small and flat in his hand. The Trimphone, with its smooth lines like something from a moon movie, had been marketed as a space-saver, although the Wandsworth house was the biggest they had ever owned. The phone almost had the hall to itself.

He went back into the kitchen where Dermot and Jack were playing a game of Six-Day War over the cornflakes packet, with Moira reluctantly cast as Henry Kissinger. Her frown asked who the early caller had been. Because she had been raised in a country of letters and yells, a ringing telephone before ten in the morning or after ten at night still meant to her an auntie with a stroke or a story that would leave her alone for days with the boys.

'A tipster,' he said, almost truthfully. 'With a story,' he

added speedily, and needlessly, as he believed that he had kept his first vice from his wife.

'So why were *you* whispering, then?'

Her scolding tone provoked Dermot to crow: 'Daddy been naughty. Smack bottom.' Jack, who was as alert to mentions of bums as a surveillance agent to the word bomb, started playing Ringo Starr with his spoon.

'Was I whispering? Oh, you know how it is when the other person's whispering. It's hard not to.'

'Yes, isn't it? I think it's called pillow talk.'

Storey knew she thought he had women. And there had been one: in the year when Moira was off sex after Dermot, the redhead in features, who he'd screwed partly to see if her muff was the same colour (which it had been, what was left of it: she had shaved it in the shape of a heart, in the style attributed to Mary Quant). His next two intended mistresses had turned him down: too old, too married or because his first lover had put it round the office that his dick had been half-limp from guilt. But, grumpily monogamous again, he still preferred his wife to hate him as a philanderer than as a spy or a gambler.

The mating call sounded from the hall again. There had been a little piece in features about how birds had begun to imitate the Trimphone, believing it to be some new suitor.

'Is she missing you already?' Moira hissed.

He was trying to work out how to shout at White to leave him alone without raising his voice and giving his wife confirmation that he was having an affair, But, this time, it was the news desk.

'Multi? Sorry to call so early, mate.'

'No, that's fine. Paper can call me whenever they want.'

'Wouldn't let that get around. Why are you shouting?'

'Am I?'

'Yeah. Look, there's a colour piece we're keen on. Wanted to catch you before you leave for the House. Wilson's staging a stunt at Marcia's place. Show of support, sending round Joe Haines and a bunch of flowers or something. All because the lady loves Black Magic. Can you get there? Wyndham Mews, off Marble Arch. Just follow the smell of hacks who've been camping out all night.'

Storey repeated the address and wrote it on the phone-pad. Moira, opening the door between kitchen and hall, asked who lived at Wyndham Mews and, when he told her, gave a smile that labelled him a liar.

'It's this slag business,' he insisted.

'I bet it is. Have a nice time with your slag, then.'

As the morning traffic crawled out towards the bridges, he listened to the 8 a.m. news on *Today*. Downing Street had again insisted the Prime Minister had no personal connection with a controversial land deal involving one of his closest aides. A spokesman had also warned that further writs could be issued against newspapers in connection with this matter. Preparations were continuing in Paris for the state funeral of President Pompidou, which would be attended by Mr Wilson, President Nixon and other world leaders. In Washington, another prominent Republican senator had called on President Nixon to resign over the scandal result-ing from an alleged cover-up of a break-in at the headquarters of his political opponents.

Storey switched over to Noel Edmonds, but he was play-ing 'Seasons in the Sun'. Perhaps it was inevitable, in middle age, that he would become intolerant of pop but it really did seem to him that something had gone wrong with the songs after the Beatles split. How was it possible that Terry Jacks's dirge about terminal illness was number one?

We had joy, we had fun, we had seasons in the sun. He

switched over to Terry Wogan, but hit the middle of the current number two, the only song more sentimental than the cancer ballad he had just escaped. *Billy, don't be a hero, come back and make me your wife.*

It was perhaps a record with a message for a troubled husband trying not to be a spy. Storey stopped at the next phone box and called to ask if Sir Hugh was free to see him.

WHAT hurt her most was the feeling that they were pulling down the fences she had built around herself. In the ten years now since Harold had won the first election, she had kept two things private: her home and her sons. Now both were under siege.

She had drawn all the curtains against the scum – she meant scrum, no she didn't – of monkeys outside but the flashes continued. She knew enough about newspapers to realize that, denied her frightened face at the glass, the snap for the splash would be the covered windows, making her look like a guilty prisoner.

She had to stay away from the hallway, in case they tried for a shot through the letterbox, which flapped open every so often as one of the hacks yelled through a question: 'Marcia, are you going to resign?' Or: 'Marcia, how often had you met Ronald Millhench?' And: 'How much money did you make from your brother's company?' Plus, inevitably: 'Has Mr Wilson rung you?'

Yes, he had. Of course he had. He was the kindest of men, when that cunt Haines wasn't making him selfish, taking Harold away from the people who looked out for him. Haines had called as well to warn her *The Times* was threatening to print some stuff about her sons. She didn't know if the hacks would rat on their dad as well. Haines had said he was sorry. She bet he fucking was. Onion tears didn't begin to cover it. A crocodile stuffed with onions.

She was glad the telephone was in the lounge but kept her voice low because she had to assume they were listening at her windows. The scum wouldn't have the equipment but there were the spooks to worry about as well.

When she dialled the study number, it diverted to the switchboard.

'This is Marcia. I need to speak immediately to the Prime Minister.'

'Excuse me, could you speak up, please?'

'No, I can't speak up. I may be in considerable danger. I must speak to Harold at once.'

'The Prime Minister's busy. I'll be sure to pass your message on.'

She heard the clank of the letterbox which had always, until now, meant the potential excitement of post.

'Marcia, had you seen the Millhench letter?' a new voice shouted, younger than the rest, but no kinder. She dialled the study number again.

AS THEY went up the staircase to the first floor, Wilson's guest looked thoughtful and stopped between the portraits of Attlee and Macmillan.

'I'm thinking we should try this in the White House. When I was here in '69, you said they hang you – ' the mistimed smile and the laugh that was more like a snarl – 'they *put you up* when you leave. But I see you're here. That must be unusual.'

'Yes, Dick. I'm one of the very few to walk past himself every morning. Of course, I *did* leave in 1970. They hung the picture then, didn't expect me back. I didn't reckon on returning either. Poor Mary had bet her life that we wouldn't have to. I was all set to be an economics don at Oxford. Even on election night, the press had written us off.'

'Writing off is how they like to write it. If I'd listened to the eyeshade guys, I'd have been an attorney in Yorba Linda since 1960, remembered as the guy who got beat by the one who got shot.' The President looked down, possibly reflecting on how he might now be remembered. 'The *Detroit Free Press* just ran the headline: Enough Is Enough . . .'

'Oh, I've had that one.'

'But Nixon is not a quitter.'

One of the switchboard girls, a stout enough lass with a solid bosom, crossed the landing above them.

'Say, is that the slag we've been reading so much about?'

'What? Oh, no. No.'

He hoped the poor girl hadn't heard.

Dick was limping. Wilson wondered if that was one reason he had stopped on the stairs. 'Is your leg OK? I'm sure you have your own medics but my chap Sir Joseph Stone . . .'

'Oh, it's just a little airplane cramp. I'll walk it off.'

Yet the President dragged his leg so horribly that Wilson was almost tempted to grab him by the elbow, as he had his da, in those last, lame days. Three years dead now, his mother seventeen. One of his dreams of retirement was the time to remember them properly.

On his last state visit, Nixon had merely sipped at wine but now he accepted the bourbon they had got in for him and drank it with some urgency.

Slouched down in one of the study chairs, flexing the tender leg, Nixon growled: 'So, no note-takers?'

'No, Dick. No, if there's a lesson I've tried to learn this second time, it's that you get more done over a cup or a glass of something than with half the civil service crouched round

the bat. I've high hopes of a few chats with European colleagues at Pompidou's funeral.'

He knew, though, that the difference must be humiliating
for Dick. Five years before, the streets had been filled with
enemies but the ceremonies grand. Now, the protesters outside the US Embassy amounted to a couple of expatriate
lawyers who had read the foreign pages of the *Guardian*.
Yet the President had been smuggled in the back way on the
absolute understanding that he had only stopped in London
for a pee and a pie on the way to burying the French President.

Joe Haines had wondered if the PM should be seen with
the President at all, with the way things were going on the
Potomac, but Wilson had insisted. He refused to see loyalty
as a weakness.

'So there'll be no, uh, uh, record of this conversation?'

I have no secret taping system in *my* study, Dick, if
that's what you mean. 'No, no. Only in our m-m-memories.'
Although you would be sensible to assume that MI5 is taping
this. 'You and me, Dick. Just you and me. How bad is it?'

'What's happening is a liberal coup d'état. In '72, we
whupped McGovern so hard, there are rumours his mom
and his dog voted GOP. So the Democrats are going after
the White House another way.'

What was said by Brother Jenkins, who played tennis with
professors from Harvard, was that Nixon had lost so many
elections earlier in his career that he had ordered the robbery
of his opponents' offices even though he was nearly guaranteed a landslide. Jenkins said the motivation had not been evil
but the corrupting fear of defeat.

Wilson, who could no longer understand such a hunger to
win, said: 'The world has been lucky to have your leadership,
Dick.'

But this support sounded like a memorial and, from the look Nixon gave him, he could believe the stories of the President turning the air blue on the tapes the Special Prosecutor was demanding. When the President next spoke, the tactic was attack.

'The Ambassador says you have to expect another election. You have no majority in the legislature?'

'Yes. I envy you knowing . . .' Knowing that you have another two years, he almost said. 'Knowing that the next election is two years away. I'll let you into a secret, Dick. When a British Prime Minister wakes in the night, it's not war, poverty or famine he's losing sleep over but when to hold the next general election.'

'Mmm. You wait for the opinion polls, I suppose?'

'Yes. But there are so many factors. Weather, for one. Our folk are less likely to have cars than their folk, so you hope to miss the northern monsoon season. I've always kept a calendar, filled with red-ringed dates. Even so, I nearly killed a man once. In 1970, I went for June. Sunny, if you're lucky. Long daylight, anyway. Schools not out yet. I'd forgotten it was what they call Wakes Week in a place called Leek. All the miners, potters, factory workers have to go on holiday at the same time. Local MP, friend of mine, suddenly has 9,000 of his voters away at the beach. Lost his seat. Never the same man again. No consolation to him that the party lost as well.'

Nixon, who frequently smiled too early, on this occasion grinned too late. He gazed balefully into his glass as if the bourbon had turned to water.

'And, Prime Minister, they say you even have your own Watergate?'

'Do they? There are no buggers in Heath's office. Not that sort, anyway.'

'No. This slag lady. What's the picture there?'

'Oh, that's nothing, Dick. Nothing at all. Fleet Street mischief. Fleet Street and friends.'

CUDLIPP was wearing one of his barber's-pole ties and a bright white raincoat lined with the colours of tropical songbirds. He was one of those men who fought the dour rules of business dress with fire.

His cockatoo hair-do, still gingery at sixty, flashed out his arrival like a police light as he pushed through the lunchtime sandwich queue at the counter of the Italian cafe opposite Parliament.

These confessionals were generally held in the Commons canteen but security had become fussy since a nutter had tried to kidnap Princess Anne and her husband in the Mall. (Storey's own view was that anyone who locked up the Queen's daughter and tried to ransom her would soon have been on the phone to the authorities offering them money to take her back.)

'Sir Hugh,' Storey greeted him. 'I know it's not quite the Savoy.'

'Listen, as a member of the Royal Commission on Standards of Conduct in Public Life, a greasy spoon's ideal. Park bench would be really pure. Good Jazz Age piece this morning.'

'Thank you, Sir Hugh.'

'Although, if I'd been editor, I'd have worried most *Mirror* readers not only wouldn't know there's a film of *The Great Gatsby* about to come out with Mr Redford and Miss Farrow, but would never have read the book. And please, Bernard, call me what you've always called me. I know that every bugger says they only took the knighthood for the missus and to make the bank laugh at your overdraft. I don't have to use it, though.'

But Storey, who had discovered that awe of mentors was no more lasting than the influence of parents, thought: you'll be Lord Cudlipp soon. Eventually, even the most bloody-minded men in Britain, when they start to wrestle with their conscience, lose.

As they tested their teeth on sandwiches of beef riddled with tough buttons of hardened fat, the reluctant knight said: 'What have they got you on today? Nixon–Wilson? Except Tricky Dicky's the madwoman in the attic this time, I gather.'

'Yeah. Actually, I did Wilson's Mrs Rochester this morning. Though she's in a mews not an attic. The desk sent me down because Joe Haines was on a cheer-up visit. I never expected to feel sorry for Marcia but it's a rat-fuck down there. Hacks are paying the local kids to ring her doorbell, try to get her out for a picture. In fact, she's the reason I wanted to see you. I'm being fed this stuff about her . . .'

'On Slagheaps? Your pieces read well. But Fatman has sat on it now?'

'Yeah. But we're being fed more. I think it's probably rubbish. Which is fine: story of my career . . .'

'Oh, no. You got a huge story one hundred per cent right when you worked for me. We just couldn't print it. You know what I have to say, Bernard: talk to Mike Christiansen. He's your editor. He's no Lee Howard. In fact, you may remember I sacked him from the Sunday for running a piece on magic mushrooms. But—'

'As you say, they've got Goodman blinding them with silks and mirrors. I'm not complaining about Mike. I just wanted a view on whether I've got caviar or fish-paste in the pot.'

'OK, then. Chatham House Rules, as they say in the circles I now move in. Take me through it.'

'Right.' Storey flipped open his notebook like a copper in court. '25th February, three days before polling day. I'm at the Golden Eagle in Kirkby. Wilson's topping up his majority in Huyton with some grab-and-grins. Phone call late at night to my room. No one I know . . .'

'This isn't the funny people? Not our famous Anon, as it were?'

'Well, I think it *was* the funny people – though also possibly the Tories – but it was a new voice to me and no name. Claimed that Wilson was involved in a dodgy land deal in Lancashire. The northern desk put in some calls. Turns out it was Marcia's brother, Tony Field, at a place called Ince-in-Makerfield, near Wigan. Field bought a slagheap and quarry there, with his own money . . .'

'This is clearer. It was hard to follow in the paper. No criticism of your writing . . .'

'The shadow of Lord Goodman getting in the way. So Field uses his profits from slag, plus a loan, to buy Ardite, another quarry owner, with Marcia as sole co-director. Neither of the companies flourish – in fact, Ardite is sold – but then Field realizes the soil he's still got is worth more than anything on it. He starts parcelling up patches of slag-land and selling it. One plot goes to Ronald Millhench, a Midlands insurance broker. There's a letter from Wilson to Milhench on Commons notepaper . . .'

'But Wilson says it's a fake? Thank you, love.' A waitress had brought two plates of a dessert called Dutch apple cake. 'So the first call came during the election. But nothing appeared then? Goodman?'

'As soon as we put in calls, he was on the blower to the editor denying it all, talking about dirty tricks. During that phoney war after polling day – when Heath and Thorpe are trying to botch together a coalition, before the Queen calls for Wilson – there was more. The Millhench letter, for a start. This morning, I was offered a dossier on Field's company, Slag Ltd. This time it *is* my unwanted friend in MI5.'

'So you have your Deep Throat. But shall you and I be the British Woodward and Bernstein, Bernard? That question I hammered into you and other unfortunate hacks under my care: *who wins from this?* Which applies to this story in two ways. Christ, this tart is gruesome. I'd rather eat Dutch cap or Dutch elm disease . . .' Cudlipp shoved his two-thirds-uneaten cake aside. 'Who wins from this? The beneficiaries of these leaks, it's clear, would be those who wanted to ensure that the outcome of the hung Parliament would be a government under anyone but Wilson. Which would make us suspicious, even if you and I didn't have memories of the events of 1968. That assumes the story to be untrue. Now, if the stuff you're being slipped is pukka, who wins from the land deals? How's Marcia involved?'

'Sleeping partner, that's all. But she went in with her brother, when he became a slag baron, hoping it would be her pension. So she was a potential beneficiary. She's done nothing wrong. But politics isn't about how you act; it's about how the voters might *react*.'

'But what could possibly be in it for Wilson? That's where Deep Throat develops laryngitis for me.'

'I know. If you believe the gossip, Hugh, he'd cross the A1 naked on a pogo stick if he thought it would help Marcia. But if you look at the kind of money he got for his first-term memoirs, why would he be investing in clinker in Wigan? The whisperers say that loyalty is Wilson's fatal flaw. Tony Field worked for eighteen months in his office when he was back in Opposition. Field's now married to Kagan's secretary. The scandal-mongers see a family tree.'

'The people around him, Bernard. That was always the blood libel, back to '68. I once asked you if what was important was the story or the fact that the story was being put about. Trying to look at this as a journalist rather than a superannuated lickspittle of the British establishment, I'd say this is the same as '68. There's a slight problem with the friends Wilson chooses. But there's a far bigger one with the enemies who choose Wilson.'

JOHN Christ Angel's last letter had mentioned a new movie called *The Conversation*. Directed by that *Godfather* chap Francis Ford Coppola – the Yanks claimed they had no class system but were practically all triple-barrelled – and had the *French Connection* fellow Hackman as a bugger who believes he's heard a murder on his tapes.

John Christ Angel raved about it, though it must have been a bloody busman's holiday for him. Wright might, though, bowl round to his local Odeon when it came over because there was no doubt that two of the biggest thrills in the game were listening and transcripts.

```
HW: Have you . . . [background noise] . . .
    damnation! Arnold, do you have any
    matches?
AG: As you know, Prime Minister, I am
    petitioning the Lord Chancellor to outlaw
    smoking in the presence of asthmatics.
HW: Ah, in this drawer . . . I . . . you've
    spoken to the editors?
AG: Higher, Prime Minister. Rothermere at
    Associated. Miles at the Mirror. I've made
    it abundantly clear that they can expect a
    writ every time they try to connect you or
    Mrs Williams to Wigan.
```

So Fatman had blotted out the sun again. Wright realized that they would have to rely on Storey giving leftovers to the Brideshead Boy.

```
HW: Arnold, the security services are on to me
    about Thorpe again . . . I . . . I'm
    sorry to have to resort to such barrack-
    room talk . . . but they have stories of
    him picking up - is 'rough trade' what
    they call it? - in London clubs for men
    who like men . . . there's talk of
    treatment for [indistinct] warts.
```

When the Olive Olivettis put [indistinct], it meant either they hadn't heard or didn't want to type it. The latter here, clearly. 'Genital' or 'anal' he would guess.

```
AG: Prime Minister, as you will realize, I may
    be at, ah, ah, risk of, ah, ah, potential
    embarrassment in this.
HW: Oh, you don't have to spell it out,
    [indistinct] Bar (?) As I always say to
    Jumbo Hanley, most of this stuff is better
    left to Latin or the imagination.
AG: I mean that I act for both Mr Thorpe and
    the Liberal Party generally. It is not so
    much conflict of interest that concerns me
    but the issue of client confidentiality.
HW: I'm asking for a wink, Arnold, that's all.
    I don't want to go out to bat for Thorpe
    and discover I've been bowled a . . . .
AG: Mr Thorpe has assured me, as his
    solicitor, that he is not a homosexual and
    will pursue with some severity any section
    of the press that suggests he is. He
```

```
           further insists that this fellow Scott,
           who is making various allegations, is a
           constituent with a grievance.
       HW: What I always say when they come in here
           with the Ipcress File on Jeremy is . . .
           look, he's a married man with a child.
       AG: Indeed. Though, as a man who has never
           married, Prime Minister, I would urge that
           the presence of a wedding certificate
           should be given no more weight in these
           matters than its absence. The significance
           lies in the personal assurances Mr Thorpe
           has given.
```

The significance lies, Fatman. Doesn't it just? Isn't that what makes it significant? And, Henry, Henry, are you really so naive? The fact that a man has paid through the turnstile once doesn't mean he won't go round the back next Saturday. And, Fatman, why so touchy that there's no Mrs F? Do you have a secret too? *Do* you? Do *you*?

STOREY was tickling up some Reuters copy on Golda Meir's problems with her Labour Party – from the dead Pompidou through the prosecuted Nixon to Wilson and Wigan, leadership seemed insecure this week (suggest possible op ed column?) – when the telephone rang in the Westminster office and he was, for the first time ever, delighted to hear the voice of 'Patrick White'.

'Patrick, I'm really glad you called . . .'

'You are? Oh, dear. Couldn't resist a trifecta at Uttoxeter? And now the missus is saying the bairns are out of shoes?'

'No, I couldn't even tell you what horse manure smells like these days. Bullshit's different. I recognize that. I wanted to tell you we're going big on the Millhench letter tomorrow.

Is this the sheet of paper that will finish Harold Wilson's career?'

'Splendid. No offence, Bernard, but I feel like a punter must when the nag his cash is on charges past the post . . .'

'Ah, no. Steward's enquiry. Urgent call for the course vet. The answer we give to the question "Is this the sheet of paper?" is: no. The Millhench letter is a forgery.'

In the silence on the line, he could hear beeps and clicks which he thought were probably bugs, but for once he hoped they were. Let them listen back to this humiliation.

'And that claim is based on what information, Bernard?'

'Handwriting and typewriter experts. Good form in the courts.'

'All I'd throw into the mix on that one, Bernard, is that specialists and experts . . . all I'm saying is . . . They sometimes believe . . .'

'Believe what they want to believe, Patrick?'

HE WAS still angry at Wilson for leaving him off the guest list for the dinner with Academician Kirillin – only adding his name when he queried it directly – even though he was one of the principal ministers involved in scientific relations with Russia and once even had Kirillin to the house in Holland Park, the time when MI5 had come and taken away the presents the Soviet delegation brought in case they contained microphones!

There had been a curious moment at the Kirillin dinner: Wilson had begun his speech with a long list of all the negotiations with the Russians – dates, places, times – as though he wanted to demonstrate his memory. His own relations with Harold were absolutely rock-bottom now; he would have to consider how to improve them. But it was so tough, when each thought that the other was destroying the Labour Party.

Benn lifted the microphone, then moved it slightly further away. There had been an interesting article in a technical journal about the elimination of microphone 'ghosting'. He clunked down the PLAY and RECORD buttons.

'Thursday 23rd of May,' he dictated. 'The amusing news tonight is that Harold has made Marcia Williams a peer!'

26

The Dog in the Fog

THE HILLS were a killer. He thought the Escort was going to stall. Not his idea of wheels at all, but you didn't want to do this kind of job in a Hertz – too easily traced if you were seen – so it had to be his lady's Escort. Maybe because of the way sex was for women, going with a chick was all about her letting you into things: her flat, her fanny, her car. Usually in that order, although he wasn't too fussy.

People bored on about Exmoor. But all he had seen so far was miles of yellow gorse and scrubby stuff and even all that was mainly covered in mist, which was another bugger. You kept expecting the Hound of the fucking Baskervilles to run in front of the car.

He was tuned to Radio 1 but the reception kept cutting out, which was actually a relief because it was David 'Diddy' Hamilton and the charts seemed to be full of joke songs, 'Funky Moped', 'Fattie Bum-Bum' and that horrible 'Una Paloma Blanca' that all the bloody passengers sang now when they were flying back from anywhere half-sunny. Ah, sweet relief. 'Diddy' had just put on 'Space Oddity', which was still a sort of joke song, but at least a good one.

The fog was dropping like smoke in a cabin-fire simulator and Newton flicked to dipped even though it must be another hour to dusk. Unfamiliar with the dash, he kept his eyes down too long and there was a moment when he thought he was going over the drop. *Here am I, floating round my tin-can.* He thought the next sign said Combe Martin.

Scott was standing outside the hotel. Though he seemed as strung as a tennis racket, he was pretty enough, Newton supposed, if you were a man who liked it up the Bourneville. Problem was he had the panting Baskerville at his side. Great browny-black donkey of a thing. That hadn't been in the contract. Only point of dogs he could see was to keep Koreans from eating each other.

Newton parked and got out of the car. Scott looked shivery but he didn't know if that was cold or some fluttery poof Larry Grayson thing.

'Norman Scott?' he checked. The reply was a trembly little smile which he'd bet his own arse Thorpe had seen from above and below.

'Peter Keene,' Newton lied. 'I wasn't expecting Lassie. I'm afraid I have a bit of an allergy to dogs.'

That was an improvised detail of the cover story, though he had the rest worked out. It was too risky for Peter Keene to be an airline pilot as well, so he would be a businessman who hopped around the Continent for his job. That covered any slip of the tongue about having been in Spain the previous day or BEA stickers on his bag.

'Well, I can't just leave her here, can I?'

Was it natural that they sounded like girls or was it something they put on?

'Norman, as I told you on the phone. We ought to talk.' He lowered his voice as a precaution against any strawsuckers coming out of the pub. 'You're in a great deal of trouble. You're going to be killed. A man has been paid a five-figure sum to shoot you. A friend of yours has sent me to warn you. But not here. Can we go for a drive?'

Scott looked doe-eyed at the shit-brown dog-donkey and shrugged: 'I'm afraid we come as a couple.'

'Can't you tie her to the bike rack or something?'

The simpering grin that had made him Greek wife to a leading politician: 'She's no trouble, Mr Keene.'

Bum-boy and the dog-donkey followed Newton to the Escort.

HE WOULD have been nervous of what he had just heard even if they had not been just a few feet from a copper.

'When you say "dispose" of her, Sir Joseph?'

'I could make it look like natural causes, Joe.' Stone always spoke in a slightly excitable voice, but now the tone matched the words. 'It will be me that signs the death certificate, so it's no problem.'

No problem? Haines glanced instinctively over his shoulder and out of the window onto Downing Street, where the duty copper would be calmly posing for the tourist cameras, unaware that a bigger crime than any threatening the building was being plotted inside.

As a matter of fact, Haines had just been screaming at Lady Slagheap on the phone when Stone, who had been checking out either the Prime Minister's ticker or his bum, came into the press secretary's office with a look on his face like he had just suffered a bungled enema. The doctor eased himself into the armchair where the pol corrs sat for their bollockings, and said: 'Lady Falkender, as we must learn to call her. She's too much of a strain on the Prime Minister. I think we should consider ways of easing that strain.'

'Well, as you'll guess, I'm sympathetic to the idea of less Marcia. But there's the tricky little matter of how to do it, even if Harold were to agree, which I doubt.'

'I think I could dispose of her, Joe.'

When you say dispose of her, Sir Joseph?

Agatha Christie in Westminster. Appealing as the prospect might be in theory, Haines would be an accessory to murder before and after the fact. And, apart from the minor matters of morality and not wanting to be soap-holder in Pentonville nick, there was another issue. His job was to do what Harold wanted, and infuriating as it might be this was the very opposite of Wilson's wish for Marcia.

'I don't think we should go down that road, Sir Joseph.'

OH CHRIST, he'd killed the bitch. It had been farcical: the whole thing was *The Day of the Jackal* remade as *Dad's Army*. Heading back from Porlock to Combe Martin, the fog had been joined by wind and rain. All three fucking lemons in a row. They wouldn't let you fly a plane in this but here he was on top of some kind of Everest of heather with Stevie Wonder visibility in a Ford Escort with a gun in his pocket and a poof in the passenger seat. And (which was the real fucking point) the hundred and second Dalmatian in the back.

In the dark, the farty car heater fugging up the windows, Newton's eyes started to flicker. He had left Blackpool not much after dawn. David Essex on the car radio. The nation's number one on the nation's number one station. *Hold me close, don't let me go*. He felt the car float across the road. Scott – just like your co-pilot suddenly saying 'OK, Skip?' when the bird lurched in turbulence, but sounding more like a steward – lisped: 'Do you want me to have a go? I know the roads.' Newton agreed. He would have more freedom if he didn't have to think about the car.

They were coming down a hill, Wales to their right. On the nearside, a scratchy expanse of gorse led down to stubby trees and, somewhere beyond them, the sea. As he swung into a rough track on the left, the headlamps swept the moor, Colditz-style, picking out ghostly ponies and then a sign: Yenworthy Farm.

Newton opened the door, forcing it against the wind and rain, which hit his face like there was a big man standing outside chucking buckets in. Suddenly, he was thumped in the back. The fucking donkey thought it was walkies and was bouncing around like Scooby-Doo.

Dogs had no hate-radar, none at all, and it was jumping up at him like he'd just sniffed its ring. Realizing the beast would always stay near Scott, perhaps that was even why Jeremy's little friend had brought the dog along, he reached into his pocket for the Mauser.

AS SCOTT ducked round the front of the car, he was blinded by the headlights and the rain but saw Peter Keene struggling out of the driver's side. 'Oh, no, no, no,' he began. He had only meant to slide across so that Rinka didn't jump out and make everything sodden. But the silly girl had got out now, wanting her run. The driver's door open. The seats will get. *Hold me close don't let me go.* 'What? . . . What has?'

She was lying on the road. He bent over her, blowing into her mouth and nose. He didn't think about the smell and had known worse. But he realized at once she was dead from the way she just let the rain hit her face. And the water couldn't wash away the blood. Oh, God.

He screamed at Keene: 'You've shot my dog . . . You can't involve Rinka. You can't involve the dog.'

The businessman grabbed his head and forced it down like. Like. Like. He felt what must, Oh Jesus, be a gun. When he had thought about such moments, or the times he had considered killing himself, he had tried to imagine praying or being brave, but all he could think was: so this is how it ends.

This was silly. Shot like a dog. Beside a shot dog. In the fog. He said a sort of prayer, not to God but a promise to himself, that whoever found the letters and the postcard in the cottage would know what to do, would know how to stop that wicked man.

'Oh fuck, oh fuck,' Keene shouted, sounding almost like he was crying now. He let go of his hold on Scott's neck. He dared to look round and saw Keene kneeling against the car, struggling with a gun that had clearly jammed.

Scott huddled over Rinka, covering her from the rain, though it could scarcely matter now. He heard a bang, which he knew was the wrong sound for a shot, and realized it was a car door slamming, followed by the wheels skidding away.

WHAT AN unsavoury detail it was that the male model had tried to give the bitch the kiss of life. Even as a dog-lover himself, Waugh could not quite imagine mouth-to-mouth with a hound. He supposed that being a practising homosexualist might increase one's tolerance of oral possibilities.

He flicked ash off the press cutting, reread it, then held the cigarette deliberately over the Liberal Leader's late and unwise audition for the role of humorist – 'Are they hunting dogs on the moors these days?' – until the words smouldered and disappeared. Smoking hands-free now, Waugh typed:

> West Somerset is buzzing with rumours of a most unsavoury description following reports in the *West Somerset Free Press* about an incident which occurred recently on Exmoor.
>
> Mr Norman Scott, a thirty-six-year-old writer, of Combe Martin, North Devon, who claims to have been a great friend of Jeremy Thorpe, the Liberal statesman, was found by an AA patrolman, weeping beside the body of Rinka, his Great Dane bitch, which had been shot in the head.
>
> Information about this puzzling incident has since been restricted on Home Office orders . . .

Part Six

1976

Kick a Blind Man

As the meeting neared its end, the Queen said one more thing to me. Looking over her half-rimmed spectacles, she said: 'Be careful, Paul . . . There are powers at work in this country about which we have no knowledge,' and she fixed me with a stare.

Paul Burrell – *A Royal Duty*

27

Years and Years of Afternoon

USUALLY HIS JOB was to make the news bigger than it was, swell a press release into a headline. Today, however, the challenge was to shrink the interest. He was about to announce the biggest political shock of the decade, at least, but had to play it down. The hacks would assume scandal; it was a gift to conspiracy theorists. The would-be Woodwards might bring up the burglaries again. And the Tories, who since the Sixties had longed for a Profumo on the other side, would smell sex.

For years, what every bugger wanted to know was if he'd fucked her: whether Wilson had, that was, not whether Joe Haines had. Blimey, that had never been a likelihood on either side. What Haines always said to people was: you've got a dirty mind. Just because a man and woman worked together didn't mean . . .

Look, he wasn't necessarily denying that Marcia was the nanny Harold never had and Harold was the daddy she'd always wanted. Still didn't mean they went to bed together. Nobody believed him, though. Even the ones who knew and accepted that Marcia's kids were nothing to do with Wilson – not least because the dad worked beside them in the press lobby – believed that there'd been something sometime.

At first, Haines hadn't been that sure himself. Harold and she both told different stories about how they'd met, although agreed it had been 1956, when he was Shadow Chancellor and she was a secretary at Labour HQ.

Wilson's line was that he'd seen her at a bus stop, recognized her as a party employee and offered her a lift in his car. That woman's version was that they'd met at a Labour Party dinner for Khrushchev (a truly bad publicity move that Haines was glad hadn't happened on his watch: wouldn't have happened, in fact).

You didn't need to be a cop – just someone who'd left a bit of shoe leather on Fleet Street – to see that these accounts of how they had become political husband and wife were, in different ways, suspicious. Harold's narrative was so implausible – would he really recognize from a moving car a typist he had seen but never spoken to? – that you had to wonder if it was a lovers' cover story for a filthier beginning. As for Marcia's yarn, her insistence that their eyes had met across a supper table for the General Secretary of the USSR only encouraged those pillocks who put it about that they had funny links with Russia.

On one detail, both sides agreed, as they used to say in *Newsweek*. Either way – in the car, or across the Labour Party samovar – the secretary had confessed to the shadow minister that she was the source of anonymous letters to him warning of an anti-Wilson plot on the party's right. That rang true. Regardless of whether they were lovers, the couple shared a passion for plots and paranoia. Between them, a trouble shared was a worry bloody doubled.

Often Haines became convinced that it was the old, old story. If Eve had allowed Adam to have a secretary, then the Fall of Man would have happened long before the apple. At other times, it seemed to him that the two were united by mutual insecurity and dependency, not anything under the covers. He wobbled between these possibilities until the day he was told that Marcia had spectacularly settled the speculation, eighteen months after they lost the election: 12 January 1972.

Haines had as usual pinned a short bulletin of Wilson's doings for the day on the Lobby Correspondents' notice-board. As they were in Opposition then, and neither the pound nor the public took much interest in the party, it was dull stuff, except for a little sop to gossip columnists: the Leader of the Opposition was taking Mary to L'Epicure, their favourite London restaurant, for her birthday.

Marcia had not been told and it was a rule of her office that Harold must never take breath or break wind without the Keeper of the Diary being consulted and the event entered in her appointments book. Discovering the unplanned lunch from a junior secretary, Marcia, according to Wilson's embarrassed account later, had telephoned Mary at Lord North Street on her return from L'Epicure and announced that she was coming round. When they met, Mrs Williams had reportedly told Mrs Wilson: 'I have only one thing to say to you. I went to bed with your husband six times in 1956 and it was not satisfactory.'

This certainly gave a new twist to that old line: let me count the ways. A panicked Wilson had insisted to wife and press secretary that his diary keeper was lying, perhaps implying that Marcia's anger came from the fact that he had refused to sleep with her.

Like most people in Harold's court, Haines had always believed that the two options were platonic friendship or adultery but suddenly faced the unconsidered possibility that they had briefly and unhappily been together. It certainly made sense of her hold over him and her intermittent warnings to Wilson that the contents of her handbag might be of interest to the *Daily Mail*. This was a secret which could have ended his career.

When the two men were alone, Wilson had said: 'Well, she has dropped her atomic bomb at last. She can't hurt me any more.' This presumably meant that her constant threat to tell Mary had finally gone off without the desired result. His calmness on the subject suggested that he had been more frightened of Mary knowing than of newspapers finding out.

It was the best political story Haines had ever got and it was one he would only tell when the Tory press could make nothing out of it. There was nothing deceitful in keeping this knowledge to himself. Being press secretary was not about deception but about selection. (He had only directly lied once, when he had told the press that Wilson was resting at Chequers after flu, rather than the heart scare it had been.)

But there was certainly a book one day in the story of Mrs Williams, the political wife. The political wife who was about to become a political widow. Haines pulled his typewriter towards him and began to write the announcement of the second biggest secret of his time at Number 10.

HE POURED a glass of brandy, deciding that it was not too early in the day. The drink was, in any case, partly medicinal. He had been up twice in the night with the squitters and had suffered again after breakfast. Sir Joseph had decided that it was time for him to see a good gut-man.

What though the night may come too soon / We've years and years of afternoon. This was his favourite version, recorded by Sir Malcolm Sargent at Abbey Road in 1956, a year otherwise unhappy with the Suez Crisis and. And. And.

Geraint Evans as Ko-Ko, Ian Wallace singing Pooh-Bah. You could hear the words better than in D'Oyly Carte's own recordings, where, even without the hiss from the primitive equipment, the orchestra drowned out the singers.

With laughing song and merry dance / With joyous shout and ringing cheer / Inaugurate our new career!

The finale of *The Mikado* ended. He dropped the needle while lifting it from the LP so that it skidded and scratched the surface. Even with the excuse that he was holding a tumbler in the other hand, he hated this clumsiness. He took smaller gulps of brandy but what had once been a pleasant warming of the throat now felt like a hot poker drilling down his middle.

Placing the glass on the desk, it was closer to the edge than he intended and the effort of steadying it splashed the last dregs of drink onto the pile of memos waiting for his attention. He signed them without reading them. When the ink met the damp paper, his name dissolved and blurred.

If there was a camera in the room – which let's face it there probably was – the spies would have seen the Prime Minister smile at this symbolic disintegration of his authority. Next they could have watched him cross from his desk to the door three times, returning the first time to collect his forgotten pipe, the next to recover the text of his address to cabinet.

Even the closest of MI5 microphones, though, could not have detected the fragments running through his head as he finally left the study. First, two phrases of Gilbert and Sullivan, easily retrieved: *years and years of afternoon* and *inaugurate our new career*. Then: Mercer, Goodall, Barkas. Barkas. Goodall, Barkas. Barkas. Bugger.

NOW WHO in their right mind would want to give a literary prize to a book about a married woman kneeling on a bed, while a young man she had only just met in a hotel pushed his 'huge' organ into her from behind? And, what's more, an Irish Catholic married woman.

It was not a view of life she recognized or felt that an

award for authorship should celebrate. It was almost as scandalous as the Rathbone. She opened her fountain pen and wrote carefully, in a notebook of the kind she usually kept for poetry: Moore, Brian – The Doctors Wife – Cape: No. She paused, then underlined the negative and added an exclamation mark.

Almost every book they had sent to her so far involved sex or adultery or both. Mary had joked to them that they should rename the trophy the Booker McConnell Prize for Describing Copulation! She hoped that neither of her fellow judges would find such fiction modish.

Mr Walter Allen had written some delightful provincial fiction himself. However, he was a schoolmate and friend of Henry Reed, who was responsible for that quite disgusting poem 'The Naming of Parts'. And Mr Francis King, she understood, wrote novels about men who liked men. She felt like Harold all the times he had worried at breakfast that he 'might not have the votes'. Well, for her part, she was determined that they would not be giving five thousand pounds to a novel about extramarital affairs.

There was one she thought Harold might like: *Saville*, about a Yorkshireman. Perhaps they could discuss it, even though he always said he had no time for novels. Perhaps he would have more time to read now. John B always said it was a little infra dig to quote your own poems, but she allowed herself in the quiet of her mind to recall the lines she had written as a silent promise and for so long read as a secret prophecy.

And a heavenly, healing silence falls / Upon my soul, and the caging walls / Melt, and the clanging voices die / And we are alone, my house and I.

Dreaming of the house at the edge of the wood, she walked to the window of the London house that had been her forced residence. At the door on Lord North Street, a second policeman had stepped into place, ready for the deluge of press that would follow the announcement.

AT FIRST, this most secret of official business looked wrong on pink paper. But since she had cut back on her time at Downing Street, wanting to be at Wyndham Mews for the boys, she had often run out of official letterheads. So, this morning, Lady Falkender was making do with the stationery she used for thank-you letters, which was at least appropriate in this case.

Delfont, Goldsmith, Grade, Hanson, Miller. The list looked like one of those fucking Harrogate City football teams Harold liked to recite although, to be honest, he had dropped that party piece entirely in recent times.

A football team, too, because every single person on it was a man. It told you a lot about this country that it almost never honoured women. The people who had sneered at her own peerage, it wasn't because she was Marcia but because she was female. When Macmillan sent *his* private secretary to the Lords, the chaps all clapped.

Between Delfont and Goldsmith, she added Frost, erased it, then replaced it. Leave it up to him. It was his fucking list. And what notice did he take of her views now? Imagining her life after this day, Lady Falkender moved the pink, scented memo aside. It would not do to smudge it.

THEIR cooperation on political matters had always been somewhat problematic, but Jenkins understood, as he listened, that he and Wilson shared an arithmetical affinity. Certainly, the emphasis of his resignation address to cabinet was statistical rather than rhetorical.

After some brisk preliminaries – 'This morning, I informed

Her Majesty the Queen of a decision which is irrevocable' – Wilson's approach was numerical rather than sentimental: he had served as premier for almost eight years, had won four separate elections (in '64 and '66, then February and October 1974 – both of these achievements ranking as world records in the Olympiad of Labour Party politics) and had presided over 472 cabinets and answered more than 12,000 parliamentary questions in that time.

Most ministers, however, were sheltered from this blizzard of figures, having paused for reflection under the canopy of a single word: 'resignation'.

The varying reactions betrayed the circulation of the secret or, at least, the rumour, which this declaration now cemented. Mellish, Short and others more distant from the core of decision-making blinked, first from disbelief and then, it seemed in some cases, as a reflex to prevent tears.

The Foreign Secretary, nodding knowledgeably, almost as soon as the Prime Minister spoke, had obviously been forewarned, and wore afterwards an expression of incipient satisfaction which dramatized Callaghan's status as the dauphin. This once improbable position had been achieved through the sudden smothering of the flames of long-time rivalry by the thicker foam of close collaboration on foreign affairs.

Jenkins himself, as was characteristic of his political relationship with Wilson, found himself required to bring a certain theatre to his features, having already been advised of the Prime Minister's impending retirement by Arnold Goodman at a gathering of Anne Fleming's before Christmas. The solicitor's indiscretion had been a kindly attempt to allow his favoured candidate a first sight of the starting pistol in the leadership race, without perhaps realizing that, even without the rapprochement between Wilson and Callaghan, Jenkins, damaged by the inevitable accidents and unpopularities of the office of Home Secretary, was now regarded as *papabile* more on the cocktail-party circuit than within the Labour Party.

Benn looked excited and conspiratorial. Ever since the burglary at Lord North Street, he had been whispering predictions in the cabinet anteroom of an impending scandal relating to documents allegedly removed. These were inferred to relate to one or more of the many rumours of security, sexual or financial impropriety which trailed behind Wilson in the latter part of his administration like a raincoat in a gale.

Wilson next seemed to address these Cassandras: 'Let me turn now to the timing of this announcement. Two years ago, I privately informed Her Majesty the Queen and Mr Arnold Goodman that it was my strong intention to leave office on the date of my sixtieth birthday: the 11th of March, 1976.'

This was the intelligence that Goodman had passed on, but, when the landmark anniversary had arrived five days ago, marked by a *Daily Mirror* interview with Marje Proops in which Wilson had insisted that he would stay for as long as there was work to do, Jenkins had assumed that the Prime Minister was guilty, not for the first time, of treating his intentions as a horse race, in which various steeds and even outright nags were set running on different conversational courses but only one would be driven to the winning post.

'However, the five-day delay,' Wilson was explaining, 'proved necessary when, last week, the pound fell below the two-dollar confidence level and precipitated a House of Commons defeat. In thirty years of politics, I have always tried to put the party first and so delayed my announcement until after we had pushed the measure through the House last night.'

Chancellor Healey glowered. The anger of the Left over

Wilson's economic policies had imperilled any possibility that Healey might succeed.

'So, whatever our enemies in Fleet Street and at the BBC may say, I want to make clear that there is nothing sinister or forced about this decision,' Wilson insisted.

Ted Short was perhaps a little lachrymose in delivering the initial speech of gratitude to the Prime Minister but there was thankfully nothing to match what Gladstone had called the 'blubbering cabinet' of 1894, when the old man had announced his departure and Sir William Harcourt had read a fulsome tribute from a crumpled manuscript. The general sense around the table was less of sadness than the destabilization which affects any workplace faced with change.

Benn was still sceptical: 'When I was young and naive, many years ago, I asked you, Harold, at Chequers, what we should do if you were run over by a bus and you said: find out who was driving the bus.'

But Wilson, who throughout his career had been the first to stir any pot of suspicion, and had more often than not brought it to the boil himself, this time cooled down the brew: 'Ah, but I haven't been run over, Wedgie. I've driven the bus away.'

As Wilson bowed his head under the compliments of colleagues, Jenkins tried to observe him with a biographer's objectivity. A man who in youth and early middle age had always appeared younger than in reality he was would now be taken for more than his six decades.

His skin was sallow and his movements slow. Although there were still the familiar jokes – 'Mary's a judge for this business called the Booker Prize. I tell you, the stuff they've sent so far, they should give *her* a prize for reading them' – they no longer seemed a reflection of excess energy but an attempt to distract from the general flatness of his manner.

The melancholy Jenkins felt in watching Wilson was, though it could not be good manners to admit it, directed at himself. The two most delicate calculations in a premiership were when to seek office and when to surrender it. Though he would offer himself for the leadership in the next two weeks, the Home Secretary knew he had misjudged the first and so would never be troubled by the second.

WHEN people asked him, as they often did, 'Joe, what's Wilson really like?', there was a story he would tell them. Once, during a crisis, he had burst into the Downing Street study without knocking and what he had seen was. He always liked to pause there because people would think it was going to be something compromising with Marcia.

What he saw was Wilson talking to one of the motor-cycle messengers, who was sitting on the sofa. Haines had interrupted but Wilson held up a hand for him to wait, so he walked to the other end of the room. When the Prime Minister eventually said goodbye to the despatch rider and beckoned his press secretary over, the explanation was: 'I had to talk to him. He's worried about his wife. Now, what did you want?'

Most politicians wore self-importance as habitually as underpants but Wilson was without it. He had been a good Prime Minister who could perhaps have been among the greatest except for his terrible alliance with that bloody woman. But he was almost certainly the kindest occupant of Number 10. History wouldn't give a toss for that but it mattered, it did actually bloody matter.

Wilson, though, had been too kind to one employee and it had weakened him. The bloody woman had written the resignation honours list on lavender notepaper. Well, Mrs Haines said it was lilac; Lady Falkender herself insisted pink.

Wilson had crossed off some names – for example, David Frost – but it was she who had sat at her desk and dreamed knights and peers into being.

A leader needed to be able to delegate but Wilson had delegated his reputation. His choice of friends had made him enemies. There was an old saying that behind every great man was a woman. Well, a woman had stood between that man and greatness.

28

H.W. and P.W., RIP

HIS WIFE had described this as a red-letter day, as opposed to Sundays, which would now be no-letter days. The spotty youths at the office, touting their computers as the answer to everything from world peace to mixing a perfect Bloody Mary, always talked as if the world these days only had a forward gear.

But every bloody year brought more reverses. Now the government, in its infinite witlessness, had decreed that this would be a country in which it was impossible to take delivery of a letter on a Sunday or purchase a stamp on a Saturday afternoon. Although the Peter Wright of wartime would never have believed it possible, he was glad to be going: from his job and from his country.

Watched by his secretary, who he had called into the room deliberately, the way a doctor summoned a nurse when he gave the thumbs-up to a female patient, Wright shredded his diaries into the burn bag beside the desk.

This was only a ritual; he kept another set at home. At the Establishments Office, he initialled the chits which removed him from the circulation of the nation's secrets: goodbye signals intelligence, farewell satellite intelligence. Entering the covert world had felt like sex but leaving it had all the glamour of cancelling a standing order.

Handing his pass to the copper in the lobby – 'That's it, then, is it, sir? Happy retirement' – he stepped onto Gower Street. A boy and girl, each as long-haired as the other, and with the just-fucked look that made you hate the young, brushed past. Walking hand-in-hand, both held those files, like giant hardboard birthday cards, that art students carried. Wright relished for the last time the thought of the reaction of all those piccolo-Picassos at the Slade, more than likely communists, if they had known that British counter-espionage was in the building next door.

Art was another reason for scarpering these shores sharpish. An American hippy had just dropped a pile of bricks on the floor of the Tate Gallery and claimed it made him Michelangelo rather than a hod-carrier. Australia might only run to Sidney Nolan but at least he painted places and faces.

No longer covered by expenses, he should have walked to Euston Square and gone on the Underground to Hyde Park. But the Paddies had put a bomb on the tube at West Ham the day before and there was no point saving on the cab fare to be sent back to the missus as an assembly kit. One of the last secret files he had taken from the Registry was an assessment of IRA strength and intentions. The intelligence it contained had made him even happier to have a pair of Qantas tickets in the bureau back home.

He flagged a cab and said: 'Leconsfield House, Mayfair, please.'

'What, the MI5 place? You a spy, sir?'

Though officially non-existent, the building had long ago become part of the London Carriage Company's knowledge.

'No, no. I'm not a spy,' Wright replied, the usual lie but, for the first time ever, true. 'I'm just going a party.'

The *News* and *Standard* billboards shrilled: WILSON RESIGNS. So conditioned to consider the politician his opposite, Wright had never realized until this week that he and Wilson were exact contemporaries, reaching sixty simultaneously and both deciding to go. It would be for history to decide if their departures were coincidental.

Already thinking like a pensioner, Wright omitted to tip the cabbie, who snapped: 'Next time an Irishman gets in with a ticking briefcase, I'm driving him right here.' Ugly manners in an ugly country; it was another justification for doing a bunk.

The Bull and Pen Club looked something like heaven tonight in the sense that everyone he had known best was lined up at the door. Tony Brooks cuffed him on the shoulder and Harry Wharton of 'K' Branch handed him a pink gin, which he then chinked with his own government thimble of syrupy red.

'May your horses' dicks be stiff and rich,' said Wharton. 'And Henry Worthington, RIP.'

'Yes, Henry,' Wright agreed. 'Who finally made a right decision for the country.'

'When did you know he was going?' Brooks asked.

'Well, Solomon Goodman's been leaking like an old man's bladder. We got word last year that Henry had told Marcia and the other Queen of England he was going. Just after he'd had a big blow-up with Jumbo over "South African interference", as it happens. Now, is that happenstance or historical inevitability? I leave it to the judgement of those of you who carry on the fight.'

'As you don't have to go to work tomorrow, Pete,' Brooks teased, 'why not motor down to the West Country? Cream tea and a quaint local court case . . .'

'Christ, I'd forgotten, Tony. "Rinkagate" is on the slate?'

'Newton – the airline pilot – was in court this morning. The prosecution are calling Scott as a witness tomorrow. He'll squeal like Edward II playing poker and then Thorpe's fucked . . .'

'Often as he wants. In Her Majesty's shower room every day,' Wright joined in.

'Get thee to Exeter, Pete. Busman's holiday, though. Bugging to buggery . . .'

Jumbo coughed to baffle the chat for the speeches. Given his bulk, the noise was like a plane taking off. Although he wore his trousers almost chest-high in Edwardian fashion, gut still spilled out. Jumbo's belly could have bagged all that undelivered Sunday post.

'Gentlemen and the occasional lady,' Jumbo began. 'As director of MI5, it is always one of my saddest duties to say farewell to a good man. For twenty years in British intelligence, and before that in the Naval Scientific Service, Peter Wright has been passionately devoted to his idea of what this country should be.'

Wily bugger, Jumbo. While sounding complimentary, the phrase covered the possibility of Wright's being enthusiastic but bonkers. Well, there would be a speech of reply and Wright kept the same make of shit shovel in his shed.

'You may be worried,' Jumbo continued, 'that Peter is being put out to grass. But, as those of you who know of his future plans are aware, he's actually being put out to stud.'

Brooks and Wharton and the few who knew of his retirement plans guffawed. The more tight-knickered secretaries flinched.

'Peter,' Jumbo now explained, 'we wish you luck in your retirement in Australia, breeding horses. At the end of a, ah, long day's mating, we hope that this' – the director's secretary handed him a rectangular parcel, wrapped in spangly blue paper – 'short-wave radio will help you to keep in touch with this country. Although, if you plan to listen to the BBC, do ask the flying doctor to check your blood pressure first.' Sycophantic giggles from the Hanley set. 'I also assure you that there is absolutely no truth in the rumour that this radio will listen to you!'

The crowd's reaction might have misled Jumbo into thinking that he had suddenly become Bob Hope. Wright took the present and, beaming insincere thanks to all four corners of the bar, scrutinized those who had come to his funeral.

His most tolerable colleagues were all here and no one, except Jumbo, would he have throttled. He most regretted the absence of John Christ Angel, his faithful deputy in the pursuit of Worthington, whose empire had finally fallen in the backwash from Watergate. John Christ had probably told one senator too many that J. Edgar Hoover was a poof with a closet full of frocks. But, through no desire of Wright's, Washington and Langley were represented here tonight. The new chief of the CIA was passing through London on a fraternal glad-hander; goofy chap called Bush.

'Could an agent have a better boss than Sir Michael Hanley?' Wright began his speech of thanks. Jumbo's toadies broke into another round of applause, although Brooks and Wharton smirked, realizing the answer the rhetorical question was supposed to imply. Jumbo's subsequent frown suggested he might also have cracked the code.

Apart from his American co-conspirator, the absence that most pained Wright was Storey of the *Mirror*. Many of his assets were here – those who had known him as Alphonse, Patrick White, Paul Waite, Paddy Witts – but Storey was lost to them. He was finally off the gee-gees, writing a column for the *Mirror* and living with his colleen and their two wee broths of boys.

Although he had helped in the King business, the hack had never been the asset Wright had hoped. The bugger had never really believed the material, sniffing the best claret as if it were meths, and had mainly proved useful in getting stuff out to the Brideshead Boy, who had always been too maverick to be an asset himself, so they needed a middle man. *Private Eye* had hinted at the Worthington allegations in 1974, finally nudge-nudged at the Mountbatten business in 1975 and now Waugh was sniffing round Thorpe's arse. Like madness in a family, a story would always come out eventually.

'I know that many of you did not accept my specific intelligence on Harold Wilson,' Wright told them. 'But I am sure that even those of you who opposed the Worthington and Oatsheaf data will consider this a happy day.' Almost everyone present, including the director's clique, gave the kind of cheer they generally reserved for the Varsity boat race.

'With Wilson gone, like Brandt and Whitlam before him, communism's three most elevated assets in the West are all now agents out of place. My opponents will say that I never actually exposed Wilson and the others and I accept that. But I would argue that, by raising the possibility and investigating it so thoroughly, I forced them to become cautious and, perhaps, inoperative. There are those who say that Wilson's behaviour in office never supported the case. I would only ask: does a hen not pull in its feathers when a fox is in the woods? To my successors, I warn that there are many other traitors out there – in Westminster, in the BBC, perhaps even in this building – who we have not seen and who we must discover. But I retire knowing that, whether or not it was I who achieved it, most of what I strove for has come about.'

But, as he walked back through the clapping hands to Brooks and Wharton, carrying one radio they would never ask him to take apart, Wright knew that the final flourish of his speech had been a final lie in a working lifetime of them. He had failed in the two major objectives of his employment: to prove that Wilson was Britain's first Soviet premier and to establish that the reason Sir Roger Hollis's long hunt for a mole in MI5 had proved fruitless was that the director's only hope of spotting the culprit was when he looked in a shaving mirror of a morning. Wright had dreamed of being a Churchill of the secret war but had been, if not a Chamberlain, then a Macmillan or even, God forbid, a Wilson.

Jumbo came over, sweaty as a Spanish navvy from the heat of all the people in the room. 'Nice speech, Peter. I hope it all works out in Australia with the horses.'

'Well, I hope stallions' cocks are more reliable than ours. But, if it doesn't work out, I've an insurance plan. An alternative pension.'

'That's sensible. Never put all your eggs—'

'Yes,' Wright said, free to cheek the old snorer now. 'I'll become the first British spy to publish my memoirs.'

'Jolly good, Peter. Sense of humour. Best way of not going bonkers in this lark.'

As Wright glanced around the Bull and Pen Club for the last time, remembering celebrations or wakes after investigations and general elections, Jumbo trundled off to talk to the tall, thin man from the CIA. Together, they looked like the Laurel and Hardy of espionage.

HOLY MOLY! In England, every speech seemed to be about sex. At the end of their face-time, Sir Michael had suggested he drop in on the drinks for Wright, who'd played Amos to the Andy of Angleton, back in the days when it was the CIA and FBI who taped conversations and broke into offices, not the Republican Party under the instructions of the President. Forgive me, Dick, but you really goofed there, let us down big-time.

Sure thing, Bush had said, figuring maybe a splash of wine and some ad-hoc bilaterals with his British counterparts. But, boy, all they seemed to want to talk about was horses' johnsons. When he'd mentioned that he liked a ride in Texas himself, they'd just ridiculed more. It was like when George Jr and his friends used to come home for chow and Barb would say they should maybe talk to a bar of soap before they said anything else!

Talking of Watergate, seemed they had their own thing going down here. 'Rinkagate', they called it. He'd asked who occupied that building. More mystificalism before they went off on this lick about an airline pilot shooting a dog – Great Dane, apparently, loving enough but always a chore to keep on the porch – on a moor.

Pooch belongs to this guy Scott, who's a Liberace, claims he used to play the vanishing bratwurst with the minority leader, name of Thorpe. They had two minority leaders here, which was different! Brit intelligence opinionated that the pilot was sent by the minority leader to get Liberace, panicked and terminated the Great Dane. The Brit spooks also claimed it was one reason the Prime Minister had resigned which was frankly where Bush tuned to a new frequency himself.

(These spies, he was finding out, could tie you in knots. Pretty much the day President Ford had sent him to the Agency, there's a call from Angleton, who's supposed to be perfecting his golf-swing by now but is sort of having trouble letting go, like those superannuated bankers in Kennebunkport, wanting to go through your portfolio at a clambake.

So he'd had Angleton round to the Washington house, wheezing like there's a sales tax on air. One minute, you're on Alger Hiss and following the story clean as a whistle. Next thing you know, it's got something to do with who the British Premier's secretary once met in Czechoslovakia and where Perry Como chose to vacation during the Cuban missile crisis.)

Hey, now, wow, the thing about Downing Street was that it was so small. 'Dainty,' they'd say here. If they reckon the White House is a wedding cake, well this is sort of a Babe Ruth. And no railings, lawns or agents, just one guy with the round blue hat, like on the souvenirs. You can walk right up to the door off the street. Wilson says he did once, back when he was a kid, which must have been a neat line for the stump speech.

They showed him into their Oval Office, which was small and square and nothing like, and Wilson was sitting at the window, looking fat and old, like those paintings of Churchill where you tell yourself it was a miracle Hitler wasn't running London by 1940.

'Prime Minister Wilson, this is a great pleasure.' Wilson's hand was clammy to the touch, like that joke slime George Jr got for Christmas once. 'George Bush, Central Intelligence Agency.'

'Call me Harold, won't you? Though I'm sure the CIA has called me much worse.'

'President Ford has asked me to reiterate the message of his cable. You will be a great loss to the world stage.'

'That's kind. But tell him I was getting to rely on the prompt corner.'

'I'll pass that on.'

Sorry, Mom. Small white lie. Sometimes you have no idea what these Brits are saying. They sat down on the chesterfield and drank real small cups of tea that smelled like scent. They drink that in England. Bush waited for Wilson to say something but he didn't so he guessed it was for him to throw the first pitch.

'Mr Pri . . . *Harold*, the President asked me to drop in on you because he knows of your security concerns and takes them seriously. He has asked me to assure you that American agencies are in no way involved in any unauthorized activity against you or your administration.'

Wilson blinked several times and twice his mouth opened without any sound coming out. He sort of had the look of a family pet at the stage that you start talking to the kids about dog heaven.

'Ah. So does that mean *authorized* activity would be OK?'

Well, hell's bells, Mom, there are still lights on. 'Harold, do you have kids?'

The blinking again, like dry crying. 'We have two boys. Grown-up now, though. They're thirty-three, no thirty-two, and twenty-seven. They both teach, actually. They're quiet, like Mary. I was the show-off. Are yours grown-up now?'

'Hey, much as they ever grow up! Barb and I have three sons. George, the oldest, we owe him our grey hairs, know what I'm saying? Hasn't quite found his way through the woods, dropped the compass once or twice. Point I'm making, Harold, is running agents is like running sons. You can hang a list of rules on the fridge but you can't tail 'em twenty-four hours a day!'

'Does the CIA have a file on me, George?'

'Hey, now, well, that's kinda hard. Look at it this way. Lady in Poodle Springs accuses me of shooting her dog, there'd be a Bush stroke Dog – sounds weird, but you get what I mean? – file. Now I might never have owned a gun or been to Poodle Springs but the complaint has to be, you know, affiliated. I mean assimilated. Do I?'

Wilson's cup shook so much as he held it that the tea slopped in the saucer. 'George, I'm interested that you used the example of a shot dog.'

'Well, I was just kind of metaphorizing, Harold. I mean, I know you've got this business going down with this guy Thorpe and the dog in the fog. Hey, there's one for Dr Seuss!'

'This Seuss. Is he CIA?'

Mom, can we go home now? Angleton might say this guy had gone over to the Sovs but he'd sure as hell gone over someplace else.

'He's a kids' writer, Harold. Cat in the hat. Dog in the fog. Meant nothing more than that.'

'I see, I see. Even so, why do you know so much about the dog business at all? Is it getting much airplay in the States?'

'Oh, no, no. Just the guys at MI5 were talking about it today.'

'Is that right? Is that right, George? What were they saying?'

'They mainly seemed to find it funny. And you gotta admit, Harold, Great Danes are kind of comical. We've always had springer spaniels.'

'What you tell me about their attitude to this is very interesting. George, does your agency have a file on South African interference in British politics?'

'Hey, well, now. That's lady in Poodle Springs again. The President took your question seriously. But I can assure you that we were unable to find any objectification of the evidence.'

Wilson smiled and moved his head slowly up and down. 'That reassures me,' he said, scratching his left ear like a bee had just stung it. The guys at MI5 said Wilson always did that when he was lying. 'George, will you join me in a brandy?'

'You know, Harold, I won't. Barb and I are off the sauce for Lent. Kinda set an example to the boys.'

29

Big Fat Spider

HE IMAGINED the crowd all shouting, like on telly. 'Steele to Gilchrist,' he said. 'Forward to Channon . . .' He was trying to sound like David Coleman. Daddy could do him better but could never get the names of the players right. 'Who passes to Osgood who shoots and . . .'

And his finger went into the carpet and really, really hurt. But, if he cried, Fat Jack would start laughing.

'Dermot,' Daddy said. 'You're pushing down. Just flick your finger gently across, like this.'

The carpet was soft and bouncy, so it made the green felt pitch all bumpy. Daddy had been saying all season that they should get a sheet of hardboard but he was always too busy to go to the shop.

'Look, you have a free kick there.'

'I bet you I score.'

'Oh, Daddy's not very good at bets.'

'If I score, can I stay up to watch *Starky and Hutch* on Saturday?'

'It's *Starsky*. We'll think about it. Now take the free kick. You can be booked for time-wasting.'

Daddy lifted three of the little Sirbootyoh players into a wall, although it didn't look right because they didn't have their hands in front of their willies like on *The Big Match*.

'Stokes and Channon line up the free kick,' Dermot said. 'Coppell, Buchan and Greenhoff are in the wall.'

They were playing last week's FA Cup Final. Dermot was

Southampton. He should have been Fulham, which was their nearest team, but Fulham had lost the Cup Final the year before and Southampton had actually won this one, so suddenly everyone at school supported them. But it wasn't quite the same in this game because Daddy was being Manchester United so they were winning. When Mummy came in, she always told Daddy that he was supposed to let Dermot win but he never did.

'And Bobby Stokes shoots and it bounces off the wall and . . . one–one . . .'

Brill. When David Coleman said they'd scored a goal, he always sounded as if he had expected it. Dermot couldn't make it come out right because his voice went so excited if he scored.

'Well done,' said Daddy but the phone was ringing. When he answered it, he always looked serious and his voice went all different when he said, 'Bernard Storey.' He waved at Dermot that he could play with Fat Jack but Fat Jack always just knocked the players over and sucked the ball like a gobstopper.

'Is this a joke?' Daddy said to the person on the phone, in that scary voice he used when Jack and him were being nasty.

STOREY'S first thought was that the subs were ringing about his column. He'd written about the latest fallout from the Thorpe resignation and Goodman was sitting on editors' heads, insisting that the decision did not imply guilt.

Bron had passed on some fantastic stuff – including a copy of a note from Thorpe to Scott, promising that 'bunnies can and will go to France' – which suggested at the very least that the Liberal leader would have benefited from the silencing of Scott.

But the *Mirror*'s duty brief, bearing the recent imprint of

Goodman's gigantic backside, would allow no reference to the correspondence, confining the columnist to the general expression of hope that Thorpe had never used phrases in letters to Scott that might be open to misinterpretation by his enemies.

Storey's fear was that the lawyer had turned an even deeper shade of yellow since he'd left the office but the voice on the telephone was not the Woodbine whine of the backbench but the soft, posh tones of a middle-aged woman who said: 'Ah, Mr Storey. Sir Harold Wilson's office here.'

He assumed he was either being wound up by some Mike Yarwood on sports or features or, worse, set up by spooks. In the years since he'd succeeded in reducing the annual profits of the Horserace Betting Levy Board (whose boss, mad Lord Wigg, had just been caught with a prostitute) he had always anticipated some revenge from 'Patrick White'. There had been an invitation to his spymaster's farewell drinks earlier in the year but he had ignored it, having said his own goodbyes to all that long before.

'Is this a joke?' he asked.

'I can't see why it would be. Sir Harold wishes to meet Bernard Storey of the *Mirror*. He wondered if you might join him for drinks this evening.'

'Sir Harold Wilson wants to . . .'

'Yes. Can we say seven o'clock? At 5 Lord North Street. It's just around the corner from the Commons.'

Storey knew this address was correct from the Goodman letters pinned up in the Westminster office, warning editors against identifying the house in case the IRA got ideas. So, if this was a scam, it took the trivial form of tricking him into ringing Wilson's doorbell uninvited.

'Your kick-off, Daddy,' Dermot said.

Storey knelt down beside the Subbuteo pitch, with its little plastic terrace of fans waving rattles and the tiny silver replica of the FA Cup waiting on a thumb-sized table, a midget dignitary ready to present it.

'Look, I'm really sorry, sweetheart. Daddy has to go to work.'

It was one of the marks of fatherhood that you suddenly started to refer to yourself in the third person, like Muhammad Ali and Idi Amin.

'But you said you'd come home early specially today to play with me!'

Leaving Dermot weeping, watched by a triumphantly cackling Jack, Storey went into the kitchen and told Moira that he was going to see the previous PM.

'Well, isn't that a bugger, as I've got the Pope dropping in for a drink. What are you doing really, Bernard?'

Though he no longer had to lie to her about either spying or gambling, and she had never been aware of either, Moira had become suspicious of him, due to the confusion of their finances. While he was working for both 'Patrick White' and William Hill, their household budget had been under constant pressure despite regular promotions at work. But, now, although wages at the *Mirror* were frozen and far out-paced by inflation, their disposable income had increased. This was a mystery Moira presumably attributed to the running and then chucking of a mistress, with the yarn about the summons from the ex-Prime Minister now covering a resumption.

'I am *really* going to see Wilson, love. He's sent for me.'

'But you'd promised Dermot.'

Cutting chips for the boys' tea, she went at the potatoes like they were Bernard's balls.

'I know. Just be glad I never became a politician. They fuck their children up even more than hacks.'

'Look, I don't really think you're lying. Just no offence but I can't understand why he'd want to see *you*.'

It was a puzzle and Storey worried about it so much that he knew he drove faster than he should. On Waterloo Bridge, he misjudged two buses pulling out and was almost crushed by them. As a reporter, he had come no closer to Wilson than being part of the pack during campaigns or state visits. He had been a photo-bylined columnist for only two months, a consolation in the reshuffle following Joe Haines's appointment as *Mirror* political editor.

Storey still missed the protection of Cudlipp, now bumped to the Lords and the author of memoirs that revealed the 2 Kinnerton Street meeting, although not Storey's role in it. But surely Wilson, in the first weeks of a freedom which had permitted long holidays in the Scillies and fund-raising junkets for the D'Oyly Carte, had not been assiduously reading the Inside Storey column.

He paused in front of 5 Lord North Street, not only from fear that he was being conned but also doubt that he had got the right house. He thought back to Mountbatten's grand private address. But Britain's former Prime Minister lived in a small Georgian terrace, its only hint of grandeur ornate railings where a young constable stood.

Even at this time of evening, sweat slicked the chin-band of the copper's helmet. Though it was only the second week of May, the meteorologists were promising a memorably hot summer. In the early county matches, the wickets were already taking spin.

Storey expected to be challenged but the policeman nodded and stepped aside, revealing a box, tied to the railings, containing several buttons.

'What happens if you press them?' Storey asked. Cudlipp had always said that too many journalists didn't ask questions because they thought people wouldn't answer but most folk liked to talk about themselves. Proving Storey's mentor right, the PC whispered: 'They won't give us guns, so I'm a sitting duck. If the Paddies charge up in their balaclavas, I hit that button to get help.'

Storey took the less nuclear option of pushing the white doorbell at the top of the steps. He had expected a lackey to answer and lip-curlingly deny the appointment but, after the rattling and sliding of what seemed to be several locks and bolts, the door swung back to reveal a familiar figure, looking more than ever like an anthropomorphized panda in a children's book. Wilson – wearing suit trousers and a white business shirt, with no tie but springy silver armbands keeping the sleeves high – glanced nervously down both ends of the street, then muttered: 'Do come in.'

Storey followed the former Prime Minister into a cluttered ground-floor room. On a long wooden table were stacks of red ministerial despatch boxes. Storey had read somewhere that defeated or leaving leaders were allowed to keep one as a souvenir but Wilson seemed to have used several for removal, although civilian packing crates and boxes also lay around. In a corner, on a tall bureau, where unknown householders would keep photos of their ancestors or children, Sir Harold had arranged a gallery of fellow leaders from his period in office: a shifty Nixon, the Emperor and Empress of Japan looking so regal as to be almost ethereal.

His host looked momentarily baffled, as if he was in the wrong place, then said: 'Do come upstairs. We must talk.'

Storey was surprised, after all the gossip of ill-health and failing faculties, that Wilson took the stairs at a run, striding two at a time. He assumed it was a declaration of potency and so matched the other man's power.

The first-floor drawing room was more impressive than

the size of the house and messy downstairs had suggested. A Victorian clock stood on a grand mantelpiece, which also held pottery figures of Gladstone and his wife. The walls were all books, neatly shelved and alphabetized, a reminder that the Wilsons had met as academic and aspiring poet.

The little other available space was dominated by a vast colour photograph of Wilson and Jack Kennedy, together in America in 1962. Storey thought one man's tragedy was that he had not lived to offer a contrast with the photograph; the other's was that he had.

A trolley at one end of the room was stacked with an array of bottles more common in public catering than private hospitality. Wilson held aloft a bottle of malt, splashily pouring two tumblers when Storey nodded assent. The politician flopped down onto a deep four-seater sofa, his weight and surrender of energy pushing the cushions even closer to the floor. Storey occupied a stiff-backed chair opposite.

Opening a wooden box on the table, which Storey assumed would contain his pipe paraphernalia, Wilson selected, slit, lit and then exuberantly blew a Castroesque cigar. For Storey, the double take was as great as seeing Charlie Chaplin with a golf club rather than a walking cane.

'Thank you for agreeing to see me, Bernard.'

'Oh, well, I'd put it the other way round, Sir Harold.' He took a small notepad from his inside pocket but his host briskly shook his head.

'I'm a great believer that the important things stick in our m-m-m-memory.'

It was the first time Storey had heard the politician stutter. He shrugged. Cudlipp used to say that shorthand was handy but the best notepad you had was grey and cauliflower-shaped.

'What do you think your next column will be on?'

'Tomorrow's on Thorpe again.'

'Ah. What do you think of that tragic business?'

It was a question which came with only one box to tick. Storey decided that Wilson would probably not appreciate the news that Bron Waugh was planning to stand against Thorpe in North Devon in the interest of the Dog-Lovers' Party.

'I think it's a personal tragedy for him. But it was inevitable he'd have to resign. With Clement Freud doing dog-food commercials, the Liberals were going to be hounded, no pun intended, by dog jokes.'

Wilson didn't smile. 'He's given me his personal word that there's nothing in it. He's as much a ladies' man as thee and me . . .' The sudden Yorkshirism was a surprise to listeners familiar with the Wilson of TV and speeches. 'I'm assuming you're a married chap.'

'Yes. Though . . .'

'This Scott is just a constituent with a bee in his bonnet. We've all had them. In this case, Jeremy's enemies were able to use him. Bernard, did you read my speech to the parliamentary press gallery today?'

No. There had been something on the wires but he'd ignored it. Thorpe was still the big story.

'No. I'd meant to be there but something else . . . You know newspapers.'

'Oh. I *know* newspapers.'

Twisting so inelegantly within the sofa's suffocating embrace that Storey feared the flailing cigar might start a blaze, Wilson pulled a wrinkled typescript from his pocket and skimmed it across the coffee table.

'Here. I said frankly that government as we know it is in grave danger. Anti-democratic agencies in South Africa and elsewhere are putting all our democratic futures at risk. Is that something that interests you, Bernard?'

Before the meeting, Storey had feared that he would find himself uninformed and bluffing on the subjects Wilson chose. But his problem on this topic was that he knew too much. He had first-hand evidence of British intelligence's desperation to remove 'Henry Worthington' yet was convinced that passing on his knowledge to the object of the plot would somehow jeopardize his three years' freedom from the whispering business.

'Well, Sir Harold, I *was* thinking of a possible subject for a column: the curious coincidence that . . .'

'Ah, yes. What's that?'

'That both Britain and America currently have leaders unelected by the people. Now, obviously, there are differences. President Nixon left unwillingly and in disgrace, whereas you chose to go and . . .'

'In *grace*?' For the first time in the conversation, Wilson gave the gravelly chuckle that had been part of his public persona.

'Well, yes. So President Ford and Mr Callaghan are in power for different reasons but both appointed, not elected. I just feel there might be something there.'

'And you'd treat this double bypassing of democracy, would you, Bernard, as a coincidence?'

'Well, isn't it unlikely to . . . ?'

Wilson raised a hand, a familiar gesture against Robin Day and Alistair Burnet in interviews, though never silencing them as directly as it did the awed Storey. The ex-Premier said, his voice much lower than before: 'For the last eight months when I was Prime Minister, I'm not certain I knew what was happening, fully, in security. Bernard, this could be the British Watergate. There are similarities. Not just this house but my colleagues' houses and their offices have been broken into. I think you should ask some questions. I can help you, though not openly . . .'

Wilson looked around the room, briefly holding the eye of the Gladstone bust as though considering the possibility that it might be a transmitter. Then he whispered: 'I see myself as the big fat spider in the corner of the room. Sometimes I speak when I'm asleep. You should listen. Occasionally when we meet, I might tell you to go to the Charing Cross Road and kick a blind man standing on the corner. That blind man may tell you something, lead you somewhere.'

Storey silently repeated these phrases until they stuck, reminded of revising for exams. In his memorizing frenzy, he was slow to notice that Wilson had stopped speaking and was now standing.

'Let me show you something downstairs,' he said. 'I've had it specially installed.'

Descending, Wilson didn't dash the stairs but took them so slowly that Storey twice bumped into him from behind. Perhaps he was more cautious after drinking or no longer felt it necessary to demonstrate his strength but the fluctuation in his movements could be seen as typical of the frequent changes in his manner: between friendliness and tension, accusation and humour, lucidity and. And what? Paranoia? Madness? Confusion?

Storey followed his new spymaster – did this make him a double agent? – into the ground-floor room that held the chaos of official papers. Wilson was pointing to a corner cupboard Storey hadn't noticed before.

'Looks like a man's wardrobe or an ordinary cupboard, Bernard, doesn't it?'

Wilson answered his own question by pulling open the pine door to reveal a steel safe taller than them both, surely seven feet high, its front studded with coloured knobs and levers, the ultimate seaside fruit machine.

'It's the biggest one Chubb do. Any document you give me, it's safe in here. You look surprised but when you've had as many robberies as we have, you'll understand. Be sure your own security is as good. Be careful, Bernard.'

As they shook hands, Wilson said: 'You probably wonder why I chose you?'

'Well, yes.'

'Joe – Joe Haines – pointed out your columns to me. There's an anger there about the spooks. I don't know why but it's there.'

Passing the policeman on the street, Storey, perhaps already influenced by Wilson's thinking, wondered if the guard's superiors would soon be receiving transcripts of everything he had said in the house.

Going home, again so distracted that a squall of horns criticized his driving, Storey reflected on Wilson. He always felt that the word 'tragedy' was not applicable to any politician except the Kennedys but it was hard not to feel regret about this differently fallen leader.

Was there another politician who had come into office with so heavy an investment of hope from the public but left with that same account in such deep deficit? At first, Wilson had seemed to have it all: youth, energy, rhetoric, ideas. But a man to whom the voters had given their belief had come to seem impossible to believe. In the end, the question was not whether he was a liar but whether he deliberately misled the electorate or suffered from self-delusion.

The angry honking of a taxi brought Storey's thoughts back to the road.

Part Seven

2004

Everybody Knows

Everybody knows that the dice are loaded
Everybody rolls with their fingers crossed.
Everybody knows the war is over.
Everybody knows the good guys lost

Leonard Cohen – 'Everybody Knows'

30

What Will Survive of Us

NARROWING his eyes against the icy brightness, he could no longer tell the first flakes of snow from the scraps of litter thrown towards the Charing Cross Road by an egg-whisk wind. The morning's newspapers had reported deaths from hypothermia, drivers deep-frozen in their cars, only six months after coroners had become used to typing on post-mortem forms that most unlikely cause of death in England: heat exhaustion. But this was weather in the twenty-first century: these seasons of extremes.

In the window of the last electronics shop on Tottenham Court Road, the stacked plasma screens magnified and multiplied the face of Dr David Kelly, his white beard and Baghdad tan giving him the appearance of a sunburned Santa. Kelly had been the ghost-face of the previous summer and now this winter.

As always when he saw the street-sign for Charing Cross Road, Storey smiled inside and wondered if he should kick a blind man, although these conditions would make it difficult to see a white stick. Wilson had been out of power for twenty-eight years now and dead for nine. Almost none of the major players from that decade of attempted coups still survived.

Checking his Psion and finding that he was ten minutes ahead of himself, Storey turned right into Oxford Street. The classical music section of the Virgin Megastore ran to a few racks of hummable extracts. They only had selected moments from the *St Matthew Passion* and the one boxed Beethoven

Symphonies in stock was not the Rattle. The single consolation of the burglaries was that many of the CDs the thieves
had taken were favourites worn almost to distortion, which
could now be renewed from insurance money.

He was luckier in Rock and Pop A–Z. Soon his basket
rattled with *The Essential Leonard Cohen, Best of Leonard
Cohen* and *More Best Of*. From the wall of the Top 100
current bestsellers, he added The Darkness and Franz
Ferdinand. He almost put them back, nervous of the wry
triumphant smile at the till from an assistant now certain of
winning the staff sweepstake for the day's saddest customer.
But then he found himself standing in line behind far older
men, with heads forcibly bald rather than shaved, bent over
their baskets of albums by Black-Eyed Peas and The Strokes.
Though actual immortality remained a laboratory dream,
cultural agelessness had now been achieved; you were as old
as you wanted to be.

Heading south down Charing Cross Road with his little
tinkling bag, Storey found time frozen in another way. The
street was the land that theatre forgot. To his left, *Blood
Brothers*; to his right, *Les Misérables*. These shows had been
birthday outings for him almost twenty years before but
seemed like kindergarten hits alongside *The Mousetrap*,
whose advertising lights, now shining through the blizzard to
his left, announced its fifty-second year. These few hundred
yards of London around Cambridge Circus seemed to be a
theatrical deep-freeze.

The best tip he had ever been given about journalism –
try to see with the eyes of a foreigner, even in your own
country – had become a habit and so he noted the latest
Starbucks-wannabe in the run of shops beside Pizza Hut.

Storey's publicist had gushed about the possibility of the
book getting a window in Murder One, so he crossed the road

to check but the only non-fiction on display among the novels
by Rankin, Rendell and Cornwell was case-histories of American serial killers. There was no copy of *Octopus* on the New
Titles table either. Storey considered asking for it but was still
too new to the triumph of being a published writer to risk the
humiliation of the trade.

Making the literary equivalent of the journey from maternity ward to crematorium, he crossed the road again to the
set of second-hand bookshops around the Chinese Medical
Centre, choosing the one that seemed to have the largest
selection, although its name was painful for a first-time
author: Any Amount of Books – Bought and Sold. Gold-
and-green barrows outside were loaded with discoloured
paperbacks, their jackets boasting low, pre-decimal prices, of
writers he remembered from his father's collection, donated
in crates to the charity shop when he died: John Masters,
Michael Innes, R. F. Delderfield, J. G. Farrell.

One of the oddest aspects of the burglaries was that
Storey's books had mainly been trashed or trampled rather
than taken. When he tried to restore order to the room,
certain favourite volumes were missing, but it was possible
the absent books had been borrowed or left in hotel rooms
or the *Guardian* office over the years.

In the politics section, he had a choice between two good-
condition copies of the Churchill biography by Roy Jenkins,
which he wanted in his library again as a memorial to the
author who had died the previous year, aged eighty-two,
more prized as a writer than a politician, although credited
and debited by opposing pundits in obituaries with liberaliz-
ing Britain.

Further along these shelves of the dead, he saw a plastic-
wrapped copy of Auberon Waugh's *The Last Word: An
Eye-Witness Account of The Thorpe Trial*, which he bought

from sentimental memory. Alone among the major players in the story, Thorpe still lived on, though his illness and public scepticism had left him entirely a private citizen in the three decades since the jury had accepted the judge's instruction that he was neither a homosexual nor a murderer.

Knowing that with the baby coming he should be watching what he spent, Storey restricted himself to one more book. The robbers of his office had curiously used Peter Wright's *Spycatcher* as a lavatory, so he replaced it with a copy soiled only with pencilled exclamation. Like the one now bagged as evidence and supposedly being analysed for faecal DNA, it came from the American edition illegally circulated in Britain during the long period when Margaret Thatcher was using the courts to keep the old spy's secrets secret.

If the Virgin Megastore had made Storey feel young, Any Amount of Books aged him. For any human, not just a new author, there was a melancholy in carrying in a plastic bag the books of three dead men. He dropped the living musicians alongside them as a psychic counter-balance.

His mother was looking around nervously as she waited on the steps outside the National Portrait Gallery. She had become frightened of London since her move back to Dublin and more so since the paranoia about a possible Islamic terrorist attack.

'Don't look so frightened, Mum.'

'Well, I do worry, Dermot. It was all over the papers again this morning. Tony Blair saying an attack by al-Qa'eda is inevitable.'

'Mother, Blair doesn't know any more than you do. I've just written a whole book about it. Politicians get given this stuff called intelligence, which is the least accurately named idea since Angel Delight or the safe period.'

She aimed a playful swipe at him. 'Rude about my cooking and the Church inside a minute. You haven't changed, Dermot. How's your Hannah?'

'She's so big she thinks it's triplets.'

'Ah. Normally it's the water. Bernard and I swore blind you'd be twins.'

Try to see with the eyes of a foreigner. London, from this perspective, was now a city in which people rattled on thirty-year-old trains towards shimmering new buildings that had opened almost monthly since the millennium. The transport was the victim of government under-investment; the galle ries the beneficiary of National Lottery cash. The National Portrait Gallery, a cube of pigeon-shitted civic stone on his previous visit, now rose in spacious layers of glass and caramel marble.

Tired from the flight and a much-interrupted journey on the Underground, his mother wanted lunch before the Beaton. They ate sandwiches so elaborate – spirals of inter-bred lettuces flower-arranged around cones of smoked salmon and topiaried chunks of tomato – that they could plausibly have been displayed as sculptures in the art galleries next door.

Conversation was slow, perhaps because any mention of Hannah risked intruding on the confusions of a devout Irish Catholic widow whose first grandchild was the product of an atheist father and a Jewish mother.

Mum suggested that she should be staying in a hotel, rather than getting under his and Hannah's feet; he lied that Hannah loved to have her. She asked to see his shopping and commented on what a good friend Bron had been to his dad and hadn't they both been taken too young?

But she really couldn't understand what he and Bernard saw in that Canadian undertaker Leonard Cohen and what on earth was Franz Ferdinand apart from a reminder of a time when they bothered to have a reason for starting wars? When he told her, she wondered if he wasn't a bit old for that kind of music. He replied that he was only thirty-four; there had been men of fifty at the tills.

When their talk was exhausted, Storey took from his shoulder bag the copy of *Octopus* and slid it across the table with a nonchalance he didn't feel.

'Oh, is this it? Your dad used to talk about the day he'd hand me this. Not that I'm not . . .'

'No, no. I felt the same, Mum, when I saw it.'

She looked at the cover, six small portraits caught in the eight tentacles.

'Ah, Diana, obviously. Wilson, Nixon. King Cecil, as your dad used to call him. That poor Dr Kelly. Sad eyes, I always think, even though those pictures were taken before he should have had any reason to be.'

She tapped the sixth picture with her finger. 'Now who's that chap with the corks hanging from his hat?'

'Peter Wright. He was in MI5.'

'Ah, well, no wonder I don't recognize him. He's meant to be invisible. I only know King Cecil because your dad worked for him. People say awful things about him but he gave us a pay rise once out of nowhere which I swear saved us from divorce that summer we knew we were having you.'

She flicked open the book and he knew from the instant pooling of her gaze that she must be looking at the dedication.

In loving memory of my father
Bernard (1936–1991)
I am his Storey; this was his story.

'If I said I wish he could have seen this, you'd tell me it was a terrible cliché, wouldn't you?'

'Oh, Mum, even journalists don't sub their own mothers.

Though, as you raised it, it's a contradiction not a cliché. If Dad had lived, it would have been his name on the cover of the book. Dedicated to you.'

It was his firm intention that his mother would never know her husband had been a spy. Or why. When he realized, reading his father's twenty-year-old manuscript, who 'Patrick White' must be, he had passed a few melodramatic days of hating his dad before understanding that Bernard Storey's two most likely motives for cooperating – that he hoped he was on to a good story or was desperate to keep his marriage together – were both difficult for someone carrying on his genes and his profession to condemn.

When he turned left on the first-floor landing of the new wing, his mother, now looking as worried as if she had just seen Osama bin Laden carrying a ticking box, said: 'The sign to the Beaton is that way.'

'Yes. I know. Don't look so alarmed. I just want you to see these pictures. I came here a lot when I was writing the book.'

She looked reluctant – his mother was such a nervous woman that he wondered if she had guessed at least one of her husband's secrets – but he held her elbow, as though she were twenty years older than she was, and edged towards Britain 1837–1990. He was familiar enough with these pictures to steer her straight to the section where the Sixties began.

After the bookshop on the Charing Cross Road, this was a second gallery of ghosts: the repertory company of Bernard Storey's anecdotes and manuscripts. Graham Sutherland, as true to the ruin of his own face as he had been to those of others, looked watchfully through crumpled skin from a self-portrait, given to the nation by his widow when he died in 1980.

Before he could point them out, his mother saw what he

had wanted to show her. 'Next to each other,' she said quietly.

Wilson, as painted by Ruskin Spear, was a tobacconist's Cézanne, the foreground swirls of pipe-smoke giving an impressionistic tinge to an otherwise figurative depiction of grey-outlined pouches under worried eyes, the politician's chubby fingers clutching the talismanic briar. It was, appropriately, Dermot thought, a Wilson of the shadows, the paint almost threatening to drift away as you looked.

To Wilson's left, Cecil Harmsworth King, as seen by Sutherland in the painting which took shape even as his empire evaporated, seemed fixed and solid. 'Tall as your dad was, he always said King Cecil made him look small. Were his eyes really as sheer blue as that?'

'Apparently. But I know what you mean. It's like one of those hardboard cut-outs at the seaside, with a real person looking through.'

King, lowered by a series of strokes, had died in a Dublin nursing home on Good Friday 1987, himself just one year younger than the century. He had reportedly insisted on his deathbed that he had never been a spy and had always done what was best for his country but the obituaries were as unkind as he had feared since 1968. Bernard Storey had not attended the memorial service.

Baron Wilson of Rievaulx of Kirklees in the County of West Yorkshire, having survived the loss of most of his guts to cancer shortly after leaving office, had lived until 1995, although the news of his death surprised many who thought him already long buried.

While two former Tory premiers, Heath and Thatcher, wrestled for their reputations through books and interviews, Wilson disappeared from the media at least a decade before he died, the holes in his memory leaving him unreliable in

front of microphones. Bernard Storey could not have
attended that memorial service as it fell four years after his
own.

(That morning, walking to his first interview at Broadcasting House, Storey had lit a candle for his dad in St
Patrick's in Soho. Bringing his mother to see these haunted
portraits seemed a second necessary ritual on the day of
publication.)

He liked the fact that the curator had a sense of Britain's
hidden history, hanging Wilson beside his thwarted Guy
Fawkes and, just a few spaces away, Mountbatten, his face
tightly framed so that he loomed down on the viewer like the
bows of a battleship.

Storey remembered, as a ten-year-old, the first time he had
seen his mother cry or swear. 'The bastards,' she had wept,
when the television news flash in August 1979 reported that
an IRA bomb had blown up Mountbatten on his boat,
Shadow V, in the harbour of Mullaghmore. A statement from
the terrorists explained that it was an attempt to tear out 'the
sentimental, imperialist heart of the British people'.

The curator's feel for history was allied to a sense of
humour. Standing back from the wall, you saw that King,
who had designated himself Britain's lost leader, had been
placed in a line of Prime Ministers, the lesser, elected alter-
natives to his desired dictatorship. As well as Wilson, there
was Callaghan, the familiar benevolent grin belying the grim
will which had allowed him to best his long rival, Jenkins.

'Is Cudlipp here, Dermot? Bernard always said he owed
him everything.'

Cudlipp, outliving Wilson, King, Mountbatten and
Bernard Storey, had made it closest to the end of the century,
dying in 1998, aged eighty-four, writing in longhand a last
note to old friends which included a final flourish of topical

populism, attributing his imminent death to 'faulty Old Labour heart valve failing adequately to supply New Labour lung with sufficient oxygen'.

'No. They have a few cartoons. But they're in storage. It's a pity but even great journalists are like their papers. Wrapping haddock tomorrow.'

The perishability of the press was the reason that his father started, and his son had now completed, *Octopus*, although the shops of Charing Cross Road had just shown him that there was an equivalent of the chippie for literature.

Mum enjoyed the Cecil Beaton exhibition more than he did. He could see the pictures of Elizabeth Taylor and Mick Jagger bringing back the Sixties for her but he disliked the photographer's glamorizing eye, his mission to remove a sitter's flaws. The determined, firm-jawed Churchill was the politician as he had hoped to be shown, rather than the startled mastiff of the Karsh of Ottawa shot. The pictures of the Queen Mother when young, however, intrigued him, disproving the tuppenny punditry that Diana had been the Royal Family's first film-star princess.

His mother was going on to the Vuillard exhibition at the Royal Academy. Dermot was keen to see the Philip Guston show there, with its vicious pictures of the ruined Nixon dragging his thrombotic leg along San Clemente beach. But his decision to show his mum the ghosts of King and Wilson had delayed them and he risked being late to give his own view of Nixon on the radio.

They separated at Eros. He had suggested they went by tube but she had read in the *Telegraph* of fears that al-Qa'eda would gas the Underground. A second gentle lecture on intelligence had no effect. Though it was only quarter to three, Oxford Circus looked like rush-hour and probably the one in Tokyo: the pavements were deep with people from kerb to shop-front. An orange-jacketed man was shouting, in a voice made tremulous by either megaphone or fear, that the station was closed because of a security alert.

This disrupting suspicion, born in New York three years before, was also in force at the BBC. Storey tried to re-use the pass he'd been given that morning for his broadcast from the same building to the outpost of BBC Suffolk but was forced to prove himself again. While he knew that it was possible to holiday quite happily in Italy without noticing that the government had fallen during lunch, Storey was still surprised that the building could feel functioning and comfortable so soon after the BBC had lost its two most senior figures.

Beside the sofa where he waited for the producer, a TV set on the lobby wall – both wide- and flat-screen: a quick history of television was that both the content and the sets had become progressively thinner – showed a news bulletin. It cut from film of the second President Bush – who had admitted that the intelligence advising him to attack Iraq might have been wrong – to a picture of Prince Charles, reportedly about to be interviewed by the police investigating his ex-wife's death.

'Mr Storey?'

The producer, carrying a copy of *Octopus* with pink Post-It notes sticking out from intermittent pages, had a nervous blink and smelled of cigarette smoke. She gestured at the television.

'Good day to have you in, all that.'

'I know. It could almost be a conspiracy.'

The producer gave the kind of staccato laugh that showed someone had spotted a joke but hadn't got it. She was right, though, about the timing. It was a season of inquiries – Butler now following Hutton – and inquests. Seven years after Diana's Paris car-smash, a British coroner was finally investigating, sending Scotland Yard on the cold and hopeless trail. Following the resumption of speculation in the press that the princess had been pregnant at the time of death, a pathologist had told *The Times* that he had looked into Diana's womb and it was empty. Dr David Kelly's death, which Lord Hutton's report had viewed as suicide, was now being considered again by the Oxford coroner.

On the way to the basement, the lift braked and seemed to fall for half a floor, before resuming its rattling regularity. The doors leading to a group of studios held a sign warning that no unopened post should be taken past this point, presumably a relic of the anthrax scares of two years before. Storey was shown to a nest of sofas – 'Can you wait here? We're having a bit of a problem with presenters' – where the 3 p.m. news was playing on speakers.

It was all Iraq again. The Labour Party was meeting to decide whether to punish Clare Short, who had claimed that British spies had bugged the United Nations during the war. Reports of recent large explosions were coming in from Baghdad. There were rumours that Katharine Gun, an employee at the government's espionage centre who had made claims similar to Ms Short's, was planning a book that might become the second *Spycatcher*. Friends of Lord Hutton had said that he was surprised that his inquiry into the death of weapons expert Dr David Kelly had led to the resignations of the BBC's Chairman and Director-General, Gavyn Davies and Greg Dyke.

The producer came back, looking even more worried, and waved Storey towards a studio that held a grand piano and a baize-covered table from which grew the peculiar blooms of microphones covered in coloured sponge. The presenter was a woman he didn't recognize – most of the radio names came from television these days – and he missed the name –

Camilla something? – in her babbled apology: 'Sorry, it wasn't supposed to be me. He's off, finishing a book. I haven't read this but they've given me questions.'

A green light on top of a wooden cone flashed and they began. 'Camilla' ran her finger along each line of the script, like a child learning to read. 'Oh, er, Bernard, I should say that it's as if we're picking up from the previous item and then we're as live. But stop if you want to cough or clarify.'

The presenter made a low growling sound in her throat, sipped from a plastic cup of water, then adopted an expression of considerable severity. '*GB 84* by David Peace is published as a paperback original by Faber. But our next subject also explores the dark side of the past. Is that a coincidence or is it – as some would say – a conspiracy? My next guest would certainly have an opinion on that. Dermot Storey, a journalist for the *Guardian*, has written *Octopus: The Search for a British Watergate*. And he's with me now. Dermot, you searched for a British Watergate. Did you find it?'

A sudden after-taste of his salmon sandwich seemed to wash across his tonsils and he knew his voice would come out croaky. 'Well, er, it wasn't me who was looking for it. The book is about how many people in Britain – journalists, politicians, spies – wanted there to be a British Watergate or thought that they had found one. It was a sort of envy of that great American story. But I came to the conclusion that they were usually wrong.'

'Right. You, er, write about a lot of different cases. Princess Diana. Two, um, plots to bring down Harold Wilson. The fall of Jeremy Thorpe. Poor Dr Kelly. Are you saying that all these stories are connected?'

Christ, she was going to read the questions from a numbered list, regardless of the answers. 'Well,' he said, gently.

The publicity department had said that listeners decided to buy books depending on whether the writer sounded friendly and nice. 'Well, the connection, as I suggested earlier – ' careful, you sound like a politician scoring points ' – the link is that these are all mysteries that people have tried to make into our Watergate. But I do also think they're connected by the business of intelligence. At different times, there are whispers. Harold Wilson is a Soviet agent who has impregnated his secretary. Jeremy Thorpe's had his boyfriend's dog shot. Saddam Hussein has weapons of mass destruction. Al-Qa'eda is trying to poison London's water. Princess Diana was killed because she was about to give the future King William a Muslim halfbrother. The government exaggerated the threat from Iraq. Now most of these stories are started or spread by MI5, with the exception of the Diana and Iraq stuff, which are stories people started about MI5. The question for—'

'Camilla', who was wearing headphones, clamped a hand to her left ear, as if she had just received an electric shock, and waved at Storey to stop. 'Sorry. Sorry, Dermot. The producer's just saying that Thorpe is still alive and we need to make clear that he was cleared by a jury.'

'Really? There's also a story that when he announced he was going to sue the newspapers for libel after he won, Lord Goodman said: "You've been a very lucky man and you should not do anything so foolish." Is he really in a position to sue . . . ?'

The presenter held her left headphone again with a scowl of pain. 'I'm sorry, Dermot. Everyone's very jumpy after Hutton.'

'OK, I think I can find a way of incorporating his definition of himself as a heterosexual whose knowledge of Great Danes was taken from *Scooby-Doo*. I'll pick up . . .' He coughed to bring back his published writer's voice. 'Now most of these stories were started or spread by MI5, with the exception of the Diana and Iraq stuff, which people started about MI5. The question for a politician – or citizen – is how many of these whispers – call them intelligence, call them gossip – to believe. Now, we see how difficult it is. The spies were totally wrong about Wilson, but at least partly right about Thorpe. Sewerage and water from the same pipe: how do you choose? Wilson didn't believe a word they told him about Thorpe, although there was more than enough to come to court, where a jury believed him, although I'd still be happier leaving my sister with him for the weekend than my brother or his dog.' The presenter paled but let him carry on. 'But history shows that much – even most – of what our spooks mutter in the ears of Prime Ministers is a kind of higher tittle-tattle. They distrusted Wilson, they trusted Tony Blair. But all Blair got for that advantage was that they hyped him a line on terrorists and Iraq. Being the spies' friend is as dangerous as being their enemy. And the general suspicion of the state raised by their mistakes creates a situation in which, long after it all seemed to have died down, people start believing again that Princess Diana was assassinated by the driver of a missing white Fiat Uno. There are people in America who believe in something called the Octopus Theory: that everything from the killing of the Kennedy brothers to the destruction of the World Trade Center was organized by five oil billionaires from a bunker under Texas. My idea of the Octopus is different: it's about how the mysteries of the Sixties and Seventies in Britain and America put out tentacles. Watergate opened the floodgates, if you like, leading to the desire to see another.'

The presenter's finger reached the third line of her brief. 'In your research, what was the most surprising thing you found out?'

Well, 'Camilla', that my dad had been a spy. 'Well, I think it was probably that, in 1968 and 1969, Marcia Williams, Harold Wilson's main adviser, was able to have two illegitimate children, fathered by the political editor of the *Daily Mail*, Walter Terry, without it ever being mentioned in the press.'

Throwing both hands to her ears, the presenter seemed to be experiencing electrocution. 'Er, the producer says is that definitely true? Can we say that?'

'Yes, it's fine. I'll pick up.' Storey coughed. 'It was only three decades ago but it feels like another world. There are two points here. One is that we have gone from a culture in which politicians were instinctively given the benefit of the doubt to one in which we instinctively doubt their benefits.' Ach, a bit Blairish, a bit People's Princess. 'The other is that the spooks and the rumour-mongers were wrong about who the father was, as about so much else.'

'I described you, Dermot, as the author of this book. But, in a way, you're the co-author?'

'Yes. That's right. It began as a manuscript called *Blind Man's Buff*, which was started by my father, Bernard Storey, apparently in the mid-Seventies. From what we can tell from his diaries, it was Harold Wilson who got him going on it. Dad never finished it. In fact, my family didn't even know about it until we cleared out an attic in Wandsworth when my mother moved back to Ireland three years ago. I think he must have knocked it out late at night on his old typewriter at the *Mirror*.'

As her finger underlined the fifth question on her sheet, the presenter swallowed hard and gripped the table with her free hand. 'Er, given, the, er, subject of the book your father was working on – how the spies tried to bring down the Prime

Minister – are you absolutely sure that it was a coincidence that he died before he could finish it?'

Storey used two sips of water to delay consideration of this possibility. 'Look, a couple of my father's colleagues tried to get that going. But people die in car crashes. I think Princess Diana's was just an accident; I think my dad's was too. It was very late at night, he'd been working on a story. He hadn't been sleeping well because he was in the *Daily Mirror* pension scheme, which Robert Maxwell had just plundered . . .'

'Wow, Robert Maxwell involved as well! That really is a conspiracy theory!'

'Yes, well, except that I'm saying to you that it isn't. I think you either tend to believe in conspiracy or coincidence. I think there *are* conspiracies – there were at least two against Harold Wilson – but the fact that my father died before he could finish his book was coincidence. An accident, in two senses.'

'Dermot Storey, thank you. *Octopus: The Search for a British Watergate* is published by Picador this week.' She paused and then spoke in less formal tones. 'They seem happy with that behind the glass. She says she can clip out the line about not wanting Thorpe to look after your dog.'

'Right. Actually, there was just one other bit I wanted to get in. There's a line in *Spycatcher* where Wright talks about them "bugging and burgling their way around London". I was just going to say that MI5 and MI6 seem to have extended that idea to the United Nations now.'

The electrocution gesture again. 'She thinks we've probably got enough.'

AFTER the posh totty had thanked Second-Storey – for what? Treachery and defamation of the state? – and told

Middle England how to buy his lies, he waved at Gandalf to stop the playback. The flickering blocks on the RealPlayer file froze, stopping the bands of sound so that they stretched across the screen as horizontal Christmas trees.

'Interesting book,' he said. 'I'd buy one if we didn't have a first edition already.'

He held up the digipen on which *Octopus* was copied. Keeping an eye on these guys was so much simpler now you just stuck a device like a tiny key-ring into their cute blue iMacs rather than arsing around half-inching floppies.

'Be nice to have a signed one, I suppose,' he told his number two. 'But the writer wasn't in when we got ours.'

The bright-eyed deputy – aka Cherie (working title) because he was the kind who sounded like he'd be up for sucking Blair's dick if he could – smiled noncommittally. Cherie was unhappy with bugging and plumbing: this intake had signed up for Spying Lite, thinking that MI5 would be like Abbey National with faster cars. Then the World Trade Center had become an airport and suddenly the old farts were called back from grass.

The nerd – kindly breaking off from watching the *Lord of the Rings* trilogy back to back on DVD with the curtains drawn to grace them with his presence in the office – looked up from the flat screen and said: 'There are five edit-points I can find. Mainly when he mentions this "Jeremy Thorpe", is it . . . ?' – yes, it is, it is, another fucker with no sense of history – 'or the war.'

'Thanks, Gandalf,' he said. Wanker seemed to take it as a compliment. In his head, he was Emperor of the Orcs or whatever. For the first couple of days, Gandalf's older colleagues had experimented with 'Kojak'. But time had played havoc with workplace nicknames. All of the new crew thought Telly

Savalas was a Greek cable station and every single one of them had fucking shaved heads, anyway.

'That's interesting. What do you usually do about that?' asked Gandalf. 'Do you try to get the edits out of the BBC?'

'Sure. Didn't you know the Teletubbies are our assets? The public's so dumb they think those aerials on their heads are some kind of joke about television. Deep fucking cover or what? No, it's a problem, Gandalf. When I joined, we had a bloke in the basement of Broadcasting House, vetting the staff. Then he left and they went Left. Still, they're running so scared after Hutton, they'll probably hand it all over if we write to *Points of View*.'

Nobody spoke for a moment and he enjoyed the perfect silence. A double-glazed grave would sound like a night club in comparison. Another advantage of the anti-listening glass, made to thwart anyone aiming a laser at the window to catch the sound-waves, was that no noise penetrated from outside.

So they were spared the screams of the peace-freaks at the gate – encouraged by that cunt Short and that other cunt Gun – waving their painted bed-sheets and singing some hippy ditty about Bush and Blair having blood on their hands. Gun was the worst because she'd come from inside GCHQ. Philby had to go and live on beetroot soup after helping the enemy. Ms Gun had the *Guardian* licking her arse all over the front page.

Everyone thought it was so fucking smart to say that they hadn't found any nuclear warheads under Saddam's bed. Questions Must Be Asked About The Quality Of Intelligence. But no doctor would say he was wrong to do a biopsy because they only found normal cells. There are no wrong answers in espionage, only questions that are always correct. As I was going up the stair, I met a man who wasn't there. He wasn't there again today but I blew up the stairs just in case. Don't come crying to us when Osama Big Hard-on blows your dicks into a different postal district.

Princess Margaret, who had sat as quietly as usual, flinching as ever at his swearing, spoke for the first time. Some of the younger ones didn't get that nickname either. 'Sir, two questions about the filing. Many of the references in the radio interview belong most naturally in the Henry Worthington file . . .'

'Crikey. Is that still open?' Cherie (working title) asked.

'An MI5 file is like a motorway service station or Diana Dors's legs,' he explained. Only Princess Margaret understood the reference to the actress and she didn't like it. The two young men looked as blank as a journalist lecturing on ethics.

'Yes. Put them in Worthington,' he told the librarian.

'And do you want a file for Storey, Dermot as well as Storey, Bernard or should it all go in the old one?'

'Oh. Beauty of computers is you can have a pouch, can't you? Kangaroo-style? Attach them. Chip off the old microchip.'

He had brought the *Standard* up with him from London and thrown it on the desk. Gandalf, his work on the *Octopus* interview done, was reading, the paper folded to a story about some peace-and-love fucker in the Commons asking questions about Saint Tony's massive new investment in intelligence.

'Do you think they'll be able to stop it, sir?' asked Gandalf.

'Nah. If the votes look dicey, a few private security briefings on how Iran's four Most Wanted flew into Heathrow last Thursday should do it.'

'One thousand new spooks,' said Cherie (working title). 'Exciting times.'

'A thousand,' Gandalf echoed. 'That should be enough.'

He thought of his old mentor in the service, long dead in Australia, and all that he had taught him. Peter Wright's tragedy had been to live in a time when people had a choice about being paranoid.

'Nah,' he said. 'Enough is never enough.'

Afterword

While this novel was based on a large number of factual sources (detailed below), the warning of the Author's Note preceding it should be repeated here: it is a work of fiction and the characters, even when recognizable from an external context, are behaving fictionally.

The plot also dramatizes innuendo, gossip and smears. It should, for example, be stressed that none of the politicians denigrated by Peter Wright and James Jesus Angleton – Harold Wilson, Willy Brandt, Gough Whitlam, Henry Kissinger – is regarded by sane, objective observers as having been a spy. The accusers were paranoid fantasists.

My general aim has been to avoid giving to any character dialogue or actions which the historical record indicates would have been impossible or unlikely. However, the dialogue, though trying to capture the cadence of their conversation as it is recorded in reality, is frequently invented, except where diaries or other archives have recorded actual exchanges.

To take a small example, it would, in my view, have gone beyond the limits of even a biographical novel to have invented meetings between Cecil King and Oswald Mosley. But, in dramatizing the established fact of their encounters, the scene expands on the small surviving record of what passed between them, while attempting to give neither man a view which he would not have held.

As a general principle, when a detail seems weird or ridiculously convenient – such as the gathering of Anglican clergy at *Mirror* HQ during King's fall, Mary Wilson's service as a Booker Prize judge or Harold Wilson's declaration to a journalist that he was a big fat spider who might command the kicking of blind men – it can be guaranteed to be true or, at least, documented.

The liberties I have knowingly taken extend to small shifts of chronology or changes of location. (While Graham Sutherland did paint Cecil King during the period depicted here, their sittings took place in France rather than England and so on.) Such changes are for reasons of narrative economy or flow.

A book which recreates so many factual characters and events is inevitably heavily indebted to works of non-fiction.

My main source on the life of James Harold Wilson (1916–1995) was *Harold Wilson* by Ben Pimlott (HarperCollins, 1992), a splendid book made even more treasurable by Professor Pimlott's recent death. Equally valuable was *Wilson: The Authorised Life* by Philip Ziegler (Weidenfeld & Nicolson, 1993) and I was lucky that as fine a biographer as Ziegler had also dealt with an important incidental character in *Mountbatten: The Official Biography* (HarperCollins, 1985).

It was useful to hear those characters speaking in their own voices in, respectively, *The Labour Government 1964–70* by Harold Wilson (Pelican, 1974) and *From Shore To Shore: The Diaries of Earl Mountbatten of Burma, 1953–1979* edited by Philip Ziegler (William Collins, 1989.) Another very useful source on Wilson was *Who Goes Home?* by Roy Hattersley (LittleBrown, 1995).

Cecil Harmsworth King (1901–1987) left a substantial account of his actions from his own standpoint in *The Cecil King Diary 1965–1970* (Cape, 1972) and *The Cecil King Diary 1970–1974* (Cape, 1975.) His vision of himself is also offered in *Strictly Personal* (Weidenfeld & Nicolson, 1969) and *Without Fear Or Favour* (Sidgwick & Jackson, 1971).

Hugh Cudlipp (1913–1998) provides a contrary account of King and a compelling one of himself in his memoir *Walking On The Water* (Bodley Head, 1976). It's a pity that the inevitable disappearance of journalistic reputation has put that provocative and well-observed book out of print, although I recommend anyone interested in the history of the British press to seek it out through on-line booksellers, as well as Cudlipp's *Publish And Be Damned* (Weidenfeld & Nicolson, 1953) and *At Your Peril* (W & N, 1962).

A useful overview of these two huge newspaper figures is provided in *Newspapermen: Hugh Cudlipp, Cecil Harmsworth King and the Glory Days of Fleet Street* by Ruth Dudley-Edwards (Secker & Warburg, 2003).

Peter Wright (1916–1995) is notoriously immortalized by *Spycatcher: The Candid Autobiography of a Senior Intelligence Officer* (Viking, 1987). There was an enjoyable frisson in the fact that the copy on my bookshelves was illegally imported during the period of the book's state-imposed ban in Britain.

The various intrigues involving the security services and the Labour administrations of the 1960s and 70s are detailed in *The Wilson Plot* by David Leigh (Heinemann, 1988) and *Smear!: Wilson and the Secret State* by Stephen Dorril and Robin Ramsay (Fourth Estate, 1991). Both books help to separate fact from fantasy in *Spycatcher* and also expand and clarify work started in *The Pencourt File* by Barrie Penrose and Roger Courtiour (Harper & Row, 1978). So does the enthralling reportage of *Rinkagate: The Rise and Fall of Jeremy Thorpe* by Simon Freeman with Barrie Penrose (Bloomsbury, 1996).

In my book, the entirely fictional characters of Bernard Storey and Dermot Storey overlap with some of the investigations of Penrose & Courtiour and are beneficiaries of some of their revelations (principally, the 'big fat spider' speech). However, the financial difficulties and many other vices of Bernard Storey – their cause and their solution – are completely an invention and he represents no actual journalist of the period. For example, though Storey covers stories actually written for the *Mirror* in 1968 by Kenelm Jenour, Roger Todd and David Wright, none of Bernard Storey's characteristics, crises or vices is borrowed from them.

Afterword

Roy Jenkins (1920–2003) gave his own typically elegant record of many of the featured events in *A Life At The Centre* (Macmillan, 1991).

The main source on the life of James Jesus Angleton (1917–1987) was *Cold Warrior* by Tom Mangold (Simon & Schuster, 1991).

Contrasting views of the Wilson administrations are provided by *Inside Number 10* by Marcia Williams (Weidenfeld & Nicolson, 1972) and *Glimmers of Twilight* by Joe Haines (Politico's, 2003). Because of the large disagreement, the novel attempts to attribute disputed allegations to the source which made them. It should be clear, for example, that Haines is the basis for the story of the suggested mercy-killing of Mrs Williams by Wilson's doctor and the 'six times in 1956' speech. The multi-viewpoint structure of the book is intended to reflect the conflicts that arise between different witnesses to history.

In most other cases, the approach has also been to balance first-person testimony against the record of external participants. Arnold Goodman (1913–1995) left the memoir *Tell Them I'm On My Way* (Chapmans, 1993) and *Not An Englishman: Conversations with Lord Goodman* by David Selbourne (Sinclair-Stevenson, 1993).

The voice and views of Richard Milhous Nixon (1913–1994) were suggested by his memoir *In The Arena* (Simon & Schuster, 1990).

The style and opinions of Auberon Waugh (1939–2001) survive in *The Diaries of Auberon Waugh: A Turbulent Decade 1976–1985* (Eye/Deutsch, 1985) and *The Last Word: An Eyewitness Account of the Thorpe Trial* (Michael Joseph, 1980).

Rebecca Marjorie ('Marje') Proops (c. 1911–1996) was brought back to me by the book *Dear Marje* (Deutsch, 1976) and the video *Learning to Love: A Frank Guide for the Young* (Mirror Vision).

The character of Graham Sutherland (1903–1980) comes strongly through *Graham Sutherland: A Biography* by Roger Berthoud (Faber, 1982), while the work is covered well in *Graham Sutherland* by John Haynes (Phaidon, 1980).

Afterword

Sir Oswald Ernald ('Tom') Mosley (1896–1980) told his own story in *My Life* (Nelson, 1968), while a more objective account, incorporating the later years, can be found in *Rules of the Game* and *Beyond the Pale* by his son, Nicholas Mosley (Pimlico, 1988).

Although Harold Wilson frequently regretted the volume of keen diarists who sat in his cabinets, they have proved invaluable to later writers on the period. For general political background and a few verbatim moments, I have drawn on *The Castle Diaries 1964–1976* by Barbara Castle (Macmillan, 1990), *The Benn Diaries* by Tony Benn (Hutchinson, 1995) and *The Crossman Diaries 1964–1970* by Richard Crossman (Cape, 1979). Barbara Castle (1910–2002) also covered the period in a retrospective record *Fighting All The Way* (Macmillan, 1993).

For general American political background, I consulted *The Haldeman Diaries: Inside The Nixon White House* by H. R. Haldeman (Putnam, 1994), *Nixon: A Life* by Jonathan Aitken (Weidenfeld & Nicolson, 1993) and *Watergate: The Corruption & Fall of Richard Nixon* by Fred Emery (Cape, 1994).

Information on a key location came from one lucky visit of my own, supplemented by *No 10 Downing Street: The Story of a House* by Christopher Jones (BBC, 1985) and *10 Downing Street: The Illustrated History* by Anthony Seldon (HarperCollins, 1999).

Important sources for Chapter 10 were *Dad's Army: The Story of a Classic Television Show* by Graham McCann (4th Estate, 2001) and *Dad's Army: The Complete Scripts of Series 1–4* by Jimmy Perry and David Croft (Orion, 2001).

Some details in Chapter 20 are taken from *Robert Kennedy: His Life* by Evan Thomas (Touchstone, 2000) and *Alistair Cooke: Letter From America* (BBC Radio Collection, 1993).

I was greatly helped to share one of Harold Wilson's main enthusiasms by the loving scholarship of Ian Bradley's *The Complete Annotated Gilbert & Sullivan* (Oxford, 1996).

For general background on the *Daily Mirror* and IPC, *Read*

Afterword

All About It!: 100 Sensational Years of the Daily Mirror by Bill Hagerty (First Stone, 2003) was entertaining and useful. The visual and typographical history of the paper was filled in by *A Century of History: A Journey Through History with the Daily Mirror* (Contender, 2003).

For specific scenes, I also consulted two specialist publications: *London Transport Buses in 1968: A Photographic Survey by Jim Blake* (Ravensbrook Press, 2003) and *Murder and Mystery on Exmoor* by Jack Hurley (The Exmoor Press, 1982).

A useful broad picture of a year important to this story was provided in *1968: The Year that Rocked the World* by Mark Kurlansky (Ballantine, 2004). Helpful in the same context were: *1968 – Marching In The Streets* by Tariq Ali and Susan Watkins (Bloomsbury, 1998) and *You Are Here: Michael Cooper – The London Sixties* (Schirmer/Mosel, 1999).

For clues to language and body-language, as well as their history, I also watched with great enjoyment Michael Cockerell's BBC television documentaries on Roy Jenkins and Barbara Castle.

Period detail was kindly provided by Graham Sharpe of William Hill and the archivists of the Savoy Hotel. The staff of the Newspaper Library at Colindale, an exhaustive and vital archive of an inherently forgettable historical source, were unfailingly reliable and courteous.

I am also grateful to Robyn Read for help with geography and his-tory; the BBC sound archives for helping me to hear the voices of so many of the central characters; and to William Lawson and Nell for restaging a notorious incident on Exmoor, although it should be stressed that no dogs were harmed in the making of this novel.

Mark Lawson
October 2004